THE MACCONWOOD WOLF PACK

WOLF PACK

Volume 2

C.D. GORRI

The Macconwood Wolf Pack
Volume 1
by C.D. Gorri

Copyright 2022 C.D. Gorri, NJ

CODE WOLF

A MACCONWOOD PACK NOVEL

USA TODAY BESTSELLING AUTHOR

C.D. GORRI

CODE
Wolf

The
Macconwood
Pack

He never thought of himself as a family man, but sometimes things changed.

Randall Graves spends most of his time writing lines of code in his air-conditioned office at Macconwood Manor. He'd rather be alone than risk involvement of any kind. Everything was going fine, until his Alpha sends him on a forced vacation.

It's all good with Randall, as long as there's WI-FI at the small, beachfront Bed & Breakfast in Bloody Point, South Carolina. What he wasn't counting on was Tulla Nirvelli. The young, single mother and her seven-year-old son, own and operate the small B &B on the island alone.

Charmed by the young family, Randall finds himself enjoying his time at *The Sea Mist* Bed & Breakfast. When trouble strikes the young mother, Randall is set to help, but that means revealing his secret. Will she accept the truth about him?

PROLOGUE

"Goddammit! Son of a bitch!" Randall ran a hand through his chest-length beard and growled in frustration. Someone was trying to hack into the Pack's secure files. And he was getting close.

Randall regretted the recent update to the system's firewall. He added an actual alarm sound, similar to that of a fire alarm, to the mountain of alerts he'd get if someone got close to breaching their system. But he never expected to hear it.

The alarm was currently screaming in the background, annoying the hell out of his supernatural hearing. He narrowed his eyes and focused. This had gone on too long, but he had yet to shut down the SOB completely.

Randall oversaw all of the Pack's technology, software and security included. No one should have gotten this far into his system. Of course, tonight was his night off. He'd been down in the music room tuning his guitar when the "intruder alert" went off on his cell phone. He got a kick out of all things Star Trek, but this was serious business.

"Fucking POS!" He slammed the keyboard down as the bastard hacker froze him out of his own machine. He stood up and raced to the next station where Dib Lowell, his fellow Wolf Guard and Packmate, sat desperately trying to double up on their security like Randall had taught him. But he just wasn't fast enough.

"Crap, Randall! This guy is getting' around everything, man!" Dib's pale skin looked green in the reflection of the monitor. He was a pretty decent developer, but Randall had no patience. He needed to end this. Now.

"Dib, will you just give me the damn keyboard already!"

"Alright, man, *sheesh*," the redheaded giant rolled his chair aside as Randall leaned forward and took control of his computer. He exhaled and went to work.

"Oh, he's good! But I am better. *Ha*! Here you are,

you bastard," Randall growled as he clicked away furiously on the keyboard with his long fingers.

He moved at incredible speed. Screen after screen flashed in front of his deep brown eyes. The hacker tried diverting his attention a few times. The traps he set were good, but Randall was too smart for that. He managed to focus on the lines of code that scrolled down the forty-inch screen like lightning despite the loud noise and thick tension in the air.

He was known for his bad temper. Especially when things were out of his control. What could he say? In his eighty plus years on this Earth, he'd become a control freak. Came from being alone so much, but he didn't care what anyone said about him needing to get out more. His world was online. He didn't need anybody else.

"Goodbye, fucker!" He punched a few more keys, then he clicked enter. The high-pitched squeal of the alarm stopped, leaving a sudden and almost unbearable lack of noise in the Pack's control room.

He turned around and sat back down in his neon green Herman Miller aluminum executive chair and let out the breath he'd been holding since his smartphone alerted him to the attempted break-in. The posh chair cradled his six-foot three frame. It made no noise as he pushed back and exhaled loudly.

Nothing but the best for Randall Graves, computer extraordinaire. The others had joked about him spending almost two-grand on a fucking chair, but it was his ass that sat in the damn thing for more hours than he liked, making sure Pack business was running nice and smooth. Hell, he might as well be comfortable.

He rolled his neck and shoulders. *Five hours.* He'd been tracking this fucker for five hours straight. The last thirty minutes had been the worst of it. The hacker had gotten past some of his more sophisticated locks. That's what set off the alarm, but he overlooked simpler ways of getting in. Various backdoors and such Randall had built into the system. He wondered why that was.

Like most of the newer computer nerds, this hacker lacked the skill Randall had honed over sixty-years of programming innovation. *Perks of being a Werewolf.* The fact he'd been around for quite a long time meant Randall was there from the beginning. He started out in the field of computers when no one took it seriously.

Hell, that was a long time. But he'd found solace in technology long before his Change. His father had worked at a Naval Air Station in Jacksonville, Florida during the Korean War. He was a mechanical engineer, a contractor not to be confused with a Navy man. Stanton Graves had no place for his own son in his heart, never mind home and country. He was a cold, solitary man, and an even worse Werewolf, forsaking his Pack for the bottle.

Sometimes when he worked overtime, Randall would go with him to the base. It was there that he met Dr. Grace Hopper. She had developed a compiler for computer languages and took a shine to the young Randall. She gave him a book that she was writing about computer code and he had devoured the pages, eager to try his hand.

Randall was no more than ten at the time, but he considered that to be when his love for technology had taken root in his heart. Now, he was an expert in the field, accomplished and learned. Some would even call him a genius, but he hated the term. But, before any of those things, Randall was a Wolf. He was on the Alpha's Wolf Guard and was ranked third in the Macconwood Pack.

Normally, he loved his work. He was a fan of technology. Overseeing the Manor's security system was a huge job. It included regular sweeps of all the in-house computers, their internet services, and the servers that held vital Pack information.

He took care of the Wolf Guard's smartphones and made sure everyone was outfitted with secure lines. He also wrote several Pack-only apps that were encrypted with software that only allowed Pack members access. Keeping the Werewolf secret was important and much harder to do nowadays with cell phones and the internet everywhere.

He also ran his personal business, Graves Enterprises, of which he gave the Pack back twenty percent as per his agreement with his Alpha who was a major investor in the firm. Rafe had wanted only five percent, but Randall wouldn't hear of it. He owed Rafe Maccon.

Randall had spent a great part of his youth consumed with Werewolf legends and stories. Rafe was the one who suggested he use it. More than that, the guy wrote an actual decree, stating Randall had permission to use Wolf legends in his work. Anyway, that was how he created the online role-playing game, *WolfMoon*.

The endeavor proved to be worth it. He initially began programming *WolfMoon* as a means for the supernatural world to communicate incognito as it were, but normals loved it. Role-playing was a huge and lucrative business.

The whole thing was an enormous undertaking, and it required a lot of time. He now had over a dozen people, Werewolves of course, on his team and they handled a lot of the day-to-day dealings. He was a success.

WolfMoon generated a lot of money for himself and the Pack via in-app upgrades and advertisements, not to mention merchandising deals. He should be ecstatic or at the very least, satisfied, but lately Randall felt restless.

"Fuck, I need a run!" Dib stood up and stretched, interrupting Randall's wandering thoughts.

"Yeah, I hear you. A long run through the back-woods and a big ass steak sounds about right. Look man, I didn't mean to snap at you," he said.

"It's cool. But, uh, we gotta talk to the boss first. You know? Come on man, don't leave me hanging!" Dib offered him a high five which he met with a loud resounding smack.

He was good at what he did. Hell, he was the best, but this hacker fuck, well, he was pretty damn good too. Too good to be working for the enemy.

Skoll's cronies were getting more sophisticated. He discovered the source of this latest attack on the Pack's system. The guy entered with a silent cloning virus, designed to duplicate information on the closed-circuit inter-Pack communication software Randall had personally developed. It was used by the entire Pack, but the section targeted was reserved for his Alpha, Rafe Maccon, and his Wolf Guard only.

The bastard shouldn't have even known of its existence. He knew how he got the information almost as soon as he realized what he was after. Liam, the youngest of the Guard, had misplaced his cell over the weekend at *The Thirsty Dog*. He informed Randall by way of Dib after the alarm started.

The Thirsty Dog was a local bar and favorite of Pack members. Probably because the owner was a Werewolf and catered to the supernatural crowd with ease and competence. Randall ventured out rarely, but on occasion he did enjoy the collection of local brewed and distilled beers and liquors.

It didn't hurt that their buffalo wings were killer. But still, he was more a homebody. He didn't like crowds and he didn't like groupies. The normals who went there, or their females anyway, were pretty much willing to bed any Wolf in the joint. He wasn't calling them out for it, but he had little use for women these days.

Anyway, he ripped Liam a new one for losing his damn cell and for not reporting it immediately as was their protocol. The kid needed to be more careful. Couldn't let a pretty face distract you when the fate of the whole Pack was in your hands. And as a Wolf Guard, it was their job to protect the Pack, be ready when the Alpha called, and heed his word.

"Come on, man. Rafe's gonna want an update like ten minutes ago." Dib was staring at him as if he sprouted another head. Randall figured he was wasting too much time anyway.

Randall understood Liam's difficulty. The pup had succumbed to the wiles of a short, red head with a tattoo of a heart between her perfectly supple breasts. She went by the name Trixie. Randall had intimate knowledge of said tattoo, but he didn't have the heart to tell Liam.

Trixie was a normal. And as with most human women, she was indescribably attracted to Werewolves without knowing exactly why. She'd made her way around the Pack Wolves pretty damn quickly. As Liam later learned without Randall's direct interference.

It was no skin off Randall's nose. He was not in love with the girl. She was a groupie of sorts, a user, and he took what she offered once. Only once, to her profound befuddlement. Randall had repeatedly said no thanks the next few times around and she now made it a point to snub him whenever he ran into her. Which was, unfortunately, any time he went to *The Thirsty Dog*. Hence his new habit of staying home all the time.

Women. Randall had one use for them and lately that had been less frequent than he'd have liked. He was losing his taste for meaningless encounters, but there had never been anything other than that in his life. Love was simply not in his cards. Except for Cat, Rafe's sister and a fellow Wolf Guard, and Charley, Rafe's wife, he could do without the entire female race.

"You coming or what?" Randall looked up at the sound of Dib's annoyed voice. He forgot the man was waiting for him. *Fuck*. He needed a nap or a coffee, or maybe he should get Trixie to give him another go. *Nah*. She was used goods and he no longer had the taste for it.

"Yeah, yeah. Let me install this new firewall I've been working on and tell everyone to turn in their phones. I'll have a new batch ready by tonight," Randall glared at his redheaded Packmate.

"Randall, come on man."

"I said I need a minute. You go ahead and tell the big man to stay calm. Those bastards should have never gotten this far into my system. Fucking hardware support asshats assured me these phones were impenetrable. *Fuck 'em*. I'm going with the new prototype from Japan. My contact there said the new phones are outfitted with a titanium core. They can't be hacked or cloned."

"Dude, I got no idea what the hell you're saying," Dib backed away from an increasingly annoyed Randall. An annoyed Randall soon became an angry Randall, and no one wanted that.

Homeboy was gonna blow a gasket if he didn't learn to relax. Dib shook his head, his unruly red mane stuck up in odd places as he walked away hands up in mock surrender. He wondered what the Alpha would say if he suggested a little vacay for the badass super geek. *Hmmm...*

"**A**re you fuckin' with me?"

"No, Randall, I assure you I am not *fuckin' with you*," Rafe Maccon eased his immense frame back into his oversized, black leather chair and narrowed his ice blue eyes at his Third and one of his oldest friends.

How long had he known the man sitting in front of him? Randall had come to Maccon City when Rafe was about ten, he looked the same then as he did now. Tall at six foot three inches, muscular, and more than a little intimidating to the Wolves under him with his long beard and equally long deep brown hair. Rafe, however, was the Alpha. He was more amused than intimidated by his surly friend.

"A vacation?! What the fuck am I gonna do on a vacation? Come on, Rafe, this is bullshit!"

C.D. GORRI

The door to Rafe's private office flew open and in strolled a very happy, very pregnant Charley Maccon, Rafe's wife. The Alpha's eyes glowed as they landed on his positively glowing mate. She wore a long, flowy dress. The shade was a pale-yellow color that, Randall admitted to himself, looked damn good with her creamy complexion and curly dark hair. Their Alpha Female was quite something. There wasn't a Wolf Guard in the place who wouldn't lay down his/her life for her.

"Well, maybe you should consider a vacation to be a relaxing experience, Randy," she dropped a kiss on Randall's cheek and walked past him, over to her husband whom she kissed full on the mouth.

The way his Alpha's eyes homed in on her when she opened the door was nothing compared to the hungry gaze that followed her across the room. Randall had noticed it took a while for Rafe to get used to his mate's habit of greeting everyone with a kiss or hug. Wolves were protective of their mates, but Randall thought his Alpha was doing an exceedingly decent job of hiding his tension.

Werewolves did not share very well. Charley; however, had stood firm. That was the way she was raised, and she wasn't going to change for any, how had she put it? *Neanderthal brow-beating husband regardless of how cute his ass was!* Randall had no direct knowledge if the "cute ass" statement was true or not. And he didn't want to know.

He liked Charley though, had from the beginning. He was musically inclined and often took to one of the common rooms to strum his guitar or play a few keys on the piano. Charley liked music too. In fact, they bonded over it. She had a good voice, and he made her an open invitation to sing with him whenever she felt like it.

Yes sir, he liked his Alpha's wife. She was one hell of a woman. He felt like a voyeur as he watched his Alpha place a large hand over her swollen belly and rub it in small slow circles, a gesture that was as loving as it was intimate. He felt Rafe's joy in their Pack bonds and couldn't help, but smile. Regardless of his own profound emptiness.

Randall had thought himself in love once, a long time ago. He was young and full of lust and promise, and of course one pretty big secret. She was a normal, she knew nothing of his world, and he liked it that way. When he suggested they marry she laughed saying that she never wanted a husband or a family. She did not want him or his children. Not ever.

Her rejection was brutal, permanently damaging something inside of him. His tale was sad, but not uncommon. His experience with love was short-lived, but there it was. He vowed then to stay away from it and any attempt at anything resembling family.

The emptiness lingered in his mind like a disease. He wondered if it would ever go away. Nowadays, his Pack was his family. It was all he needed. Randall didn't believe in happily ever after for anyone. Except maybe these two. He wished a long healthy life for them both. He sat quietly as Charley perched on her husband's lap. She smiled as she turned to face him.

"It'll be fun, Randall. Warm sand, cool water, a couple of weeks to unwind, all by yourself with no one around to bug you. You could get room service day and night, a deep tissue massage, new movies on demand, and some real privacy! I mean, wow! I'd kill for a vacation like that!"

"What do you mean you'd kill for a vacation like that? Are you unhappy? Is something wrong?" Rafe looked mildly insulted and Charley rolled her eyes before swatting him on his huge bicep.

"Oh shush, I didn't mean that!" She giggled like a schoolgirl, her big brown eyes laughing, as she turned and kissed her husband on his nose before looking back at Randall, "Well, where are you going?"

"How the heck do I know? Excuse me, Charley, I didn't mean to snap, but *shi-*, I mean, I don't need this, Rafe. I'm fine!"

Rafe leaned over carefully so as not to disturb his

wife in her delicate condition. He picked up an envelope and tossed it to Randall, a small smile played at the corner of his mouth. *Uh oh*, thought Randall. He got the joke when he opened the envelope.

"Oh yeah, this looks relaxing!"

"Well? Where to?" asked Charley.

"*Bloody Point*, South Carolina!"

"*Daufuskie Island is the southernmost sea island in South Carolina. The history of Bloody Point begins in 1715, when the native Yemassee tribe clashed with the European settlers over a variety of reasons, such as unfair trading terms, ending in battle which ran the waters red with blood,*" Randall read the brochure to himself as he squeezed into the too-small coach seat on the airplane. He'd thank Dib later for conveniently forgetting to book him first class.

He stretched as discreetly as he could, but his six-foot three-inch frame and his two hundred-fifty pounds of solid muscle simply didn't fit. The older woman beside him gave him hard looks as he jostled her elbow for the tenth time since they took off from Newark International Airport. He smiled and mumbled an apology, but she only widened her large blue eyes under almost non-existent white eyebrows and looked away.

He forgot he could be sort of intimidating to normals. After all, he was a beast of a man. *Literally*.

Even in the best situation, Randall hated planes. It was too close, too crowded, and too damned bumpy. His Wolf was restless and unhappy with the conditions.

He felt his Wolf closer nowadays. Ever since the curse that kept Werewolves from Changing and even hearing their Wolves until the full moon was losing power, Randall was still savoring the unpolluted joy of feeling whole. But that meant he had to work harder at keeping his Wolf in check.

He imagined how he looked smiling at the lady next to him and grimaced, maybe it was time he trimmed the beard. Or the hair. *Or both.* He looked like a damned lumberjack out of a fairytale in his worn jeans, brown leather boots, and flannel shirt. It was April, but in New Jersey the weather was unpredictable at best.

Besides that, Randall worked in an office with servers and computers. It was vital to keep the temperature at a steady fifty degrees for the health of the equipment. Werewolves ran hotter than most normals, but fifty degrees was still only fifty degrees. His clothes were practical and comfortable.

It had been a long time since he paid attention to his appearance. Maybe he'd do some shopping on the island. He looked back down at the travel brochure Charley gave to him before he took off that morning. She kissed his cheek goodbye and stuffed it into his travel bag before he could protest. He only brought a duffle bag and his carry on with him. Some shorts, t-shirts, running shoes, and a ukulele.

The guys had hidden his laptop and his tablet, but he still had a Chromebook. And his phone. And if he got really desperate, he'd buy a damn computer. Lord knew, he had enough money.

WolfMoon was the most significant source of his income, but he also developed various bits of code and patch-ins that he sold to big name corporations under a sub-branch of *Graves Enterprises* called *Upward Compatible*. He wondered how long he'd be able to list his name there before he needed to change it.

He was older than he looked. Some Werewolves were, not his Alpha though. Rafe was young, but he was also strong and good. Wise beyond his years and a much better man and Alpha than his father, Zev Maccon. He shook his head at the difference in them and silently thanked the universe for it. It was a long time since Randall had thought of that old bastard. *Must be the plane.*

"Excuse me, would you like a drink?" Randall looked up at the steward and shook his head. He was not in the mood to talk. He was too anxious. The young blonde man almost dropped the can of soda he was holding when he looked at Randall.

He felt his cheeks burn at the blatant interest in the man's eyes. Under the beard, Randall was good looking. It was a fact that most Werewolves were attractive and prime physical specimens. He was used to getting looks by men and women alike, though it had been a while since he had left his "coding cave" as the guys called it. The older woman next to him ordered a soda and the flustered steward almost dropped the plastic cup right on Randall's lap. Good thing for fast reflexes or he'd be soaked.

"I am so sorry, sir, did you need a napkin?"

"No harm done, son," Randall smiled kindly. The steward couldn't have been more than twenty-four years old. Probably just out of college. His name tag read Brian.

"Brian?"

"Um, yes, sir? I am so sorry-"

"No worries, I was wondering if you had a bag of peanuts?"

"Actually, we no longer carry peanuts because of allergies, you know? But I do have a few organic cranberry acai granola bars if you are interested?"

"That'll be fine, thanks," Randall took three granola bars from the basket Brian held out to him. He had just about as much interest in eating the overpriced rabbit food as he did in eating the biodegrad-able wrapper, they came in.

What was the world coming to? No more peanuts on airplanes? He shook his head and bumped the woman next to him with his elbow again. *Damn these coach seats!*

"Sorry," he mumbled and ate the first granola bar. It tasted like sawdust, but he chewed until it was swallow able. He chased it with a bottle of spring water that he accepted from Brian who assured him he'd need it. The kid was right.

Randall needed to consume a lot of calories during the day to satisfy the beast within him. A hungry Werewolf was not a friendly one. And wasn't that the understatement of the year? *Ha!* He closed his eyes and tried to clear his mind for the rest of the flight.

Okay Randall, he told himself, *only two hours left in this flying tin can. Fuck me.*

$\approx$ 2 $\approx$

"**M**ama! Look here, mama!"

"What honey?" Tulla Nirvelli turned around on the small outlook where she stood waiting for their first guest of the spring season. The wooden dock was old, and the paint was chipped off in most places, but it was sturdy just the same.

Her eyes found the small blonde whirlwind that was her seven-year-old son and she felt that familiar pang in her chest. She pushed all bad thoughts out of her mind as she listened to his excited chatter. Danny loved *guest day*! That's what he called it when the small Bed & Breakfast she owned and operated got new arrivals.

Her Daniel was always getting into something. Right then, he was perched on top of the rickety wooden railing, staring out at the big blue sea. His left hand still had the slightest impression of a dimple from his chubby little toddler days. *Was that really so long ago?*

"Mama, I think my dog is coming today!"

"No, love, no dogs today. Just a new guest!"

He giggled and spun in a circle shouting about his dog! He'd had a dream about some dog saving his life or some such, she couldn't keep up. He was into so many fantasy themed games and online activities it was difficult to determine which one had a dog in it this week. *Oh, my sweet Danny.*

Any day now, he'd be a man. And that was something Tulla was simply not ready for. Her baby was special, and not just to her. *Eight years*, Tulla thought to herself. Her heart squeezed painfully in her chest. The cold, abiding fear was ever present in her heart. Ever since she had found out just who, or rather *what*, her late husband was and what he had promised to those who were used to having their way. The knowledge plagued her every day since he died.

The man said they'd come back in eight years to see if the child, *her child*, was their anointed one. Time was almost up. She shivered as she recalled the man's low, eerie voice over the phone.

It was rainy and dark that night, just a few hours after the police had knocked on her door to tell her the unimaginable. Her husband of under a year had died in a boating accident. She was alone in the world with her newborn son and terrified of her uncertain future. Little did she know there was so much more to fear.

The phone rang as she sat at the counter with her hand on her still swollen belly. She had just come home from the hospital with her newborn son to discover Tom was gone. She'd called for him during the two days she was in labor and the two days she spent in recovery.

He never answered, never came to see her or his boy. That was when she alerted the police. After they investigated, they informed her that Tom had been killed in what appeared to be an accident.

"It was no accident, Mrs. Nirvelli, I killed your husband and now it is you who bears the weight of his promise. I will come to visit the child in his eighth year."

"No. who are you?"

"Who I am is of no consequence. If the boy is the chosen one, he will return with me to be trained. Consider yourself lucky, Mrs. Nirvelli."

"Lucky? You want to steal my baby, how am I lucky?" She asked him, the true horror of his words not penetrating the fog that clouded her brain. Tom was dead, a stranger wanted her son, and she was lucky? How could this be happening to her?

"You're still alive. The child needs his mother right now, otherwise I would have sent you to meet your husband already. Enjoy the next few years while you can, Mrs. Nirvelli. We will be watching you."

After the call, Tulla packed up her few material belongings. She let the landlord keep the security deposit on the house she and Tom rented, and she left. With the mainland town she had lived with her husband, Tom Nirvelli, for a little under nine months in her rearview mirror, she and Danny headed to Daufuskie Island. To the small cottage her great-aunt owned on Bloody Point.

She was grateful for the warm welcome Great-Aunt Mildred had given her. They lived together for two years until the old woman had suffered a stroke. She could no longer handle the rough sea winds of the small island and she went to live in a senior center in Charleston to Tulla's great dismay.

It was better for the old woman, Tulla knew that deep in her heart. Still, she was the only family Tulla had left except for Daniel. Aunt Mildred was a kind and sweet soul. She was cared for by the friendly staff and nurses at the senior center. Tulla made sure of that.

Tulla loved Aunt Mildred for her warm spirit and boundless hospitality. She opened her heart and her home to a grandniece she had very seldom seen. Oh, and how she had welcomed them! She doted on Daniel and became a surrogate grandmother to them both.

Six months after her stroke, Mildred died. She left Tulla, her only living relative, her tiny cottage. By then Tulla had already started taking in week-enders to the island. After a few months and some modest renovations with the small inheritance she received, she turned the place into a cozy B&B. Nothing could replace the old woman in Tulla's memories, and she planted little annual flowers outside to remind her of Aunt Mildred every spring. She loved flowers.

The Sea Mist Bed & Breakfast sat right on the corner of the island's south side, on a stretch of sandy beach that was almost completely isolated except for a few widespread neighbors. The waters were rougher on that side of the island with the south wind constantly blowing, but larger developers have already come around sniffing for cheap land to build larger resorts for their golfers and vacationers.

Tulla had no wish to sell. Not when she felt safe on an island with only a couple of hundred perma-nent residents year-round. She had come to appre-ciate Bloody Point's beauty despite its gory name. The moss-covered oaks and oceanic birds that nested on the shores, the alligators that you could sometimes spy sunbathing in the summertime, the clam bakes and friendly faces made it a lovely place to live.

She made decent money with her B&B. She had four, single-bed, guest rooms. Two had spectacular views of the ocean, the other two faced a row of oak trees that were equally pleasing to the eye. Outdoor attractions at her B&B included a pair of beachside hammocks hung together under a group of transplanted palm trees, a wood deck off the kitchen that sported a huge outdoor table with an umbrella surrounded by oversized chairs with cheerfully colored cushions and pillows, and a large outdoor fire-pit. She had a small rowboat for those who enjoyed fishing when the weather allowed and a handful of cushioned lounge chairs lining the beach.

She was a good hostess. Her natural warmth and honest face inspired people to loosen up around her. Business was good and steady, and she prided herself on keeping her guests happy. A novice chef, Tulla provided her guests with three home-cooked meals prepared daily and served promptly at eight, one, and six. A constant supply of fresh cookies and sweet tea were available in the kitchen for anyone in need of snacks along with healthier options like sliced fruit and yogurt.

Danny loved the island though he asked to go on trips to the mainland. There was a small school on the island where Danny attended classes. Their private rooms were set apart from the guest quarters. In fact, she had renovated the garage into a mini apartment for them. They each had their own bedroom and a small play/living room area with a television, gaming system, loveseat, and small table with a computer she had gotten secondhand.

Danny loved computer games and was always fiddling on the used laptop she bought to keep track of their guests, their bank accounts, and their inventory. Danny was a smart boy. Inquisitive and a delight to his mother. The pair of them had carved out a nice little life for themselves on Bloody Point.

As every mother of curious little boys knows, he was prone to asking a ton of questions, and therefore, had strict instructions not to pester the guests. Especially until Tulla got a good look at them. Well, a good listen anyway. She tried to instill a sense of security in their lives, but her nerves were raw. She was always dreading the day she'd hear that voice again. The one belonging to the man who wanted her son.

She shivered and looked at her towheaded boy with that panic still gripping her heart. It took her a moment, but she willed herself to breathe. Danny knew nothing about his father or the man who terrorized her dreams. She never told him. How could she? *It was impossible.* Tulla wanted to keep him safe and innocent of whatever madness Tom had been a part of.

"Mama, can you see it?" Danny pointed and almost lost his grip on the railing. Tulla reached out and steadied him.

"Look, it's coming closer!" She smelled his soft hair and the fading scent of the baby shampoo he used.

Her son was caught between that inevitable transition from baby to boy. She held him a little too tight and he squirmed to get free, caught up in the excitement of a new guest.

Tulla wasn't focused on their new arrival. She was lost in thoughts of her son. She wanted to pick him up, to hold him close to her heart, like she did when he was just a baby. *Not in public though*. He would be highly offended if she didn't take into consideration his manliness when they were out and about. *The little devil!*

"My dog is on that boat!"

"Hush, silly, he's a guest not a dog!"

"Right there! Right there!" She nodded as he pointed out to sea at the small image of the water taxi coming into view.

It was so far away it looked more like a toy bobbing up and down in the unusually rough waters. She inhaled the salty air and steadied herself, trying to relax into her usual guarded, but friendly professional face. The boat would be carrying her guest for the next four weeks.

A Mr. Randall Graves, if her memory served. He was coming alone and staying at *The Sea Mist* for what his colleague had said was an overdue break from work. The man who phoned her and made the initial reservation was quite insistent on giving her details of Mr. Graves' poor overworked sense of duty and dedication to his job.

The man hadn't had a vacation in years! His coworker, a Mr. Lowell, described the poor old man as married to his desk. No family, no children, no one to care for him! That only made Tulla more sympathetic to his lonely plight.

She was so moved by the thought of him all alone that she put on a pot roast complete with mashed potatoes and glazed carrots. She even baked two dozen double chocolate chip cookies with walnuts just for her guest. The man probably hadn't had a home-cooked meal in ages! She felt a certain responsibility to her new guest and wanted to make sure he was pampered a little for all his arduous work.

Poor old thing, she thought. She had instructions to give him his space, which she would naturally. Except for doing his laundry and preparing his meals, of which he preferred substantial portions of organic meat, fowl, or fish with every meal, he required no other services. No guided tours, golfing, or chauffeuring. *Except for today of course.*

There was one other thing she was asked to do for her guest. She was to tell Mr. Graves the internet connection was down for the duration of his visit. Normally, Tulla did not like to lie, but she was told it was a matter of significant importance to the man's health. She had struggled for a moment or two before acquiescing. To be honest, she still wasn't sure she could pull it off.

She worried it over and over in her mind until inspiration struck! She knew she could never lie with a straight face, so she disconnected the modem and "accidentally" dropped it in the kitchen sink when it was full of soapy warm water.

The thing would need to be replaced, but to do that she'd have to go to the mainland or head on down to the library and use their computer to order one for herself. So, *technically*, the internet was down. She worried her lower lip as she imagined the conversation between her, and her guest should he ask for her WI-FI password.

Oh Lord, forgive me for fibbing, she thought as she rubbed her hands together. She hoped Mr. Graves found *The Sea Mist* relaxing and distracting enough to forget about work. He would certainly owe his colleagues for thinking so highly of him to arrange for his comfort up to the finest detail.

She wondered at the large cardboard box that arrived for her guest early that morning. It was huge, but surprisingly light. She had placed it on the chest at the foot of the bed in the room she picked out for him. *Magazines and stuff like that.*

"What's he look like, Mama?"

"We're lookin' for a businessman type, older I should think, my sweet Danny. I was told he needed a break from work, poor thing."

"I bet he's a million feet tall, with long hair, and he likes to play frisbee on the beach, and he can play guitar too, Mama!"

"Now, Danny, you know you aren't supposed to bother the guests. And no, I don't think so, I believe Mr. Graves is more the indoor type. A computer programmer. You know, a stuffed shirt!" She whispered into Danny's ear and tickled him till he gasped for breath.

"No way, Mama! You are so wrong!"

"*Nuh-uh,* your mama is never wrong! I bet he is bald with a big round potbelly and his skin is as pale and white as a sheet of paper!"

"No way! Hey look, I think that's him! Maybe they do stuff his shirt?" Daniel tilted his head to the side as if trying to measure the figure staring at them from the deck of the water ferry.

Tulla turned and looked to where the ferry was now docked. A couple of men set the metal plank in place and connected it to the side of the boat. A moment later she noticed a man carrying an over-sized army duffle and a sleek black backpack.

If only this was her guest, she thought to herself and bit her lower lip. His long hair was pulled back high on his head in an elastic band, a long beard hung down to an impossibly broad chest that narrowed to a slightly tapered waist. He was tall, well over six-foot and the muscles in his arms and legs spoke of an outdoorsy type of guy. *Too bad*, she thought to herself, *but this here is no rusty, old programmer*.

The stranger took off his black wraparound sunglasses and if Tulla was interested before, she was positively speechless now. They were a color she had never seen on a man. One moment they were dark as roasted coffee beans, the next they were a light, shimmery brown, kind of like caramel sauce.

Molten, whiskey-colored pools in the sunlight inviting her to dive in and lose herself. Her heart thudded in her chest, Tulla could drown in those eyes. He didn't blink, didn't move at all. Just stood and stared at her. It was like being caught in the eye of a predator, one from whom she wasn't necessarily certain she wanted to escape. She managed to break eye contact and looked over the boat again, waiting for her guest for the next month, but there was no one else onboard.

If this was Randall Graves, she was in trouble.

3

few hours earlier...

Randall sat in the back of the black limo Dib had arranged to pick him up from the Charleston airport. The two-hour car ride from there to Bluffton went by quickly as he used the time to test and make notes on a new app, he was building for the Macconwood-Nighthawk Teen Outreach Program.

He was happy for Cat and Tate. The two of them had been in love for as long as he could tell, but they had only recently gotten married. Together they opened the youth center with the hopes of helping teens in trouble, most especially teen Werewolves.

Randall more than understood the need. Young Werewolves were susceptible to bouts of severe depression after their first Change. The Curse of St.

Natalis, though waning, was still present and kept Werewolves from connecting with the other side of themselves. The exception being during the full moon.

The separation caused some to despair. *Too many*, Randall thought. He recalled his own severe anxiety after he experienced his first Change. His father had beat that out of him. Hopefully, Tate and Cat had a different approach. He growled at the thought of his father then looked up to find the driver staring at him wide-eyed.

Randall stared the man down for all of two seconds before the driver's eyes went back to the road. He shrugged, *oh well*, he was no good at small talk anyway. He tipped the man a fifty-dollar bill when they arrived at the dock even though he retrieved his own bag from the trunk. He tried not to notice as the limo hightailed it out of there.

Look at me, making friends and everything. I am rocking this vacation! Randall exhaled as he walked to the counter and got his ticket for the hour-long water taxi to Bloody Point. He sat like a statue in the small indoor seating area for the entire ride. He hated the noisy motorboat. Not that he hated the sea, he just preferred sail boats or even the occasional rowboat to the noisy excuse for water transportation he was trapped in.

The boat docked abruptly, and he walked outside desperate for some fresh air. He stopped breathing the second his eyes found her. It was like time stood still and everything else just faded away. The woman on the dock wore a gauzy sort of blouse that revealed a sliver of her slender, tanned waist. She had on a pair of fitted jean shorts that stopped just above her knees. Impossibly small canvas sneakers graced her feet as she stood on her tiptoes searching around him with her eyes.

She was deliciously curvy in all the right places with toned calves and shapely thighs. Her skin was lightly bronzed from her time in the sun. From where he stood it looked smooth and clear too. *Damn*, he wanted to reach out and feel it for himself. Her heart shaped face was beautiful. She had full lips and big eyes the color of stainless steel. He'd never seen eyes like that before.

Her honey-streaked hair floated around her shoulders as a warm breeze drifted off the water. It swirled around her, making her look like a fairy or some such magical creature. The breeze carried her scent to his nostrils and Randall's stomach muscles clenched.

She smelled as good as she looked. *Like coconuts and sea salt, the good kind.* He licked his lips thinking of all the ways he'd revel in that scent, when a little whirlwind with red sneakers and blonde hair wrapped himself around her tiny waist.

Oh shit, he knew as soon as he saw her that she was the owner of the B&B, it was printed on the tote bag she carried. But if she was married then he needed to get right back on that damn boat before he did anything stupid. He didn't wreck happy homes. It wasn't his style.

One thing he knew, the guy who called that woman his was one damn lucky son-of-a-bitch. He shouldered his bag and walked towards the woman and child, the least he could do was introduce himself and apologize for the error. He tried not to let his disappointment show.

"Hey there, I'm Randall Graves, I, uh am sorry Mrs. Nirvelli-"

"Mama, that's funny! He calls you *missus* like *Missus Clara*! That's my teacher!"

"Hello. Yes, I heard him, sweetie. I'm sorry, this is my son Daniel and he just loves *guest day*. It's actually Ms. Nirvelli, I'm a widow."

Randall felt those muscles in his stomach tighten again. *Widow huh? Well, widow wasn't married.* He wanted to kick himself for the turn his thoughts had taken. Only a heartless bastard would think those kinds of thoughts about a single mother. Then again, no one ever accused him of having too much heart.

Besides, she was an adult and could make the choice herself.

It's not like he was animal or something. He rolled his eyes at the irony and followed his hostess off the dock towards her car. He suddenly wished he'd taken the time to dress better. At the very least he could have had a haircut and a shave before embarking on this vacation. *Damn,* he must look terrifying. The little boy grinning at his heels seemed to think otherwise. He extended a chubby little hand and smiled.

"You can call me Danny, sir. Gosh, you are big! How big are you?"

Randall stopped walking and narrowed his eyes. He focused on the little whirlwind instead of his captivating mama and thought before replying. He didn't have much experience with children, he'd never been around them much, but he imagined he was pretty darn big to a boy that size.

He dropped smoothly to one knee and accepted the boy's hand in a manly shake that he couldn't help but be impressed by. He liked the kid. He liked his mother too. Randall figured the best way to address the situation was to tackle it head on. It was more than probable that he'd be on intimate terms with the boy's mother by the end of the trip.

Randall acknowledged this as a fait accompli. Not

because he was conceited, but because he felt a burning desire flame inside of him when he looked at her. He hadn't experienced that in decades and if he was reading the signs correctly, she was not averse to the idea. The way her eyes lingered as they roamed over his body told him so, even if she didn't realize it yet herself. At any rate, he wanted to be able to look the kid in the eye when the time came to leave. *Straight shooting from the get-go*, he thought to himself.

"Hello, Danny, it is nice to make your acquaintance. To answer your question, I believe I am six foot three inches tall and I weigh around two hundred and fifty pounds. You look pretty big yourself for a boy of, what are you seven or eight? How big are you?" He tried to keep his voice light and easy going as he had no wish to frighten the child. He was rewarded with a smile for his efforts.

Randall's heart squeezed inside his chest. He was struck by the child's open expression and wide-eyed honesty. The way the kid shook his hand all proper-like was just another point in his favor, Randall had to fight to hold back a grin of his own. The boy smelled of saltwater and sand, crayons, and if Randall wasn't mistaken, a grilled cheese sandwich that made his stomach growl. This was some kid.

"How'd you know I'm seven? I'm gonna be eight soon though! Oh, and I'm four feet two inches tall, but I only weigh fifty pounds! I can get my shirt stuffed like you? Mama said you must stuff your shirt; how do you do that anyway?"

Randall raised an eyebrow at the red blush that crept across the boy's mother's cheeks. He was intrigued more by the pretty pink color that was now across her entire face then with the actual question that was put to him. He turned back to the child.

"Uh, what was the question again, Danny?"

"Oh, well Mama said businessmen have stuffed shirts-"

"Danny, let's not bother our guest with questions, come on now, get in the car. Uh, if you will just follow me Mr. Graves."

"Lead the way. Uh, will your boyfriend be joining us later?"

"Oh, um, no, no, I do not have a boyfriend at the present time, Mr. Graves, but I assure you the B&B runs smoothly and will suit your needs."

"Well, that's good news for me," Randall smiled to himself, grateful the boy had run ahead.

"I'm sorry what was that?" She asked him while searching her tote bag for what he assumed was the car keys. He clearly got to her considering said keys were already in her other hand. He smiled as he took them from her and clicked the unlock button before handing them back.

"I was just saying how wonderful that is for me, Ms. Nirvelli. I'd hate to be caught staring at another man's girl."

Her steel-colored eyes sparkled in the afternoon sun with little hints of silver. She wrinkled her nose in a futile attempt to hide her smile, but his wide grin must have been contagious. She shook a finger at him in that way mother's do at spoiled children and shook her head as she rounded the car.

"I do believe you are flirting with me, Mr. Graves," she cleared her throat and closed her bag as she walked. Her canvas shoes made little noise on the graveled floor of the dock parking lot. She stopped and met his eyes when he answered, his deep voice little more than a rumble.

"Not yet, but I intend to."

"Well, I'll consider myself warned."

❧ 4 ❧

"**G**et in, Mr. Graves! You can sit up front with Mama!"

"Thank you, Danny, I think I'd like that." He grinned as the mama in question dropped the keys on the car mat before she finished buckling her seatbelt. Her response delighted him.

The tempting Ms. Nirvelli wasn't exactly immune to his charms. That was a good sign. *A damn good one!* She regained her composure and turned to him with a professional expression on her face.

"Well, I guess I should tell you that *The Sea Mist* is mine and Danny's of course. Your colleague, Mr. Lowell has rented all the rooms out for the duration of your stay. You won't be disturbed, Mr. Graves."

"Call me Randall. So, Dib rented them all, huh? And, uh, was this on the phone?" He couldn't help but wonder if his Packmate had been up to something when he booked this vacation for him.

He smiled at the formal way his hostess addressed him. Now that he knew she was not married, Randall decided to put some effort into exploring the electricity that seemed to spark between them. Surely, she noticed too.

"Oh no, he insisted on video conferencing through the internet. We chatted quite a few times. I have to say he led me to believe you were much older than you look," she took her eyes off the road for a moment to look him up and down and he felt the weight of that look like a thousand-pound brick.

"A few times, huh, I bet," Randall discreetly adjusted himself and tapped his fingers on the dashboard. A nervous habit of his which was why he usually played an instrument.

It gave his hands something to do. Right then they were itching to do all sorts of things, and all to the delectable woman sitting to his left. He inhaled and got a whiff of her scent, *sea salt and coconuts*. He licked his lips.

"Um, here, let me turn the radio on. Is country, okay?"

He nodded his assent. He wasn't sure he'd be able to hide the need that was taking over him, body, and mind. If he opened his mouth, he couldn't be sure he'd do more than grunt. He wanted this woman. And badly.

She was a businesswoman, surely too astute to mistake the raw attraction he felt for her. He watched through heavy lidded eyes as she drove the old hatchback through the narrow tree lined street. It drove well for an older model, but it was a tad too small for his long legs.

The drive through the main part of town was quick. From what he could see it was pretty and clean, quaint was a better word. He tried to settle into the seat, but he just could not get comfortable.

He turned and looked down the narrow streets. He saw a couple of older people in golf carts, but that was pretty much it. There were few families out and about. It must be lonely for the kid, he thought to himself. He wondered how she came to live in such an isolated place.

"Ow," he banged his knee on the glove compartment in his effort to find a suitable position.

"Oh, uh, there is a release just under the seat there," Tulla motioned where the release latch was located after observing him moving around in his seat, but damn him if he could reach the thing. There was simply no room for him to bend over.

He struggled once and twice to the sounds of laughter coming from the munchkin in the back.

Finally, his driver and hostess for the next month put the car in park at a stop sign and leaned over him. He gulped as he got another fresh wave of her scent. He had to fight the urge to touch the wavy tendrils of hair that stuck to the side of her face in the South Carolina heat.

She was beautiful all right. A small dimple sat on her right cheek as she pursed her lips, he wanted to kiss it. She held her breath as she reached down between his knees with her small, elegant hands. Randall closed his eyes, his brain taking liberty with all sorts of images he should not be thinking but couldn't help. He cleared his throat. His body trembled with anticipation.

He opened his eyes. Certain she'd see the Wolf inside of them, Randall was wary of her reaction. Their eyes locked, but instead of fear, she smiled, a wicked sort of grin. He swallowed. *Holy Hell!*

He was about to speak when he found himself flying backwards. The seat moved quickly and heavily as she pulled the lever. She tried to look ashamed as he banged his head on the slight indent on the ceiling of the car, but her giggle gave it away. He muffled a curse under his breath and rubbed his head.

"Uh oh, you need to put a dollar in the swear jar now, right Mama!"

"Oh, I'm sorry Mr. Graves," she said. But Randall

knew better. It was as if she had guessed the lasciv-
ious nature of his thoughts and got him back for it!
The minx!

"Now, Danny that swear jar is for us, not the
guests!"

"No, no he's right," Randall said. He looked at her
hand, the one that was still resting between his knees,
her fingers still gripped the seat adjustment bar.

He looked back into her eyes with all the smol-
dering heat he felt in every part of his body. He gave a
satisfied smile when she sat up quickly before taking
the car out of park and stepping on the gas again.
Randall's smile turned into a grin, *let the games begin*.

"So, I owe a dollar, huh, Danny? Is that right?"

"Uh, huh! You said a swear word, so you pay a
dollar!"

"Alright then, here you go. Now, you be sure and
put it in the, uh, swear jar for me, okay?"

"Yes, sir, I can do that. Right, Mama?"

"Okay, Danny, thank you. I'm sorry Mr. Graves, I
didn't mean for you to get involved in my attempt to
break from the terrible habit of swearing."

"Not at all. I may find myself attempting to
reform as well. Led by your fine example of course,
Ms. Nirvelli," Randall smiled genuinely for what
seemed like the first time in ages. He enjoyed their
banter and wondered if she did too.

He rubbed a hand along the length of his beard and wondered how on *Earth* he had let it grow so long. He looked out the window and was surprised to find himself interested in what was outside. Werewolves generally liked being outside, but he had spent the last twenty-years or so behind closed doors.

He'd been determined to make a success out of *Graves Enterprises*. Nowadays, it was rare for him to spend time outdoors in the daylight. *Hell, when was the last time he felt the sun on his face and the wind in his hair?* He'd been hiding away with nothing, but computer code for company for so long, maybe he'd forgotten to take time and live.

His reaction to the fine woman sitting next to him was proof that he needed to get out more. He felt like a freaking puppy around her. He couldn't remember a time when his body had reacted so quickly to a member of the opposite sex. *Dammit*, he may owe Dib a thank you for this trip after all.

They rolled into the driveway of *The Sea Mist Bed & Breakfast*. The wooden sign outside was thickly lacquered and hung from a post surrounded by newly planted flowers. It was larger than he expected for a seaside B&B.

The ranch style house was painted a bright white with pale yellow shutters and plenty of potted plants dotted the gravel driveway and the windowsills. An old-fashioned mailbox sat at the end of the drive. That too was cared for with little yellow and white flowers planted all around the post. He was charmed and intrigued. He almost felt guilty for the Chromebook he had smuggled in his backpack, but maybe it was for the best.

He found himself looking too often at the curvaceous Ms. Nirvelli on the ride over. He may be a Wolf, but he wasn't a scoundrel. The woman had a son. He needed to be sure she knew the rules before he became more than a guest while staying here.

A little flirting, maybe a little more, but he wasn't going to get in over his head. A ready-made family wasn't what he signed up for. *Hell*, he didn't even want a vacation, but here he was just the same. Might as well enjoy it.

He grabbed his bags and followed the sway of Ms. Nirvelli's hips all the way inside. When she opened the door the smell of something good made his stomach rumble again. He was hungry. *And not just for food.*

"I put you here in the *Blue Room*. It's the largest and has a jacuzzi bathtub as well as a sliding door that opens up to a small wooden deck with a wraparound fence that overlooks the sand dunes, but you get a great view of the ocean as well," Tulla turned around expecting to see pleasure on his face, but he was unreadable.

She put a hand to her stomach and continued, "Of course, you are welcome to any of the other rooms as they won't be occupied while you are here,"

"No, this is fine, *real fine*," he said quietly. He wasn't smiling because he was too focused on the way she moved when she spoke.

The woman was a beauty. He couldn't help but watch the expression of her face as she smoothed a hand over the sky-blue coverlet on the king-sized bed. She turned and opened the matching curtains to reveal the sliding door to the patio she spoke of. The white sandy beach and the blue of the Atlantic behind her was dazzling to his eyes, but not quite as dazzling as the woman in front of him. The sun was low in the sky and its rays shone through her hair, lighting it as if she were some sort of ethereal being. *A sea nymph right here on Earth. Just for him.*

"Good, I'm glad. Would you like me to bring you a tray with a snack before supper? I have some fresh made cookies?"

"Uh, nope. I'll just settle in first."

"Sure thing, see you at dinner, then. Don't hesitate to let me know if you need anything."

Tulla walked quickly out of the room. She had to squeeze past him as he had not moved since entering the bedroom. Her heart pounded as she brushed lightly against his chest and muscular thighs. *Oh my!*

He was enormous. She wondered if that were true everywhere. *Oh Lord, forgive me.* It'd been so long since she experienced anything other than mild attraction for a man. And the sparks that were flying between her and Randall Graves were much more than just mild attraction. Tulla was in trouble!

She exhaled and walked to the kitchen. Her son was waiting on his promised snack of cookies and milk before going off to his scout meeting with the neighbor's boys. He had already eaten a grilled cheese with sliced tomatoes and cucumbers on the side before they left to pick up their guest.

Tulla was proud of his love for vegetables and added another cookie to his plate. He needed to be quick or he'd miss his ride. Mrs. White often took Danny with her twins, Mark, and Matthew, to their weekly scout meetings.

They were one of the only other families in the area and the twins were in Danny's class. Mrs. White was friendly though a good fifteen years older than Tulla. She and her husband had their children later in life. Still, they were always willing to help with carpooling and she liked to reciprocate with fresh baked goodies and things like that.

She smiled as she packed some cookies for them

as well. Danny was out the door five minutes later with his scout bag and the goodies she packed. Tulla waved to Mrs. White from the doorway.

Now, what was she going to do for two hours while he was gone? *Think, Tulla, you have a new guest. What do you always do?* She scolded herself for her behavior, she would not be a bumbling idiot for anyone. Especially not a guest.

But she felt like a high school girl again. Mr. Graves was just so big, and not just his size, but his very vitality. It was if he spoke to her without saying a word. How was she going to get through a month of him without throwing herself at his feet?

It was going to be an exceptionally long month.

5

"Um, Ms. Nirvelli?"

"What?" She gasped as Mr. Graves placed a long-fingered hand on her shoulder.

"Oh, Mr. Graves! You startled me."

"I'm sorry, I called you twice, but you seem to have drifted away for a moment," his concerned gaze was nearly her undoing.

"I apologize. Wa-, was there something you needed?"

"Well, I stubbed my toe putting my things away and I may have used a word or two I shouldn't have. Since I promised to keep my language PG while I'm here, I believe I owe that swear jar of yours a couple more dollars. Where is Danny?"

"Oh, you just missed him," she laughed and shook her head.

Of course, he wanted to put money in the swear jar because of Danny. He did not want her for anything. That explained it. She continued when he stood waiting for what she could only assume was an explanation.

"Oh, uh, he went to his scout meeting, but don't worry about it. I won't rat you out."

"No, please, I insist, a promise is a promise."

"Okay, I admire you keeping a promise to a boy when he's not even here. It's this way," she walked across the kitchen to the part of the house that was reserved for herself and her son.

She opened a door right off the kitchen to reveal a small living room area that looked more playroom than anything else. There were drawings hung up with care, a half dozen fluffy colorful pillows on a snug loveseat, and a black teddy bear with one eye that looked extremely loved sat waiting loyally for his boy.

"Nice," he said looking about the place.

"Oh, hardly, but thank you."

"Hey, you have a computer, oh good. I'd like the WI-FI info and password when you have a second."

Tulla turned around after rummaging around on a small bookshelf with a large mason jar filled with coins and singles. She could have kicked herself for inadvertently showing him the computer, especially when he hadn't asked about it before. Randall walked close to her and stuffed the folded bills he carried into the jar in her hand. *Oh well, it was show time.*

"Oh, uh, the modem is broken. I won't have time to get a replacement for a few days."

"Days?" Randall realized he should be angrier about this, but honestly what was a few days. He'd certainly have enough to distract him here.

Like right now for instance, he was distracted by the dusky pink of Tulla's unpainted full lips. Come to think of it she wore no makeup at all. He liked that about her. She was real.

The golden glow of her skin was all natural and appealed to his senses. She smelled like sunshine, salty sea air, and a hint of coconut underneath it all. He wanted to get closer. To smell her all over.

"Please, um, let me get you a glass of sweet tea."

She turned abruptly and he was left to follow in her wake. A trail of sunshine and maybe a hint of sadness underneath. He wanted to take whatever it was that made her sad and crush it under his boot.

This woman should never be sad, he decided. She should smile all damn day. *If only he could be the one to ensure that she did. If only it was his right to make her happy.* Dangerous thoughts for a Wolf who was alone as long as he was.

"Would you like me to serve you outside or in the sitting room?"

"Thank you, but I'd much rather you join me. Please, sit with me and have a glass yourself. It is very warm out."

"Alright, thank you, I, uh, have to tend dinner so if you'd like my company it has to be in the kitchen."

"Perfect," he said, and she nodded her head and poured.

They sat at the kitchen counter with two glasses of homemade sweet tea and a plate of fresh baked cookies between them. Randall groaned when he bit into one. They were delicious.

"*Mmm*, these are good. I love walnuts."

"Oh, thank you."

"So, tell me about yourself." *Smooth, dude, real smooth*, he rolled his eyes at what obviously sounded like a line coming from his lips.

"Oh, there's not much to tell," she was clearly uncomfortable talking about herself, but he was interested.

"Come on, beautiful young woman like you, great kid, the two of you all alone on this island? How'd you come to be here, anyway?"

"Oh, my great-aunt lived here."

"So, you used to visit her often? This great-aunt of yours?"

"No, actually I didn't know her until after I lost my husband."

"Damn, I'm sorry, you don't have to talk about that."

What an idiot! How could I bring that up?

"No that's, alright. I don't mind. It's really not a unique story, I mean I married young, had a baby, and then he died. I came out here to live with my aunt. She passed a little while later and left me the house."

"And now you run a Bed & Breakfast. Did you always want to do that?"

"We needed to live, to eat. It just sort of fell together, I guess. I mean, I'm a born nurturer," she tucked a strand of hair behind her ear and looked down at her tea glass as she spoke, "I mean I was always taking care of things when I was a kid. Mending birds with broken wings, taking in strays, that sort of thing."

"I can see that about you. What about family?" he said willing her to look up at him. When she did, her eyes held that sparkle of silver he glimpsed before. *Beautiful.* His eyes took in every inch of her from head to toe.

"Thanks. Anyway, my parents, they had me late in life. They uh, died in a car accident before I started my freshman year at college. I was alone for a while, I worked various places and went to classes, then I met Tom."

"Tom?" he couldn't help the jealous feeling that welled up inside of him.

"My husband. I admit I was foolish. I didn't know him very well."

"But you married him," he wanted her to continue.

"Um, yeah, I'm sorry, I am talking way too much right now. Let me just go check on dinner."

"Please don't stop, I'd like to know more about you."

"Why?" She looked directly into his eyes and asked her question.

There were a million reasons why, he thought to himself, but before he got a chance to speak, she narrowed her eyes. He smelled her anger and raised his eyebrows.

"What is it, huh? Why do you want to know about me? You want me to tell you how I got pregnant, quit school, and stayed home to keep house like a good little girl? I married my husband because that's what I was taught girls did when they got pregnant," she pushed back her hair angrily, but turned to face him as she continued.

"I didn't know him very well. He was bookkeeper.

He was gone so much of the time I never really got to know him either. I liked reading and cooking, so I took a few culinary classes at the local community college where we lived. One or two adult education classes on business management and of course childcare and CPR. I never did pick a major. I just like learning about everything, but to answer your original question, as I am sure you are so interested in the answer, yes, I run a B&B because I want to raise my son and here, I can do that and earn a living. But before you get any ideas you rented my rooms, Mr. Graves, not me," she pointed a finger at him and continued her tirade.

"I am not part of the attractions here and neither is my son. I'm aware that a man that looks like you must be used to getting his way, but I am telling you now that I am not on the list of activities for you to enjoy on this trip. Leave the plate and glass right there when you are finished," she broke eye contact and turned her back on him. Randall was almost embarrassed to admit how much her little speech had turned him on.

"*Holy Shit*, you are fucking amazing," and *can I add, I think I just fell in love with you*, but that part he kept to himself.

"No, I'm not. I'm just a mom who wants the best for her son. Nothing amazing about it. It's nature. All parents feel that way. And you owe the swear jar two more dollars."

"No, you're wrong. Trust me. But I hope you understand that I do not think about you as some means to tickle my fancy. I want to get to know you. Hell, just about everything about you intrigues me. And it's not some diversion or vacation attraction. I want to know about *you*."

"All you need to know is that I serve meals on time, I'll make up the bed and do the laundry if you leave it in the right basket and I will do my best to keep things between us professional for the next few weeks. If you are so interested in me personally, then here's some trivia about me, if I could while away the hours studying classical literature I would. I like Keats, Byron, and Shelley. I read the Bronte sisters when it's raining outside, and I usually cry when I do so. I have neither the time nor the inclination to have an affair with you or anyone. Now, I hope you enjoy yourself while you are here, Mr. Graves, excuse me."

Oh, my Lord, I have gone and lost my mind, Tulla's heart was pounding as her tirade ended. She couldn't help herself. The second she saw the man step off that boat she knew she was in for trouble. Everything about him breathed sex appeal, but she was gun shy and not in the market to be seduced by the likes of him.

He was what her Aunt Mildred would have called *too damned good-looking for anybody's good!* Tulla thought for sure he was going to walk out the door and she'd lose the whole month's income, but if that's what it took to preserve what was left of her sanity and her heart, so be it. She didn't hear him walk over to her, so it was something of a surprise when she felt his hands on her waist.

"My name is Randall," he turned her around and pulled her up against his hard body. Then his lips crashed down on hers and Tulla held on for dear life. He tasted like the dark chocolate she used in her cookies and sweet tea and mint. He broke the kiss abruptly and steadied her with his hands. *Thank goodness for that*, she thought, or else she'd be in a heap on the floor. And just from a kiss.

"Okay then, *Randall*. As long as we understand each other," she tugged down the hem of her shirt it had somehow crept up her stomach revealing the underside of her white lace bra, "I've, uh, got some laundry to take care of. Dinner is in a half hour."

"Of course, I'll just unpack my things then. Here's the two dollars for the swear jar. Until dinner, Ms. Nirvelli."

6

Randall walked to his room with the taste of her still on his lips. It had been touch and go there for a second. He didn't think he'd be able to stop, but then he remembered the boy. It wouldn't do for Daniel to come home to find his mother and him, well, anyway.

He went back to his room and forced himself to shut the door even though his body was screaming for him to go back and claim that woman for his own. The growling voice of his Wolf echoed inside his head. *Mine.*

Randall distracted himself with the cardboard box that had been shipped to *The Sea Mist* by some of his more daring Packmates. *The bastards!* He grinned as he tossed the contents onto the bed and shook his long hair back.

The first thing he pulled out of the box was a bright yellow swimming thong wrapped in blue tissue paper. *As if he'd be caught dead in that!* He chuckled and unwrapped the next surprise. It was a superhero themed mask and snorkel set, more appropriate for a kid than for a grown man. *Perhaps that could be passed on to Danny.*

Next, he opened a large envelope. Inside was a porno magazine inside, a small tube of lotion, and a mini pack of tissues. He guessed that was from Dib. The son-of-a-bitch had gotten a good look at Tulla on the video chat! Probably figured Randall would be in dire need of some relief the second he saw her. *Wait till he got a hold of him.* He tossed the contents on the bed with the rest of the stuff.

Finally, he pulled out a hard, plastic box that was sitting on the bottom. He opened it to find a salon worthy grooming kit for men. It included scissors, clippers, shaving cream and a brand-new razor. He tugged on his beard and raised an eyebrow. *Maybe it was time.*

The spacious bathroom was clean and well-lit. The faint smell of bleach lingered in the air underneath the fresh linen scented potpourri that sat in a glass bowl above the toilet seat. He opened the window to the sound of the surf, but he still felt as if he was in a shoe box. He'd had the beard for about two decades. He wondered if he'd even recognize his face anymore without it.

"Fuck it," he said and grabbed a handful of dark facial hair. He took the scissors and went to town. Once it was short enough, Randall held the clippers to his face and began clearing away the hair that had been his constant companion out of sheer neglect.

He'd never been overly concerned with his looks. He knew he was physically attractive to the opposite sex. It was a Werewolf thing. His body was muscular and fit without him even trying. He did love to jog, but he rarely hit the gym for anything other than the treadmill.

So, he wasn't quite as trim as Conall, who was kind of in love with himself, nor was he as buff as Rafe. His Alpha was almost twice as wide as he was, but that kind of went with the job. *Hmm.* Maybe he should try harder.

Then again, Tulla had mentioned his good looks when they were having their *discussion* earlier. So, she did find him appealing! *That was good!* Well, if he was being totally honest, as a Werewolf usually was, he'd admit it was more like she had drawn a line in the sand as opposed to simply admitting her attraction. Okay, the woman basically told him to back the fuck off. But damn it, that just made him want her more!

He turned off the clippers and splashed freezing

water on his face. He patted it dry with one of the several cotton washcloths that sat folded on the marble bathroom counter. She thought of everything! There were little bars of soap shaped like seashells in a little ceramic dish next to the sink and a note that read "Thank you for staying at *The Sea Mist*!" in yellow and blue ink. *Dang, she was cute!*

He put down the washcloth and got a good look at himself. His skin was paler than he remembered, but his mouth was wide and full as ever. His jaw was square and even. He ran a hand over his neck to test the smoothness. *You'll do,* he thought to himself, *you'll do.*

Tulla splashed cool water on her face from the large plastic sink inside her laundry room. She grabbed the small towel that hung on a hook next to it and patted her skin dry. There was no mirror for her to check herself. She'd just have to deal with it.

Okay Tulla, nice work. You sure put him in his place, she exhaled and closed her eyes tight for a second. There was no denying the attraction between her and her new guest, but she thought her little speech would have put a stop to any and all advances he thought to make. Was he crazy or did he simply not care that she was a single mom and his hostess for the next month? She was not about to have a fling with a strange man, no matter how damn cute he was!

She rolled her eyes and shook her head. *Idle hands and all, none of that now. Get to work, Tulla.* The pep talk helped motivate her to start the wash that she had gone in the room to do. Tulla loved the busy work of washing, drying, and folding clothes. It helped ease her mind when she was worried or anxious. Like she was now.

One of the first things she upgraded when she decided to open a Bed & Breakfast was the laundry equipment. She had a top-of-the-line washer, a commercial strength dryer, all energy efficient of course. She had an amazing iron with a million settings, and an extra-large ironing board set up in the corner.

Her personal favorite was the home dry cleaning machine! She bought it at an auction on-line and paid less than she did for the washer. She was profoundly serious about laundry, both for herself and her guests!

She pushed the start button on the stack of beach towels she just placed in the dryer. She liked to provide her guest with fresh towels every morning. These were her favorite. They were patterned to look like mosaic tile in bright aqua, white, and yellow squares. *Look how you go on about a set of beach towels!* Oh well, anything to take her mind off the way she lost it in the kitchen with her new guest.

What was she thinking? *Four weeks!* How was she

going to last in the company of that man for four weeks without melting into a puddle at his feet! And how was she going to look at him again after the way she spoke to him? He must think she was the most conceited woman in the world. As if he'd look twice at somebody like her.

She was twenty-eight, already had a child and been married. She wore sneakers and shorts just about every day of her life and never, ever got her nails or hair done. She never finished school and made her living essentially cooking and cleaning for strangers. He would never think her interesting or smart, after all, he was some sort of computer wizard.

What the heck was he doing here anyway? This was a place retirees or serious golfers came to visit. Not gorgeous men alone and looking to hook up. She certainly made it clear she wasn't available as some sort of side attraction for him and he'd just have to deal.

It was done now, she couldn't un-say it. So, what if she made a fool out of herself with that declaration? So, what if he never intended to make a move on her and she was just being uptight? *He did kiss you. Hmm.*

Well, yes, there was that. He had kissed her and held her steady in his arms until she could stand on her two feet again. *Holy cow!* The man had lips designed for sin. Even under all that hair. She was curious to see the rest of him without that beard, the sound of the clippers coming from his bedroom meant she just might get the chance. She only hoped he wasn't shaving his head too. She kind of liked all that long dark hair on a man. Okay, maybe not on every man, but on him, it fit.

He looked like some kind of knight from days of old with all that hair. His eyes were what really captivated her though. They were warm and dark when he was thinking or smiling, but every time he looked at her, they seemed to glow like molten caramel.

When he was in her kitchen, he took up all the available space. He just had one of those larger-than-life personalities, though he was quieter and more unassuming than she would have thought for a man who looked like him.

Tulla's stomach did a somersault when she thought of that kiss. It'd been so long since she felt even the inklings of desire, she almost didn't recognize it. Oh, why did she have to go and feel that way about a virtual stranger and a client?

She had to shut this down. She had a son to care for and a business to run. She couldn't afford to get mixed up over a guy who would sail out of her life the same way he sailed in. And it simply wouldn't do for Danny to get involved either.

The sun was still burning in the sky and Tulla

wondered if the temperature was to remain hot and sunny the next few days. It was usually warm on the island, but the constant breeze cooled things off so she rarely ran the AC.

She wondered if Randall found his rooms too warm. Did he want the AC on? She'd have to ask him. She was surprised when he got off the water taxi in his flannel shirt and long jeans. She guessed the weather where he travelled from must still be cold despite it being spring. She never travelled north but would love to visit a place like New York City. Not to live mind you, but just a visit would be nice.

She wondered what it would be like to go there with him. A real night on the town with her in a fancy dress and him in a tux. No doubt he'd look good, muscular, and tall as he was, he'd fill out any suit like a model. And after he wined and dined her, they'd go back to his suite overlooking Central Park and she'd help him take off his jacket and shirt. She wondered if his skin would be soft and smooth or if that dark hair of his was everywhere? She liked a little hair on a man. And then he'd peel off her dress and their bodies would touch and...

Yikes! Fantasizing about the man was no way to get him out of her head! *Okay, what was I doing? Towels! Do the towels, Tulla!*

7

Tulla served his dinner in the formal guest dining room. The room was cheerfully decorated in pale yellows and blues. It was homey and clean, and the food smelled amazing. Pot roast was a favorite of his, but Randall couldn't help feeling disappointed. Especially when she retreated to the kitchen.

He always ate alone. No big deal, right? Except lately, Charley had insisted that the Wolves in residence at the Manor eat meals together as frequently as possible. It was good for morale and kept Pack ties healthy. Randall tried to accommodate the Alpha Female, but his work often left him eating at his desk.

He should be used to it, but he was twitchy throughout his meal. It was as if, for some reason unbeknownst to him, he felt his isolation keenly. Maybe it was because of the sound of laughter coming from the kitchen? Maybe it was because he couldn't stop thinking about Tulla and her shy smiles and wicked silver eyes?

Another bout of giggles came from the kitchen. This time they erupted out of Danny. He must be back from his scout meeting. The boy was growing on him. There was something about the kid. Now that he had time to reflect on it, he could sense the boy was special. *Oh hell, you just have the hots for his mama. Shut up and eat your dinner, man.*

He had no right to intrude. He had no rights to this family. The thought left his Wolf snarling in his mind. He'd heard of Werewolves who had instinctively chosen their mates based upon less intense feelings than the ones he was having, and he stopped with the fork midway to his mouth. He needed a run.

He left the plate on the table, unsure of what else to do with it and threw on a pair of sneakers and a pair of sweats and left the house. He set off towards a stand of huge oaks that lined the road opposite the house. It would be good for him to do a little recon-naissance anyway.

He usually did that as soon as he arrived at a new place. *Man*, he must have it bad. When was the last time a woman had interfered with his common sense?

He ran double-time in a miles-wide perimeter around *The Sea Mist*. The expulsion of energy was good for him. He felt alive and far more in touch with his Wolf than he ever had.

The wilderness held secrets normals couldn't begin to understand. Randall's supernatural senses allowed him to commune with nature with a great deal more intensity and honesty than the average person could imagine. He moved throughout this part of the island as if he were invisible, leaving no trace of himself. Randall could stay hidden if he didn't want to be seen.

He wasn't here on a mission, but he'd sleep better at night knowing the area was secure. *That Tulla and Danny were secure.* His strong connection to the family of two would have been disturbing if it didn't feel so damn right to him. They were both special and they were his to protect. Even if only for the time being. *Mine,* his Wolf growled the word in his mind and Randall stopped moving. *Mine.* This time the thought was his.

Overall, it was a good run, he decided. He'd tracked a few more aggressive members of the local wildlife. He made sure the alligator nests were far enough away from where he traced the scents of Danny and his mother.

It made him smile to circle the grounds where

they took walks and played games. Bloody Point was a beautiful place. Full of mystery and legend. He'd read about the massacres that gave the place its name on the plane ride over. The Yemassee Tribe often quarreled with the European settlers over such things as unfair trades and he imagined, a general unrest at being evicted from a place that was their home for centuries.

History, for normals as well as supernatural beings like him, was often full of bloodshed, wars, genocide, and any number of atrocities. Bloody Point was simply one such place. The one thing that he noted on his walks that would not be in any history book was the fact that Bloody Point rested on a strong vein of magic.

In fact, it was by tracing the direction in which Tulla and Danny walked that he discovered the place where the magic was at its strongest. Just a few miles west of *The Sea Mist*. The small cave sat on a part of uninhabited shore where the ocean constantly crashed into the huge rocks that covered the sand.

It was the one or two times he noticed their hikes took them a little too close to danger for Randall's comfort. No good ever came from playing too close to magic. He discreetly moved a couple of fallen trees to discourage any further exploration in that area.

Other than that, and a few near run-ins with wildlife they were fine.

The sun had already set by the time he circled back. He slowed to a jog and headed for the shore, taking his shoes off, and slinging them over his shoulder. There was a section of the beach that smelled as if it had been used recently by one or two people.

He inhaled, he caught a whiff of too much cologne and a trail of human urine. The guy must have been hanging out for a long time behind the coarse grass that grew on top of the sand dune if he had to pee and couldn't make it to the shore to do his business. Randall poked around the area. The traces were faint, a month old at least.

He would have normally been able to pick up more after such a brief time, but the wind and surf had altered the scene. Whoever it was, the person hid behind this dune for a reason. Randall raised an eyebrow. It was too close to *The Sea Mist* for comfort. Too close to those he now considered his to protect. He'd be keeping an eye on it.

All that travelling must have caught up with him because he laid down on the bed just after he got back from his run. There was a mint on his pillow which he popped into his mouth before closing his eyes. The next time he opened them it was two o'clock in the morning according to the small alarm clock that sat on the nightstand. *Fuck*, he shouldn't have gone to bed so early. Now he was wide awake.

It was too early to go wandering through the house. He didn't want to cause a commotion, so Randall walked over and opened the sliding door to the small patio. The air coming off the water was cool and refreshing. He breathed it in greedily. The sound of the waves tempted him to get a little closer. He leapt over the short gate that enclosed his private deck.

His feet landed soundlessly on the sand. Randall closed his eyes and felt his Wolf in his mind, strong and clear, closer than he'd been in years without it being a full moon. He listened with his supernatural hearing to the sounds all around him. The loudest noise belonged to the waves crashing on the shore. It was a soothing melody. It had been years since he let the sound of nature creep into his mind. Years of staring at code and cracking down on enemies of the Pack.

Randall loved his job. Computers were his life, but lately, ever since Rafe and Charley had gotten married, he'd felt hollow. Computers were all fine and good, but they were cold and lifeless. Randall wanted more.

He'd never felt that way. Not in all his years on this Earth, and yes, they were adding up. Werewolves had longer lifespans than normals, that much was true. He just never realized how long it felt when you had no one beside you to share it with. Emptiness had become too familiar to him. He worked himself hard lately, to the dismay of the rest of the Wolf Guard, the Alpha's elite set of Wolves who acted as his right hand with the rest of the Pack. They wanted to see him settled.

He was annoyed when they suggested a vacation a few weeks ago. *Hell*, he'd been dead set against it. Then Rafe called him into his office and ordered him to spend no less than a month, *a whole freaking month*, away from their home in south Jersey.

He inhaled the warm night air rich with salt and sand and exhaled just as slowly. *Hell*, Randall wasn't sure he even knew how to relax. He even snuck a Chromebook with him on vacation! He figured he'd at least work on *WolfMoon*. When the lady of the house informed him that the modem was busted, and he wouldn't be able to use the remote desktop access he had so carefully set up he almost didn't know what to do. But then he'd been distracted by her soft curves and plump lips to really care.

He spied two hammocks snug in the shadows of a couple of palm trees and walked silently over to them. He was a predator and he moved like one. He did not make a sound unless he wanted to, and he did not want to. It was dark and quiet, and he fell into the night like he was a part of it which he guessed, he was.

He chose the hammock with the most cover and sank into it with all the natural grace he possessed. Well, he may have been roped into this vacation against his will, but he was here now, and he might as well enjoy it. *If you can't beat 'em...*

He sat there alone, in the dark quiet of the night with the waxing moon and the ocean to keep him company. His Werewolf eyes saw perfectly fine in the dark and his hearing was focused on the perfect silence. Which was why he stilled the hammock and held his breath the second he heard the screen door from the kitchen swing gently open.

8

Randall dropped from the hammock and rolled onto the floor hiding himself behind two palm trees whose trunks were intertwined. The vantage points from there gave him an optimal view of the person tiptoeing across the back deck and onto the sand.

There were electric lights outside on the deck, but they were turned off at night. His enhanced night vision allowed him to see clearly, he only hoped whoever was stalking about the place wasn't as adept to the surroundings as he was. He was no stranger to fights, and he would gladly engage in a war if it kept those inside that house safe.

He held his breath and waited. The second he recognized the lithe silhouette he exhaled. Her scent, that seductive combination of sea salt and coconut that was unique to her, drifted into his nostrils on the cool night breeze. She enticed him with her potent fragrance, he admitted it freely to himself.

He could get drunk on that scent. *On her. His. Tulla.* Her name felt good rolling over his mind. He longed to feel it roll off his tongue. He longed to do other things with his tongue. To lick and taste those secret parts of her body that he'd been dreaming of since he laid eyes on her.

She's a widow and a single mother, he tried repeating that over and over in his brain, like a mantra to keep her from his lusty thoughts. He should leave her to her moonlit walk, he thought but he was rooted to the spot like the trees he hid behind. *Shit*, he bit his lip and craned his neck, *what was she up to?*

The mystery that was Ms. Tulla Nirvelli fascinated him. Why a woman as intelligent, capable, and drop-dead gorgeous as her would hide themselves away on this remote island was a puzzle to Randall. Like most computer programmers, Randall's mind thrived on solving puzzles. He wanted to solve this one alright. *All night long.*

He watched greedily as she walked across the sand to the shore. She was wrapped up in a thick, oversized robe that fell all the way to her ankles. Her feet, he noticed, were bare. He frowned at her hair piled up the way it was on top of her head in some kind of long, clippy thing. He liked it better when she wore it loose around her shoulders.

As if she read his thoughts, she reached up with her hands and removed the clip shaking her hair loose. He inched forward, curiosity getting the best of him. When her hands dropped to her waist he almost cursed aloud. She tugged open the belt of her robe, her back towards him. He craned his neck and almost fell face forward in the sand when she lifted her heart shaped face up to the sky and closed her eyes.

It was as if she were drinking in the soft moonlight. Pulling it into herself. As if she too were a part of the night, the air, and the water around her. Her hair hung down past the graceful arch in her back in soft cascading waves. Randall itched to run his fingers through it, to test its softness.

This woman was wreaking serious havoc with his brain and he'd barely met her twenty-four hours ago. The dull thud of the robe hitting the sand was nearly his undoing. Randall's mouth hung open at the sight of Tulla Nirvelli bare and beautiful with only the moonlight touching her supple skin.

Her body was womanly, soft, and elegant with dips and valleys aplenty. Her toned curves were enough to make him bite back a growl. She was a damned knock-out. From his position, he saw every inch of her. It should have felt wrong and maybe a little bit perverse, *okay, maybe a lot*, but it didn't.

The act of watching her unguarded in this moment was something he would cherish always. Beautiful did not begin to describe how she looked to him. *Strong. Fierce. Goddess. Desirous. Lovely. Fire. Mine.* To his Wolf, she was already his.

The tension in his body increased. He felt himself harden inside of his sweats and tried to ignore the instinct raging inside of him to take her and claim her without delay. Inevitable as it might be Randall wanted her to have a choice in the matter. He had secrets to share with her when the time was right. He couldn't just pounce on her for God's sake!

His mind went blank as she straightened. He focused. Something was about to happen. Anticipation made him grow harder. She stretched and rolled her shoulders as if ridding herself of all the stress from her day. He particularly liked the little wiggle of her hips. *Damn, she was cute.*

He could have watched her for hours, but his perusal was over far too quickly. The object of his intense study walked or rather jogged straight into the waves without flinching at what he assumed was seasonally cold water. Her satisfied sigh carried over the sound of the surf to his waiting ears.

Damn, he wanted to make her sigh like that. *And*

more. He felt his growl reverberating in his chest. The need to go to her was growing stronger with each passing second. He watched her stretch out her long, toned arms over her head. One second, she was there, her back curved, head tucked, like any seasoned diver, and the next second she was gone, under a wave of frothy saltwater.

Randall's heart skipped a beat. His little vixen dove straight into the ocean in the middle of the night without a stitch on! Carefree and fearless as anything he had ever seen! He waited a few seconds and was about to jump in to look for her when she resurfaced a few dozen feet from shore.

Brave. Maybe reckless. He couldn't help but admire her. Still, he pushed back his long hair and finally released the breath he was holding. The Wolf in him was having a tough time with her being so far away. The man in him was struggling not to strip down and join her.

Hell, he was more than tempted, but Randall stilled himself. This place was her home. It was where she lived, and this was clearly a ritual of hers. He had no business intruding. His Wolf snarled at him in his mind's eye, but Randall controlled him with his own dominant stare.

She was not his. *Not yet*, came the reply. He forced himself to sit back and admire the view. He could keep watch from afar. The thought settled the Wolf in him, but only slightly.

She swam around in the cool night air for a good twenty minutes before making her way back to shore. She stopped and whipped her head out of the water. Tiny clear droplets sailed across the night sky like diamonds being tossed to the wind. *God*, she was beautiful.

She looked like an oil painting he'd once seen somewhere in Greece of a sea nymph returning to her home in the dead of night. He'd travelled to Athens once for a gaming convention, but he managed to steal away a few hours to explore.

Randall appreciated art in the sense that it was not the chaos or happy accident some people thought it was. No, art was something much more sacred to him. It was order, planning, mathematics, perspective, logic, fractals, and symmetry or the absence of it. The human soul expressed through calculations that sometimes only the artist could understand. Few people recognized it, but software development and programming required that same kind of artistic skill.

He'd like to spend more time studying art someday, but right then he only wanted to explore one thing and she was swimming around completely naked in the Atlantic Ocean under the light of the moon, not forty feet from where he crouched against the sand. She was more captivating than any painting or code Randall had ever seen.

He bit back another growl as she stood up and stepped free from the surf. Water rivulets rolled down her luscious curves in places he longed to follow with his hands and mouth but had to be content with just his eyes. The woman was a goddess. *Mine.* This time it wasn't the Wolf who snarled in his mind. It was all him.

He wanted her in a way he'd never wanted another person in his whole life. The level of possessiveness was new and kind of disturbing. He needed to get out of there. He had to stop watching her before he acted on his baser instinct to claim her succulent body for his own.

His Wolf demanded he go to her. It was like an ever-growing wave of noise and yet there was nothing but silence around him. This roaring sensation was inside his head. It made every nerve in his body stand on edge, screaming at him to take her, to dive into her the way she did that cool saltwater, to cover her in his scent. The scent thing was to ward off any other males who came sniffing around her. They would know she belonged, that she was taken. *Mine.*

He ran a hand over his smooth face and almost groaned aloud. The changes in him in a matter of hours were unbelievable. He shaved! Of all the things, he never thought he'd do, he shaved off that long beard of his. That beard was a part of him for years and years, camouflaging his expressions, hiding him from the world so he could easily sink back into the screens of code he wrote and analyzed for weeks at a time.

Randall excelled at keeping himself separate from other people and Wolves. He had for some time now and the beard made it easier to keep away. It made him seem aloof and maybe a little scary. He used that to his advantage. He was not a coward, but he preferred to remain at an emotional distance from others. Even his Pack. It was something of a shock to discover that, after all this time, he no longer wanted that.

He didn't need the beard anymore. Not here. Not with her. He wanted the foot-long growth off his face the second he landed on this island. Well, *not really,* he admitted. He wanted it gone the second his eyes landed on Tulla.

He needed to slow down. The Wolf wanted her now, but the man knew better. Visions of her body, cool and wet, fresh from the sea water, pressed up against his, made his mouth water. *Mine,* growled his Wolf in his mind's eyes. But Randall needed time to approach her properly, to test the mutual attraction he felt between them. *You don't force a connection. You have to proceed with a smooth and steady hand.*

It was funny how he recalled advice he'd given to the junior developers who worked for him while he sat crouched against the sand looking at the first woman he wanted in years. He sunk farther into the shadows and backed up a little further.

He intended to wait for her to go inside and then he would return to his bed where he was certain he'd toss and turn all night long. It would be worth it if he dreamt of her though. Just as his mind started to wander through all sort of delicious images, his acute hearing picked up the sound of someone breathing heavily.

He whipped his head around, homing in on where the sound was coming from. He inhaled and picked up the scent of deodorant and something akin to sour cream and cheese flavored chips. Someone was definitely close by and the guy brought a snack. *Grrrr.* The Wolf was on edge. Randall went into protect mode.

He reacted before he could even think to stop himself. He stood quickly and knocked over the small side table that sat next to one of the hammocks. He ignored Tulla's gasp and moved out from behind the palm trees racing silently across the sand. The culprit was thirty feet away and, apparently, he didn't sense the immediate danger he was in. *Good*, thought Randall, *which should make this more fun*.

He held his fingers to his lips while a stunned Tulla grabbed her robe and wrapped it around herself. He needed her to remain quiet so he could catch whoever it was doing all the heavy breathing. Whoever it was, he didn't have the sense he was born with to leave himself so exposed. One thing Randall knew for sure. This guy was going to get the message that he didn't belong here and after he was through with him the fucker was never gonna forget it!

Randall moved with all the stealth and speed a Werewolf in his human form possessed. The sand dune was about four feet high off the ground level where he stood. He stilled for a moment and listened to the sounds of a cell phone being used. *Was that the camera app?*

The rapid tapping of the screen told him someone was typing. *Oh crap.* It had to be a kid, no adults he knew could type that fast and with their thumbs too! *Ah, blessed technology!* He rolled his eyes. He could probably set off a bomb and the kid wouldn't notice, as long as his attention was focused on his phone.

Randall decided to surprise the little punk. He crouched down and vaulted over the four-foot-tall sand dune in one pretty damn impressive jump. He reached out and grabbed the kid by the collar of his sweatshirt and hauled him off the ground into the air. The kid screamed and kicked his feet to no avail, Randall narrowed his eyes and shook him before telling him to shut up.

"What the hell are you doing creeping around at this time of night?"

"Nothin' man! Let me go! You can't do this! Put me down or I'll call the cops."

Randall raised an eyebrow. The kid was fifteen years old at most, his Bieber wannabe haircut hung over a pair of scared blue eyes, but his mouth was yelling all sorts of nonsense. It was quite the show, but Randall ignored him. the Wolf had no interest in fighting children. However, the little creep had a cell phone and Randall could just imagine what he'd been doing with it. He let the Wolf out a little and brought the kid closer to his face.

"I asked a question. What were you doing out here?"

"Let me go, man! I swear I'll tell the police you attacked me!"

"Yeah, let's call them and tell them what you've been up to, you little perv! Give me that phone!" Randall was finished with the games. He dropped the kid on the ground without hurting him and took the cell phone. It was a fairly new smartphone and the little fucker had definitely been up to no good.

The camera app was open as was his *UrShotz* account. His handle was *PayaDaPlaya*. He had a PayPal account link in his profile and accepted private messages. A little more poking around and Randall's gaze flew to the creepy little entrepreneur.

"For real, bro? How much you make a month?"

"Couple of bucks, it's no big deal, man."

"No big deal? This is some seriously illegal shit right here. You do this here before? Tell me-" The sound of footsteps brought his head up.

"Oh, my Lord! Brayden White is that you? What on Earth are you doing outside this time of night? Oh, let him go, Mr. Graves, he's my neighbor's nephew!" Tulla tied the belt to her robe tightly and brushed back her wet hair with her fingers trying to make sense out of the scene in front of her.

"Not so fast," Randall's voice was barely more than a deep growl as he looked through the kid's cell phone and opened it to find the video of Tulla's night swim.

"This is what he was doing," he flashed the screen to Tulla who gasped, her eyes going wide with embarrassment or horror he couldn't tell, but he wanted to pummel the pimple-faced brat with his fists to make that look go away.

"Shame on you, Brayden! How could you do something like that? I am going to have to talk to your aunt! Can you erase it?"

"Well, the good news is he didn't get a chance to upload it anywhere, so it is just local to his camera. However, it seems Mr. White here is a businessman. He's been selling images like these online and making money. Tonight's photos and videos haven't been sold yet, but the bad news is, it looks like he was here last month and took a couple of photos of your uh, night swim. He did upload those to a few sites. They are pretty grainy images though."

"Oh, my Lord! Brayden! How could you? Is there anything I could do?"

"Well, I'd need a computer and a working modem, but I'm confident I can trace them and get them down. Now, I deleted everything from his phone-"

"You can't do that it's my personal property!"

"Brayden, you have invaded my privacy, you are trespassing on my property, and I'm sure it is illegal to take nude pictures of someone without their knowledge never mind selling those images!"

"She's right, kid, not to mention the fact that I will personally beat you to a bloody pulp if I hear one word about Ms. Nirvelli's fondness for swimming at night anywhere on this island, do you understand me?" Again, the Wolf surged forward, and he knew from the way his face turned a sickly shade of gray that the kid got the message.

The boy nodded his head up and down like one of those bobble-headed figures and shuffled his feet. His nerves were like a treat to Randall's Wolf who wanted nothing more than to hunt down the culprit who disturbed the sanctuary of Tulla's privacy and peace of mind.

"Okay, I'm sorry I won't do it again, just give me my phone back."

"I'm afraid I won't do that, Brayden. Not until you have your aunt come by for it in the morning and you tell her what you were doing."

"But–"

"No buts. You messed up, you got caught, but what you were about to do was so much worse. You were going to betray another human being's trust and privacy for your own selfish needs, you were going to exploit naked images of my body that you had no right to, to get a few dollars and maybe some more friends at school or 'likes' on your social media pages. That is despicable behavior from a young man like you. Now, go on home to your aunt's house and I will see you both in the morning."

Randall didn't approve of letting the boy go, especially after Tulla finished her speech. He wanted to howl his frustration into the night air, but that wouldn't do. It was too late anyway; the kid ran off like a shot towards his aunt's house. Randall squeezed the offending phone in his hand until he heard Tulla's gasp.

"Randall! Your hand!" She reached for him little electric shocks seem to emanate from the place her hand touched his. He lowered his eyes. He liked the way his name sounded coming from her lips.

It wasn't until she gasped again that he realized he had crushed the damn cell phone in his fist. Glass from the screen pierced his palm and he was bleeding. She tugged him into the kitchen, and he followed meekly as she pulled him past the kitchen and into his room. Randall was keenly aware of the fact that she was standing awfully close to him in very little clothing in what was essentially his bathroom.

Fuck, there was no way she'd mistake the, uh, condition he was in considering he wore nothing, but a pair of thin sweatpants. Thankfully, she was too intent on his hand to notice.

How could she not notice, maybe you are losing your mojo there my man, his voice taunted him inside his brain and Randall narrowed his eyes. His other hand hovered awkwardly on the counter. *Should he say something? Do something?* He felt like an idiot! He closed his eyes and tried to quiet the rather rare moment of panic and doubt he was having.

The sound of her soft, shallow breathing was loud in his ears. That coconut scent of hers increased. Tulla shuffled a little on her bare feet though she stood on the plush little bathroom rug, so he knew she was neither cold nor uncomfortable. She carefully plucked tiny shards of glass out of his palm, but all those other little things told him she wasn't as unaffected by his proximity as she seemed. *Good.*

"How in the world did you do this to yourself? That piece of junk could have sliced open a vein! What do they make those things out of anyway," she muttered as she worked on getting the last pieces out. Her mothering stirred something inside his chest.

He watched as she reached for a first aid kit under the sink and held his hand firmly in one of hers as she searched through a small magnifying glass to make sure all the pieces were in fact out. She withdrew some sort of wound cleansing wipe and gently swabbed his hand. He didn't feel a thing. He was doing his best to remain still, afraid if he moved, she'd break that delicious contact that was making every hair on his body stand up.

The second she touched him it was like a punch to his solar plexus. He couldn't breathe. He didn't want it to end. Her ministrations were efficient and careful. He liked watching her tend him. It humbled him and made him want to return the favor. Nothing had ever felt so right.

"Well, you must be made of pretty strong stuff not to flinch after all this."

He grunted and she smiled and, damn, if that wasn't another punch to his gut! Her smile was like the sun coming out after a long hard winter. It was the most beautiful thing he had ever seen. Bright enough to take over the whole damn room.

She turned on the faucet and let the warm water pour over his cuts. She patted them dry with some gauze and applied antibiotic ointment to it before wrapping a band aid over it. Most of the cut would be gone by the morning, only the deepest ones might remain another day or so, but he didn't stop her. Hell, he'd do anything to keep her touching him.

"Mr. Graves," Tulla's voice didn't shake, but her wandering eyes made it obvious she was aware of the shirtless man in front of her. Randall smiled slowly. He liked the way she watched him under her long eyelashes. Her voice interrupted his train of thought.

"I asked what you were doing outside? Were you, uh, spying on me, like young Brayden White?"

Randall gulped. *Oh shit.* "Uh, no, no I was not. I, uh, was relaxing in one of those hammocks you so thoughtfully provide for your guests and was quite surprised when you came outside to, uh, swim."

It sounded lame even to his ears, but it was the truth. Werewolves didn't usually lie. Well, maybe except about being Werewolves that is.

"Uh huh, so why didn't you announce yourself?"

The question was direct and honest, and Randall was in even deeper shit than he imagined. He expected anger or annoyance, but she seemed amused by the whole thing. He wondered for a split second if maybe she orchestrated it, but the thought quickly vanished from his mind. Her enjoyment of the night air and the cool water were far too real for her to have made it up.

"Well, I didn't want to intrude."

"Obviously. Well, you're not a horny teenager looking to put pictures of me in my birthday suit on the web so, I have to assume it was accidental. At any rate, thank you for so chivalrously coming to my aid."

"Anytime," he said and leaned a little closer. *Damn*, she smelled like coconut oil and sandy beaches and a little like laundry soap. *Fresh and clean and Earthy*. He wanted to roll around in that scent. *In her*.

"Goodnight, Mr. Graves."

"It's Randall."

"Goodnight, Randall."

"Goodnight, Tulla."

9

The next day was relatively quiet. Tulla placed an order for a new modem online at the library and it was delivered next day as promised. She had planned to wait till the next time she ventured to the mainland, and she hated to go back on her word to Mr. Lowell, who made the reservation for Randall, but she had no choice.

The little teenage cretin who sometimes visited his aunt, her closest neighbor, had crept onto her part of the shore and took photos of her engaged in her little habit of skinny dipping in the ocean at night. And worse, the little creep posted them and possibly sold them to other creeps wanting a sneak peek! Thank goodness Randall, uh, *Mr. Graves*, caught him before he uploaded the latest video he filmed.

Her cheeks grew warm as she realized again that

Randall had also seen her naked. Her embarrassment went out the window when she thought of how he'd found Brayden's hiding spot! He was some hero alright. He looked positively enraged at the teenager when he discovered what he was up to. Tulla hoped he scared the crap out of the kid. *Really scared the crap out of him!* She couldn't believe he was selling nude pictures of unsuspecting women without their knowledge or consent!

The worst part of the night wasn't the fact she'd been seen and potentially exploited. No, she'd get over that, but her stomach flipped over itself when she realized Randall had been hurt. Tulla was glad she still renewed her CPR/First Aid certification every year. The knowledge had certainly come in handy.

Of course, there was nothing she could have read in any book or taken in any class that would have prepared her for the jolt to her system she got just by touching that man. *Was it only two days ago?* She felt as though she were walking on hot coals ever since.

Especially when a certain pair of caramel-colored eyes found hers across the room. She tried not to meet them, did her best to appear unaffected and courteous. Tulla treated all her guests with the utmost respect for their privacy and needs.

She made sure he had fresh towels every day, home-cooked meals and snacks, a glass of sweet tea in the afternoon with a slice of a fresh peach the way she noticed he liked it, and some brochures for the local golf resorts, fishing expeditions, and the few restaurants on the island.

He was always polite and thanked her properly, but she swore he was picturing her naked every time he looked at her. She'd be lying to herself if she said she didn't like it. Still, she was in trouble and she knew it.

Her tall, dark, and too-handsome-to-be-true guest made her quiver in places she had long since forgotten about. Now that the weekend was over, and Danny was heading back to school she wasn't sure what she would do if he didn't quit making eyes at her. *Put the reins on Tulla girl, you've been a fool once in your life for a man and once was enough!*

She would never regret her marriage to Tom Nirvelli. The man didn't deserve her praise or even a mention really, but he had given her the most precious thing in the entire world. He'd given her a son.

Daniel was amazing in every sense of the word. He was her entire reason for being. She loved that little boy to pieces. *Focus on your boy*, she told herself firmly as she packed his lunch into a plain brown bag. After misplacing several rather expensive lunch boxes, Tulla had decided old-fashioned was some-times the best way to go.

She now packed Danny's snack and sandwich in a brown paper bag and found that the boy was just as happy with those as with the more expensive kind. She filled his sports bottle with ice and filtered water and set both on the kitchen counter.

She grabbed a felt tip pen and drew a mini comic strip on the front of the brown bag. She pictured his smile when he saw it! Today she drew a picture of a frog jumping on lily pads and then missing the last one. Only the frog's eyes and droplets of water were visible in that square. *Cute.* She signed it with hugs and kisses. *Always.*

That's how Randall found her, bent over a brown paper bag with a marker and smiling at the cartoon she was drawing for her son. Randall's heart thudded in his chest. It had been hell the last few days trying to forget the image of her swimming in the moon-light out of his mind.

For a few wonderful minutes, she had been completely unaware of his presence, naked and free in every sense of the word. Her soft skin glowing, her hair loose and curling around her shoulder. When she emerged dripping from the cool, salty waves of the Atlantic he had to bite his tongue to keep from growling aloud. *Beautiful.*

She was still beautiful now, with her hair pulled back in a low ponytail and a smile on her soft plump lips. He didn't move a muscle, didn't even breathe. He loved watching her, observing the tiny sparkle in her eyes that came from the genuine happiness it gave her to care for her son. In his entire life, he couldn't remember looking upon anything as lovely as Tulla. *My Tulla.*

"Good morning, sir," a small voice behind him broke the spell. He met her eyes as she turned to see him standing there. Daniel raced in with his backpack open spilling its contents along the way.

"Hurry up, Mama, the bus is coming!"

"Easy there, champ, you're gonna need this," Randall smiled and scooped up the pencil case and folder that had fallen out of the bright blue backpack.

"Thanks, Mr. Graves!"

"Call me Randall," he smiled at the kid and laughed when his eyes grew big and round. He looked at his Mama who nodded first then he said, "Thanks, Randall! I'll see you later maybe we can play catch or something."

"Wait a second, young man, here's your lunch and what about my kiss?"

The boy threw his arms around his mother's neck and gave her a loud kiss right on the mouth before scampering off to the front door. Tulla followed him and waved to the bus driver as her boy set off for another exciting Monday of school and recess.

"That is one lucky boy," Randall said watching her blow a kiss and wave goodbye to her son.

"Are you kidding? I'm the lucky one. I get to be his mom."

"That is a lovely thought and I admit much more noble than the ones I've been having, Ms. Nirvelli," Randall's eyes ate her up from her bare feet to the top of her head. She was something alright.

"I thought we were on a first name basis now, Randall, after all you've seen me naked," she waked past him and made her way back to the kitchen with that subtle sway of her hips that kept him staring. If he didn't know any better, he could swear she was flirting with him. *Hmm. Interesting.*

"By the way, the modem is here, I'll connect it after breakfast then if you wouldn't mind terribly will you show me how to track the images that Brayden took of me?"

"Yes, ma'am, but I can set everything up while you do what you gotta do."

"Oh no, please, breakfast is part of the package. I feel terrible about this already, the least I can do is feed you first. Come on, I'll get you some coffee."

Randall nodded and followed her. He was hungry

all right, but not just for eggs and toast. This woman stirred feelings in him he thought were long gone. She poured him a mug of dark, rich coffee. When he raised an inquisitive eyebrow, she just smiled.

"I noticed you take it black. You never use the cream I put out when I serve coffee."

"Thank you," his voice was deeper than usual. He was pleased by the fact that she knew what he liked. Silly and old-fashioned, but he wasn't as young as he looked. Werewolves rarely were.

"Alright, you know you can take that to the dining room, and I'll bring out your breakfast."

"Is it okay if I stay in here," *with you,* he added silently. She looked startled but nodded and smiled at him a little nervously. The beat of her heart told him she was just as nervous as he felt. Maybe there was something there after all.

A timer went off and she walked to the oven carefully putting mitts on her hand and bending down to take out a mini casserole dish. The contents of which made his mouth water.

"This is a South Carolina staple, my great-aunt taught me this recipe. I hope you like shrimp and grits," she smiled and set a clean plate down with utensils in front of him. Then she set down the casserole dish with the drool-worthy shrimp and grits and a serving spoon. She walked backed to the oven and took out a tray with some homemade drop biscuits and piled them into a basket. Next to it, she set out a bowl of sausage gravy.

Tulla went to the fridge as he piled food on his plate and came back with a small bowl of fresh cut fruit and a dish with various jams, jellies, and whipped butter. Lastly, she placed a small plate, with a warm cinnamon bun oozing pecans and icing, to his right. Randall's eyes widened. Everything smelled and looked good if she did say so herself.

She bit her lip as she watched him take his first bite. He closed his eyes and exhaled with pleasure sending little tingles up her spine. She was a good cook, she knew it too, but for some reason his opinion really mattered.

"This is amazing!" He exclaimed and took another bite before using his napkin and sipping his coffee.

"Do you really like it?"

"I love it, we don't usually do grits up in Jersey, but Charley, that's my uh, boss's wife, she makes a polenta dish that's not half bad, but this knocks it right out of the park!"

"Thank you. You seem fond of her?" He heard the question and nodded.

"Oh yeah, she's great. Rafe, that's my boss, and his wife, Charley, are an amazing couple. She cooks most of our meals even though we have staff at the Manor who do stuff like that."

"You live with your boss?"

"Um, yeah, well, part of the job is to live on site at Macconwood Manor. There's a huge main house and a bunch of guest houses on the complex. We have everything, a gym, a pool, game room, gardens, playground, woods for hiking, and a private beach that is really close."

"Is it just you and your boss and his wife?"

"Oh no, there are several of us who live there, and we often have guests. Business related, that is," it wasn't a lie, he consoled himself with not being able to tell her everything. After all, one didn't just stand up and say *Oh yeah, I'm a Werewolf and I live with my Pack Alpha because not only am I in charge of Pack technology, I'm also a Wolf Guard!*

"Wow sounds interesting! I don't think I ever heard of a company quite like that. Is the whole company about computers or is that just your department?"

"Uh, just my department. Technically I have my own corporation. That's where I do most of my code work and where I file technological patents and such. But I, uh, sort of subcontract a greater portion of my time to Rafe. He got me started after all. We, uh, do a lot of different things."

"Wow! So, you have a contract with Macconwood Corporation, that's the name, right? Wow! That is amazing. I think I remember reading about a youth center too. Am I right?"

"Oh, Cat, my boss's sister, and her husband Tate, started a non-profit youth center for troubled kids and teens. Community is particularly important to us."

"That's really wonderful! And very necessary in these times. I lost my parents when I was a teenager. I came here to live with my great-aunt the summer before college, it was the best three months of my life. Then I started at a state school on the mainland. I waitressed my way through most of it. Then I met Tom, my husband and, well, now I'm here."

The tone of her voice held something he couldn't quite place. *Sadness or regret?* He wanted to ease her mind or at least turn it to something else. It didn't do any good to dwell on the past.

"Why don't we get started on that computer now? If you'd show me the way?"

He followed her to her private quarters and sat at the small table in the chair she indicated. The smell of coconut drifted into his nostrils as she leaned over him to give the old laptop's monitor a small smack on the side.

"Sorry, this thing is temperamental," she backed

up a little self-consciously and Randall felt the loss of her body heat immediately. *Damn*, she smelled good.

"No worries, um, do you have the modem?" He cleared his throat and accepted the cardboard box from her. It took him all of three minutes to set things up.

The computer sat on a small card table against a wall in what he imagined was Danny's playroom. There was a tiny, worn loveseat with a colorful blanket thrown casually over the back. A coffee table with stacks of little storage boxes containing toys underneath it took up most of the floor space, and a TV with an old gaming system hooked up sat against the opposite wall.

The room was clean and tidy, everything in its place. The smell of furniture polish and glass cleaner lingered despite the open window. It was a happy space. Full of care and love, nothing like the house he grew up in.

"I'll just grab some stuff from my room," he mumbled and retreated to his room. He needed a moment to clear his head. He grabbed his phone and Chromebook, both of which were more powerful than her older laptop.

"I'm sorry, I know my computer is old, but it works for our needs," she shrugged apologetically as he strode back in.

"It's a fine machine, mine is just a bit faster," Randall downplayed the difference in their computers as he sat his down and powered it up.

"It's second hand, my laptop that is, I got it at a church sale. You don't have to spare my feelings, Mr. Graves, I've got a little boy to clothe and feed, computers are not exactly a priority for me, but Danny does enjoy his games and it does help in running the B&B."

He was a jerk. A total freaking POS. He didn't mean to make her feel self-conscious. Especially not when it was obvious that she gave everything she had to taking care of her boy. Hell, the room he sat in was evidence of that.

"I'm sorry, I didn't mean to imply anything. My work is programming, I need the newest and fastest machines to get anything done. I was in no way trying to ridicule you. I think you are an amazing person, Tulla."

"Thank you," her cheeks turned a dusky pink at his words, and he found it quite charming. He wondered if she turned that same color in any other circumstances.

"I'll be right back," she said and walked out of the room.

He felt like an interloper sitting there. Tulla clearly loved her son and took exceptionally good care of him. He smiled as he thought of the little boy with his blonde hair and blue-gray eyes. He had the look of his mother. An angel's face with a good mind and kind heart.

What would it be like to have a little carbon copy of himself running around? The thought made his pulse speed up. He never had a family of his own. He was raised by his father. The two of them were alone those first few years of his life. He left home at sixteen and never looked back. His dad was a hard man and he had none of the warmth for his son that Tulla obviously had for hers.

She left the room for a few moments while he logged onto the teenager's various social media accounts after receiving a list from his Aunt that morning. She was exceedingly grateful they didn't alert the authorities and in turn gave them all the information he asked for while on conferencing in the boy's parents on her cell phone.

Tulla insisted on a written letter apology and a promise to never trespass on anyone's privacy again. He was surprised when Tulla informed the boy that should she find out that he ever did anything like this again she would be informing the authorities for his own good. He smiled at the memory of her stern words. She had grit. He liked that.

He found the offending images, thankfully they

were grainy, and her face was not visible in them, and he erased all traces of them. It was more difficulty tracking down the IP addresses of every person he sold images too, but Randall got all the information he needed in a matter of minutes.

The Chromebook was in no way as powerful as his own laptop, but he could hack his way into the servers where the kid's customers kept their files. One by one he deleted the images Brayden White had sold. There were five total videos and forty images of various women. If Randall had to guess he'd say they were neighbors or maybe even mothers of the kid's friends.

Randall deleted all of them. He then put a bit of hacker code on the kid's PayPal account that would alert him if the boy was receiving payments again. The little bastard deserved a beating for this shit, but Randall had to make do with happily erasing every image he had ever saved. The kid's collection of pornography was damn big, and it took a moment to delete all of it.

He was happy the parents gave him remote desktop access to the boy's computer without too much coercion. Randall searched his caches and tracked all of his online movements for the past six months. The kid wasn't all that savvy, but he managed to keep this from his parents and the parental locks they had placed on his machine. *Garbage code.*

Randall grunted and made some private changes to the device. If the punk decided to take up photography again not only would Randall be alerted, but a copy of the images would be immediately sent to the boy's parents. If such an infraction happened again Randall put a virus in the machine that would cause it to begin to erase itself. *Nice.*

Freaking teenagers! He remembered when he used to swipe a look at his father's girlie magazines just to see a female form. He supposed the internet made for easier access, but didn't these kids know that every move they made could be watched and traced back to them? *Idiots.* Making money off of illegally obtained pictures of naked women was not only stupid, but it was also criminal. Randall just shook his head.

"Any luck?" her voice interrupted his thoughts, but he didn't mind not one bit. She handed him a steaming mug of coffee, black just how he liked it, and smiled. *God*, he loved her smile.

"Uh, yeah. I've traced the image and erased it."

"I guess boys will be boys, but my goodness! Imagine my body plastered all over the internet! How embarrassing! Every stretch mark and freckle just exposed to the entire world, ugh! It would make people sick!" She shook her head and patted her stomach self-consciously,

Randall stood up so abruptly he knocked the chair he was sitting in right over. He closed the space between them in two long strides. He took the mug from Tulla's hands, ignoring her wide-eyed stare, and placed it on the table. Then he brought his hands to either side of her face and met her lips with his.

"You are beautiful and even though I'd want to tear the eyes out of anyone who would look at nude photos of you, they'd be damn lucky, *hell*, they'd be blessed, if given the opportunity to gaze upon the vision that is you, naked in the moonlight."

His statement was met with a look of disbelief. He needed to erase that look. He pulled her flush against his body and delighted at the way her heart thudded in her chest at the contact. She went still in his arms, but she didn't move away. In fact, she leaned into him ever so slightly.

He felt himself grow hard at the small submissive movement. He flexed his hips, pressing his manhood against her soft belly and brought his head down to meet hers again. *Mine.* The word sounded like a roar in his ear and brought a rough growl to the back of his throat as he kissed her.

His lips were soft, teasing her mouth with their gentleness. The contrast between his rock-hard body and her soft sigh of acceptance against his mouth made his heart sing with wanting her. He penetrated her mouth with his tongue, licking and tasting, drinking her in.

She was warm and sweeter than honey. He wanted more. Her small hands reached around his waist and she pulled him closer to her. Randall almost lost it at the small gesture of possession. He wanted to be hers, hell he'd just about roll over if she asked him to.

"This is the only thing I've wanted to do since before I watched you jump off the sand and into the water like some sea goddess in the middle of the night."

"I can't believe you've seen me naked," her shy whisper was accompanied by a sudden dropping of her eyes.

"Hey, none of that now, sweet Tulla. Every inch of you is beautiful and I don't know anybody in their right mind who wouldn't say the same if they saw you the way I did last night. Bathed in nothing but moon-light, you looked like a goddess."

"Oh please, I did not–"

"I never lie. You can believe me when I tell you, you are incredible."

She stared at him dumbfounded. Did he just tell her he found her beautiful? She couldn't be sure of his exact words. Her mind was being torn between listening to him and trying to keep up with every feeling she was having as he kissed and touched and talked.

She felt the pressure of his lips and then his tongue was dancing with hers again in a kiss so damn sexy she was liable to swoon at his feet. *Oh my!* She had never been kissed like that in her entire life. *But he's a guest. A client. OMG! What was she doing?*

"Excuse me, I'm sorry, I have to go," she ignored his call and grabbed her car keys before sprinting out the front door. The sight of him gorgeously disheveled standing in her living room with his lips swollen from their kisses was sharp in her mind as she started the car.

❧ 10 ❧

Tulla drove home with Danny safely buckled in the back seat of her car. She'd been gone five full hours. She needed some time to think, that's what she told herself when she hightailed it out of the house after Randall kissed her. *Okay, you kissed him too and you know it.*

She couldn't deny that she responded to his touch. The thought of his deliciously aroused body pressed up against hers made her pulse speed up and her knees grow weak. Tulla didn't care if she was an affront to feminists everywhere, the man had some serious skills, worthy of weak-kneed swooning women everywhere. And all he did was kiss her!

He could probably make her orgasm within five minutes of contact if they ever got really hot and heavy. Not that Tulla would know much about that.

The only man she'd ever been with was her late husband and Tom was not what you'd call a generous lover. They'd only completed the physical act of sexual intercourse the one time and she hardly remembered it.

Besides, Tulla couldn't afford to entertain even hypothetical visions of Randall Graves in bed. *Nope. No way.* No matter how eye-opening or earth-shattering such an event might be for her. She was too busy for fantasies! She'd leave that to the authors who wrote those clever little eBooks she downloaded on her tablet regularly, her own guilty little secret. As for her long-haired, caramel-eyed guest, well, Tulla was determined to keep him at arm's length.

Her life was far too complicated for an illicit affair. She could not afford to be reckless. The one time she made the decision to throw caution to the wind she got pregnant. She was married before she knew it and then poof, her new marriage was over. There'd been no other man in her life since then.

Tulla simply didn't have the experience necessary to deal with a man like him. How would she survive an affair with him? All she had to do was look at him to know she was out of her league. She was a mom for Pete's sake! She wore her hair in a pony tail most days and preferred jean shorts, loose tops, and sneakers to slinky little outfits and heels.

C.D. GORRI

He, on the other hand, looked like a model. Not one of those skinny little guys with too much eyeliner and hair gel. *No sir, not him!* He was more like one of those tall, lean, and cut athletic types who modeled underwear or motorcycles. He was gorgeous.

Tulla thought he was handsome even before he shaved off the beard. Once the facial hair was gone, he went from nice looking to serious hottie. She could picture him now, standing in her kitchen with his long, shiny locks down around his broad shoulders like it had been earlier that day and, well, she had no words. *Sigh.* The man was dreamy, as Aunt Mildred would say.

Sometimes, when he watched her, his deep brown eyes would lighten to a molten caramel color that she found purely hypnotic. He had high cheekbones, a strong, square chin, straight nose, white teeth, and full sensuous lips that made his face sinfully handsome.

Then there was his body. Tulla sighed under her breath when she thought of his herculean build barely hidden under loose athletic pants or shorts and t-shirts. His long, tall frame was corded with tight muscles and a smattering of chestnut colored hair that dipped beneath the waistband of his sweatpants.

His thighs were something else! Tulla felt his thick muscles press against her when they kissed. She had to stop herself from running her hands up and down them to his no-doubt, hard as steel backside. She had a weakness for men with killer legs! She was startled out of her daydream when a horn sounded behind her. *Oops!*

Shame on you, Tulla! He's a human being not a piece of meat! She stepped on the gas and her little car moved down the road at a steady speed. Of course, she could always think about his pleasant conversation, his quick wit and charm. That was probably more dangerous than mooning over his abs. But Tulla did enjoy talking to him as much as she did looking at him. Randall was funny and refreshingly forthright in his speech.

It was obvious he was exceptionally bright. *Like Danny.* Her sweet boy was buckled in his booster seat sipping on a peach smoothie. She glanced in the rear-view mirror and chided herself for not paying attention as her son chattered away about his day of school from the backseat.

"How come I didn't take the school bus today, Mama?"

"Oh, I just had an errand to run," it wasn't a lie exactly, but she couldn't tell her son she'd been too scared of what she'd do if that man kissed her again. Truth was, she forgot to prep for dinner and stopped at the market for a couple of fresh porterhouse steaks

C.D. GORRI

for her guest. She was going to grill them along with some fresh asparagus and wild rice pilaf.

"Mama! My backpack is stuck again! I wanna show you my artwork from today! We made honey-combs out of pasta and glue, I put some gold glitter on mine," his excitement was contagious.

She laughed as she stopped in their driveway and put the car in park. Tulla turned around in her seat to pull it free. That little blue backpack often wound up halfway stuck beneath Danny's seat when he was in the car.

He scrambled up the graveled path as she exited the car with her bags of groceries. She paused when she saw Randall standing in the front door. He was big and so masculine looking with his hair pulled back and a black t-shirt on with gray sweats. He had a high five ready and waiting for Danny who jumped in the air to deliver it, his blue eyes sparkling with delight. *Uh oh. Don't go there. Oh, please, don't be nice to my son. Don't make it so easy for me to fall for you.*

"Here, let me take that for you," Randall reached out and took the grocery bags from her. He smelled good, like soap and that same earthy spice she'd noticed earlier that day. She wondered if she could discreetly discover the name of the cologne or after shave or whatever it was he used. The scent made her nerve endings tingle.

"Thank you."

She looked down and noticed he was bare foot. His feet were nice, she mused. He had short, clean toenails. It seemed such an intimate thing, looking at someone's bare feet. She paused as guilt overwhelmed her. He must have stayed indoors on the computer all day! *Damn it.* She walked inside with him following behind as she wrestled with her conscience.

"I hope you got outdoors today, it was so nice and sunny."

"I did, actually, I went for a run on the beach. It was a real nice day for running, though I'm not sure how many more of those we'll have."

Her back went ramrod straight as she caught his meaning. *Play it cool, Tulla.* She smiled politely and turned to start taking groceries out of her bags. His deep chuckle sounded behind her and she realized he was teasing her. *The gall of the man!* Danny came inside with his picture in his hand and Tulla praised his work before sticking it to the fridge with a magnet.

"Wow! That is some honeycomb you designed there, pal! Do you know what they call that shape in math?"

"A hexi- no, a hexagon!"

"That's right! High-five! Come on, don't leave me hanging, bud!"

The scene was so homey. The two guys talking

and fooling around. Tulla almost allowed herself to believe it was real. *It's temporary, don't forget that* she thought to herself, *he doesn't belong to you.*

"Mama, what's an orphan?" Danny's question made the two adults in the room stop cold.

"Huh? Why are you asking that honey?"

"Today at recess Marcus said I was an orphan. I asked him why he said that, and he says it's because I don't have a daddy."

"What!" Tulla covered her mouth as she bit back and expletive. She was so angry. She was spitting nails!

"Ooh, that little jerk. You tell him, well, just tell him, ugh, I can't-"

"Hey, hey, hey. Come here, calm down, it's okay," he rubbed her arms up and down and faced her before nodding to Danny, "May I?"

Tulla was so angry she couldn't form a coherent sentence. She didn't think he'd say anything to harm her boy so, she nodded and pushed her hair out of her face. Her hand covered her mouth as she tried to register the fact that he was kneeling on her kitchen floor to address her boy on eye level. Her heart squeezed in her chest.

She'd fight the world for her son, take on beasts or man, it didn't matter to her. But how do you deal with other children when they were perhaps even more cruel than anything else out there? Randall's voice was steady and calm as he spoke.

"Danny, an orphan is someone without any parents. You have a mama so, you can't be an orphan, right? Now, there are lots of people out there in this world that don't know what they are talking about. The next time this Marcus or someone else says anything like that to you, you inform them that they need to learn the definition of a word before they use it, okay bud?"

Tulla smiled through tears at the patient explanation Randall gave her son from on bended knee. *He was right too,* she thought. She laughed out loud when he continued.

"And if Marcus or anyone else insists on using words like that despite all your trying to persuade them otherwise, then you punch them right in the nose." He proceeded to fake punch Danny until the little boy roared with glee.

"You are funny, Randall! Hey, when are you gonna show me how to use the *ukulele* again?"

"It's pronounced *ukulele*, bud, and I'll show you after supper, if it's okay with your mama?"

"If you're sure," she nodded and turned her head before the tears in her eyes threatened to fall.

"No problem, but first I think you have things to do, little man!"

"*Nuh uh*, I don't have any homework today," was the quick reply.

A tickle fight erupted behind her and wails of laughter followed as Randall picked up Danny and tossed him in the air. She wiped her face and listened as man and boy began talking about music and then games.

Before she knew it all six-foot three inches of Randall was curled up on her tiny loveseat next to her towheaded son playing an old spaceship themed video game on her tiny, battered TV instead of the one she used for her guests.

The scene warmed her heart. It touched some-place deep inside of her. It was as if the tiny shield she had erected to protect herself was crumbling. This man was breaking down her barriers. He was dangerous to her peace of mind. *It won't last,* she tried listing the reasons why in her head. *He's leaving soon*, she repeated inside her head again and again as she prepared dinner. *This isn't real for him, it's a vacation. Like a kid playing house.*

The next few days passed by in a blur. Tulla managed to treat Randall with all the politeness and courtesy she could muster. It wasn't easy to remain distant when his smile was ever at the ready for both herself and Danny, who seemed to have developed a bond with the tall stranger.

She was surprised when he came out of his room one day with a ukulele kind of like the one, she'd gotten for her son at a garage sale. He'd been teaching Danny the process of playing the four-stringed instrument ever since. It was just another thing they bonded over. Gaming, music, old TV shows. Danny had started watching the original Star Trek series when he'd come down with a bad case of the flu that past winter. Homebound for two weeks, the little boy had watched every DVD they had so, she got a subscription to one of those streaming video apps and he'd gotten hooked.

Tulla could take it or leave it, but Randall it seemed was a devoted *trekkie*. Between that and the ukulele, the man had grown about ten more feet to her son. She only hoped he understood that it wasn't forever. Being a person with no musical talent at all, despite a persistent love for singing along with the radio now and then, Tulla was surprised at her guest's ability. Was there anything he couldn't do?

He was patient, kind, and generous with his time when it came to her son. The sounds of a happy little tune met her ears and she smiled. He was teaching Danny to play the small instrument in record time, but her son always was a quick learner. She admired Randall's eagerness and willingness to help though he was on vacation. Even when she attempted to get

Danny to leave him alone, he would hear of no such thing.

Tulla had to admit she appreciated his candor. It was refreshing. If she was being truly honest with herself, she'd also admit that it didn't hurt that Randall was breathtakingly beautiful to look at. *Seriously.* He was gorgeous. He had smooth, creamy skin that was growing more tan by the day. Even though he shaved regularly, she liked the five o'clock shadow that was visible on his cheeks by noon.

His laughter was deep and rich, and she liked the feeling she got in the pit of her stomach whenever she heard him. It was addictive, that feeling of anticipation and desire. It was desire, after all. She finally admitted that to herself days ago.

Tulla also noted that despite his re-connecting her modem, he spent little to no time on his Chromebook. He seemed to be enjoying his stay at *The Sea Mist*. He didn't go for any of the usual tourist attractions, but he seemed to like the island.

He went for daily runs on the beach. He even went swimming regularly. She sometimes caught a glimpse of him from the laundry room as he swam out into the Atlantic, past the buoys, despite her frequent warnings. He'd just smile at her attempts to caution him and reply by saying he was a good swimmer. He took the rowboat out fishing a time or two.

One day he came back with a huge sea bass that he then cleaned and grilled for the three of them. *Yep*, the man cooked too. He was damn near perfect.

There was just one thing she didn't get. With only two weeks left of his vacation, Tulla found herself wondering why he didn't make another move to kiss her. She caught his caramel gaze staring at her time and again, but he never did anything more than look. She admitted she was a little bit confused and, maybe a little disappointed, though she should have been relieved. After all, she couldn't afford to fall for a man like him.

She shouldn't even be having thoughts like these. It wasn't safe, it wasn't smart. She knew better. Tulla wasn't a kid anymore. If she could only stop thinking about those lips of his and what it would feel like to have the right to kiss him every single day!

She felt like a teenager daydreaming over him. Maybe it was hormonal? Maybe something happened to a woman after being alone for years? Tulla had gone out on the odd date here and there, but no one moved her the way this man did. It was a simple fact. Not even her late husband. The thought made her feel ashamed of herself.

Tom wasn't a good husband. If she were being brutally honest, she'd recognize he wasn't even a good man, but he gave her Daniel. For that, she would always be grateful to him. *Rest in peace, Thomas*, she thought to herself. A loud bout of laughter coming from her small living room jostled her from her morbid thoughts.

Time to fess up, she thought as her heartbeat increased wildly by just listening to the deep rich laughter coming from the man who was interrupting her thoughts, even her sleep. This man had gotten through her armor and he did it with his easy smile and soul-shattering kiss.

"Hey, can I help with anything?" Her thoughts were interrupted by the deep baritone of Randall's voice. *My, oh my, even his voice was sexy!*

"What? Oh no, I got it under control. I am sorry if Danny is bothering you, I can send him outside for a little while until dinner is ready–"

"No way, that's my buddy in there! Seriously, that kid is some little gamer!"

"Oh, he spends too much time on that thing–"

"Look, you are his mom and I'd never go against anything you say where it concerns your son, but he's really good. I mean he understands the rules and he's got better eye-hand coordination than most adults. Outdoor play is important, but there is nothing wrong with being good with technology. For some kids, it's all they have."

She was prepping that night's dinner and stopped

to listen to him, noting the sadness in his brown eyes and the tightness of his voice. She put a hand on his and gave him a small smile. She should have been frightened of the way she felt, the desire welling in her to soothe his mind, but she didn't. She felt calm and right. The skin under her hand was warm and she felt an overwhelming need to touch him again.

"Anyway, uh, he sent me in here for some drinks, and he said to call you, ma'am," he gently pulled his hand out from under hers and thumbed his pants, shrugging as if hadn't revealed a little bit about himself to her just then.

"Oh, he did, did he?"

"Yes ma'am," his smile was infectious.

"Um, well, you tell that little man, only water on the couch! Here you go," she handed Randall two small cups of water. Her fingers brushed against his in the exchange and she sucked in a sharp breath.

It was like little sparks of awareness were shooting up and down her arm from that one, tiny, little touch. She only had to look in his eyes to realize he felt the same charge of attraction. *Uh oh.* Tulla licked her lips.

A nervous habit from when she was younger. She realized her error when his gaze locked onto the small movement. Heat flooded her body, and she felt a wave of desire rising inside of her like the tide. If her heart survived this man intact, she'd be surprised.

"You and I are gonna have a chat about this thing between us, one day when Daniel is tucked in his bed or at school. There's not gonna be any more running, okay?" Randall sucked in a breath and closed his eyes. His large body seemed to sway under some kind of magnetic pull that existed between them.

She felt it too. As if the stars and fate had deigned that they would meet like this. *Here and now.* She nodded absently. *Yes,* a reckoning of sorts was bound to happen soon. They were going to have to do something about this attraction for lack of a better word. If only to get it out of their system. He left the room and she stood there for a moment or two until the sound of the timer going off made her turn. *Time's up!*

Dinner was a cozy affair. After those first few nights of eating in the formal guest dining room Randall had insisted, they take their meals together. She agreed, but that was before the tension between them was thick enough to cut with a knife.

The three of them ate their meal outside on the clean wood deck overlooking the Atlantic Ocean. Tulla loved eating out there, though she and Danny rarely did as the space was reserved for their guests. Daniel decided to mimic Randall bite for bite and nearly ate the entire tuna steak she had grilled for them. He was supposed to share that one with his mother, but she would make do with the vegetables and rice.

She was surprised when Randall took half his tuna steak and placed it on her plate. He continued talking to Danny as if it were no big deal, but she felt the gesture all the way to her toes. Naturally, she'd grilled him a larger portion than the one she had cooked for herself and Danny. Food was part of the package and she prided herself on her ability to cook satisfying meals for her guests. It'd been a long time since someone had taken care of her. Even in such a small way.

"Danny, you are going to get a tummy ache if you eat all that," she chided gently but he shook his head.

"Uh uh, Mama, I need protein so I can grow up big," the innocent hero worship in his eyes as he looked at their houseguest made her chest tighten.

Her boy had grown up without a father. She wondered when he would start to feel it. When he would yearn for a man to look up to, to teach him things, to be a role model. Had it happened already? She tried her best to be everything to him and it stung that she simply couldn't be. She was certain to fall short. It was one of her greatest fears as a parent.

The other, well, she'd rather not think about that. So far, the man who had called her that night so many years ago had stayed away from her and Danny. Maybe it was all a prank? Maybe he couldn't find them on the island? Tulla didn't care the reason as long as he left them the hell alone.

Danny seemed to bond with Randall, a virtual stranger, right off the bat. She watched him replace his fork for his glass of sweet tea and take a long chug like their guest did. Randall's eyes twinkled when he looked at her. *So, he did notice,* was her only thought as she watched him switch from his fish to his grilled Brussel sprouts.

She silently applauded his tactics as the little boy ate every single vegetable on his plate. If only she could let herself indulge in the fantasy that the three of them were a family, but that was too dangerous. She only hoped it wouldn't be too bad when it came time for him to leave *The Sea Mist*. She prayed that she and Danny would be okay when the dust settled.

Randall's promise to have a chat with her about the minor problem of their growing attraction for each other stayed foremost in her mind all through dinner. *Maybe he was just teasing? Maybe it was time she take a little something for herself? Would that be wrong of her?* She was not sophisticated enough to keep on pretending she didn't want him, but she wasn't quite sure how to go about telling him.

The one and only time she'd engaged in a sexual

relationship had been with her husband. Once she told Tom she was pregnant he insisted they marry. Afterwards, he told her they needed to wait until she got approval from a doctor to have sex again.

She'd seen the OB/GYN and was told it was okay to proceed with that physical aspect of their relationship. She wasn't exactly jumping for joy, but still, she told Tom what the doctor had said hoping it would improve things between them. Tom had shown less enthusiasm than she at the prospect of sleeping with her again. In fact, he seemed to grow tired of their marriage bed before he even made a dent in the mattress.

He said her lack of sexual knowledge was a buzzkill. Her innocence was not enough to keep him interested. His exact words were something like "*the novel of fucking a virgin is gone, babe*". He preferred a more skilled and experienced lover. She was glad when he began working longer hours and going away on frequent business trips only to return home to sleep in the guest room. The only thing he really asked of her was that she stay home.

She was more than happy to give up her waitressing job to stay home and grow their baby while he left for work. She learned to appreciate the days he was away on business the most. When he was home, he was always unhappy, discontent, blaming her for why he had no money. She stayed because she believed they could be a family. That was all she wanted, but Tom was never the family type. She could see that now.

Not like Randall, she thought to herself. He seemed to like everything about playing with her little boy, but he wasn't afraid of the tough questions either. She liked that about him she really did. If she were being honest, she'd admit she could picture herself falling for the man. *Head over heels.*

It was one thing to be lonely and foolish when you were twenty, quite another when you were widowed and a single mother at twenty-eight years old. One thing was certain, she could not afford to lose her heart to Randall Graves. Her body; however, was another thing entirely!

❧ 11 ❧

A warm breeze drifted in through the open window. South Carolina was starting to grow on Randall. After all, he was a southern boy at heart, born and raised in Jacksonville, Florida.

He called New Jersey his home these days, but for some reason he wasn't looking forward to going back to his cold office at the Manor or to his one bedroom in the most isolated part of the big house. Indeed, he found nothing about returning to his solitary life appealing. Even his company could survive without him. *Hell*, except for the Pack and his position as Wolf Guard, he had nothing.

Don't get me wrong, he thought to himself, *I'd die for Rafe, Charley, heck, for any one of them, but just once it'd be nice to have something to live for too.* He inhaled deeply as he took a long sip of the deep red wine Tulla served him after dinner.

Werewolves didn't get drunk as easily as normals. *Heck*, it was damned near impossible for them to get drunk at all. But still, he enjoyed the taste and the feeling of the dark liquid as it slid down his throat. Things like taste and smell were heightened for Werewolves. The wine was really good, he acknowledged.

He listened with his supernatural hearing to every giggle and whisper of clothing coming from inside the house as Tulla helped Danny get ready for bed. She tucked him in, sang to him in her fine if slightly off-key voice that made Randall smile, and kissed him goodnight. *Damn.* He was jealous.

He wished he had the right to go in and join the fun. Imagine him, *tucking in his child and kissing his mate on the lips before turning in for the night. Lying beside her, knowing she was his to protect, that they were both his. To keep safe, and fed, and warm. A lovely dream*, he thought as he tossed back his head and downed the entire glass.

The tightness in his chest was from the wine, he told himself. It had nothing to do with the fact that he wanted that dream. *So, fucking much.* He wanted to march right in there and stand by her side. He wanted to drop a kiss on the little boy's head and whisper goodnight to him before turning on the little dinosaur nightlight at the foot of the bed. Then he wanted to gather the little boy's mother in his arms and kiss her until she moaned her pleasure.

It's definitely the wine, he told himself. Randall wasn't a family man. He was a computer hack. He had no time or room in his life for complications and that's what women and children were, right? Isn't that what his father had called him. A complication that caused his mother to die.

He winced at the sharp pain he felt in his heart as he remembered the cold words his father had spoken to him all those years ago. Werewolf or not that man was a drunk. He poisoned himself with Aconitum, or Wolfsbane as it was commonly known.

He added the stuff to his liquor so he could feel the effects. He was a cruel son of a bitch. He had strict rules and was quick with his fists if they weren't obeyed. Randall admitted now that his reason for never wanting a mate or family stemmed from his fear that he would be like his father.

That was an idea he could not tolerate. He would deny himself the right to be a father before he'd harm a child with either fists or words. Children were to be protected and cared for by someone worthy. *Was he worthy, though?* He'd lived a long life and done a lot of things he wasn't exactly proud of. He'd been selfish, mean, and sometimes even petty with his time and his feelings. What right did he have wanting things he didn't deserve?

Then he thought of Tulla. With her sun-streaked hair and golden-tanned body. She made him forget about all the promises he ever made to himself to stay away from women, to never have children. The thought of her body swollen with his baby made him hard with need. He readjusted himself in his shorts and shook his head.

Damn, Randall, you're not a kid anymore. Someone should tell his dick that. Fuck, he ran a hand through his hair and stood up. Sure, he'd spent plenty of nights with women whose names he never got and faces he didn't remember, but this was different. Tulla was special. She was the only woman who made his Wolf stand up and take notice. The only one to make his blood sing. *My God*, he wanted her. And badly.

They both felt it. That much he was sure about. Her little gasps and wide eyes whenever they accidentally brushed past each other coupled with the pounding of her heart told him everything he needed to know. She wanted him too.

It was a heady thought, being wanted. But was it enough? Desire was not anything to scoff at. It was an important part of any relationship. If he happened to long for true love, well, he'd keep that secret buried deep inside of him. He wasn't the loveable type. But he could make her want him. That much he knew.

He stood by the open screen door and looked past the wood deck with its table and chairs and colorful pillows to the waves that crashed onto the shore. It really was a nice little spot. The house itself was cozy and quaint or maybe that was just Tulla's influence that made it appear so.

The structure was nothing fancy. Randall had certainly slept in enough high scale hotels and been in enough mansions to compare it to, but still, he didn't think he ever felt as comfortable and at home as he did at *The Sea Mist.* He'd driven through South Carolina plenty of times, maybe even stopped for lunch there, but this was his first time ever staying in the Palmetto State. He'd had to look that one up.

Tulla kept a fine house. Little bowls of potpourri and candles sat on dust free shelves, yellow and white flowers filled pots outside and in, and she cooked like a professional chef. He never was one for beaches and sand, but he liked the look of the palms swaying in the constant breeze and he liked the taste of salt on his lips.

The rocky shore and rough waters accounted for why a bigger corporation didn't swipe up all the property on this side of the island as of yet, but Randall could tell it wasn't too far off. Beachfront property was big business. A few man-made improvements to the coast and this place would be a hot commodity. Not that he approved of many so-called man-made improvements, but one thing he learned in his long life was that you could not fight progress.

This little house and others like it along this stretch of beach, though separated by miles, would one day be gobbled up by some greedy hotel chain or other. It was a damn shame. He wondered if Tulla would ever sell the place. He wondered if she could ever be at home in a place with cold winters and hot summers. Would she be willing?

It was dangerous, this idea of having Tulla and Daniel with him in New Jersey. It would change everything, but maybe that was what he needed. Picturing them with him, by his side filled his heart to near bursting. *Mine.* Inside his mind's eye he heard his Wolf. The statement was made independently of Randall's own mind. His *Wolf* wanted them both. *His. Family. Pack. Mine.*

It was dangerous, but Randall needed to admit that his Wolf had already claimed the two of them as his. Tulla was the mate his Wolf had been searching for, and her son was the son of his heart. He would be cared for and protected as his own. The man in him agreed with both assessments, but it wouldn't be easy, convincing her that they belonged together.

He had never shared his secret with a normal. Would she be able to handle it? It all worked out for Rafe and Charley. *Heck,* better than worked out, the couple were wildly in love and they were expecting their first child in a couple of months. Randall was happy for them both. His Alpha deserved a family of his own, to love and cherish and shelter. Their mate-bond was the stuff of legends. The need to protect was strong with Werewolves and Randall realized he was already past that point with Tulla.

Damn, if he wanted her, he was going to have to do something about it. That would mean facing his fears and doubts and showing her how he felt. Then he'd tell her the truth about himself. A Wolf denied his mate was not something anyone wanted to be around. He would have to tell her and soon.

He was so lost in his thoughts he almost didn't hear her approach. Her shoes were gone, and her bare feet hardly made a noise on the floor. Her scent reached him before anything else, coconut, saltwater, and the cool ocean breeze. They all seemed to be a part of her.

"Hey," she smiled up at him and he forgot to breathe. It was like the sun coming out. Or in his case, the *moon*.

Her silver eyes and whiskey colored hair captivated him. His palms itched to hold her. A deep longing started to grow in his belly. She licked her lips, a small flash of her tongue, a subconscious invitation, and that was all he needed.

Randall put his glass down and did the only thing he wanted to do right then. The only thing he'd been thinking about for the better part of two weeks. He pulled her tight against his body. She felt good there, like she was made for him. When she didn't show any signs of protest, he lowered his head, his eyes locked on hers as he slowly moved in. Their breath mingled and he felt her shiver against him, Randall's nostrils flared as the scent of her arousal flooded his senses.

Slowly, he told himself, *go slowly*. His lips settled on hers, testing their softness. He met hers once, twice, and again. Tulla sighed against his mouth and opened for him, allowing him access inside. She tasted like the chocolate mint ice cream pie she had served for dessert. *His favorite*.

He deepened the kiss, twirling his tongue with hers, drinking her in like a man dying of thirst. She moaned into his mouth and he tightened his hold on her. He felt his cock harden against her soft belly, but he did nothing to hide her effect on him.

No more hiding. He reveled in it. He was proud of the way she affected him. She made him feel like more of a man than he had in years. He growled deep in his throat when she pressed herself fully against him and held on even tighter. *Damn*, this woman was killing him. Randall held her face and rained kisses down her throat and neck, licking her from the open neckline of her shirt back to her mouth.

Their pants and moans were like music to his ears. He wondered what other noises he could pull from her. His long-fingered hands roamed over her ample breasts in their thin cotton covering to her shorts and around to that luscious ass of hers that had been driving him crazy for days now.

He squeezed her body, grinding her against him. Randall was thrilled with her reaction to him, the way she flexed her hips into his, an invitation to explore the mysteries that were all Tulla. *Mine*. He growled deep in his throat. With his right hand, he circled around to the apex of her thighs.

He felt her heat seeping through the thin material that separated them, and his growl grew louder. She moaned then and he searched for the fastening at her waist. He needed her out of those clothes, but the porch was too well lit. He wanted her, but he wasn't going to put on a show for anyone who happened to be out stargazing.

As if she knew what he was thinking she backed up a step, her gray eyes glazed with pleasure, sparkling like stars in the moonlight. Tulla took his hand in hers and tugged. He mimicked that small smile that played on her swollen lips. A dusky rose tint visible to him in the soft moonlight, graced her smooth cheeks as she lifted a finger to shush him and raised her eyebrow. *A question, was it?* He swallowed, nodded his head, and allowed her to lead him where she would.

He followed her down to where the B&B small rowboat sat in the sand. It was tied to an anchor and flipped upside down on the still warm sand. She pulled the dry sheet off the boat's bottom and laid it down on one side. Anyone trying to peak wouldn't see anything other than the twelve-foot fishing vessel.

"Come here," she laid down on the sheet and held her arms out. Randall obeyed her command without hesitation.

She looked like a goddess lying there, offering herself to him freely. Her eyes sparkling and her mouth tempting as hell. He claimed her lips again and again, his hard body pressing down on hers as he undid her shorts and eased them down her smooth tanned legs. Uncomfortable with the clothing that still separated them, Randall took off his shirt and was satisfied to see her wide-eyed fascination. Her small hands trembled as she smoothed them over his chest and abs.

"I'm glad you approve," he smiled and kissed her again.

"Approve? You're gorgeous," Randall could feel his own blush staining his cheeks.

A woman had never called him that before, but he was pleased that she liked what she saw. It satisfied him to know his appearance tempted her and the Wolf in him approved wholeheartedly that she found him appealing.

"I need to see all of you," he growled as she kissed his neck sending shivers up his spine.

She lay before him in a button-down shirt and a pair of purple cotton panties, but it was still too much clothing. A second later, the buttons to her shirt were flying as he ripped it open baring her full breasts to his eyes. Randall moaned as he reached out with one trembling hand to touch her.

"Perfect, you are perfect," he groaned as he felt the smooth softness of her breasts. They were round and high on her chest, tipped with plump, dusky nipples. Her chest moved up and down as she breathed in and out, faster now with her growing arousal. She was a goddamn work of art.

He bent his head, compelled by the need to taste her. He licked and sucked at one glorious mound while caressing the other with nimble fingers. Her moans of pleasure told him all he needed to know. He lavished attention on the next breast as his hands crept downwards moving inside of the tiny cotton barrier to her most feminine parts.

Tulla wound her hands in his long hair and held him to her, arching up towards his mouth as he suckled her and teased her with lips, tongue, and teeth. He enjoyed her reaction to him, growing harder with every gasp, every sigh. He needed more.

"You're so beautiful. I have to taste you," he whispered.

"You are," she gasped.

"No, I need more. I want to really taste you, sweet," he lowered his head from her breast and dipped his tongue into her navel. She arched and he held her down with firm, but gentle hands. Randall grinned and spread soft kisses and playful nips along the way as he moved down her body.

He watched her wondrous expression as he travelled down her stomach to her soft inner thighs. Her heartbeat was like a drumline in his sensitive ears. He loved the rhythm, became attuned to it instinctively, and played her body like a finely tuned guitar.

He stopped when he reached her tiny cotton panties. Randall looked up. His eyes met hers as she watched him wide-eyed. Tulla bit her lower lip and he grinned from ear to ear looking more like his Wolf than even he knew. He glanced down and was stumped for a second. A small picture of a cat curled up in a ball sat on the front of her tiny purple cotton panties. Underneath the image were the words "pet my pussy".

"I, uh, didn't know when I put those on-" her embarrassed whisper made his heart swell.

"That's fine with me. I like a little instruction," with that he gripped the sides of her underwear with his hands. He had intended to rip them off, but he decided he liked this pair, so he very carefully tugged them down her legs and tucked them into the pocket of his shorts for safekeeping.

She moaned when the movement brought his breath into contact with her core and all thoughts of being embarrassed seemed to vanish from her mind. Randall growled as her scent flooded his nostrils. She was ready for him, desire and pride mixed with a fierce need threatened to choke him. he steadied himself with a deep breath.

She was his for the taking. *Finally*. His fingers inched up her thighs to find her wet and ready for him. He didn't hesitate, he bent his head and licked a path from her left thigh to her center. The growl reverberating in his chest acting to increase her pleasure.

Randall held her in place when she would have sprung up off the sand. He kissed and licked and sucked as her short nails raked his shoulders. The action only made him more attentive, he smoothed one hand along the top of her belly, effectively holding her in place while he entered her with the other hand. First one, then two fingers. Licking, sucking, kissing, and penetrating her all at once while she moaned a glorious symphony to his ears.

The sound of her pleasure only increased his own as he drank her in much like the fine wine, he enjoyed earlier that night. But wine had nothing on his Tulla. She was sweeter and smoother than anything he'd ever had before in his life. She shuddered against his mouth crying out his name as his tongue continued to lave at her swollen nub. When he felt her release skyrocket through her body, he slowed his speed, but didn't stop.

Randall was a generous lover, but he never wanted to please a woman more than he did *this woman*. In that moment, she was both *everything* and *the only thing*. He rained kisses on her thighs, her belly, and her breasts before settling himself between her legs. His shorts long gone. He pressed the full length of his arousal against her.

She instinctively wrapped her legs around him as he aimed his swollen head at her sleek entrance. With one final questioning glance Randall waited until she arched up and opened for him. Then he entered her welcoming heat in one hard thrust.

He felt her stretch to accommodate him and stilled himself so she could adjust to his length and thickness. He'd never felt anything so fucking right as when he sank himself into her. Tulla arched her back and pulled him closer, her hands gripping his firm ass as he flexed his hips, going deeper inside. He loved the feel of her muscles flexing around his shaft, the perfect way she sheathed him, surrounding his hard length. She flexed her hips experimentally and the uncalculated movement sent delicious shivers up and down Randall's spine.

His need to pound into her was overwhelming, but he restrained himself. He wanted to care for her, not just fuck her into oblivion, though if he were being honest, he wanted that too. This woman was his now, in every sense of the word. He smoothed the hair out of her face and kissed her chin and neck and lips reveling in the way she opened her mouth for him. Their eyes met and Randall held her stare.

"Beautiful," his whisper surprised even him as he moved inside of her.

"This is the most incredible night of my life," she whispered. He allowed her to pull his head down and kiss him.

"It's all you," Randall answered and flexed his hips again.

He groaned as he pumped his body. Attuned to

her every desire, he kissed and licked, and yes, even bit while she gasped and moaned and ran her hands all over him. Sweat covered them both as her inner muscles tightened around his cock, stroking him with each hard thrust.

She was tight and slick and perfect. His body hummed with energy as he pumped himself into her and for the first time in his life, he knew peace and perfection. He meant to slow down, to savor the moment, but he was acting on instinct now.

His Wolf's scent, his unique combination of musk and spice, enveloped her as they made love. The rush of emotion that went with it was undeniable. He felt the Wolf in his eyes, rising up, telling him to claim her. He wanted to wait, to ask her first, but there was no stopping now.

He felt her body tighten around him and Tulla moaned her orgasm even as he bit down on her shoulder, marking her as his. She cried aloud as his mark increased her pleasure. Randall pumped himself harder. He couldn't think, he didn't want to, he just wanted to make her come again, this time with him. And they did. They came together, her glazed eyes met his as she called out his name to the night sky.

The sudden knowledge that she was his now, filled him. His heart thudded in his chest as he kissed her on the mouth, deeply, knowing that if he kept looking into the silver pools of her eyes, he'd never find his way out. He got up on his knees, still inside of her and stroked her legs as he placed them up on his large shoulders.

He was still hard inside of her and he needed more. He loved the sound of Tulla's gasp as he found her bud with his fingers. He pumped slowly this time. Long, hard strokes, in and out. The feel of her, the smell of her, Tulla, his own Tulla overwhelmed him. He moved faster then, wringing another orgasm from her, and finding his own.

"Randall," she cried out, her head moving wildly back and forth.

The sound of their bodies, skin on skin slapping each other as he thrust in and out of her body was nothing compared to the sound of his heart in his ears. A resounding roar filled his head as he felt his second release and he spilled everything he had to offer of himself inside of her. He'd meant to withdraw, but he was too far gone to have the presence of mind to do it.

The sound of their ragged breathing filled his ears. He remained upright, on his knees, his cock still buried inside of her, until her shiver brought him out of his reverie. He grabbed his shirt and draped it over her cool skin before settling down beside her and pulling her into him. The temperature had cooled off dramatically since the sun set, but Randall used his warmth to comfort her in the aftermath of their lovemaking.

He marked her. Shit. Randall hadn't meant to do that just yet, but he'd lost control somewhere along the way. He inhaled and noticed his own musk mingling with her coconut scent. He wondered if she would regret leading him down here once she knew what he was, what he did, not that it mattered. It was done. She was his. *Mine.*

❧ 1 2 ❧

Tulla almost dropped her basket of groceries as she walked carefully down the supermarket aisle. It was still a bit early, but she'd already had her coffee so that wasn't it. She was distracted. And with good reason.

Her mind was still in replay mode. *Did that really happen last night?* She must have been temporarily out of her mind. She had seduced a guest! Or she let him seduce her! Whichever way she looked at it, the fact remained that last night she'd had *literal* sex on the beach! *Not the drink*, and with a man she barely knew!

Images of Randall's molten caramel eyes peering into hers as he rained kisses all over her body kept her awake for most of the night, after they had made their way back to his bedroom. He'd insisted she come with him and, boy, did she ever. Three times on the beach and once more in his bed before he fell asleep. She'd waited to hear his steady breathing before she went back to her own room. She didn't want to go, but she had Danny to think about.

By then it was nearly dawn and she needed to shower and get dressed. Danny was still sound asleep when she crept past his room. *Thank goodness.* It would have been difficult to explain why his mama was walking around in a man's shirt covered in sand when it was still dark outside. *My oh my, what a night!*

Tulla was a grown woman, she totally understood the consequences of her actions, but she had no idea when she went to Randall last night that he would take her to heights she had never seen before. To think she'd been married and given birth, but she was, for all intents and purposes, a virgin up until last night.

She'd seen plenty of movies and read tons of books that detailed sexual encounters that left the women gasping with pleasure, and the men strutting like gods, but she imagined it was some sort of conspiracy designed to pander to the fragile egos of men who suffered from some psychological trauma about their penises that only Freud could name! However, after last night, Tulla knew better. Whoever wrote those books or screenplays must have had a lover like Randall Graves. Her heart sped up just thinking about the man.

Last night was the single most satisfying sexual experience of her entire life. *It wasn't just sex and you know it,* she ignored that pesky little voice. She didn't want to ruin things by overcomplicating them too soon. She was still basking in the afterglow of it. She bit her lip as worry and doubt crept inside of her mind. He was still asleep when Danny went off to school and she was unsure now of going back to face him alone.

What if it was just a one -off for him? What if it didn't mean anything special to him at all? She recalled the sounds of his satisfied groans and the way he'd kissed her from head to toe as if she were something he cherished. It had to mean something, right?

It just had to. She'd been certain of it last night. She'd seen it in the way his eyes seemed to glow gold in the darkness, in the way he made her body sing under cover of moonlight and a million dazzling stars. It was daytime now and time to face the music. She was no coward. She would face him, alright, head high, and she'd ask him what was what. What were her other options? She bit her lower lip as she piled groceries on the conveyor belt.

"Good morning, Tulla, my, don't you look lovely today!"

Tulla turned and blushed as the wife of the owner of the small grocery store rang her up. Mrs. Atkins was a small woman, petite with medium length brown hair and trendy thick framed glasses. There was always a sparkle in her eyes and Tulla knew what that meant! She was on to something. Unfortunately for Tulla, that something was her. *Best play it cool.*

"Good morning, Rainne! It's Danny's birthday at the end of the week, I guess I'm just excited is all."

"Oh, that's nice, you sure you're not excited about that new guest of yours? Mr. Atkins and I have seen him out running along the shore and such. He is a handsome man if ever I saw one! A hottie as my daughter would say!"

"Rainne, I am surprised at you! He's just a guest is all. I don't get personal, you know that. And what would your husband think if I told him you were drooling over another man!" Tulla winked as Mrs. Atkins blushed and giggled. She waved goodbye and headed to the car with her groceries.

Oh, my Lord, Mrs. Atkins knew in all of two minutes that something had happened between her and Randall! Tulla was completely transparent. She felt her face heat up and rushed all the way home. The way everyone looked and smiled at her when she waved off Danny this morning and went shopping, well, she wondered if she had a sign on her forehead that said, *why yes, I did get lucky last night.*

She even had a tough time looking at herself in the mirror that morning. That is to say, she didn't recognize herself at all. She had a smile from ear to ear and her hair was mussed, and her skin had all the signs of a good night of loving. She even had a small hickey at the bottom of her left breast. She could barely walk, but she admitted with a sigh, she felt damn good.

Randall had been fast asleep when she got Danny ready and off for school. Then she'd run to the market for coffee after drinking the last cup. She got fresh rolls and more eggs as well. He was still technically her guest and she had to prepare breakfast. She didn't know whether to feel awkward or not, but what was done was done. She had no choice but to face him.

She pulled into the driveway to see a furious faced Randall. He was just pulling on a sneaker when he heard the car and his head shot up. All the warmth of last night was gone from his dark eyes. Until he saw her, then he exhaled, and it was as if all his tension eased. He strode to the car looking like a force to be reckoned with, Tulla had no idea what was wrong.

He opened the door for her and before she stepped out, he practically lifted her from the seat and had her in a hug so tight she thought she was going to pop. *Oh my.* Her heart pounded in her chest. He'd been worried! *About her.*

"Hey, it's okay, I just had to run to the market," she spoke in the same quite voice she used to soothe Danny when he had one of his nightmares.

She ran her hands up and down Randall's back in an effort to calm the big man. Something had gotten him all riled up, and though she had no idea exactly what that was, her first instinct was to ease his mind, to comfort him. Tulla smiled with the knowledge that he obviously felt something for her.

"I woke up and you were both gone. No note, no car, uh, I'm sorry. I just, uh, I just needed to know you were safe."

"I'm okay, honey, look I'm alright. Now, come on help me inside with the bags," she kissed him on the mouth, and he hugged her close to his body again.

So much for taking a step back, thank God, she thought while a profound sense of relief flowed through her. He kissed her on the top of her head and squeezed her shoulder before taking the two bags out of the car. Tulla had never felt so cherished before in her life.

Tears stung her eyes as she walked ahead of him into the house. This was so much more than a one-night stand. Her head tried to warn her, telling her to use caution, but her heart was singing inside her chest. *I love him.*

He set the bags down on the counter then turned to her. All thoughts of wanting to comfort and calm him turned into something else. Heat pooled between her thighs and her heart skipped a beat or two. He had that same predatory gleam in his eyes that he had last night when he tore her blouse open. Tulla's lips parted, she watched as he undressed her with his caramel gaze.

"Uh, would you like breakfast?" She hoped he'd say no. Not yet anyway. What she wanted was so much more fulfilling than eggs and toast.

"I think I'll skip breakfast and go straight to dessert," one step was all it took for him to reach her. The second his hands landed on her waist her mind went numb.

All her resolve to maintain a professional relation-ship melted away as he reached for the hem of her sleeveless shirt and drew it up over her head. The front clasp bra was a little tricky, but he made short work of it as his mouth claimed hers. She was impressed and maybe a little wary. Did he have much experience with these things? As if sensing her doubt, he placed his large hands on either side of her face and kissed her lips with his warm and generous mouth.

Tulla moaned. She wanted to feel his skin against hers. She tugged on his t-shirt. He got the message and broke their kiss long enough to whip the offending fabric off his body and met her skin with his. Tulla sighed. *Mmmmm.*

His skin was hot and smooth and hard. Like the rest of him. Nothing had ever felt as good or as right as when his arms came around her and he pressed his fully aroused body against his. He seemed to know exactly where to touch her, where she wanted it, how much pressure she needed. It was as if he read her mind.

Tulla gave as good as she got, her hands roamed all over the hard contours of his superb physique. She dipped her hands inside the waistband of his sweats and came into contact with that long, thick part of him that she had so intimately acknowledged last night. The velvet skin of his shaft felt good beneath her hands.

She explored with the knowledge that he seemed to enjoy her touch almost as much as she enjoyed touching him. He was hugely aroused, and his shaft throbbed in her hands. If anything, he seemed to grow harder under her touch. His groan was as deeply satisfying as it was confidence inspiring.

She pushed him towards the couch, and he went willingly. Tulla wiggled out of her shorts revealing a pair of blue cotton panties. She ran her hands along his chest and over his pants before tugging them down his long-muscled legs. She tossed them to the floor and moaned her appreciation.

He wore nothing underneath, his glorious body revealed itself to her and she had to appreciate the raw power that emanated from his sleek form. His jutting arousal glistened at the tip with his excitement and Tulla dropped to her knees in front of him. Ready to worship his body with everything she had.

He growled deep in his throat as she pressed herself against him, licking and nipping his neck and chest, and abs with her mouth. When she reached that most masculine part of him, Tulla sighed with approval. His cock was hard and long, and beautiful. As fine a form as any that graced museums the world over. His golden eyes watched her as she ran her hands over him, exploring every inch in the bright rays of sunlight that poured in through the skylight of the B&B's guest living room.

She sat back on her heels as she continued her study of every curve, every vein, every delicious inch of him. Her hands ran up and down his length again and again. She increased her speed, building momentum and enjoying the groans of pleasure that came from his lips.

Then she did something she'd never done before.

She leaned her head forward and kissed the gleaming pearl of moisture that beaded at the tip of his head. Her eyes remained focused on him as she opened her lips and took him inside. Tulla claimed him with her mouth. Loving the feel of him, the taste as she licked, and kissed, and sucked. His gasp gave her the courage she needed to take him further, deeper inside of her throat.

He throbbed and she hummed, sending deep vibrations over his sensitized flesh. Randall hissed and wound his hands through her soft, whiskey colored hair as she took him. She felt him stiffen. He tried to pull her up, but she had no intention of not finishing what she started.

Tulla's eyes met his glazed ones as he arched and pumped inside of her mouth. He called her name as his climax took him and Tulla felt a fierce pride as his orgasm rocked through his large body. She was ready for him, for all he had to give. When he finished, Tulla smiled placing small kisses across his abdomen before reaching his lips, a small smile on hers.

Holy fuck! Randall's mind was completely blank. When he woke up to find himself alone that morning fear and panic gripped his chest. *What if she just disappeared?* Ran away after the exquisite love they had made under the moon on the sand just steps away from her back door.

He couldn't explain his overwhelming need to find her, to make sure she was okay and safe. Without thinking he grabbed some clothes and was still shoving his feet into a pair of sneakers when he heard her car.

He'd grown accustomed to her comings and goings the past few weeks and recognized the sound of her vehicle. He had barely managed to control himself enough to open the car door without ripping it off its fucking hinges.

Thinking back on it he could have simply called her cell phone and asked where she was. But that wouldn't have satisfied him or his Wolf. No, he needed to see her, feel her, taste her. She was his to protect. His to touch. He could think of nothing else. *Mine.*

He was almost embarrassed by his need for her. His desire for this one woman was taking him over completely. It should have worried him, but the second he laid eyes on her sitting innocently in the driver's seat all thoughts left his mind. The only thing he knew was that he needed to touch her, to get inside of her as quickly as possible.

There was always a chance she would reject him, but Randall was too far gone to weigh the risks. He followed his instincts and strode to her car door with one purpose. *Get the girl.*

When she saw him, her light gray eyes opened wide and he readied himself for a battle. He wasn't going to give up, *hell no*. He couldn't let her go. Of that he was sure. Instead of demanding he back off, she took one look at him and wrapped her warm loving body around him. Caressing him, kissing him, reassuring him she was okay.

That was all it took for him to know he was right. She was *the one*. He knew it the second her coconut scent now laced with his own bonding musk hit his nostrils. He wanted her. He needed her. And to his complete and total surprise, he loved her. *Mine*.

She was intoxicating. When she knelt in front of him and proceeded to rock his world, he didn't know what hit him. He could sense her uncertainty at first, but the second she found her rhythm, *holy fuck*, he was a goner. He was prepared to love her for her kindness, her warmth, her honesty, but he had no idea she was a goddamn sex goddess!

He wanted to move her before he came, but she took him and everything he had to offer and damn him if that wasn't the sexiest damn thing he had ever experienced. Her satisfied smile told him she had loved it almost as much as he did.

"Was that okay?" The tremor in her voice belied the smile he had seen a moment ago. His heart squeezed inside his chest as he nuzzled her neck.

"Are you kidding? There's only one thing better than that," at her frown he stood up with her cradled in his arms.

"What?"

"That it's *my turn now,*" Randall strode with her towards his bedroom.

She bit her lower lip and he frowned replacing her teeth with his own. He ran his tongue along the soft-ness of her lips, soothing where he'd just bitten.

"*Ooh,* look out," she moaned directing him around a side table while he continued to kiss her.

He was perfectly able to kiss her and walk at the same time, but somehow, she managed to snake her hand down his stomach and run her fingers across his balls when he almost bumped the damn thing. He hissed out a breath before moving her hand. She giggled then gasped as he tossed her on the bed.

"*Uh uh,* I said, my turn," he felt the Wolf in his eyes, but made no move to quiet the beast. He was as much a part of Randall as the man and both had claimed her.

The spicy scent of her arousal was thick in the air. He sucked in a breath. Anticipation made him trem-ble. Randall grabbed her slender ankles and slid her slowly down the bed. The sound of her gliding over the coverlet made him harden all over again. For her, he knew he'd always be ready. He didn't stop pulling until her legs hung over the sides. He picked them up and swung her thighs over his shoulders as he knelt on the floor at the foot of the bed.

"Oh my!" She gasped, her eyes round as she guessed his intentions.

He looked at the flimsy blue cotton panties and tore them off her with one flick of his wrists. Then he parted her soft lips with his fingers and ignored his own throbbing member, concentrating on her pleasure only. *Damn,* he wanted to pound into her sweet warmth, but for now he was going to taste her with his mouth. *Hell,* he was going to eat her alive.

Randall growled as he lowered his head. No soft kisses now. No, he used his tongue to lick her slit long and hard. She was all honey and slick passion. He roamed over her, lapping at her folds, *tasting every inch of her.* Tulla gasped and pulled at his hair, but he was immovable.

He blew on her swollen nub and she groaned and squeezed him with her thighs. He watched from heavy-lidded eyes as he spread her legs wide with his hands and used his tongue to pump in and out of her core. He fucked her with his mouth the way he wanted to with his cock, the way he was going to as soon as he made her scream his name.

It was as honest and raw a sexual experience as he had ever had. Only with her. She was everything.

Randall had never been so completely taken over by a female. He felt her muscles tighten around his tongue and he knew she was seconds away from climaxing. He replaced his tongue with his fingers and stroked her clit with his mouth as she rocked her mound against him.

"Randall!" her shocked eyes met his and he growled as she arched her back and moaned his name again.

He climbed on top of her and she opened for him as he placed the head of his cock at her slick entrance. He buried himself deep inside of her with one hard thrust. The feeling was alien and yet more familiar than his own name. As if he was made for this.

To be with this one woman. Like coming home. *Home.* He'd never had much of one, but with Tulla it was everything he could have ever imagined. Warm and safe, hot, and sweet, a communion of love and sex that was simply perfection.

He covered her in his scent as he rolled onto his back, taking her with him. Tulla stretched out on top of him, sitting up and running her hands over her breasts and into her hair, his hands followed.

He thrust upwards as she rode him, her heat seeping deep into his bones. He sat up as she continued to move her hips, harder and faster than before. He reached out and took one plump nipple in his mouth, the taste of her tantalizing him with her salty hot sweetness.

"Tulla! You're mine, *mine*," his voice shook as he said her name. Pressure started to build inside of him, and he knew without question he was going to explode. He gripped her hips and moved her faster and harder over him. He felt the familiar tightening in his loins, she gasped and reached her hands over her head, riding him with pure abandonment.

Randall had never seen anything so fucking gorgeous in his life. He'd keep that picture in his mind for always. She opened her eyes and tossed her head back, Randall thrusted upwards, burying himself inside of her heat. Her sex squeezed him until finally, the two of them shattered together in an explosion of white-hot pleasure that seemed to last eons. *Never like this.*

❧ 13 ❧

"Tell me about how you grew up," Randall's voice was deep as his soul-touching satisfaction. It was barely recognizable, even to himself.

That kind of contentedness had always been outside his reach. He never dreamed he'd feel whole or complete, but there he was, right next to the woman who made his heart feel full, with his Wolf, as close as he had ever been, in his mind and a sense of peace inside that he didn't think he'd ever feel in his lifetime.

Randall pressed his face against her shoulder and kissed the smooth skin there. She was curled up on her side next to him, her body completely relaxed, her breathing soft and even. He wrapped his big body around hers, to keep her warm and safe. He couldn't stop touching her, even after they were both spent.

He traced the curve of her hip and the swell of her breast. He ran his fingers over the dimple at the base of her back just above her sweet, supple ass. She was golden tan all over with only the faintest trace of bathing suit lines. Her legs were long, toned, and lovely. He couldn't get enough of them.

She had the tiniest feet he'd ever seen on a woman. The way she looked walking around barefoot in a pair of cutoff jeans, *good God*! And the way she wrapped those legs around his waist when they made love, *well damn,* he didn't think he'd ever get enough. He was in deeper than he ever expected to be, and he was loving every minute of it.

You need to tell her. The nagging voice in the back of his mind had been whispering in his head for the last hour. Growing in volume, it reminded him that it was unfair to keep such a secret from one you claimed as your own.

A Werewolf was permitted by Pack law to tell his/her mate the true secret of his/her dual nature. And hadn't he already marked her as his mate? And just now, when they made love repeatedly, didn't he wrap his scent all over her, claiming her for himself. Yes, he needed to tell her.

"Oh, I don't know if that's such a nice story."

"I don't need a nice story, Tulla mine, I just need you. I want to know everything about you."

She turned around to face him. He loved the way she looked. His Tulla was beautiful all the time, but most especially when her lips were soft and swollen from kissing him and her gray eyes shone with sleepy satisfaction. *Fuck beautiful*, she stole the breath from right out of his body.

"*Mm*. Okay, well, you asked. So, my parents are gone, died in a crash when I was starting college. I had to sell the house to cover costs of the funeral and settle their debts, there was nothing left, but I managed to work my way through it. I, uh, got an associate degree in business management while I worked as a waitress at an upscale seafood bar and restaurant in Charleston."

"You waitressed?" He smiled at the image he had of her in his mind. She undoubtedly had a bright smile and easy demeanor for the patrons of the restaurant where she worked. She was just that kind of person. Hardworking and enthusiastic.

He'd have left her a huge freaking tip that was for sure, but *damn*, his heart squeezed a little as he thought of her all alone like that. His Tulla was undoubtedly a sweet kid and she shouldn't have had to work so hard all alone. *Not alone anymore, baby. Never again.*

"Yeah, I did. It was fine. I didn't mind the work. It took my mind off things. My classes were okay, I mean, I liked school."

"What about Danny's father?" Randall couldn't help the pang of jealousy that shot through him when he thought of Tulla's dead husband.

True, he was indebted to the faceless man in his imagination for the gift of the son he gave to her. And Danny was a gift. He believed that one hundred percent, but he still couldn't help the growl building up in his chest when he thought of another man putting his seed inside of her. *Grrr. Mine.*

"Danny's father was a charmer. I was barely twenty, he came into the restaurant one night with a large party and just about swept me off my feet. I hadn't dated much up till then and well, what can I say, I was flattered by his attentions and just so tired of being alone."

When she would have stopped, he kissed her shoulder and gave her hip a soft squeeze. He traced circles from the back of her knees slowly up her back to her neck. She continued.

"One night he took me out on this boat for an evening ride and a meal. We drank some wine, ate something I can't recall, and before I knew it, we slept together."

"And?"

"And?"

"*And* were their fireworks or something what? Were you in love? When did you decide to get married?" *Jeez, I sound like a fucking idiot.*

"I just want you to keep talking, baby, that's all." He tried to keep his voice even and calm, carefully hiding all of his jealousy. She smiled and kissed him on the mouth before continuing.

"Well, um no, no fireworks. Actually, it was awkward and a little bit painful, my first time, you know. And then I didn't see him again for about a month. By then I knew I was pregnant and when I told him, he proposed. Looking back on it, it was a mistake. Not Danny, I would never call my son a mistake, but I shouldn't have married his father."

Randall stilled as he listened to her tale. It all sounded so cold. Too unemotional for his Tulla. That man didn't deserve her. If he was alive Randall might have killed him just for the chance to make her his. He placed a possessive kiss on the mark he left on her neck and she arched into him.

"*Mmm.*"

"Tell me more," he said as he kneaded the flesh at the base of her spine. He turned her on her side and spooned in behind her, massaging her ass and pressing his hardened length against her.

"It didn't last long. He was away a lot. I gave birth

alone. Tom died before ever laying eyes on Danny. Oh God, Randall, I can't keep talking, -" he smiled into her neck as he licked the sensitive spot on her earlobe. Still, he wanted to hear more so he retreated a bit and held her away when she would've turned into him.

"Oh, you tease," she laughed and tried swatting him. He pinched her ass playfully and laughed when she yelped.

"I'm sorry, baby, let me rub it better." He cupped her and massaged the flesh he'd just pinched until she was leaning into him again, a little breathless when she spoke again.

"Okay, but, *mmm*, that's the whole story though."

"What about love?" Her eyes opened, the soft gray a little blurry, as she looked at him over her shoulder. His heart stopped for a moment, he needed to know if she mourned her dead husband. If he was simply a replacement.

"I never loved Tom Nirvelli. I am sorry he's dead. Sorry he didn't get the chance to meet his son. But I don't miss what we had. It was a shallow, cold union. He didn't love me. After that one time on the boat, that I hardly even remember, he never touched me."

"What? How can that be?"

"He didn't want me. He said making love to me

was like banging a cold dead fish. I couldn't keep him aroused."

"Was he a fucking moron?" Randall's sudden surge of anger was outdone by his sincere confusion. The man must have been fucking dead inside not to respond to the searing passion of his Tulla in bed.

"Thank you for that, but I think I know what you are asking me. The answer is no, I don't see him when I kiss you. I don't imagine him when you're inside of me. I don't want to think of anyone else when we are like this. Only you. Is that what you wanted to know?"

Randall's heart sounded like thunder to his ears. He pulled her into him and locked his lips over hers. Their position made it difficult, but he needed to taste her lips as he entered her from behind with one controlled flex of his hips. She cried out into his mouth and he held her as he joined their bodies and loved her with everything in him.

His hands roamed everywhere, her breasts, her neck, the sweet little nub that made her buck and moan under his skilled fingers. Her response to him was raw and natural and made him want to howl. Randall couldn't get enough of her.

Maybe theirs would be a union based on physical compatibility? Maybe he'd be able to keep his heart separate from what they had? Who the hell was he kidding? His head swam with the same words over, and over again as he pushed and pumped and finally, with one last, hard thrust, he spilled himself inside of her pulsating core.

Love. Mine. Love. Mine. Love. Love. Love. Love. LOve. LOVe. LOVE.

❧ 14 ❧

The cheerful wall clock announced the time with three little bells and Randall frowned. Danny's bus was late. He and Tulla had long since taken a shower and dressed. Of course, they would've had more time to clean up the wreck that was his bed if they hadn't taken that shower together. Not that Randall minded in the least. *You still didn't tell her.*

He shook his head and bit back down his guilt. He'd gone and done the unimaginable. He'd fallen in love. For the first time in his long life. He marked her as his mate, and still, he didn't tell her his secret. Ice cold fear gripped his spine every time he thought about telling her the truth about himself, that he was in fact a Werewolf.

It wasn't something most normals could even

comprehend. He'd heard stories from other Wolves, men mostly, of women, wives even, walking out on their men or husbands after hearing the news. Some could not reconcile their men with the beasts inside. They saw them as monsters.

Randall was old enough to know that the Were-wolves who were monsters started that way as men or women. Their evil was not brought on by their Wolves, no, it was something else. Something dark and twisted that lived inside of their human selves first. The Wolf made the human stronger, but he/she was not evil or good on his/her own. That came from the man or woman. *Geez,* it was exhausting being politically correct, even if he was only working things out inside his own mind.

One thing remained true throughout all his musings. The thought that Tulla would possibly leave him, that she would look on him with disgust or disbelief, tied his stomach in knots. He'd only just found her. He could not lose her so soon. *Mine.*

Tulla paced back and forth in front of the large bay window that looked over the driveway. Randall listened to her footsteps as he wiped down the stone kitchen counter and put the recycling outside the back door. He surprised her when he suggested that he cook while she take some time to herself just to relax.

He wanted to impress her by preparing a home-made Neapolitan tomato sauce and a couple dozen handmade ravioli stuffed with a blend of finely chopped spinach and ricotta cheese. The recipe was courtesy of his time spent in the kitchen back at the Manor with Rafe's mate, Charley.

It was good, he'd made it before, but this time it was special. He had never prepared a meal for someone he loved. *I love her.* He'd repeated it in his head a hundred times since they made love that morning.

"I can't wait till you try these *ravs*," he called out to her from the kitchen.

"Mm, it smells amazing," she turned and smiled, but he could sense her worry.

He looked at the clock again. It was ten minutes past the hour. Randall frowned again. In his brief time at the B&B he'd never known Danny's school bus to run this late. He turned off the stove and walked into the living room.

"Tulla, do you have the school bus driver's cell phone number?"

"No, just the schools. I should call, right? I mean it is getting late."

"Yes, I think that's a good idea. You call. I'll wait by the window."

As if his words were the sound of the gun going

off at the start of a race, Tulla sprinted from the room and came back with her cell phone. Her hands shook as she tapped the screen. He smelled the acidic scent of her fear and he felt his Wolf surge forward. *Protect. Mine.*

"Hi, this is Tulla Nirvelli, I'm wondering why the bus is so late today with Danny? It's 3:12 and he hasn't come home yet? What? No, no, that can't be! His father is dead! No! Oh, my God!"

Randall didn't need to be on the phone to hear the conversation. His heart thudded in his chest at what he'd just heard. Someone had picked up Danny from school, someone claiming to be his father.

"Tulla look at me, take a breath and go over everything you just heard."

"Dan- Danny isn't there at the school! Someone took him! They just walked into school and took my son! I have to go," she was running to the door when he stopped her and pulled her close to him. She was in a state of shock and panic. Tears spilled from her gray eyes as she shook her head back and forth.

"Do you want to call the police?" Randall asked the question, but he was against the idea. He wanted to go now, get to the school, get the scent of whoever it was that had taken her precious son. The boy he'd come to think of as his to protect. A loud roar was going off inside of his head, this one cried out for blood. If one blonde hair on that boy's head was harmed someone was going to die that day. He swore it to himself.

"No police. They can't help."

"Why not? Tulla look at me, what's going on?"

"His birthday is Friday, I was gonna keep him home Friday. This is too soon, he's not eight yet, the man said he'd come when Danny was eight, but I was gonna keep him home with me! No! No, this can't be happening!" Tulla was screaming by the time she reached the end of her tirade. Randall struggled to understand what she was saying.

Did she know her son was in danger? Why didn't she tell him? The scent of her terror enraged his Wolf, he wanted to rip apart the bastard who did this. The bastard claiming to be Tom Nirvelli. It was time for answers.

"Tulla, I need you to breathe, baby. Come on, get in the car. We need to get to the school now."

He was gentle with her. He spoke slowly and carefully led her to the door. Every instinct, every cell in his body in protect mode. His Wolf demanded to take over, but it was too soon. Randall needed to remain in charge for a while yet, to discover what had happened to Danny, the child his Wolf had already claimed as his own. *Mine to protect.*

Tulla followed him without question. Her eyes

wide with terror. She could not believe this was happening to her. For the first time in her life, she discovered passion and love and now her boy was taken.

Was it a punishment? Maybe she was destined to be alone. She didn't deserve happiness, not when she couldn't keep her son safe. *Oh no, Danny! Please, please let him be okay.*

Tulla knew she wasn't making any sense, but she couldn't stop her thoughts any more than she could stop the changing of the tide. *How could she? He had her son!* A fresh wave of fear flowed over her, threatening to drown her as Randall pressed the button on his cell and spoke into it. She didn't quite understand his words though she heard them clearly.

"Danny was taken from school by a dead man. I am going to catch the man's scent at the school. Send backup, now, and yes send a fucking clean-up crew. I've marked her, she is mine. Yes, my Wolf too!" Wolf?

"Buckle your seatbelt, baby," Randall's words were clear in her ears. He reached forward and buckled her seatbelt when she made no move to comply.

She could feel his empathy, his emotions far more controlled than her own and she clung to that. His strength would get them through this. In that moment, Tulla had no doubt that he would do all he could to help her get her son back.

Randall stepped on the gas and drove the ten minutes to the boy's school in half the time. He was out of the car before she undid her seatbelt, but he knew the moment she stood beside him. Danny's teacher came forward to meet them. The middle-aged woman's name went right out of his head, he sniffed and acknowledged the truth of her statements.

"I am so sorry, Ms. Nirvelli, he had a note in your handwriting! Look, I even compared it to the one you sent in last month when Danny was sick! He said you gave him permission to take him!"

Tulla was still talking to the woman as Randall made his way to the office where the man who took Danny had given her the note. He inhaled and closed his eyes, his supernatural senses working overtime to discover the culprit. He breathed again and ran a hand through his hair. *Concentrate dammit!*

His heart thudded in his chest as he called his Wolf forward. He knew if anyone saw him, his eyes would be glowing a light shade of gold as that other part of himself took in the scene before him. He saw scattered fragments of Danny's cheerful aura left behind, and another next to him. The other was dark and murky to Danny's bright white. *Not human.*

The Wolf in him inhaled and growled deep in his chest. *Magic. Witch. No, an oath-breaker!*

🦊 15 🦊

Warlock! A fucking Warlock took his boy!

Randall took four seconds to calm himself before taking his cell out of his pocket. He relayed the information over to the only other Wolf in his Pack who would understand the height of his terror.

Dib Lowell and his brother Kurt had more than their fair share of run-ins with the loveless bastards who wielded dark magic for their own personal gain. Warlocks were a nasty bunch of fuckers. And now they had Danny.

"Randall! Dude, you hear me? I already sent back up. They're coming to you in a helicopter. Some of our Wolves from Charleston. Tate was already there doing some work for Rafe. He's got Doug O'Neill with him. You know him, right?"

"Yeah, I know Doug. He's a good Wolf."

"Listen, I know how much this means to you, but don't do anything stupid, Randall. Warlocks are fucking evil, man. Wait for reinforcements."

"Thanks, man, I really appreciate, *fuck*, you know what I mean," Randall saw red. His vision became skewed as he tried to give his thanks to Dib over the phone. His emotions were raw, and it was making him jumpy.

"We're Pack, brother. We help each other, you know that. Hang in there," the call dropped, and Randall crashed to his knees. His Wolf howling in his chest, demanding to be let out. There was no way in Hell he was sitting around doing nothing until the others arrived.

That was when he noticed something on the floor. A piece of thread or yarn. He picked it up and squeezed it in his hands. It was a piece of string from the ukulele he was teaching Danny to play. He was going to get his boy back. *Now.*

"Let's go," he moved outside to where Tulla was now trying to comfort the distraught teacher. The moment her steel gray eyes met his, he knew she was made of tougher stuff than even she had thought.

"Look, Tulla, I found this, it's from Danny's ukulele."

"*Oh, my God! My baby, Danny*! But how will this help you find him?"

"It will. Listen, I need to know what you are keeping from me," the hitch in her breathing when he said those words told him he was on the right track. She knew something.

"*Oh no!* The night Tom died, or the night I thought he died, I got a phone call from some guy with a creepy voice telling me I had till Danny's 8th birthday. They were gonna come for him on his 8th birthday to see if he was their anointed one, but I have no idea what he meant. I thought he was crazy! Just some weirdo Tom owed money too. The next day I took my baby and ran all the way out here to be safe from them!"

"Anointed one? *Fuck*, alright look Tulla. I know you are gonna find some of this hard to believe, but I'm gonna say it anyway. Danny has been taken by a Warlock and we need to find him now."

"*Warlock?*"

"Yes. Warlock. If he was talking about an anointed one, that's not good news, but I swear to you I'm gonna get Danny back before anything happens to him."

"*Oh God!* But how? And where are we going?"

"We are going to the one place I can think of on

this island that has a strong enough connection to magic that a Warlock would find hard to resist."

"How do you know about any of this?"

"I'm going to tell you something Tulla, that you are bound to find out any second now anyway. *Shit.*"

Randall struggled for control as the Wolf inside of him demanded release. Once he knew Danny had been taken by a Warlock it was all he could do to keep the beast contained within him. He was losing all such control and pulled the car over before something happened that he never thought he'd live to see.

"You need to drive," his eyes were glowing, he could feel it. Any moment she was going to see what he was. He had to tell her. *Now.*

"So, what you are telling me is you are a Werewolf?" Tulla hopped over the seat as Randall got out of the car and circled around to the back seat. He pulled his shirt over his head and when her eyes met his in the rearview mirror, she understood everything he had just said was real. *This was real.*

"Yes. I am," he growled the words as the Wolf fought to come out.

The Change was painful and could take some time. He was older than he looked, with more than half a century of Changing under his belt, Randall could make the transition from man to Wolf in usually under five minutes. But in all his years, he had never Changed on a night other than the full moon.

He'd had reports that the teenage Wolf from Northern, New Jersey had taken huge strides in breaking the curse that kept Werewolves on two feet for all nights except that of the full moon. He just never knew how far the girl had come. He'd have to thank her when he got his boy back.

"Tulla, you need to drive to that cave where you and Danny go hiking sometimes. The one west of your house. Can you drive close enough?"

"How do you know about that place? Oh, my God! Is that your bones, does it hurt?"

Randall growled as his body began cracking and twisting under the pressure of the Change. He panted with the effort it took to answer her. His skin felt as if it was burning off of his very body.

"Roll the windows down. Get me close. Don't follow. Wait for back-up."

"Randall! What— *Oh my God!*" Tulla pressed the pedal to the floor of her little car and opened the windows as far as they'd go. She kept her eyes on the road, but the noises coming from the back seat had her looking in the mirror more often than not.

The sun was still shining though it was almost five o'clock. Two hours. Her son had been gone for two hours now and the man who had been staying in her

B&B. The one she'd opened her body and more, her heart too, was currently writhing in her back seat like a man in agony.

She heard a deep growl reverberating behind her and looked up to find herself eye to eye with the biggest Wolf she had ever seen. His molten caramel eyes were familiar though they burned gold with an intensity that was almost hard to look at. His fur was dark and thick, almost black.

He was as gorgeous as the man who sat there a moment ago, but Tulla had no time to appreciate the Wolf. She pulled the car over next to a clump of trees that would give way to the rocky sand path she and Danny had walked before to what her boy often called "the secret cave".

They had discovered the place a few years back and Danny sometimes asked to go there for picnics and such when the tide allowed. She didn't know how Randall knew they walked there. She certainly had never discussed it with anyone.

Then again, the man she'd shared the most amazing sex with, only hours earlier, was now covered in fur and on all fours banging against the car door with all his might. Any second the door would break. So, she did the only thing she could do. She opened it.

The Wolf leapt out from the back seat onto the

dirt floor. His head reached almost as high as her shoulders. He was enormous. She instinctively backed up a step, but his growl was not for her. He seemed to hesitate, looking at her with gold eyes until Tulla understood. She nodded at him.

"Go! I'll be fine. Go get Danny back!"

The gigantic Wolf shook his fur covered body, now that he was in the light it looked a lot like Randall's long dark locks. He seemed to understand Tulla's words and he gave her one last look before running off in the direction of the cave. He was faster than any animal she'd ever seen.

Tulla gasped before falling to her knees on the rocky floor of the forest that bordered the beach on this part of the island. She was familiar with the area, but there was so much she didn't know. But now was not the time to think about that. She had one goal, one job, to get her son back.

Tulla recalled what Randall had said to her before his Change took over. He told her his phone password, *1848*, and told her to hit redial. She took a second to gather herself. She could afford herself no more time than that, her son needed her.

Tulla stood up and ran to the car. She grabbed the fancy smartphone off the floor where he'd dropped it earlier. It was still warm from his touch and she prayed silently that he would reach her boy in time while she went about typing in the password. As soon as she was able, Tulla hit the little green button that would call the last number dialed.

"Randall, the helo just landed! Where the fuck are you, man?!" The voice at the end of the line was familiar though he sounded a tad exasperated. Tulla had no time for introductions.

"This is Tulla Nirvelli, Randall just took off on four legs to find my boy. I'm following him on foot. Now, you tell me what the hell is going on and how he's gonna get my Danny back!"

"Oh shit! I'm sorry, ma'am. Look, did he, uh, you said four legs?"

"Yes! I know what I saw and, apparently, the man I've been sleeping with is a Werewolf. I suspect you're one too!"

"Um, let's not jump to any hasty conclusions here, Ms. Nirvelli, wait a sec, did you say you've been sleeping with Randall?" She could almost hear him smile through the phone.

"Will you concentrate, please, my son is in danger! It's going to take Randall at least thirty minutes to get to where Danny is, even running like that and it's gonna take me a damn site longer! Now, talk."

"Look, just stay on the phone I'm sending your coordinates to my guys. They've got ATVs with them and they'll pick you up. If you wait for them-"

"No, I'm going to follow Randall. Danny will be afraid-"

"Tulla, I promise you Randall will find him, and he won't harm a hair on that boy's head."

"I know that! I'm not stupid, Randall would never hurt him! But that man who took him-" She tripped over a tree root and tore her knee open, but she hardly felt the pain. She picked herself up and half-jogged through the trees.

"Are you okay? What happened?"

"I'm fine. Randall said he was a Warlock, the man who took him. I just can't think. I have to hang up. I can't run and talk on the phone-"

"No, no, look, they're almost there, please, just another two minutes. Stay on the line with me."

"I'm sorry, he's my son, I need to go."

"Wait!"

Tulla clicked off the phone and shoved it in her pocket. Her knee ached, but she ignored it and picked up speed. She knew where she was headed, but her fear for her son increased with every passing second.

Oh Danny! She tried to calm herself, but tears fell down her face nonetheless as she hurried along the wooded path as fast as she could. The sound of engines behind her made her turn and she stumbled again right onto a patch of rocks. She felt searing pain in her hands before a pair of strong arms helped her up.

When she was on her feet again, she was face to face with a man with short black hair and dark eyes. He looked Native American, but his eyes had that same glow Randall's did earlier. Her fear subsided as she gave into her instincts. This was Randall's friend and she'd trust him to help.

"Tulla? I'm Tate Nighthawk. This is my team, are we headed in the right direction?"

"Yes, it's just that way. Another twenty minutes or so on foot. Randall's probably not even there yet."

"He's there. I can sense his rage and more, there is dark magic afoot. Let's go, get on the back of my ATV, and hold on to my waist. We'll get there a lot faster than walking."

Tulla did as he said and held on. Her heart thudded in her chest. It was difficult to breathe. There were five men all together, each one huge and muscular. *Are they all Werewolves?* She knew the answer in her gut. It should have scared her, surrounded by monsters, but she was not afraid of them. Not of them, nor of Randall. How could she be when she loved him? *Oh God, I love him.*

A lump formed in her throat. *Yes*, every fiber of her being was concentrating on her son, but there was another worry growing too. Would Randall be able to take on a Warlock?

They just have to be safe. Her frantic mind was moving a mile a minute. *Danny, oh God, not my Danny! Randall will find him.* The thought was clear in her mind and more surprising was that she believed it. She believed in him. He would find Daniel and he'd bring him home to her.

Randall pushed himself harder than ever before. He ran like the wind, leaping ten feet at a time over bushes and rocks and fallen trees. Normally, he didn't like to leave a footprint, but time was of the essence.

Danny was in trouble. The boy had already become the son of his heart and mind. He'd die before he let a single hair on his blonde head be injured. And he'd kill the fucker who dared take what was his. He growled as he ran. Rage replaced concern. He needed to kill that son-of-a-bitch who took his boy.

Warlocks were an evil bunch. True, Dib and Kurt knew more than he did, but Randall knew enough. They dealt in dark magic, pacts with Demons, blood sacrifices, that sort of thing. They broke the one vow that all Witches and beings who used magic made upon receiving their gifts, to do no harm. Randall made a vow to himself right then, the *Oath-breaker* would not survive meeting him. *Hell fucking no!*

The sound of the surf crashing against the rocks below told him the tide was changing too fast. He crouched against a boulder, hoping to take in the scene instead of charging in there blind. He breathed in through his lupine nostrils and caught Danny's scent.

His increased senses were normally something he reveled in during his Change, but not now. His Wolf's sole focus was on Danny, and the boy was afraid. Randall had to fight the Wolf to keep from charging down the side of the hill to breach the mouth of the cave. That could prove fatal for them both, so he bit back the urge and watched.

He needed Danny safe, out of the clutches of those who would harm him, and he couldn't be sure of that if he got himself killed in the process. He shook his head from side to side and refocused. From his vantage point he couldn't see inside the cave, but he heard voices. *Plural.*

Whoever took Danny wasn't alone. Randall crouched lower on his front legs, silencing the deep growl that was coming from his throat. He inhaled again. The rotten stench of dark magic invaded his space. Someone was casting a spell.

He looked and saw a figure come out of the cave. He was dressed in jeans and a button-down shirt. A faded black baseball cap sat on a head of white streaked gray hair. The man's skin was a blotchy, unhealthy shade of pink. Like a bad sunburn on a fair-skinned person.

He looked like every other middle-aged tourist on the island. Except this man had a crazed look in his eyes as he held his left hand up to the sky, like he was some kind of religious zealot or cultist. With his right hand, he took a wicked looking knife out from behind his back.

The blade glinted in the sun. *Sharp and hungry.* The blade seemed to emanate feelings that Randall's Wolf picked up on. With quicker movements than Randall thought possible, the man sliced the blade across his left palm. A look of pure ecstasy crossed his face as the sound of his blood hitting the sand reverberated in Randall's ears.

The man mumbled something that Randall could not quite make out, then he called out behind him. Another man, thin and disheveled, wearing dirty ripped jeans and an equally stained t-shirt came out of the mouth of the cave dragging something behind him.

It was Danny! The boy's arms were tied in front of him, his blue backpack dragging behind him in the sand. His face was tear stained, but he was pulling back against the ropes. Fighting his kidnappers with all the strength in his eight-year-old body.

"Shut up, kid! Come on, move it. And no more crying, I can't take it!"

Randall heard Danny's whimper at the sound of the man's frustrated voice and everything in him wanted to go down there and rip the guy's throat out. *Not yet,* he forced himself to stay put. He couldn't help but feel a surge of pride in the little boy who struggled against his captors. *Attaboy!*

Whoever he was, the guy that was yanking on the rope around Danny's arms was not in charge. That much was clear. No, this man sounded scared and he looked worse. *Definitely a lackey.*

"Tom, is that any way to talk to your son? Tie him to the post there and finish making the circle. Now, just a few more hours, Daniel, and this will all be over."

"I want my mommy!"

"Yes, I know you do, and what did I promise you?"

"You said if I went with you, I'd see her again soon, but that was hours ago! And these ropes are hurting my arms."

"Yes, well, we can't have you running away now, can we? It's like I told you, when we tied you up, it is for your own protection."

"You're a liar! I want my mommy!"

"*Hahaha!* Do you know what I am doing? No? I am granting you your destiny, boy! Do you know who your father is?"

"No! I want my mommy! My father is dead!" Daniel's chin jutted out defiantly as he argued bravely with his kidnapper.

"No, he is very much alive. See that man there, that filthy excuse for a man? That's your father, boy. But don't think bad of him, you see when he made you, he was just a tool, a host if you will, for something much bigger than the small pathetic creature you see before you."

The man he pointed to, the man Randall guessed was Tom Nirvelli, squirmed under the stare of the man in the baseball cap. The stink of urine and body odor clung to him, but it was the smell of his fear, sour and pungent, that stood out to Randall. The man was a coward and a pawn. He'd get what he deserved.

"No! My father is dead! You're a liar!"

"*Liar* is one of my names for sure, but you *son*, ah, you have the potential to be the *king of the liars*! How would you like that?"

"No! I won't! I won't!" Daniel struggled with his ropes pulling them as far as he could, but the wooden stake that he was tied to was unrelenting. He fell in the sand as the Warlock hovered over him laughing at the spectacle. He reached down and yanked the boy up. He lifted Danny's shirt revealing a star-shaped birthmark on the boy's stomach.

"Yes! You are the one! I am sure of it! Tom, grab his head!" The warlock leaned forward and smeared the still wet blood from the slice on his palm across Daniel's forehead. That was enough.

The rumble of engines was faint in the woods behind him. *My back-up is here.* But Randall wasn't going to wait any longer. He crouched low and leapt down the twenty-five-foot drop landing on his paws with a small thud on the dry sand. He announced his presence with a loud snarl, snapping his jaws at the two men.

"Oh, my God! What is that?" The man Randall guessed was the supposedly deceased Tom Nirvelli dropped to the ground cowering like a child when he got a glimpse of Randall in Wolf form.

The Wolf fed on that fear. He growled, dripping saliva, and baring his fangs as he advanced on the real threat. The Warlock turned and met him with wide, crazed eyes. He pushed Danny down into the sand and crouched to face Randall.

"No! You'll not take him from me! The Master is come! He is here, you are too late!"

He lunged forward with a sick look on his face, the knife gripped tight in his right hand. Randall ducked away from the Warlock's careless advances. The man was no fighter, but he was relentless and the angle he stood made it impossible for Randall to get to Danny.

He had no choice. He stepped into swinging distance and took a hit. With one swipe of the blade the Warlock made contact and Randall made his move. He ignored the pain of the blade as it sliced his shoulder and bit down on the man's wrist.

"No! Ahhhhh!"

His scream soothed part of the Wolf that demanded he pay for taking what was his. But still, Randall held firm. His Wolf bit down with all the power in his mighty jaws, through muscle and tendon, sinew, and bone, until the man's hand lay on the bloodied sand beneath him.

"No, you can't! You will ruin everything! The Master! Get the boy, Tom!" He crumpled to the ground, cradling the ravaged stump that was all that was left of his hand to his body.

Randall turned to see Tom pulling on Daniel's ropes once again. The boy struggled and Tom drew back his hand and slapped him hard across the face.

He tried to drag Danny away, but he wasn't fast enough.

Grrrr. Randall used all the muscles in his legs and leapt forward cutting off his retreat. Tom dropped the rope, but he must have hit Daniel too hard, the boy was lying in the sand. *He's not moving.*

The roaring growl that erupted from Randall's jaws seemed to drown out the surf. He lunged forward, his jaws locked on Tom's throat and he crushed the man's windpipe beneath his teeth. A noise from behind him got his attention. He spit out the foul blood of the pitiful excuse for a man and turned to see Tulla jump off the back of an ATV a few feet ahead of him on the sand. She ran straight for her son.

Randall's heart swelled at the sight of her. She gathered Danny in her arms just as his blue eyes opened, and he hugged his mom. She was safe. Danny was alive. *They were both safe. Mine.*

He lunged forward as Tate moved towards them. He had a gun in his hand as he assessed the scene. He nodded at Randall and halted his steps. He averted his eyes in reverence to the more dominant Wolf. Randall took his due respect.

He sniffed out Doug O'Neill and a few other Wolves cleaning the scene and binding the Warlock in what Randall guessed was some kind of magic blocking equipment. They proceeded to duct-tape the man's mouth shut. Doug completely averted his gaze as he came forward.

"I'm not looking to move in on what's yours, man, but we'll be taking this one back to headquarters and I'll get a report to Rafe ASAP. 'Kay?"

Tate nodded and Doug backed off. That was when Randall realized that he was still crouched in front of Tulla and Daniel ready to attack any that went near them. His fangs were barred, and he was still growling. Tate took a step back and nodded behind Randall.

He felt her there, standing right at his back before he heard her approach. He turned not knowing what he would find and was surprised to see Tulla, Daniel cradled in her arms smiling through tears as she looked at him. Randall was overwhelmed with emotion. He whined and snapped his jaws.

"Randall? It's okay, man. They are okay," Tate's muffled voice did nothing to soothe him. His head moved back and forth. They were his in his heart, but he'd never asked her. He bonded with her sure, but she never agreed. *Never said the words.*

He howled his frustration. He needed to go. Had to run off his anxiety. The blood in the air was making him agitated. They took the Warlock before he could finish him. Suddenly, he was consumed with the need to hunt something, anything to take his mind off of what could have happened.

"I'll take care of her, of them. *For you, my brother.* Go now, run."

Randall felt the power of Tate's promise and it was the only thing that gave him focus. He barked and looked back once to the family that was not rightfully his, the one he would cherish above all others, then he took off down the beach running as fast and hard as his legs would carry him.

❧ 17 ❧

Tulla tucked Daniel snug as a bug in his twin bed. The pale green and blue comforter was soft and fuzzy. It smelled faintly like fabric softener and even more like her boy. She kissed him on the head and moved to the doorway as his breathing became deep and even, but she couldn't move any farther than that.

Maternal instinct kept her glued to the spot. She'd almost lost him tonight. She couldn't believe it. She hugged herself and exhaled silently. *He's so brave!* Her little boy hadn't fussed in the aftermath of the scene on the beach near the "secret cave".

He didn't argue when she gave him a bath and put him in his pajamas, her own motherly way of discreetly checking every inch of her baby to make sure he was whole and well. She watched him intently after he was warm and dry as he ate a few bites of the chicken soup she heated up.

He asked to go to bed right after and she laid down with him while he settled in, something she hadn't done a whole lot of this year. Daniel had insisted he was too big to sleep with his mama. Tears rolled down her face as she watched him sleep. What was he dreaming of? She hoped to God it was something nice and not about what had happened to him that day.

Kidnapped by a man who turned out to be his dead father! Told by a madman, a Warlock, that he was their king! And witnessing a Werewolf rip them both to shreds! And yet the only thing her son had asked about the whole incident was where had Randall gone?

"What do you mean, baby?" She had asked him.

"Well, Randall was a Wolf, and he ran away, where did he go? Is he coming back?"

"What do you mean, baby?" Tulla didn't know what to tell her son about the fact that Randall was a Werewolf. Evidently, she didn't have to explain anything.

"He's a Wolf, mama. My Wolf. I dreamed him, remember, only I thought he was a doggie. I knew he'd come for me."

"How did you know that?"

"I dreamed him for a long time. Is he coming back?"

"I don't know, baby."

She hated not being able to answer him. Two hours and still he hadn't come back. The man, Tate, sat in her living room like living statue refusing her offer of food or drink. He was polite enough, but he looked preoccupied. As if he were waiting for something. She left him there and excused herself to go be with her son.

Her poor baby! The red marked that had stained his little round cheek was almost completely gone by the time he closed his eyes. The time since Tate had brought them home after Randall had rescued him from the monsters that kidnapped him from school felt like eons.

She had so many questions. So many things she wanted to tell him, but he took off after he had saved her boy. *A Werewolf.* A real, *honest-to-God*, Werewolf. *Wolf-shield,* that's what Danny said.

It was certainly a lot to wrap her mind around, but was it any more than the fact that her supposedly dead husband had turned up today and taken her son from school? That he was a player in some Warlock cult that believed her sweet boy was destined to be the ruler of those evil bastards!

Her entire body shook with anger at the thought of Tom Nirvelli. That low-life skunk had stolen her boy! Lied to her for years about his death! Tricked her into marriage! *Ugh.* If he wasn't dead, she'd kill him herself. Once again, she pushed all that anger aside as she gazed at her son. He was safe. Alive and well. Home with her. *Because of Randall.*

She wanted to talk to the man, but, where was he? *Out running.* That's what Tate had said when she inquired after him. He tried to explain that it was not usual for a Werewolf to Change without the full moon and Randall's emotions were no doubt all over the place because of said Change and the events that brought it on.

Tulla didn't have the chance to really think about that before. All her attention was on her son, as it should be. But he was fast asleep now and no worse for wear. She walked back to find Tate standing at the back door. He seemed to be listening. He opened the door wide and in walked the four-legged version of Randall.

"They're here. They are safe." Tate's first words seemed to be to reassure the beast before them. He was panting heavily, his caramel eyes glowed as he gazed past Tate to where Tulla stood. She came forward slowly, but the Wolf backed up a step.

"Careful, he's Changing back now. It is painful and he feels vulnerable. I'm going to go outside, but I wouldn't touch him until he is himself again." Tate raised a hand and without looking at Randall he went to stand on the back deck.

It took ten full minutes for the cracking and popping sounds of Randall's flesh and bones as they stretched from Wolf to man to subside. When it was all finished, he lay there on the hardwood floor unmoving. The sound of his breathing told her he was still alive though what she had just witnessed seemed excruciatingly painful.

His naked body was covered in sweat, his eyes were closed, there was a gash on his left shoulder that was leaking blood. Tulla did not think, she acted. She removed some hydrogen-peroxide and gauze from under the sink and went to his side.

"Randall? I'm gonna clean this out, okay," her whispered words seemed to reach him because he turned to give her easier access to the wound. Once cleaned and wrapped she sat back on her legs.

He held himself still under her careful ministrations. She moved to brush back a strand of hair that clung to his cheek with trembling fingers. Warm brown eyes opened and met hers, the color changed to gold for a second and Tulla gave him a shaky smile. She hadn't had the time to worry about him, not since she was looking after Danny, but now that he was here, she couldn't hold it in any longer.

"Randall? You came back," she held her hand to her mouth to hold in her sobs just as he sat up and reached for her murmuring words of comfort in her ears.

"*Oh baby, God, Tulla, my Tulla.* Of course, I came back, I'll always come for you," he rained kisses on her face and down her neck as she clung to his neck crying harder now that she had him to lean on.

"It's alright, everything is alright."

She allowed him to comfort her, she even loved the way his body responded to her. His hardness pressed against her belly as he cradled her on the kitchen floor. But his words sank in and she was angry again.

"It's alright? You lied to me!"

"I never lied-"

"You never told me you're a Werewolf!"

Randall stilled as she stood up out of his embrace. He dropped his gaze and she felt more than saw his shame and guilt. She felt bad for causing it after all he'd done for her, but if they were going to have a future, they needed to clear this up.

"Well?"

"You're right. I lied by omission. I didn't tell you what I am because I didn't think-"

"What? You didn't tell me before because you thought I wouldn't believe you? Thought I wouldn't accept you?"

"That was part of it, but mostly I didn't tell you

because I had no right to you or to Danny. And I, I wanted the both of you more than anything I've ever wanted in my whole damn miserable life. I fell in love with you, Tulla. I didn't plan it, but I did. I'm sorry."

He stopped talking almost as quickly as he started. Tulla's ears were ringing. *Did he just say he loved her? And did he just apologize for it?* That was it.

"You are a Werewolf, correct?"

"Yes," Randall's head flew to the side as Tulla slapped him squarely on the jaw with every bit of muscle she possessed. Her hand stung afterwards.

Randall's shocked brown eyes met hers, but before he could speak, she pointed directly in his face. Her best angry mommy pose.

"That's for lying to me and for not believing in me."

"I guess I deserve that—"

"Shut up! It is not your turn to talk. Now, where was I? Oh right, now this, this is for saving my son," she kissed him on the lips. A soft and sweet gesture, but she pulled back before he could wrap himself around her, before his tongue could enter her mouth.

"Tulla," his eyes were glowing again, and she felt the pain and longing well up inside him.

"Just a minute, now that was for Danny, but this, this is because I love you too."

Tulla stepped back and pulled the cotton nightshirt she was wearing right over her head. Her breasts were bare underneath, her nipples pebbled in the air-conditioned room. She watched with heavy lidded eyes, her heart pounding in her chest.

His reaction was instantaneous, Randall's eyes lightened to that molten caramel color she loved, and his lack of clothing did nothing to hide the fact that he was aroused just by the sight of her. Tulla bit her lip.

18

When Randall walked back into *The Sea Mist,* he had little concept of where he was or how much time had passed. The Wolf in him demanded he get away from the scent of blood and death that permeated the air by the cave on the beach. He needed to distance himself from the other Wolves there who were too close to what he'd marked his.

His Wolf recognized Tate's promise, a sort of Pack bond magic that allowed him to trust in his Packmate, to see the truth in his words. Otherwise, he might have done more damage than he cared to. His Wolf trusted Tate to care for his mate and son. Randall's mind was working overtime just to comprehend the events as they happened, he was in no position to rationalize the Wolf's need to leave.

He'd never felt so out of control as Wolf or man as he had on that rocky shore. Truth be told, he didn't care to feel that way again. His brain couldn't imagine what Tulla must think of him now. *Had he lost her already? Lost his only chance at love?*

That fear brought him to her back door before he knew where he was. It was time to face the music and Randall had never looked forward to anything less. There was simply no way Tulla could ever love a beast like him. And without her or Danny in his life, well, Randall didn't even want to think about it. Suicide was hard for Werewolves. Living with a broken heart was even harder.

He wasn't surprised that his Packmate was still there to let him in. Tate, always true to his word, had stayed to watch Tulla and Daniel. He opened the door for Randall before the Wolf even made it to the top of the deck. Randall padded into the kitchen. The room looked slightly askew from his Werewolf eyes, but he recognized it.

The coconut, sea-salt scent that was Tulla permeated the air. He breathed it in deep, allowing it to invade all his senses. The image it evoked of his heart's own true mate was there in his mind's eye until, suddenly, she stood before him. She looked beautiful in her long t-shirt with her whiskey-colored hair loose around her shoulders in soft waves. Her gray eyes were slightly red from the tears she undoubtedly shed that night for her son.

Randall wanted to comfort her, to shield her from everything she'd witnessed the past few hours, but he couldn't undo the past. All he could do was try to mend the damage he'd done. There were things he needed to say, but he couldn't do that in his present shape. He closed his Wolf eyes and concentrated. It wasn't long before he felt that familiar hum of magic surround him.

He was still shocked at the way he was able to call the Change to him. Indeed, his Wolf was with him in a way he'd never experienced before. Stronger, unified, full of purpose. He finally believed that soon, there would be a day when Werewolves the world over would no longer suffer from the curse that kept them separate from their Wolves except for the full moon. Today was the first time he'd felt real hope for their species. The entire day had been a series of firsts. Not all of them good.

He hadn't meant for her to see him go through the lengthy process of Changing, but he had little choice in the matter. He knew it wasn't pretty. It was downright disturbing, maybe even disgusting. But he couldn't wait to face her any longer. Whatever blows she dealt, he knew he deserved them. He'd take them all, everything she had. The pain, the hurt, the disbe-lief, the anger, and then he'd beg if he had to.

The slap was surprisingly hard. She walked over to him and landed a blow right across his cheek. He felt the sting all the way through his body, sensitized as it was after Changing so recently. But he didn't object. He deserved her anger.

It was the kiss that shocked him. Tulla's declara-tion of love after everything had left him speechless. When she pressed her sweet body against him wearing nothing, but his favorite pair of purple panties with a certain kitty on the front, he damn near lost his mind. Any semblance of self-control flew right out of the proverbial window.

"Oh, thank God," he answered and took her mouth with his own. His moan of pleasure reverber-ated in his chest and only grew louder as their tongues tangled and she ground her hips against his. *Damn*, she tasted so good. Like salted caramel and Pina coladas on the beach.

"Say it again," he growled against her neck.

"I love you, Randall, I love you," she smiled against his mouth and he sucked on her lower lip loving every single inch of her.

"I never thought I'd hear you say that."

"I still haven't heard you say it," she bit her lip as his hands came up to capture each side of her beautiful face. Her silver eyes sparkled with desire and Randall worked to keep still. She deserved nothing, but the truth from him.

"Tulla, I have loved you since the day my eyes landed on you at that pier, hell, maybe even before that. I love you. Do you hear me?"

"Yes, yes, I hear you," she laughed and moved to kiss him, but he held her still.

"I love you, woman! *So fucking much!*"

"Show me," she arched into him and Randall thought he'd explode right then. This was his woman, his to love and cherish and protect. He kissed her face then her neck and shoulder. He used his tongue next, tracing a path along the curve of her jaw to the base of her neck where it met her collar bone. He tasted the sweet salty scent of her, delighted in the feel of it on the tip of his tongue.

He needed more. He dipped his head and cupped her breast with one hand, raising the dusky pink nipple to his mouth. Tulla's groan was his reward. He suckled her in his warm mouth and felt her knees buckle. His hold on her was strong and he swept her into his arms his mouth still busy at her full breast.

He used his large, long-fingered hands to hold her naked body against his. The curve of her ass fit perfectly in his left hand, while his right hand ran along her spine and neck and chest. He couldn't get enough of her, but the kitchen was too small for what he had in mind.

"Hold on," he growled, satisfied when she held onto his neck. She dipped her head and stroked his ear with her tongue and Randall bumped the two of them into the counter. Tulla laughed and tugged on his hair, kissing him within an inch of his life. He damn near swooned. Her tongue was wicked when she used it like that!

"Darling, I could hold you here all day with you kissing me like that if you want, but I got bigger plans."

"You do?"

"Yes, ma'am."

"Then what are you standing here for?" Her sultry gaze ignited a fire in Randall's belly. There was nothing in the world he could compare to the feeling of this woman in his arms.

There simply wasn't a big enough word for the emotions sweeping through him body and soul. He felt as if he were caught in a tide he never wanted to get out from. If this was love, then Randall wanted it, he needed it, all of it. She was everything. *Mine.*

The sound of someone knocking on the door reached his ears a little too late. When the doorknob began to turn, he twisted his body, shielding Tulla from whoever it was that had a fucking death wish.

Randall growled out loud, a snarling sort of noise that caused Tulla to gasp.

"Don't open that fucking door," his deep voice was answered with a chuckle, but the doorknob abruptly stopped moving. *Shit*, he forgot about Tate.

"You guys are good? Alright, man, I'm out," Tate was gone before Randall could say thank you, but he'd make sure the guy knew he appreciated everything he'd done for him. Pack was Pack. He'd do the same for Rafe and Charley, Tate, and Cat, and any one of the Wolf Guard. They were brothers, well, brothers and just recently, a sister. A family. Families cared for and protected each other.

He had a family of his own now too. The thought made his chest swell with pride and happiness. A true happiness he never thought he'd feel. He ground Tulla against his arousal and kissed her long and hard. She let out a slow, deep moan that he found insanely tempting. *Oh yeah*, he was going to make her moan like that for hours yet.

He used his memory of the house to carry Tulla across the way to his room. The door swung open and he carried her across the floor to the bed. He landed on top of her in a tangle of arms and legs and lips and tongues. He needed to feel, needed to taste every single inch of her luscious body, but that would have to wait.

C.D. GORRI

"I need you, right now, I need you inside of me," Tulla's whispered plea made Randall momentarily forget the feast he was going to make of her. *Well, not forget*, he'd just put it on hold.

"I love you," he said as he settled between her legs. The swollen tip of is cock sat right at her warm opening. She was ready for him, hot and slick with her arousal. He leaned down and kissed her full on the lips, his eyes boring into hers.

Randall pushed her thighs wider apart. He thrust into her warmth until he was buried inside of her. Tulla moaned and arched into him, gripping his waist and then his thighs with her hands, pulling him closer to her. He kissed her mouth and eased almost all the way out of her before pushing himself in again. In and out, in and out, slowly, and deeply each time. A rhythm old as time, but completely new for them both. *Every time like the first.*

He'd never had this kind of connection with any of the women he bedded. They were nothing, just bodies to ease an ache. His Tulla, she was everything. Her body fit him like a glove. As he pushed inside of her, he held her gaze steady, what he saw reflected in the silver pools of her eyes was nothing less than love.

It was more arousing than anything he'd ever felt. His thrusts became harder and faster. He'd marked her already, but that was mostly his Wolf. This time it

224

was the man who needed to make her his, this time he'd ask her first.

"Tulla?"

"Oh, Randall, you feel so good," her pants were coming faster and faster. He sensed her near completion and wanted to beat his chest with pride that he could make her orgasm so readily.

"Tulla, I want to mark you, now. Please, I know I did it before, but this time I want to ask you first, before I do it, I want to make you mine, *forever.*"

"I am yours, Randall, sure as I was destined to be the day I was born. I love you. Yes, you can mark me," she turned her head to the side and bared her throat for him.

Randall wanted to howl out loud. She was so brave, so open, and true. He felt her muscles contracting around him as he moved inside of her. Their bodies were slick with sweat, but he'd never felt so damn good in his life. Anticipation made his hands shake as he reached forward and swept her hair back across the pillow.

Tulla moaned and arched her body, her full ripe breasts pressed against his chest making him ache with need. He could hardly contain himself. Tension rose with each and every stroke of his body. He was going to come inside of her, *soon*, it was all he wanted to do, *but first.*

Randall kissed the spot where he already marked her. Small indents from his teeth were still there. He licked it once, twice, then he bit down. He knew when the feeling hit her as she raked her nails down his back and groaned against him. Her body shuddered, skyrocketing him into similar spasms that rocked them both into one long, shared, sweet as sin orgasm.

White hot lights exploded behind his eyes as he poured himself into her. Her cries told him she was experiencing the same, and his male pride made him want to howl with joy at giving his mate the most intense orgasm of her life, but he was too caught up himself.

It was never ending, like being caught in a hurricane of feeling. Pleasure, sharp and poignant, only to be overcome by emotions so intense Randall thought he'd weep. Joy, love, a sense of home, of belonging, and intense pride filled him. *Mine.*

19

The trip to New Jersey was long. They decided to drive along with a caravan of her belongings from *The Sea Mist*. Randall insisted she keep the property, even though she offered to sell. She was glad. It made her feel good to have something of her own. For now, she hired a local couple to run the place for her. Mr. and Mrs. Atkins readily agreed to manage The Sea Mist in her absence. They said they needed a new project.

It was a little scary leaving the life she'd built for herself and Daniel to move across the country with a man she barely knew, but what else could she do. She belonged to this man and he belonged to her. Werewolf or grizzly bear, Tulla was in love with him.

He laughed when she told him that, he also told her there were people, Werebears, who would think it quite funny too. There was so much she needed to learn! One thing was certain, Randall Graves was the best thing that ever happened to her.

The fact that her son had readily accepted the news that she and Randall were getting married told her she'd made the right decision. Her little blonde whirlwind looked at her with his guileless blue eyes as if she were crazy when she asked him if he would be okay with her marrying him.

"Mama! That's why he came here! Right, Randall? Would it be okay if I called you, Dad?"

Tulla's eyes teared up when she thought of how that big man of hers fell to one knee in front of Danny and opened his arms out to his son who readily jumped into them.

"Danny, it would just about make me the happiest guy in the world if I got to be your mama's husband and your father!"

"Really?"

"Yes, really."

"Well, okay then!"

After that, the two of them were inseparable. Danny loved having a new father and just about went nuts at the thought of having uncles, which is what all seven of the huge men, who were all actually Were-wolves, who lived at Macconwood Manor, insisted he call them.

Their suite of rooms were pretty much isolated from the rest. Randall liked his privacy. Lucky for them, there were several bedrooms unoccupied next to his. It was almost like having a townhouse.

They now had a master bedroom and bath that they both shared. Charley had invited her to feel free to redecorate however she liked to which Tulla said thank you. Daniel had his own bedroom and bathroom. And there was a living room area just for them, and even a mini-kitchen and office. It was incredible.

Charley, Rafe's wife, was warm and friendly. She'd welcomed Tulla and Danny with open arms. She was especially interested in any story or bit of advice Tulla could give her on childbirth. The woman's belly was just about ready to burst, Tulla was shocked to hear she was only halfway through her pregnancy.

Rafe Maccon was not as open as his wife had been, but Tulla understood he was the man in charge, the Alpha, as Randall referred to him. Still, he greeted her cordially and respectfully. He even got down on one knee when he was introduced to Daniel in order to shake the boy's hand at eye level. It was a sweet gesture.

Randall told her the man, the Warlock, who had kidnapped her son had been taken by a Witch Tribunal to be questioned and held accountable for his crimes. He was not satisfied, she could tell, but she managed to calm him with a few softly spoken words. It was important they discover just what the man wanted with her son.

All of the men, and Cat too, seemed to have a real affection for children. It wasn't until later that she understood why. Randall explained that to Were-wolves, young were precious. It was everyone's job to ensure they grew up feeling safe and secure so they could grow with pride and a good sense of morality.

This world was new to her, but she was going to do her best to get by in it. She'd made a vow and she would never go back on her word. She couldn't. Her heart would surely break in her chest without him. There was no place she'd rather be.

She looked down at her hand. The white gold band was plain except for an engraving of a sea star. Inside were their initials, T and R. written in Daniel's sturdy little block letters. Both she and her son changed their names to Graves. She wanted to shed all connection to Tom Nirvelli as fast as possible.

The ring was beautiful, and it meant so much to her. She liked how it looked, it went well with her short nails where a flashy diamond would have seemed wrong somehow. She liked that Randall knew her tastes, he paid attention to her likes and dislikes. *All of them. In the bedroom and out of it.*

The wedding ceremony had been cozy and romantic. Just the members of the household and Daniel and the two of them. They decided to hold off on a honeymoon, though Daniel went to spend the night at his first real sleepover with Uncle Tate and Aunt Cat who lived in one of the guesthouses at the Manor.

They'd come back to his room, *their room now*, and Randall stripped her out of the ivory lace dress she wore. He worked slowly, insisting she turn and give him every angle of what she wore underneath, a matching silk bra and panty set with sheer hose that stopped at her thighs. She wanted him out of his tux, but he refused to let her undress him. Insisting this was his wedding gift.

"God, woman, I need to taste you," His low growl had the desired effect for sure. Moisture pooled between her thighs and her stomach muscles clenched in anticipation. His hands were rough on her body, groping, tugging, teasing, and she loved every minute of it.

He dropped to his knees and lifted one leg, draping it over his black clad shoulder. The rustling sound of his tux as he moved his arms, one to push her silk panties to the side, the other to grip her ass as he moved forward and tasted her. That tongue of his was wicked, indeed. Tulla felt her body react to just the memory of his sweet mouth between her thighs.

He'd licked, and kissed, and tasted her for what seemed like hours. Once she felt the familiar tremors of her orgasm start, he'd pull back, a devilish smile on his face. She'd thrust her hips forward, but he simply parted her lips with his fingers and blew cool air over her sensitized flesh. Tulla had moaned.

Then he went in for the kill. He brought his mouth down over her clit and he suckled, long and hard. She bucked her hips against him and fell backwards onto the bed. Where she landed, he followed, his tongue not quite finished with her.

Tulla wanted to be as close to him as she could get, she hated that her panties were separating them. As if he read her mind Randall's big hands gripped the sides of her ivory silk panties and he tore them off. She groaned aloud and the beautiful man mistook it for regret. She recalled his apology with a stifled giggle.

"I'm sorry, baby, I'll buy you more, I promise. I just have to taste all of you with nothing in the way."

"I don't mind, I liked it."

"Then I'll buy you a truck load just so I can tear them off your sweet body, every single fucking day for the rest of my life."

"Yes!"

Tulla had no problem recalling the shudders that went through her entire body as his tongue was soon joined by his finger, and then another. Seconds was all it took for her to shatter against his mouth. And that was only the first orgasm. She'd lost track of how many times Randall had made her come ever since.

The moon was bright in the sky now and they'd been married and in their bedroom since one in the afternoon. He'd showed her in every way possible that she was loved, cherished, and desired. It was something, being wanted as much as all that, but the thing was, she wanted him just as much. She sighed and stretched feeling completely satisfied before glancing over at her husband.

His skin looked as soft as it felt in the moonlight. *Like silk,* she thought, even though it covered an expanse of muscles. His breathing was soft and even as she cuddled closer to him and ran a hand over his back up to his face. *Mine,* she thought and reached out to kiss his lips.

Caramel colored eyes opened to meet hers and he smiled. The love and desire he had for her always there now for her to see. She smiled back at him, the man she loved.

"Hey baby, I'm sorry, did I fall asleep?"

"That's okay, I did too for a while."

"You hungry?"

"A little. Someone dropped off a tray outside the door about an hour ago. I put it on the table by the window."

"Mmm, come here," he pulled her against his body and kissed her sweetly on the mouth. Tulla loved the feeling of being wrapped in his embrace. Like she was treasured.

"Have I told you I love you today, Mrs. Graves?"

"I think I can stand to hear it again," she smiled against his mouth as he kissed her deeply and with intent.

"I love you, my Tulla, always."

EPILOGUE

"**D**aniel! Come on, buddy, it's time for school!" Randall called out to his son and listened for the boy's fast feet as he ran across the hallway.

His Danny loved school! He was a good student and made friends with the other kids almost as soon as he started a few weeks ago when he'd married the boy's mama and brought them back to live with him in New Jersey.

"I'm coming, Dad!" Randall's heart swelled with pride at the sound of his new title. It rolled off Danny's tongue as naturally as if he'd been the boy's father since the second, he entered this world.

His wife walked in and he straightened to his full height. She was a vision, as always. Her hair was down and full of soft, glossy waves just the way he liked it.

She wore a dusky pink blouse and loose skirt dotted with flowers and leaves across it. She looked as fresh and lovely as ever.

"Good morning, baby," she bent and kissed Danny's head before her silver gaze found her husband. He groaned as he pictured what the two of them were doing just an hour ago under the full spray of the shower. Thank God, it was big enough for two in there!

"Hey, darling," he pulled her against his side and kissed her forehead as she hugged him around the waist.

"Hey, are you ready?" He scented her nervousness before he saw it in her face. Today was a big day. They were going to meet with the Witches to find out what they had learned about Danny's kidnapper.

Tulla had agreed with him that they should take Danny to school as usual before discussing the matter with him. There was no point in upsetting him when it might be hours before they had any answers.

They got in the large black SUV that was the standard mode of transportation for the Macconwood Wolf Guard. Randall nodded and the two vehicles discreetly followed them as they drove to the closest elementary school in Maccon City. About twenty minutes from the Manor.

He'd wanted to insist on a tutor, but Tulla had

discussed it with Danny and the boy wanted to go to school. He'd given in, but not without a few compromises. One was they'd drive him and pick him up every single day, with an escort, and two, was the school would be under Pack supervision. Tulla had agreed to everything and even suggested Danny be given a cell phone of his own.

The boy was smart and good with modern technology. It took Randall all of five minutes to show him the right buttons to press in case of an emergency. He'd also installed tracking device so he and Tulla could track him at all times. He probably wouldn't appreciate that when he was a teenager, but they'd deal with that when the time came.

"Bye Mom, bye Dad!" Danny was out of the car and running up the stairs to school before Randall put the car in park. Still, he and Tulla were out of the car in seconds after and followed to watch him go in. His teacher, Mrs. Jones, waved from the door. They had explained in a rather roundabout way the need for extra precautions and security, she'd complied without question.

An hour and a half later, Randall and Tulla sat in the offices of Tanner Global Enterprises where a Witch named Archie Tanner was waiting for them.

"I have news for you Mr. and Mrs. Graves, please sit. Can I offer you any refreshments?" The man was good-looking with perfectly kept hair and a killer business suit. His smile was kind though, causing Randall to instinctively trust the man.

"No, thank you, Mr. Tanner, we'd just like to know what you have to tell us."

"Right, well then let's begin. Mrs. Graves, are you aware of any magical blood in your family?"

"Excuse me? No, no, I mean, I would know, right?" Tulla's panicked eyes met Randall's and he could hardly contain the growl that came from his throat at his mate's rapidly increasing heartrate because of what the man was saying.

"I apologize, please, both of you. Look, from the blood sample you so kindly provided Mrs. Graves of both you and your son we've concluded that the boy does in fact have some unique markers in his blood."

"Well, that would be from his biological father, wouldn't it?" Randall hated the word biological, but nothing would change the fact that he did not claim a biological relationship to Danny. Still, he was the boy's father and he intensely disliked all mention of the slug that was Tom Nirvelli.

"Yes, well actually, we examined the remains of Tomas Nirvelli, and um, he was a normal."

"Excuse me?"

"Mr. Nirvelli was a *normal*. A non-supernatural, completely human. You, however, have traces of magic in your blood. It's fascinating really, whatever claim the Warlock made of Mr. Nirvelli being a host for something greater was all nonsense. Those oath-breaking bastards often deny the power of the feminine. Foolish really."

"I'm sorry what are you saying? I am a Witch?"

"Oh goodness, no! No, you are not a Witch, Mrs. Graves, but your ancestors were. I've had the markers in your DNA traced by experts in the field and your bloodline goes all the way back to Catherine Monvoison, she was burned at the stake in 1680 in France. She had the power to see the future, but she crossed someone and eventually it led to her death. Tell me, Mrs. Graves, have you ever experienced anything like that? A glimpse of something before it happened, a dream about something that later came true?"

"Well, no, not really."

"What about Daniel then?"

"Well, yes actually," Tulla reached for Randall's hand and he squeezed hers encouragingly, "Some-times Daniel gets these feelings, and he can sort of guess when something is gonna happen. He's had dreams like that too."

"He has?" Randall asked while Mr. Tanner listened.

"Yes. He, uh, dreamed about you before you arrived at Bloody point. He told me about a great big dog with sharp teeth who saved him. He said the dog was his shield. I thought it was just a dream, something from playing too many online games. I never put it together until now."

"I see," Mr. Tanner wrote something down and handed it to Randall. It was a phone number.

"That is the number of someone I have trusted with my own daughter's life. I know this is scary and seems impossible to you, but I believe the boy has a gift. Call this number when you are ready to find out for sure."

"Okay, but what should we do for now?" Randall asked his question though his mind was already moving a million miles a minute.

"For now, just enjoy your son. Call the number anytime. She'll help you."

"She? She who?"

"Her name is Sherry Mo-"

"Sherry Morgan?" Randall's face broke out into a smile as he sat forward and looked at Tulla reassuringly.

"Yes, do you know her?"

"Yes. The Pack has had dealings with her before," he decided to tell Tulla later that Sherry was a friend of his and the Pack's. The Witch had actually dated Seff. He was one of the Wolf Guard and acted as Rafe's Beta, his second hand. Their relationship had been a turbulent one, he recalled Seff being head over heels for the woman, but for whatever reason they called it quits.

More importantly, to Randall anyway, was that he liked the Witch. She was honest and good. Even Rafe consulted her on magical matters that concerned the Pack. She would not harm their son. Tulla looked worried and he squeezed her hand again, admiring her strength and courage.

This must all seem so strange to her, but there she sat, back ramrod straight and eyes fearless. She trusted him to do what was right for herself and for Daniel. It was an honor unlike any other that he'd ever been given. The right to love her and to protect his family made his heart swell with fierce pride. Tulla's voice interrupted his thoughts and he turned to face her as she spoke.

"Mr. Tanner, I need to know if the Warlock said anything about his cohorts, who he was working with? I need to know if anyone else is coming for Daniel?"

"Unfortunately, we don't know if he was working alone. He took his own life before we could find out that information. We will keep looking, do not worry on that front."

"Do not worry, my love, I will never let anything bad happen to him or to you," he'd made that vow a

C.D. GORRI

thousand times in his head since that morning and now he said it aloud. He meant every word too.

"I know," her unwavering faith in him was a testament to their love. Tulla would never risk her child, the fact that she recognized the level of Randall's devotion was just one more point in their favor. He rose from his seat and shook hands with Mr. Tanner.

"Thank you, we will be in touch."

"Anytime. Good afternoon, Mrs. Graves, Mr. Graves," he nodded and sat back into his chair just as his assistant came in with a pile of papers.

Randall shook his head and tucked Tulla's hand into the crook of his arm. He loved the feel of her, needed to touch her at all times. He wondered if that would ever go away and hoped to whatever God was listening that it didn't. *Mine.*

"But I don't understand," Tulla said as they left the office building.

He waited for her to buckle her seat belt before explaining to her the facts as he saw them. Daniel was special; therefore, he deserved a special kind of tutoring. Randall knew and trusted Sherry, but he would have them both meet with the Witch before bringing her around their son. *Their son. Our son. My son.*

That night they tucked Danny into his bed. As a wedding present, they allowed him to pick out all new décor for his room and Randall's eyebrows went all the way up to his hairline when the kid opted for a mix of all his favorite things.

It was like a comic bookstore threw up in his room! He had everything from Luke Skywalker sheets, to Fred Flintstone decals on the walls, Thundercat curtains, a TMNT lamp, and Voltron shower curtain, a Pokémon throw rug, and six different character pillows crowded around him. It was a mishmash of every superhero and cartoon the kid had ever seen.

Tulla had fretted over the cost, but when he shared his net worth with her, he was embarrassed to say her jaw hit the floor. He half expected her to slap him again for keeping it a secret that he was filthy rich, but instead she raised one eyebrow and looked at her son and told him to pick out anything he wanted.

It was the most fun he ever had, letting the boy fill up shopping carts online and clicking the "buy" button. When the large boxes arrived, the three of them, Randall, and his family, had had one hell of a time putting it all together. Afterwards he set up a special computer area and entertainment center for him. It was pretty sweet. But not as sweet as the six-string guitar Tulla had picked out for Danny.

"Teach me to play, Dad?" Daniel asked, his bright blue eyes fixed on Randall.

"You got it, pal."

Randall kissed the blonde head of his precious son and walked over to where his mate, his wife, his everything was waiting for him by the door. Her silver eyes looked over him a thread of worry in them. He took her hand and kissed it then settled it over his heart as they moved into the living room.

"He's going to be fine, Tulla. I swear it."

"Oh, I know that. I know you'll keep him, *us*, safe, but I was just thinking we've made such huge changes in your life. Are you okay with them all? I mean you are stuck with us that's for sure, but are you positive we are what you wanted?"

She looked so damn cute standing there biting her lower lip the Wolf inside of him wanted to take over and nibble on the plump little tidbit himself, but Randall reigned him in. *Mine.*

"I've never been so positive about anything. You and Danny are my life. I love you, Tulla mine, love you till there's not a breath left in my body and possibly even longer than that."

"And you won't ever get tired of us?"

"Never, how could you say that?"

"And you'll never get tired of this?" She stepped back from him and pushed the straps of the flowy, yellow sundress she was wearing off her shoulders.

The material made a swoosh sound as it landed in a soft pile at her feet.

Randall's arousal was instantaneous. His bulging erection obvious in the thin black shorts he usually wore around the house. His wife's breasts were full and ripe, he growled deep in his throat as his gaze swept past them, down the curves of her waist and the flow of her hips. His attention was brought to a certain little kitty demanding attention and he grinned that wicked grin he reserved for the nights she wore the special little swatch of purple cotton just for him.

"Well?" she asked bringing her hands up to caress herself from the tips of her breasts to that sweet juncture between her thighs that he couldn't wait to taste.

"Tulla! Come here," he advanced when she backed up a step, her left hand going under the elastic band of her panties.

"I'm waiting for an answer," she pulled her finger back out and ran it up her belly, over her nipple, and into her mouth. Randall felt his cock throb in his pants. *Fuuuck meee.*

"I'll never ever get tired of you, that is a fucking promise! Now come here, baby," he reached for her again, but her eyes held a mischievous gleam.

"I think we need a bigger swear jar." She winked

and turned around giving him room to chase her as well as a tantalizing view of her supple ass as it bounced with every step.

Randall let her think she was getting away, then he chased her down. He feasted on her sweetness before entering her from behind, her breasts filled his hands as the woman herself filled his heart. Hours later they lay in a tangle of arms and legs, so spent he wasn't sure where one began and the other ended.

"Tulla?"

"*Mm?*"

"I love you."

"*Mm.* Show me."

"Now?"

"Yes, please."

"Yes ma'am." And he did. Every day of the rest of their lives.

The end.

THE WITCH AND THE WEREWOLF

A MACCONWOOD PACK NOVEL

C.D. GORRI

THE *Witch*
AND THE
Werewolf

The
Macconwood
Pack

BLURB

Once upon a time magic tore them apart, now it's the only thing that can save them!

The Covens are demanding she choose a mate to continue her magical line, but there has never been anyone for White Witch Sherry Morgan except him. She spent years mourning the past and the only man she's ever loved.

Seff McAllister is a Werewolf and the local Pack Beta. Years ago, he allowed prejudice to stop him from claiming the only woman who made his beast howl. His cruel rejection has plagued him ever since. Now, Seff is in trouble and the only person who can save him is the last person he'd ever ask for help.

Will Sherry do what she can to cure Seff of the Dark magic that is slowly killing his Wolf? Or will old wounds get in the way?

PROLOGUE

T*en years ago.*

Shereen Morgan, or Sherry as she preferred to be called, crossed the bare wood floors of her small apartment. She came to the small seaside town on a whim.

She'd needed a change. *A major one.* Moving next to the sea seemed like an excellent idea at the time. *If only she knew.* Despite her nomadic past, Sherry had immediately fallen in love with the beautiful landscape that comprised the Jersey Shore. For the first time in her life, she wanted to settle down, grow roots.

The apartment she'd rented was small, but it suited her immediate needs. She had one goal when she chose the space, and that was to rest, relax, and recuperate some of the energy she'd spent over the past few months. But all of that changed when she'd met *him*.

Her body still tingled from their fevered embraces, but still, sadness threatened to overwhelm her. She inhaled a deep breath and allowed the energy in the room to settle over her.

Don't be a coward. Sherry frowned. It wasn't like her to dawdle. She usually preferred to rip off the band-aid so to speak. *Not this time.*

Slowly, she exhaled the breath she'd been holding. Sherry glanced down at the note that sat unobtrusively beside the silverware caddy. She grimaced as she picked up the surprisingly light paper off the tiled counter inside her small kitchen nook.

She'd decorated the small space with cheerful yellow paint and brightly colored curtains. But the happy décor did nothing to soothe her soul in that moment. Her hands trembled as she fingered the smooth edge of the paper.

He'd methodically torn it off of the legal pad that still sat on the clean wood table. Carefully as if not to rip it. *And yet he's ripped my heart from my chest.*

She took a moment to observe just how deliberately he'd folded his missive. His placement of it, propped up to ensure she'd see it almost as soon as she entered the room, just as thorough. *How like him.*

The familiar and neat, yet very masculine hand,

had scrawled her name intently across the back of the page. *Oh Seff.* Dread filled her. She hated her own weakness. The fear she felt in the pit of her stomach that accompanied the pain that squeezed her heart.

She was not a true clairvoyant, but sometimes Sherry had psychic hits that proved all too accurate. Especially where *he* was concerned. She sighed and replaced the note without opening it. She knew what it would say, but *dammit*, she wished she were wrong.

She'd thought that he of all people would have at least listened to her side of things! True, she couldn't expect him to ignore the edict of Zev Maccon, his Pack Alpha, but still. He could have talked to her.

Zev Maccon. The man was an all-around bastard. He hated everything and anything to do with magic. Especially the creatures who'd been born to it. *Like me.* The irony of the situation wasn't lost on her.

Sherry was a Witch. A fact of her birth that she could not control, nor deny, even if she wanted to. Magic was indeed real. Seff, as a Werewolf, had undoubtedly known about its existence.

Still, he hadn't connected it with her until they'd already become involved. *My fault*, she thought guiltily. She'd kept the truth of her powers from him.

Sherry recognized Seff was a Werewolf from the start. Surprised by the sheer force of her undeniable attraction to him, she'd delayed telling him the truth about herself. *Foolish Witch.*

At that time, she'd only heard rumors of the Macconwood Pack's Alpha and how adamantly he warred against magic. In fact, it was part of the reason she'd ventured to Maccon City.

To find out if the rumors were true, and to advise the *Elders Trust* on how to proceed. She hadn't really believed the accounts that a Wolf could object vehemently to magic. *After all, what was a Werewolf if not magical?*

When supernatural factions had disagreements, there were special forces called in to weigh on them. Guardians to be precise. But before they were sent in, a third party was sent to gauge the situation. Sherry had needed a break. She'd heard about the trouble and offered her services to the Order of the Guardians.

Having little contact with Werewolves before, she'd expected most of what she heard to be gross exaggeration. Her plans were to watch from afar while drinking in the sun and enjoying the cool waters of the Atlantic.

Then she'd met Seff. And the rest, as they say, was history. Had she known then that his Alpha had decreed to his Pack that no Werewolf of his would associate with Witches, she might have prevented this entire mess.

Still, Sherry could not help the shake of her head at the irony of it all. *Rejected for her magic.* Anger coursed through her veins. Zev Maccon absolutely refused to acknowledge the magic that worked within his own Pack.

He debased her and her kind as filthy abominations. *Witches are not worthy to live let alone to be trusted.* And as part of his Pack, Seff had no choice but to submit to Zev's fanatic views.

Sherry had spent years of her life steering clear of unnecessary strife. She'd rejected that part of her magic that was prone to violence and war. She had no desire to fight or to police other supernaturals.

It was inevitable that she'd run smack into a fight when she'd only been there to do some research and rest her weary bones. *The Fates strike again.* She wondered what she'd done to tempt them to break her heart.

It would have been so much simpler had she just said no when the Elders trust asked her to gather information on the Pack. Werewolves in general were secretive, but none so much as the Macconwood. Sherry's curiosity had gotten the better of her. She'd been thrilled at first. She'd never seen so many Wolves in one place.

The small town was ripe with them. After spending the last few years stuck in a damned desert doing the bidding of the *Elders Trust*, that pesky council of the leaders of the White Covens of the world, she'd been looking forward to some down time. This had seemed like the perfect assignment.

She waved her hand and the teapot on the table filled with the steaming herbal concoction that she favored. The note sat heavy in her hand. *Coward. Open it.*

Instead, she thought back on when she'd first met *him*. Seff McAllister, Werewolf, and all-around good guy with his boyish charm, exquisite, good looks, athletic build, and confident yet gentle nature.

Sherry had fallen for him. *Hard.* How could she not? He was made for her. Or so she thought. She thought she'd found her mate. Her true love. She had believed Seff loved her enough to get through the whole difficulty with his Pack. *I was wrong.*

The shock of her admittance was nothing compared to the words written in his *Dear Jane* letter. Her eyes closed on a wave of pain that shocked her to her core as she read his departing note. *Oh Seff, we could have been great together.*

She knew she should have told him as soon as he walked into her life that she was a Witch. And not just a Witch, she was a Morgan. Hers was one of the most powerful magical lineages known. She was a direct descendant of *the Morrigan*, once worshipped as a goddess amongst the ancient Celts.

Her famous ancestors also included Morgan Le Fay, that wronged half-sister of the legendary, but no less real, King Arthur of the Britons. She came from warriors, supernatural magistrates who'd brought judgement, and oftentimes death, to the lands they'd touched. They were both feared and revered, sometimes worshipped, by the Covens they'd served.

When Shereen Morgan was born it had been under a Blue Moon during a lightning storm. An omen, they'd later told her. Her mother had sacrificed her life for her child. She had been taught the ways of the Morganna by her grandmother.

Sherry was bright and powerful. Gifted by the Fates. Her skills unmatched, she'd wielded her power for whatever Coven her grandmother had assigned her to.

Once her grandmother's health began to decline, Sherry had put down her sword. She chose to nurture the healing arts instead. She was proud of her magic and her history. Especially once she began her journey as a healer and a guide to others looking for truth and peace.

Still, despite how far she'd come and how good she felt about herself. Neither feeling stopped her from withholding the truth about her magic from the one person she should have been honest with. And now, it was too late.

She had already given her heart to the young, incredibly handsome Werewolf by the time she'd whispered that she was a Witch in his ear. Seemed she'd been right in hiding that fact. Once he'd discovered the truth about her, he'd left.

Not that she could really blame him, though she tried. Seff had been raised to hate magic. Werewolves didn't trust Witches. Zev Maccon had declared all Witches the enemy of the Macconwood Pack. *Seff's Pack.*

Sherry had been curious about him from the first. Her intense attraction to the Werewolf shocked her.

She hadn't lied about what she was. Well, not exactly.

She simply hadn't flaunted her powers. The scent of her *anima magicae*, the heart of her magic, was easily masked with perfume and her constant baking. She'd always loved to cook.

She wanted to weep when she thought of all the time they'd spent together. Didn't it mean anything to him at all? *Especially these last few days.*

They'd cooked Szechuan in her tiny kitchen, watched game shows where he blurted all the answers, danced in the living room to the sound of the rock band that practiced next door.

He'd brought her small gifts every time he dropped by. Candied apples, licorice whips, the red kind not the black, and of course, flowers. Potted ones so she could water them and watch them grow from their perch on her windowsill.

The weeks had flown by. It really hadn't been a surprise when the first real chill of October had set in the previous evening, that Sherry had opened her arms and her heart to him. After dinner, she'd turned on a horror film and brought them dessert to share in front of the screen.

She'd fallen in love over apple pie and ice cream. He'd turned to her after lowering the volume and feeding some more wood to the already roaring fire in the hearth. Those clever hands of his swept away her blouse and bra without her even noticing.

Before long, Seff had stripped off her skirt and her underthings, baring her flesh to his eyes and mouth. He'd murmured words of praise and tender endearments as he kissed and touched her in the most wonderful ways. Her body trembled at the memory of how he'd made the sweetest love to her.

Sherry's eyes stung, but still she felt no regret. It had been mutual and wonderful. Seff had skillfully seduced her willing body, building pleasure until she could no longer hide who and what she was.

The magic that had always been a part of her had pulsed from within as her senses became lost in his touch. In the end, it was her eyes that had given her away. In her ecstasy, they'd changed color as they were known to do. First hazel, then gold, and finally, to a deep, glowing amethyst.

"Sherry? Are you okay? Your eyes are different. They're changing color and glowing, but you, you're not a Shifter? I'd smell it on you. Oh God, you're a Witch!" He'd been surprised at first, but still, he had not scurried away.

"Yes, it's true, I am a Witch and I know you are a Werewolf."

"Why didn't you tell me?" his voice was laced with sadness and awe.

"Because I know how your Alpha feels about us. Are you going to stop?"

"I don't think I can," he whispered.

"Are you not afraid?"

With his thickness still buried inside her pulsing cleft, Sherry had feared his withdrawal more than she'd cared to admit. He'd looked at her with his own brilliant brown eyes glowing, his Wolf shone brightly in them.

Caught up in wave after wave of passion and desire, he'd kissed her lips, claiming them with his own. Seff played her body like a master. Every touch, every movement, every meeting of their lips had culminated into a symphony of pleasure that grew and grew until she could no longer bear it.

"The only thing I am afraid of is how much I want you."

He pushed himself deeper inside of her heat. Grinding into her core while his lips did marvelous things to her neck and, finally, the tips of her breasts that ached with need.

He seemed to know instinctively how and where to touch and kiss. His hips drove in and out of her, the friction of his muscular body against her soft one created a feeling of pure ecstasy with each powerful thrust.

He sucked her tongue into his mouth, his teeth nipping the sensitive flesh of her lower lip. Electric bolts of pleasure zipped down her spine, right to her core as he swirled his hips and stroked her deep inside. His scent filled her nostrils, clean and fresh with a spicy musk that was all him. She wondered briefly if she would ever wash those sheets again. She could breathe in the scent of him forever.

"Oh God. Sherry, you feel like fucking heaven. So damn good." *He growled and thrust faster, losing himself in her heat.*

She welcomed his loss of control, reaching up and scratching her nails down his back. Whispering words in his ear that she'd be embarrassed to say in the light of day. But not right then and not with Seff.

They spent the entire night together. Between

bouts of exquisite lovemaking, they'd talked, really talked. She'd told him of her magic, and he'd told her of his brother and his place within the Macconwood Pack. He'd been young when his parents had died, and he'd had to rely on Zev Maccon to provide for them.

Sherry could have wept for the little boy he'd been, but he'd silenced her tears with more kisses. They came together again on the rug and once more on the bed. Their bodies spent, but still hungry for one another.

Seff was a fantastic lover. Just as she'd expected. Each encounter more passionate, more urgent, until Sherry was certain she'd declared her love for him aloud. How could she not when every fiber of her being wanted to shout it from the rooftops?

Expecting him to be skilled was one thing, losing her heart and soul in the span of one night was quite another. She'd never felt that way in all her long years on the earth.

Being magically inclined, she did not age the same as normals and was older than she looked. Not that age mattered, Wolves and shifters shared similar traits and Seff was also older than any normal would have guessed. Still, it was the first time she wanted to claim and be claimed in turn, by anyone as *mate*.

Though more modern in marital practices than

most Shifters, Witches did still believe in the concept of true mates. Some went so far as to blame the Fates who they said sometimes took a keen interest in the bedfellows of one Witch or other.

One thing Sherry had heard all her life was that when the mating instinct began in a supernatural being, it was difficult to quell. Sometimes impossible.

Sherry had grown up with tales of Witches gone mad when kept from mating with the one the Fates had chosen for them. One of her own ancestors was such a Witch. Others of course, did not believe in true mates. Still, they married, had children, and lived productive lives. And others still, wasted away for wont of their true mates, choosing solitary lives until they perished from the loneliness.

Being magical in no way guaranteed happiness. As she could now attest to. Sherry stemmed the flow of tears that threatened to overcome her as she watched the play of sunlight on the folded note. She inhaled and caught his scent on her skin and in the air.

It was unfortunate, that she, one of the most powerful Witches of the last age, one who had denied the whims of her heart for many years, had finally let the blasted organ free, only to have it betray her.

Her foolish heart had chosen most unsuitably. A Werewolf who would put his Pack before her. *Oh Seff.*

The object of her desire had slipped away during

the night. *Slipped away like the thief he was.* True, he left her a note. *A note! The dog!*

She opened it and could have howled her rage. He told her to forget about him, he explained that he had nothing to give her.

We have no future. Last night is in the past. Forget me.

Sherry grieved for what could have been, but she was not one to wallow. Head held high, she set the note aflame with but a wave of her ring adorned hands. She packed up the small apartment with another flick of her wrist and was gone within the hour.

Forget the Wolf and move on.

If only it was that easy.

Present Day. Macconwood, the property owned by the Pack just outside of Maccon City, New Jersey.

Seff sighed as he got out of Charley's fully loaded, cherry red, Range Rover. How his Alpha's wife loved that freaking car! He shook his head as he ducked against the rain.

Loved it so much, that he had younger members of the Pack washing the thing by hand every other day. Seff grimaced at the thought that he might scratch the highly polished paint when he lugged out the massive spare and the flat tire kit from the trunk of the SUV. *Better be careful, or Rafe will have my ass.*

Cold rain assailed him like stinging pellets, and he shivered despite his being a hot-blooded Werewolf. His beast chortled in his mind's eye and Seff grunted. *Real funny!*

His Wolf was quite the character lately, especially with the gap between man and beast narrowing with every passing day. *You go, Grazi!*

She was the teen Wolf who was battling to end the Curse of Natalis. The curse kept all Werewolves from their Wolf side except for nights of the full moon. The young girl, whom Seff had met on occasion, was working tirelessly to demolish the ancient edict.

Seff had no doubt the fearsome she-Wolf would emerge victorious. The evidence was in the fact that he could clearly see and feel his buff-colored Wolf round the clock. A first for him.

Seff reveled in the closeness of his other half. He was learning to control the sensory overload that came with having his Wolf on hand twenty-four hours a day. It was not always easy, but he'd manage and so would the others.

A huge wet drop flopped into his left eye and he blinked to readjust his sight. *Stupid rain!* Perfect weather for a flat! He rolled his eyes and took in the obviously deflated tire. *Well, shit on my luck!*

The sound of the window rolling down caught his attention. He looked back and smiled encouragingly at his Alpha's mate. The former deli-worker, now Alpha female, regardless of the fact that she was a *normal*, was hugely rounded this late in her pregnancy.

That was the reason why he was standing outside in the biting wind and rain changing a tire. Charley had been restless and uncomfortable all day and was about to go for a ride alone when he'd offered to take her. Otherwise, he'd have been warm and dry at home. *Yeah, cause being home and alone was so much better.*

Of course, he didn't have to be alone. He could've gone with some friends to *The Thirsty Dog*. His Wolf growled inside his head.

Not that he didn't enjoy hanging out in the local Werewolf owned bar. His brother and Packmates certainly did. It was just that lately, he didn't feel like putting on a show for the guys at the bar.

Who needed their shit when he refused to take home any of the willing women at the place? And there were many. Normals couldn't help being attracted to the natural vitality of Werewolves, but he was not interested.

Casual encounters had lost their appeal long ago. They left him feeling empty and, oddly enough, guilty as hell. *Don't go there.* Seff was alone in the world. It was past time he accepted it. *Not true. There is one person who could make you feel again.*

A phone call and an apology wouldn't be enough

to cure him of his lonely state. No matter how much he feared it would become his permanent state. Still, it wasn't like he could just drop her a text. Not when he walked away like that. *Shut up and grow a pair*, he told himself firmly.

This was becoming a regular thing for him. He pushed his hair out of his face as he grabbed the tire iron and missed the first time. *Fuck*, when would he stop thinking about her? *Never. Duh.*

His old Alpha's voice infiltrated his mind and he growled as he worked the flat tire free. *The only good Witch is a dead Witch, my boy. Pack first, Seff, you put the Pack first and you can't go wrong.*

And isn't that what he always did? He left the girl, *the one*, he was sure of it, for his Pack! He had turned his back on her and on his heart. And he'd never looked back.

Nope. Seff had responsibilities. He needed to look out for his brother, and it was with that in mind that he had set to work. He'd busted his ass studying Pack politics and making use of his unassuming appearance to turn himself into the perfect Beta.

He stood just about six-foot tall, as most Wolves did. His build, however, was wiry and lean, unlike most of the hulking dominant Wolves he knew. He preferred his hair cut short, his face cleanly shaved, and his clothes neat.

His affable exterior meant others let their guard down around him. A mistake that often led to their downfall. He was brutal to the Pack's enemies and when hot tempers and thick heads within their ranks needed a smack down, he was the one to initiate that delivery.

Seff was a good and loyal Beta to Rafe. Stronger and smarter than he looked, he was a valuable asset to the Pack. His knack for diplomacy and his ability to read people was vital to his position.

His old Alpha was a right bastard, and he couldn't have been happier to see him go. Especially, when Rafe Maccon stepped into the position.

Seff believed in Rafe and his plans for the Pack's future. It was why he worked tirelessly to aid Rafe and his Packmates in any way he could. It was also why he was outside in the freezing rain in the dead of night.

In her state, Charley was in no condition to drive by herself. Heck, he wasn't even sure she could get behind the wheel. *Not that he'd tell her that. She'd probably feed him Chef Boyardee for a week if he did. Sad whine.*

No way. He couldn't risk her taking it out on him by denying him her delicious pasta sauce. He'd kept his comments to himself. But with their Alpha away and her in her delicate condition, Seff had gently insisted on accompanying her.

Good thing too. She'd never have been able to change a flat by herself. Not with her "precious cargo" and certainly not in this weather. Feminism aside, even if she were the heartiest female, Seff would still be the one to change the tire. He'd been raised to treat women with a certain amount of courtesy and chivalry.

Not that *she* noticed. Damn it. Just when he thought he stopped thinking about her, she would creep into his mind again. Sherry Morgan was the one mistake in his otherwise pretty damn impressive history with women.

Not that she was just a woman, no, that would have been too easy. She was a Witch. A White Witch, but still, she practiced magic. Magic *is not to be trusted.* The words of his former Alpha rang clearly in his head.

Zev Maccon had been a madman and a bit of a sadist, but after Seff had lost his parents, Zev had seen to his education. He made sure Seff and his younger brother, Liam, were taken care of. Sure, the old fucker he'd stuck him with was a little mad with age, but they had had a roof over their heads and food in their bellies.

Because of his keen mind and unquestionable

loyalty to the Pack, Seff had been quickly promoted within their ranks. He'd soon made friends with the Alpha's son, Rafe, and the rest is history. With Rafe Maccon's ascent to Alpha many of the old ways were cast aside. *Good riddance!*

Including one edict that had declared all magic and magical practitioners as enemy of the Pack. In other words, the old Alpha had deemed all magic evil, and in his zeal, forbade Wolves to mix with Witches. That sort of anti-magic sentiment had reigned supreme amongst Wolves for some time. *But not anymore.*

In fact, Rafe insisted on breaching the gap between Witches and Pack. He'd breathed new life into the Pack and made Seff proud to serve him as Beta. He was honored to stand beside Rafe and the rest of his Wolf Guard and to provide whatever was needed for the Macconwood.

But what about what I need? He tried to stifle that nagging thought with a grunt as he pushed the tire iron to loosen the bolts that held the flat secure to the rim. The rain made it difficult to see what he was doing. It was coming down even harder now. There was something almost unnatural about the whole thing. He was sure the skies were supposed to be clear tonight. *Oh well. Stupid weather channel was always wrong.*

But seriously, the wind seemed determined to get every blasted drop in his eyes! He squinted to try and minimize the effect, but the effort was wasted. Thunder cracked overhead and Seff strained to hear beyond it to the inside of the car where Charley waited.

Once again, a loud roar of thunder echoed in the skies followed by the strong smell of ozone. It infiltrated his nostrils and tickled his senses, but he ignored it. A trick of the storm. They were on Pack land, after all. They were safe.

He shook the rain from his hair and resumed his task. The noise of the storm grew to deafening heights, and he worked faster to change the bloody tire. Ignoring the little voice of warning in his head, Seff focused. He didn't hear anyone approach until it was too late.

He turned as the sound of someone coming breached his senses, but he was too late. Even as disbelief rang through him, he felt the pain begin. *Someone would have to be mad to attack him here.*

Next thing he knew, he was lying on the cold asphalt. Pain, *a burning, scorching pain*, ripped through his entire body.

He could not move as the hooded figure bent down and forced a foul-tasting liquid into his throat.

He wanted to growl and fight, but his body would not obey him. He groaned with the effort.

Fire raced through his veins, black and unnatural, it burned down to his soul. His Wolf howled grievously in his mind's eye. He struggled to reach his Wolf, but his beast was gone. The pain of the forced separation threatened to render him unconscious.

No! NOOO! Through the torture, he had one thought only. *Sherry.* He needed to reach her somehow, to tell her he was sorry. He'd waited too fucking long. And now his time was up. *No! No! Sherry! Sherry! SHERRRYYYY!*

Inside his mind, he screamed the words his lips could not say. He roared her name over and over again as the veil between him and his Wolf closed. It was there, trapped inside his mind's eye, shrouded in the cold darkness that he saw her. *His Sherry.*

He howled his rage and frustration as he watched her with his head thrown back and her purple eyes glowing. He roared until his voice stopped working. And it was then that he heard her scream his name. *Seff!*

Then, the darkness took him.

2

Sherry! SHERRYYYY!

A voice from her past screamed loudly inside her head, shattering her inner calm and startling Sherry from her repose. *Could it be?* She gasped as she heard him call her name loud and clear. *Sherry!*

She'd been attempting to reach a new level of self-transcendence. In her deeply meditative state, Sherry had even managed to levitate more than a few feet off the ground when she'd heard him calling her name. *Seff?*

The pain of her bottom as it slammed down onto the hardwood floor was unpleasant, but not so much as the torment she felt coming from him. Surely, something was very wrong.

Sherry!

"Seff?" She spoke aloud, though she knew the voice was in her head alone.

It's so dark. Sherry, I can't see or hear anything. I need to tell you...

"Oh no," she gasped and tossed her head back, drawing on the connection forged between herself and the only man she had ever loved.

Her heart squeezed as she opened herself up to that connection. *The same one that had broken her heart so desperately before.* But she had no choice. He was in trouble.

Sherry envisioned the silver threads of magic that connected them, that would lead her to him. She was mildly surprised to see that they still pulsed with life and feeling even after so many years.

Her perusal halted when she beheld a malevolent darkness as she neared the end of the path that led to Seff. Within the darkness, Sherry felt its cold and evil intentions engulfing the otherwise bright aura of Seff's being. She advanced but was unable to get much closer.

The menacing, inky blackness surrounded him. It threatened to extinguish the beautiful light that was all him. A purely evil spell, she acknowledged the Dark magic with a toss of her own light and prayed it would be enough to hold it at bay.

Regardless of the past, as a Witch, a Keeper of

the Light, and a descendant of the Morganna, she would not allow this attack on her ally. The Macconwood Pack had officially acquired her aid months ago in the form of a contract that bound them as allies.

You may lie to everyone, but not to yourself, Sherry. You are bound to the Wolf. Admit it. She opened her eyes and yelled into the empty room.

"Seff! I'm coming for you!"

She jumped to her feet. The tiny silver bells that lined the bottom of her harem pants jingled as she crossed barefoot over the wood floor. She picked up the phone and dialed quickly. When it continued to ring, she clicked off and started packing.

"Why do people even have cell phones when they don't answer?" She slammed the thing down and walked to her bedroom. She would need enough personal items and magical stores for about a week or so until she learned more.

She grabbed a canvas bag decorated with a bright green elephant on the front and began tossing in an incredible array of items. Way more than should have been able to fit in the bag, but that was magic for you. The inside of the canvas was as large or small as she needed.

After tossing in some clothes and shoes, her cell phone and charger, laptop, and a variety of dried herbs, candles, potion bottles, her favorite chardonnay, her cast iron tea kettle, bunny slippers, and of course, her grandmother's grimoire, she snapped it closed. She didn't normally transport herself through time and space, but without the benefit of a more traditional means of transportation, *meaning her car was currently in the shop*, she had little choice. This was an emergency.

Are you sure you should go? Will he welcome your help? She dismissed the stray thought almost as soon as it entered her mind. This was Seff. He was in danger. She felt his pain, heard him cry out her name. Whatever happened between them, it was in the past. He needed her now. Of course, she would go.

Besides, she had a treaty with the Macconwood now. Their new alpha was not opposed to magical help. *Much like a certain young teenage Werewolf she knew.* Grazi Kelly was closer than ever to breaking the curse and Sherry was proud to have aided the young woman on her quest.

In helping the young she-Wolf, Sherry had opened herself up to helping other supernatural factions. She dealt with Werewolves, Vampires, Dhampirs, and of course Witches, on a revolving basis.

Rafe Maccon and his new *magic is cool* policy resulted in her being called in to work with his Pack on more than one occasion. Her fees differed among the groups from money to hard to come by magic ingredients and other boons. Above all things, magic demanded balance and, therefore, she was required to accept payment in return for use of her many talents.

Sherry got results and she was in high demand. Which is why the leader of the largest Pack in the world had his legal team draw up a written retainer whereby she was acknowledged for her considerable skills as a magical consultant on call to the Macconwood Pack.

They were now her top client, after the Covens of course. In a sidebar, she had informed Rafe that she would prefer to have little to no dealings with a certain Pack Beta. The same one she was now rushing to help. The irony was not lost on her, but she was too wound up to pay it any mind.

She recalled how Rafe had proven willing to negotiate, but Seff had not agreed. In fact, he scoffed at her request. He was the Beta and matters of diplomacy were his domain.

Meaning, she would have to deal with him regularly. However, Sherry was nothing if not tenacious. She'd been firm in her request. She even lessened her standard fee by ten percent. Magic did have its price after all, and Rafe agreed. Much to Seff's chagrin.

Idiot. He should have fought harder. But he never had. Not where she was concerned.

It didn't matter now. Old disappointments aside, Seff was hurt, possibly dying judging from the hollow ache of his pain that still throbbed inside of her own chest.

Her heart shuddered at the dreadful thought. Seff had no time for doubts or personal insecurities. Sherry would simply have to swallow her pride. She bit her lip and lit the rare red flame candle that she kept hidden in the magically enhanced safe under her bed and invoked a spell to keep her home safe from intruders.

Then she stood in the center of the room and spoke in a soft voice, *"Ewch â mi ato."* Roughly translated it meant something like take me to him.

Her native language being a mix of Celtic and Welsh, Sherry was able to bend and use magic with commands that other practitioners could simply not grasp. A supremely powerful Witch, she chose to keep most of her talents hidden. It was safer that way.

Modern Witches new little of the ancient arts and the world was a better place for it. Greed and treachery were abundant, and it was her duty as the Morrigan to keep their secrets safe. A Witch with too much power and too little control could too easily forget their number one rule, to keep their magic hidden from the normals. It sort of fell under the whole, *do no harm* thing.

The fragile beings could not comprehend the forces that gave birth to the universe and made it work. Heck, most supernaturals did not understand either, but Sherry did. More than most.

Her level of skill was not easy for many to conceive. Especially since magic was thought to be finite. In a way, the Covens were correct. There was only so much magic allotted to this universe at any given time; however, the ability to tap into that power differed amongst them.

A Witch was born with Magic, it could also be inherited, freely given, and in some cases, stolen. Sherry had a very large store of magic herself, more than most Covens combined, but she kept it very well hidden. It would not do for the *Elders Trust* to know the extent of her powers.

Still, her history was widely renowned, and the Covens now demanded she ensure the passing on of her gifts. It was the reason she was doing so much mediation lately. *Drat it.* She'd almost forgotten the deadline they had given her.

She had managed to keep them at bay the last few decades with promises that she was searching for her mate, but that didn't stop them from sending yet another demand that she choose a mate and beget an heir by the next cycle of the moon. *As if she were some broodmare! The fools!*

She pushed her impending deadline as far from her mind as she could. The only man she'd ever loved needed her. She needed to focus on Seff and to stop whatever it was that dared to hurt him.

Whoever the transgressor was, he had no idea what she could do once she found him. First, she had a Wolf to tend to.

"*Ewch â mi ato.*" Her voice reverberated around the room as a large oval shaped portal began to shift in front of her. Sherry exhaled and stepped through to aid the one who'd left her with a broken heart. *Too late to turn back now.*

Sherry was on her way. *To Seff.*

3

"Ms. Morgan, I am shocked to see you," Rafe Maccon extended a hand to her. The fact that she had appeared in his study just as he opened the door was not lost on him.

She was extremely powerful. Almost to the point where he should be worried, but she was a friend. *Or so he hoped.*

"Where is he? I must see him," she didn't have time to waste on formalities. She let go of his fingers and walked past him to the hallway.

"He is in the medical wing, come this way," the immense Wolf led the way, undisturbed by her forthright manner. He felt Sherry bristle behind him as she followed.

Impatience had her lips pulling downward in a frown. Still, she knew better than to try and skirt around the Alpha. She was not often intimidated by size, but if anyone could manage to do so, it was the Werewolf in front of her.

Rafe gave the word big a whole new definition. Sherry preferred her men a little more manageable in size. Lean and lithe. *Like a certain Pack Beta.* She only hoped she'd get to admire the man again even if only from afar. *I hope I'm not too late.*

Something tickled her senses. The atmosphere of the Macconwood Manor was charged with energy. Not all of it good. Sherry gasped as she realized there was more to this than Seff being attacked on Pack property. Blood tinged the air. Magic too. Dark magic. She scowled at the bitter taste of it.

"I see you have had more trouble than just Seff tonight? And you did not call me?"

"Yes, well, a lot has happened. You would have been my next call, but you beat me to it."

"I see," she waited for him to continue.

"Earlier this evening, my mate was kidnapped and Seff was attacked-"

"How is Charley now?" She gasped at first, then remembered herself enough to ask after Rafe's wife.

As a normal, she should have been excluded from attack, but this crime was initiated by one without honor. *One I will dismember should Seff be harmed beyond my skills.*

She could hardly stop the violent turn of her thoughts. Seff may have left her, but not before she imprinted on the man. Her heart squeezed inside her chest, it had been a decade since she'd admitted as much, even if only to herself. *I still love him.*

"Thank you for your concern, Ms. Morgan, but I found her and eliminated the threat."

"I take it the *threat* to your wife is not something we shall hear from again?" She shook herself from her reverie to ask the question.

He studied her quietly for a brief moment, but in the end, he nodded his head. Sherry understood. Some would not approve of the shedding of blood, but she was raised in the old ways. Sometimes violence was the only end.

"Do not worry, Rafe, I find no fault in your actions, you were right to defend what is yours. Is Charley well then?"

"She is, as are our children?"

"More than one? Delivered safely?"

"Yes, by the side of the road. That amazing woman of mine delivered three healthy young! Two lively boys and a precious daughter!"

"Many congratulations to you both. What of Seff? Do you know what happened?" She kept her voice calm, but on the inside, she was anything but.

"Before his demise, our enemy, Skoll, said he had a

Dark Witch perform some sort of spell or potion on Seff. We don't know what it was, and we can't wake him with medicine or through our Pack bonds. He has been unresponsive and remains unreachable."

Sherry gasped and missed a step, but strong hands reached her before she stumbled. She looked at Rafe and saw the concern in his gaze. *Unreachable?*

"I know you have made strides, Rafe, to trust Witches. I assure you, regardless of the past, I would never harm Seff. Not him or anyone else, less they harm me or mine."

"I believe you, Ms. Morgan. It's the only reason why you're still here. Come this way," he opened the door to a pristine hallway that led to a series of rooms that would have looked perfect in any hospital.

Sherry breathed in the antiseptic. Beneath the strong scent, there was one scent she recognized. Tears pricked her eyes, but she quelled them. This was no time for hysterics.

She walked through the door of the nearest room and saw a short brunette, *a Wolf*, bent over Seff. She couldn't help the flash of jealousy that made her reddish gold hair swirl angrily around her shoulders.

That sort of thing happened whenever she was riled or about to do magic. She closed her eyes and counted to ten before joining the woman who was talking to Rafe and looking at a tablet at the same time. She was a doctor, her interest in Seff purely scientific. *That's good.*

"There has been no change, sir."

"Thanks, doc. You can go now."

"But-"

"I am afraid this is beyond medical science," Sherry's voice was shaky.

She dismissed the Wolf doctor and walked to the prone figure lying still as death in the hospital bed. *Oh Seff.* He looked deathly pale. His cheeks appeared gaunt. His breathing raspy.

He looked alien with all the tubes and monitors attached to him. Sherry frowned and began peeling them off.

"Hey, you can't do that-"

"Yes, I can."

"Those tubes are necessary-" the petite doctor interrupted again, but Sherry shot her a warning look.

"These are not helping and will make it only more difficult to get a true reading. All this, these electronics must go, *now*," she said.

The doctor held onto the one that was forcing oxygen into Seff's nostrils and Sherry rolled her eyes. She had no time for this. She waved her hand, agitated beyond reason, and the small Wolf was flung to the side as plugs and tubes detached themselves from Seff's prone body.

Oops, she'd cast too much into that little spell as plugs came out of electric sockets and machines flew across the room. The tubes closest to him wound themselves back up and the IV currently attached to Seff withdrew its needle and scurried away from the bed.

"What the-"

"You can go now, doctor," Rafe said and looked at Sherry with narrowed eyes.

"Yes, sir," the she-Wolf growled and left the room.

"You will see that he recovers?" Rafe asked.

"I will do my best to bring you back your Beta,"

"Seff is more than that, he is Pack, he is family."

"Yes, I know." *It is why he left me.*

"I need him moved someplace that is *his*."

"It will be done as you say, but I don't have to tell you to be cautious," he growled the last and she could see his Wolf in his eyes.

"I vow here and now, Rafe Maccon, that I am a friend to Seff McAllister, regardless of our past, no harm will come to him by my hand," the magic imbued in her words shook the room slightly, but the Alpha seemed appeased by the gesture.

And that was how Sherry Morgan found herself

safely ensconced in Seff's wing in the rather remark-able Macconwood Manor.

The place was a veritable fortress. A huge, stone structure with the best possible security measures from the outside. Inside, the place was immaculately cleaned and built to last.

The furniture sturdy, the floors highly polished, and every room spacious. Each of the Wolf Guard seemed to have his or her own wing or *lair* as Shery thought of them. With the exception of the Nighthawks, who lived in an outlying guesthouse.

Seff's wing was much like the man himself. It had a reserved, yet classy style to it. Modern technology blended fluidly with the sturdy leather and solid wood furniture. He preferred clean lines and an uncluttered look. Except for the living room area where books, hundreds of them, lined the many shelves.

There was no television in sight, and she smiled, recalling how he preferred to read or talk to watching shows or movies during their brief time as a couple. A beautiful chess board sat in one corner.

It was carved from the finest mahogany and lovingly cared for, she could tell from the lack of dust on each of the gilded pieces, they were Wolves versus Dragons. *Nice.*

The palette was very masculine, but still somewhat sedate. Something she would have scrunched her nose at. She preferred vivid colors to the dull grays and beiges. She could imagine adding a plush throw rug with deep maroon hues and a gold and blue blanket for the couch with accent pillows in all three colors. Some curtains, a few candles here and there, it would be lovely. Not that she would be doing any of that.

This place is not yours. He is not yours. Well, no duh, stupid inner monologue. She was all too aware that the Wolf in question was not hers. No matter. She was bound by her vow to help him and she would.

Sherry entered the bedroom and sucked in a breath. It smelled like him, a combination of the masculine soap he preferred and the subtle scent of fresh cut spearmint that she'd always associated with him. Delicious in tea or on the tongue. Especially after dinner. Yum. *No, bad girl.*

She looked over her charge who was now lying comfortably in his own bed, the clinical hospital gown removed, but his modesty still preserved under a crisp white sheet. *Of course, the sheets are white.* She'd prefer printed or some flamboyant shade of orange or yellow.

Anyway, she sat at the foot of the bed, not quite touching him, but close enough for her to get a reading on the type of cast that had him locked under its spell. This part of her talent was highly developed over the years as she tended to flock from Coven to Coven when and where her services were needed.

Sherry was a healer, a trainer, and so much more. The *Morganna* Witches wore many hats and, she had tried them all. Healing and teaching were her true callings and Sherry preferred to do both, unobserved.

She frowned as she became aware of the presence lurking just outside the bedroom. The pacing back and forth of Seff's younger brother Liam was pronounced in the quiet quarters. She concentrated hard, tuning him out.

It was almost easy after living above her latest entrepreneurial endeavor, most recently named *Hair and There*. The beauty salon offered treatments to all beings, normals and supernaturals. That said, her employees were a rowdy bunch of young supes, and they loved to blast all sorts of music during the working day which went from nine in the morning to nine at night, except for Saturdays when the remained open till eleven.

It was easy to minister to people under the guise of offering beauty treatments. How many times had she discovered a skin lesion on a normal and washed it away with an elixir? How many times had she eased a broken limb or sprained muscle? Not to mention those cursed or afflicted by a cast gone awry. Sherry enjoyed her work. She always had.

She bit her lip as worry welled up inside of her. This time it was different. This time she had a vested interest in the outcome of her craft. She exhaled and pushed away all her thoughts and fears. There was only one way to trace the spell the Dark Witch had cast. She'd have to get a reading first then proceed from there.

Sherry closed her eyes and sat cross-legged on the exceedingly comfortable mattress. She let the scent of Seff and the sound of his steady breathing wash over her. He was here. With her. Safe, but not out of danger. *Yet.*

She furrowed her eyebrows and focused on the smoky black tendrils of dark magic that circled his immobile frame. Caught in the web of the evil spell, his Wolf had been cut off from his body, leaving his human side to deal with the effects of the cast.

Sherry went deeper into the mind of the man, touching the edges of his consciousness with the lightness of a butterfly's wings. She could have cried for the agony Seff was in. All of it endured in tortured silence.

It tore at her heart to witness the man struggle so desperately under the dark weight of the spell. He cried out again and again to release his Wolf, but it was to no avail.

He could not break through the magic. Sherry, just a visitor in this sense, was powerless to help him. *But not for long.* Her fierce determination was a plus on his side. She pulled herself carefully from the plane where his consciousness dwelled and opened her eyes not surprised to find tears there.

Sherry never understood the temptation others spoke of when they turned to the Dark. What pleasure could be derived from such evil casting? It truly boggled the mind.

Dark Witches were pawns in her eyes. Used by the Demons and magics they tried to control, but they were never the ones in power. Why could they not see that?

Like addicts, they concentrated on their next fix, but failed to see they were simply pawns of the substance they coveted most. In this case, power and greed.

She looked across the bed at the pale image of Seff, his skin almost the same shade as the pristine sheets that covered his bed. *I will not let him struggle alone.*

She would find a way to fight.

4

Seeking answers, Sherry sat on the turquoise and gold mediation rug that she'd pulled from her canvas bag. She rolled it onto the bare floor in the living room of Seff's quarters.

Her solitude was disrupted by the invasion of Liam, Conall, Kurt, and Dib. The Werewolves would normally crowd the smallish room, but in deference to her, they attempted to curb their natural physicality by being still. They filled the seats surrounding the room and waited for her to speak.

She knew better than to use her magic blatantly in front of them, but still, a girl needed her tea. She rose as the electric kettle she had plugged in began to whistle and poured the boiling water over one of her special blends designed to open the senses and replenish the soul. She waited as the tea steeped.

"So, what have you found?" Kurt spoke up first. The red-headed giant was the more easy-going of the two identical twins. Dib, his brother, simply grunted and waited with narrowed eyes.

"Would you like some tea?"

"No, thank you. We don't have time for niceties, Ms. Morgan, now about Seff?"

"Seff has been bespelled by a Dark practitioner. That you already know, but I am afraid his condition is truly dire. You see, the spell has cut him off from his Wolf. His human side tries to free the beast, but he is weakening at an alarming rate. It is a sort of double attack, while his Wolf is jailed, his human half is being drained of his life force."

"But how is that possible?"

"Anything is possible. I do, however, agree that this is beyond the talents of most Dark practitioners. If you can locate the Witch who created this odious spell, then I would of course be able to end it swiftly. However, without more to go on, I must try other means to free him," she poured tea into a clear mug as she spoke, setting a cinnamon stick to stir as she resumed her seat.

"Will you try?" Liam asked, his voice held a bit of a whine and Sherry couldn't help but feel for the young man.

"I will not leave him until he is able to tell me to go himself." *Like he did once not so long ago.*

"Thank you," she heard the words, but it was his Wolf, the Wolf of Seff's brother who whined with worry, that softened her towards him.

"I will do all I can. I swear it. Now, I have a list of things I will need. Can someone get me these items?" She nodded her head and a small index card with the various things she needed printed on it, floated through the air towards the men.

"Yes, I'll go," Conall plucked the card from the air without any hesitation.

"Thank you. Also, I need one of you to also give my report to Rafe. He is with his family and I am not prepared to leave Seff until he is awake."

"He will wake then?" Again, the question from Liam who seemed so young and so very angry. In fact, he seemed angry with her. Sherry grimaced, not that she could really blame him.

He'd been taught to hate Witches to distrust all magic. *If only he knew how much magic is in him.* All Shifters were part of the magic of the universe. How else could you explain two beings inhabiting one body? Then there was Pack magic, the special bonds that allowed Packmates to sense and sometimes communicate with one another.

"Of course, young one, I will stake my life on it," Sherry sighed her response. She nodded her head at the younger version of Seff.

A few days later...

Seff still remained unconscious and Sherry's normally positive attitude had somewhat diminished. Liam was openly growling his frustration at her and the Alpha was not around to rein him in, busy as he was with his new family. Never mind, she could handle one pup.

"Light the candles," she commanded. Candles served many purposes in casting. They acted as representatives of the four elements, and sometimes God or the gods, depending on one's beliefs. They also increased the power of A Witch's spells. They were used to channel magic, and sometimes they even helped open doorways of communication.

Sherry used candles often when casting. It was one of the few material items she relied upon in her craft. She was pleased she didn't have to ask twice. The pup may not like her, but still, Liam walked around the room and did as she'd commanded.

She was keenly aware of his unhappiness with the situation, but after extensive research she'd come to the conclusion that this was the only thing she could do to help Seff without having access to the Witch who cursed him.

She'd tried the basics already. She bathed him in herbs, bled him, questioned the runes, cast numerous counter spells, fed him potions, she even tried scrying for the Witch with crystals, but to no avail. She, *the Morrigan*, was at a loss.

There was one thing left for her to do. It was tricky and, it broke more than one rule. What's more, she'd need the help of someone she could trust. Her hands itched to take action, but she needed patience.

She needed to cast her own spell, one strong enough to tap into Seff's consciousness. Once there, she could possibly give him the strength he needed to fight and possibly wake. *One way to find out.*

It was risky, especially for her. But, it was a risk she was willing to take. How could she not? He was the only man she had ever truly cared about. It was time she admitted it even if only to herself.

She was confident of the outcome, but what worried her was his reaction afterwards. If she pulled this off, they would be bound together. Would he be able to handle that?

She bit her lip as she weighed the consequences in her mind. It was an unavoidable side effect of the magic needed to wake him. And he needed to wake sooner rather than later. With each passing moment, Seff was fading. His Wolf was dying.

Sure, she wondered how he would feel about

being bound to her and about her having used magic to save him, but she had no choice. She would do what she had to to keep him alive and she'd worry about the consequences later.

"Will it work?"

"Yes. But just in case of complications, I have called for reinforcements. Ah, there he is, let him in," Sherry pointed to a raven that flapped its great, black wings just outside the window of Seff's bedroom.

"What the fuck? How did he get there without setting off alarms?"

"Really Liam, what birds do you know set off alarms?"

"That's no bird!"

"Very good. Yes, that is not a bird, now open the window, please."

"Is it a Witch? How? Witches can't shift?"

"Not true shifters, but some Witches are blessed with *spirit animals*, I myself have no animal, but I can sometimes travel in the shape of a weeping willow seedling. But he is a friend, Liam. Please, let him in."

"I should call Rafe-"

"You are wasting time!" She felt magic glow in her eyes as she raised her voice to the pup.

The young Wolf growled his displeasure, but after hearing a whimper from his brother's still form he acquiesced. The raven flew into the room, but where the bird had landed, there was suddenly a tall, slender man in dark clothing.

"You called me to this place, Sherry?"

"Vasco," she nodded.

After a brief explanation she told him why she summoned him. To say he was upset was putting it mildly. Still, she'd expected the outburst from her longtime friend and colleague.

"Are you completely mad now, Sherry?" he wailed and paced as he pulled on his black hair.

"You'll be penalized! You know this!"

"Vasco, will you help me?"

Once upon a time she thought to mate with the Witch, but they proved better as friends than lovers. Still, she knew he cared about her and, although it might've seemed cruel to anyone looking at it from the outside, she called on him because she trusted him. A higher compliment she couldn't have paid him.

"Well?" she asked watching the play of emotions over his hawkish features.

"Are you certain? The Covens will go fucking berserk, Sherry! If you do this, you may never find yourself mated! How then do you propose to pass on your talents? They won't stand for it!"

"I should have never told you of their foolish demands! But that is not the point. Vasco, it is the only way I know to bring him back. Please, help me," she begged.

There were many things her colleague and childhood friend could resist, a blatant plea for help was not one of them. He was her one confidant.

After she'd foolishly given her heart to the Werewolf in question, who was it that came to her aid? *Vasco.* He had listened while she cried. He'd aided her when she buried herself in work. He was, in all things, her friend. She trusted him.

"Oh, come now, Shereen, you're still a fool for this *dog* then?"

"Watch it!" growled Liam who, up until then, had been taking in the byplay without comment.

"Guess I'd best set up the protection then. *Save me from foolish women,*" Vasco ignored the young Wolf and grumbled as he went about his work.

Sherry wiped the tear that struggled to come out and smiled. *Here now, I have friends yet.*

He was not wrong. Sherry was taking a huge risk. One Seff might not like. Sherry slipped out of the robe she wore over her simple, light cotton gown.

She needed to be free of the excesses of the modern world for this to work. The cotton was undyed, organically grown, and woven by hand. It was imbued with magical spells handed down from the female Witches of her line. She rarely donned the rare garment. Vasco sucked in a breath upon seeing it.

"By the goddess, Shereen, you look just like your grandmother," he bowed his head in reverence and looked away quickly. He continued to place protective crystals about the room.

Sherry understood and appreciated the respect he paid her. She did not answer, as he knew she wouldn't. She needed a clear mind to concentrate on preparing herself.

She took off her many bangles and rings and placed them in a silver bowl. Next, she freed her long hair until it curled in a riot of hues from the darkest brown to the palest blonde and all shades of red in between. The thick mass of hair reached all the way down her slender back to curl around her hips.

She rarely wore the mass down and felt power flow freely through the strands. It swirled and lifted on its own.

She exhaled as she relished the tingle of magic as it swept through her less encumbered body. Each piece of jewelry and clothing she wore acted as blocks or funnels for her talents.

Free of them, her power simply flowed. It was heady and dangerous, but she knew what to expect and braced herself for the impulse to wield magic without consequence when it came.

She ignored the seductive voices whispering to her, demanding she use her powers to free them, to join them. Instead, she focused her breathing and kicked off her flats.

Darkness and light struggled for power in the room. So much of it flowed through her. Sherry allowed herself to enjoy it only briefly.

All the magic in the universe was there. Parts of it revealed itself slowly to her eyes and she watched, willing it to show her the way to reach Seff.

She was aware of Liam, who stood in the back of the room, quietly intent on her, ready to act should he suspect her of hurting his brother. She could almost laugh at that. As if she could ever hurt Seff.

She was also aware of Vasco. He walked silently to each corner, placing several small crystals as he moved about the large bedroom. *Seff's bedroom.*

A moment of wrongness passed through her when she observed her friend. She quelled what was surely regret and began to access the magic in front of her.

Sherry did not speak to either of the two men. She'd best forget they were there.

Yes. Focus, child. The whisper-soft voice of her *grandmere* spoke to her as she exhaled the breath she'd taken.

Help me in my effort to save him, mamie, she thought. The ghosts of those who passed were always there and, sometimes, they were eager to help. This she knew for a fact. Her *grandmere* would have known the danger she faced. *She is here to aid me.*

Sherry felt the power of her magic pulse through her veins. She was no novice. This battle would be a long one. *And deadly too.* But she had to try.

"What now?" Liam asked, but she ignored his query.

Her eyes and words were for Seff alone. She approached the bed and took a place next to him, lying down with her head by his feet. Mirroring his position, she closed her eyes and spoke to the magic that pulsed all around her.

Ignoring the seeking tendrils of darkness that swarmed all over Seff, she choked down her fear for his safety and called upon her talents.

"*Deffro fy rhyfelwr, deffro fy blaidd, dewch yn ôl ataf,*" she chanted over and over again. *Wake up my warrior, wake up my Wolf, come back to me,* her cast spoken directly to the man and his beast, a command for him to obey.

He shuddered and cried out. Sherry cringed and gasped as she felt the Darkness which kept him trapped tighten. It choked him as she cast again to go around the magic that had frozen him inside his mind.

"Wake up, Seff, come to me now. Leave the prison of your mind and join me here," using her mind to speak to him, Sherry repeated her chant in English.

She could not control the spell of another, that was not how magic worked. But time was running out and she could not wait for the Wolves to find the Witch responsible. She had to appeal to Seff directly.

She had to place a bond on him. He would not be happy, but it was the only way. A direct link between the two of them would bring him back to their plane of reality.

"With my will I bridge your life force to mine, with this vow, I take a piece of you into me, and give in turn a piece of me to set you free, tis my pledge, by my honor we are linked, trapped within no longer, out now to be stronger, as I will so mote it be," she switched from English to Welsh to Ancient Greek and even Russian in her casting. *There was nothing like truly putting forth your best efforts.*

Heat poured into her. She felt sweat pool down her spine, soaking the cotton of her gown. Then came a bitter, icy chill that had her speaking through chattering teeth.

She'd prepared for this, but still, the change from hot to cold and back again was creating havoc within her earthly body. There was something nagging at her, something familiar about the magic she was battling. If only she could put her finger on it.

Sherry gasped as she felt her cast waver. *No, better leave it for now.* She could not afford to lapse in her concentration and so she ignored it.

She gasped again as heat scored her flesh. Magic sometimes asked for concessions that non-magic folk could not comprehend. It was all about balance and willingness. And yes, Sherry was willing to go through any amount of pain to bring Seff back to the realm of man, a little fever or chill was well worth it.

The amount of magic she was expending was great and it was paying off. The darkness was starting to relent. She could see the inky tendrils that surrounded Seff weaken, but that damned break between him and Wolf was still there. Nothing she vowed or spoke could mend the bond with man and beast.

She gasped and cringed when the pain of the separation cut into her heart like a blade. But before she lost her grip entirely, she reached him. Golden tendrils of her magic spiraled between them, binding them tightly together.

Sherry sighed with contentment, not fear, as she felt Seff enter her mind and heart, as never before.

She cast back the dark magic that dared trap him.

She felt the curse that caged the man crumble before her will. *Success! He is safe! But his Wolf...*

Suddenly, Seff sprang up from his prone position. His golden-brown eyes flew to Sherry and he blinked as if trying to clear his head.

"What the hell did you do to me?"

5

Seff grunted and groaned as he used more strength than he should have needed to sit upright. *Where am I?* He opened one eye cautiously and took in his surroundings. *My sheets, my bed, but how?*

Pain shot through the left side of his head. He groaned and pressed his palm to his eye hoping to dampen it, but it didn't help in the least. *Anybody get the license of the truck that hit me? Fuck, that hurts!*

He tried getting up, but his legs weren't listening to his brain. *The fuck is going on?* The pounding in his head was nothing compared to the underlying weakness of his body.

Something had happened to him. Something bad. But fuck him, if he could recall whatever it was that left him weak as a *normal*.

He closed his eyes to try and jog his memory. One thing struck him as more than probable. Seff wanted to howl in rage. *Magic.* He'd been bespelled by some Witch or Warlock or *something! Dammit!*

He tried to free the memory that swam just beneath the surface of his consciousness, but it was no use. He had no fucking idea what had happened to him. He only knew one thing, Seff was alone in this. *Where is my Wolf?*

Fear made him tremble as he tried to stem his rising anxiety. He couldn't allow himself to give in to the wave of panic that threatened to drown him. *You're the Pack Beta. Calm the fuck down.* But it was an impossible ask. Anything could have happened when he was under.

The absence of his memory meant trouble. The acrid taste of terror filled his mouth causing him to gag, but Seff forced himself to swallow. He'd suffered worse in battle. He could handle this.

He inhaled. The familiar smell of ozone crept into his nostrils. *Fuck!* There was no denying it. Someone had cast a spell on him.

Seff tried to recall who had attacked him, but he remembered nothing of the person who cursed him. He did, however, remember calling out to the woman who'd haunted him all these years. *Sherry.*

Shit. He must be really hurt because he swore it

was her lightly accented voice that had called him back from his own private version of hell. *Sherry.*

Warmth spread through his cold limbs at the thought that she still cared for him. *Stupid dream.* But wait, he inhaled deeply. The scent of cinnamon and spice drifted into his nostrils. Hell, he tasted it on his tongue too. As if she were there, with him. That couldn't be right, could it? He opened his eyes and pinched himself hard.

Sherry was lying in his bed, rumpled yet beautiful as always. Sweat clung to her forehead as she smiled at him, relief evident on her pale face.

"What the hell did you do to me?" He wished he could've stopped the words, but they tumbled unabashedly from his lips. Something had just gone down and he needed to know what.

He felt her in his blood, tasted her on his lips, but *what, when, where?* How did the woman who wouldn't even return his phone calls come to be at his side? In his bedroom?

No, this isn't right. He didn't call Sherry. He'd had no plans to meet her. He'd gone out, *yes*, but not with her. Who then? *Wait*, held his palm up to his left eye as he tried to force himself to remember.

Pain exploded in his head and he growled as he pushed through it to reveal his last memory. He'd gone out with Charley! That was it! They went for a drive when they got a flat and, when he went to see about it, something attacked him.

He growled deep in his throat as anger came rushing through his veins, but something was wrong. Usually his Wolf took over when Seff's temper became roused. *The fuck?* Where was his Wolf?

"Agh," he groaned and almost collapsed back down on the bed as he sought within himself for his other half. Panic, the full-blown kind, set in as he tried again and again to confer with his beast.

His Wolf, who had been coming to him all the more quickly now that his kind were almost free, was not answering, he could not feel him. *No!*

"What's the matter with me?!" *Was that him?* That weak hoarse sound? *Pathetic!*

His eyes met her sometimes-hazel ones. Seff gulped in air as he read the understanding in them. Trapped in her stunning gaze, Seff wasn't at all shocked when her eyes shifted from greenish blue to glittering gold, and finally, to a deep brown that simmered like molten chocolate as they looked over his face.

She wore a simple gown, her glorious hair curled around her face in a riot of reds and golds, her lips were slightly parted, and perspiration beaded on her pale skin as she tried to catch her breath.

"Seff," she smiled as she breathed his name.

She tried to sit up, but some hidden weakness stole her strength. Seff lunged forward to help. He was a tad slower than he was used to, but he managed to catch her before she toppled off his bed. The sheet covering him dropped to below his waist, but he was more than comfortable with nudity. *Werewolves often were.*

Besides, this was Sherry. *My Sherry.* He cradled her against his naked chest and tried to clear out the fog that once again clouded his brain. That and the fact that she always did wipe every thought he had right out of his head whenever he'd held her close only added to his addled state.

She smelled so good. *Mmm.* He inhaled her scent deeply. Like some heavenly combination of cinnamon and spice and fresh apples. Sort of like apple pie, but like, to the tenth power.

Sweetest fucking pie I ever had. How long had it been since he held her this close? Too damned long in his humble opinion.

"Oh, my word, that took more from me than I thought it would," she murmured against his skin.

Her soft breath tickled his bare chest, but she didn't seem in a rush to move. Inside, he preened at that small revelation.

"What, um, what are you doing here?"

"Well, I brought you back, of course," her eyes were dilated as she looked up at him.

Seff frowned. She looked pale. Her soft, ivory hands reached up and she ran her fingers from his brow, down his jawline, to his firm lips. He kissed the tips and she trembled in his arms. Seff's nostrils flared.

He may have forgotten a lot about what had recently happened to him, but he would never forget how good Sherry felt and tasted in his arms. *It's been too long.*

"Sherry," a husky voice he barely recognized as his own reached his ears as he lowered his head, greedy to taste her soft pink lips. The door slammed open, snapping them both out of it.

A strange man burst into Seff's room and he reacted predictably. He dropped Sherry gently to the bed and, naked or not, he sprang to his feet and had the intruder by the throat before either of them could blink. Whether his Wolf was speaking to him or not, Seff was still fast and strong, if a little bit wobbly.

"Wait, please!" Sherry cried out weakly, "He is a friend, Seff."

Seff stiffened at her use of the word. He didn't recognize the man who'd just come bursting into his room. The guy was lucky Seff was weak or he'd have ripped his head off.

He'd gotten a reputation as being somewhat docile as his Pack's Beta, but nothing could be further from the truth. Seff's role required diplomacy and a certain genteel exterior, but inside he was all Wolf.

At least, he usually was. *Fuck. What is wrong with me?* Either way he wasn't dropping his guard without reason. And right now, the reason was pale and beautiful and still in his bed.

Whatever their past, one thing was true, he wanted to keep her there in his bed, in his room, and this guy was not welcome!

"Who are you? What are you doing here?" he growled and gripped the man's throat tightly.

Never mind that the action stopped the guy from answering. He rolled his eyes and loosened his fingers before continuing, "Tell me what is going on!"

The only sound was that of his captor trying to breathe and Sherry's soft gasps. He tried calling his beast, but there was still no answer. It took all his strength to remain upright, but he wouldn't allow himself to appear weak before this skinny, black-cloaked, *sniff*, Witch, who dared trespass in his bedroom!

The bastard was ignoring Seff's death grip on his

neck! His beady eyes remained riveted to Sherry. *Sweet Sherry*, in a fucking transparent night gown in his bed! *WTF? Wait. How did she even get here?*

"One of you answer me! What the hell is going on!" Seff bellowed on shaky feet and held the stranger tighter for one instant before tossing him away from the bed, in the direction of the door.

Just then his brother, Liam, walked in, his eyebrows raised as he hurried to his side. Like the stranger, his brother's gaze went straight to Sherry.

"Whoa! You did it! Thank you so much! Seff, I can't believe you're back!"

"Ha! You owe me twenty bucks! Told you she'd deliver! Damn, you look like shit, Seff," Conall shouted as he walked in after Seff's brother.

"I am glad you are satisfied with my service," Sherry replied to Liam, but her eyes were smiling.

Clearly, something had passed between his brother and the Witch. Something that made Seff want to roar in frustration and smack his brother upside the head. *Mine. Grrr.* Unfortunately, he was in no shape to do either.

Fuck. Every inch of him felt as if it had been put through the ringer. His whole body ached. Even his brain hurt. None of this made sense. He took in the crowd of people in his room and one thing was clear, he needed them gone.

"Out! Everybody out," He fisted the sheet and growled his orders, when Sherry made to move he stayed her with a look, "Except you."

Seff could hardly get a handle on what he was feeling. He knew he was weak. He knew his Wolf was not answering. He knew he needed answers.

He felt tired, angry, hungry and, confused. The only thing that was not a complete fucking shock, was that he still wanted the woman in front of him like crazy.

That ship has sailed, buddy. The reminder that he had fucked up that relationship years ago was as unwelcome as the temptation she represented. It was almost too much for him to bear.

He groaned as pain shot through his chest all the way up to his head. He sat down hard on the rumpled bed, covering his half-erection with the bundled-up sheets. In pain or not, his body didn't seem to notice anything else but her, especially when she was close enough to smell. *How about taste? Down boy.*

No matter how sternly he spoke to himself, the second he was within a mile of the Witch, he reacted with the same insufferable desire. A lust so strong that it couldn't be dampened with a month of ice-cold showers. *Shit. If she was there, he could probably still get it up if he was buck naked in Antarctica.*

Working in close proximity to Sherry over the

past year had left him with the bluest balls he'd ever had, but he'd always managed to hide it. *Not so much now.*

With nothing but a sheet to shield him from her gaze his physical condition was more than obvious. Given the way her cheeks heated when he caught the direction of her stare, he'd say she damn sure noticed. *Hey, I got nothing to be ashamed of if I do say so myself.*

The pretty pink glow of her skin gave him the strength he needed to control himself. *Sherry Morgan is finally here in my bedroom and not totally immune! Too bad I can't fucking remember how she got here.*

He took a long, hard look at the woman whose face had invaded his dreams for the better part of a decade. Seff drank in every curl of her long, wild hair, every tiny freckle that crossed the bridge of her slightly upturned nose, and delicate tilt of her oh-so-kissable bow of a mouth.

Like a starving man, he devoured every nuance of her superb countenance. All the reasons he'd told himself why they couldn't be together vanished. He might not know what had happened to him, but he knew it was bad. *And possibly fatal.* A thing like that changed a man's opinions.

He blinked hard. He couldn't afford to have his wits scrambled by her beauty regardless of how easily she continued to dazzle him with her perfection. *She is still as gorgeous as ever and just as unattainable. Keep telling yourself that, Seff, old boy.*

She was part of his past and no matter how he regretted his actions, nothing he could say or do would bring her back to him. She'd made that perfectly clear the last time she came to aid the Macconwood.

"Thank you for coming, Sherry. It's so good to see you again. Maybe we can talk over a cup of coffee or glass of wine," he'd said to her.

"I do not do this for you, Seff McAllister. I have a contract with your Alpha. That is the only reason I am here," and with that parting retort she'd left in a swirl of colorful scarves and skirts, like a fleeting glimpse of a rainbow behind the clouds. She'd left., and everything was gray again.

"Seff, you must have some water, let me fetch it for you," she said, but her words were spoken in a voice that trembled. *So, unlike her.*

"No, no water. First, tell me what's going on."

6

Sherry gasped at the sight before her. Still so damned perfect. *The beast.* How unfair nature was to give such lasting beauty to the man who tore her heart out with a single written note. Still, that didn't stop her from taking in his perfect *and lusty* form. Given the tent he was pitching, Seff McAllister still found her desirable. *Isn't that interesting?*

It was a shame he'd given her up without so much as a conversation. He'd never even bothered to call her up after he'd left his blasted note. There was a time when she would have gladly dropped to her knees and begged him to listen to her.

She would have worshipped every glorious inch of him with her eyes and hands and mouth. Anything to prove her love for him. Hadn't she welcomed him into her willing body? Given him her heart? *But it wasn't good enough.*

She bit her lip. What would he say if he knew what she'd done to bring him back? If he knew that not only had he broken her heart, ruined her for any other man, but now, she'd given him access to her soul? And in turn, gained entry to his.

She doubted it would please him. *Best break the news gently.* Lying was out of the question. It would taint the magic she weaved to protect him.

Besides, Seff was not wholly unreasonable, just biased against magic. And even that was hardly his fault. He'd been raised to think Witches were evil, untrustworthy beings. But, that said, Seff possessed an innate goodness that would surely lead him to the correct conclusion that she'd had no other choice.

Perhaps, *goddess* willing, he'd even come to the conclusion that she acted as an impartial contractor working at the behest of his Alpha. Then he wouldn't have to know how, to her unending shame, her heart still longed for him.

The one who got away. But maybe not this time? No. He is not for me. After all was said and done, Seff was the one who had left. If Sherry knew anything about life it was that *choice* mattered. He chose to leave her.

Still, she'd come to help him. She couldn't refuse. How could she? Sherry might be a powerful Witch, but she was also a woman. A woman in love with a man who did not, could not love her back.

It was such a terrible cliché. She was smart enough to acknowledge it, even if she admitted to being powerless to help it.

"I will answer your questions," Sherry attempted to stand with one hand on the still warm bed.

He needed answers that only she could provide, but for some reason she didn't think she could do that in his bed. She wobbled on her bare feet.

Not as steady as she'd have liked, she closed her eyes and breathed deeply. *Weak and empty.* She needed to restore her physical being before she tried to replenish her magical stores. *Balance in all things.* His gravelly voice interrupted her thoughts.

"Sherry?"

"Yes, yes. Let's see then, you were bespelled by a Dark Witch while out with your Alpha female-"

"Charley! I'd forgotten! Is she okay?" His frantic eyes pleaded with her and she felt her heart pull.

Poor Seff, she should have known his first response would be to duty. He'd surely blame himself if anything had happened to his Alpha's mate. *Pack first,* she'd almost forgotten his creed.

"Do not fear, she is well as are the young-"

"Young? She had the baby then?"

"Yes, three actually. Triplets. And the mother is

THE WITCH AND THE WEREWOLF

doing very well too," she couldn't help the smile on her lips and the small trace of envy in her voice.

To have a family with one that she loved and chose as her mate was something she'd never know or have. The *Elders Trust* saw to that. Damn fools.

She envied Rafe and Charley their obvious love and their new family. She was happy for them of course, but it saddened her to think she'd soon have to pick a male Witch to bed and father an heir to the great Morgan magic.

It was either that or leave it to the Elders Trust to choose a mate for her. *Ugh.* That idea was not appealing in the least. In her opinion, greed and time constraints were not good reasons for getting with child, and yet she'd agreed to their terms otherwise face a Tribunal made up of many Covens who would, no doubt, seek to strip her of her magic and divide it amongst themselves. *Bastards.* Sherry would not be the end of *the Morganna Witches. I swear it.*

"They are doing well then?" Seff's voice interrupted her thoughts and she refocused on him.

"Yes, parents and children all healthy and well."

"That's good. No, thanks to me," his fist clenched, and she could read the torment in his eyes.

"No one blames you. Seff, you executed your duty to the fullest of your power, as always. You could not have countered the attack against you."

"I should have scouted better. I should have known not to trust anything or anyone with our Alpha female even on Pack land! I should have-"

"Please, calm yourself. There is no peace to be found in looking back on what could have been, Seff. You risked your life," she choked back tears, then started again, "You conducted yourself bravely. You did very, very well," she spoke in a soft voice hoping to take the edge off his anxiety.

He gritted his teeth at her praise, his eyes were still a bit wild, but at least he'd stopped degrading himself.

"Now, I have managed, after several days of trying out many, many different things, to rouse you from the Dark spell that held you in its grip. It has been a long fight and I am depleted, I am afraid, but I must tell you all of it. There was a price for your recovery, partial as it is-"

"What price?"

"It was for me to pay, do not worry yourself."

"I can't allow you to do that-"

"You can't stop me either, besides I have a contract," she said.

"The hell with the contract, Sherry, you will not put yourself in danger for me."

"Before you fly off the handle, listen, *please*," it was the please that stopped him when arguing wouldn't.

He'd always been a stickler for manners. She waited for him to calm down before adding, "I can't fully cure you of this Dark magic without getting my hands on the foul Witch who cast the spell. It is why you can't reach your Wolf, Seff, and I am afraid this is far from over."

"You mean, I'm still in danger."

"Yes, but I am not ready to give up yet. There are other things to try," she said.

"No, I can't let you. You are obviously weak from this fight. I won't allow you to put yourself in danger," she frowned at his choice of words, but he continued, "That is, what I meant to say is, *thank you, Shereen*, but I can't accept any more help from you-"

"You remember my full name?" Hardly anyone called her Shereen anymore, and she was stunned to hear it on his lips.

"Of course, I do," he said, his voice deep and sincere.

He had the kind of voice that made a woman's toes curl. Strong and deep, confident and gentle. Sherry was not immune. No matter what she told herself. *He's got a voice to make a woman fall in love all over again.*

"Well, that's a surprise then, Seff *Andrew* McAllister," a smile teased around the edges of her bow of a mouth.

"I see you've got a knack for names as well. Truth is, I haven't forgotten a thing about you, Sherry," his whispered words sent shivers down her spine.

Neither have I, she answered in her mind, afraid to voice the words. *Enough foolishness. He is still in danger.*

"Anyway, you have no choice. You are not clear of the cast yet."

"Sherry, I mean it. I can't allow you to–" The sound of heavy footsteps from outside the bedroom had them both turning their heads towards the door.

"I need to get in there."

"No way, bro, you heard the man," one of the Wolves spoke.

"My mistress will need sustenance. You can't imagine how much she is spent–"

"Don't care. You're not getting in there until Seff says so."

"I could turn you into a frog, little dog–"

"And I could use you for a chew toy, bird-man!"

"This is going to get ugly, please allow Vasco in to see to me," Sherry turned to Seff.

"Fine. Your boyfriend can enter, then we will continue this. Enough, Conall, let him in!" he bellowed towards the closed door.

"Sherry?" Vasco entered the room with a steaming mug and ignored Seff's angry glare.

"Here you must drink this now," he held it out in front of her and Sherry smiled at him and squeezed his arm before accepting the brew.

Vasco was no fool. He frowned at the nearly tangible undercurrents in the room. But what was a Witch to do? She could hardly stop herself from reacting to Seff's nearness and vulnerability. The usually tough-as-nails Werewolf was so deliciously frazzled. She wanted to soothe his brow and ease his confusion.

Okay. So, she was still a sucker for the tall and handsome brute. She couldn't help it. Disapproving looks from Vasco or not. Sherry sipped her tea and allowed him to fuss over her, running a hand along her forehead and checking her pulse.

Vasco had always been a reliable friend and at times, even an apprentice. Their families had known each other for ages and though they were of different Covens, they often worked together.

His concern for her was touching. She smiled as she reassured him that she was perfectly fine. Just a bit tired. All the while she ignored the elephant, or should she say *Wolf*, in the room.

Well, she tried to anyway.

7

"Are you feeling better?" The tall skinny Witch stared at Sherry with guarded eyes.

He looked over her face with far too much interest for Seff's peace of mind, but he didn't comment on it.

It was all he could do not to vault over the bed and deck the guy. Truthfully, Seff wanted to rip the skinny fucker's throat out. How could he let another tend her? *Calm down. She is not yours.*

Like fuck she isn't.

Besides, he still needed to figure out what the heck was going on and blowing a gasket over the male Witch's overly familiar manner with Sherry wasn't going to help his situation. *Nope. Not at all.*

Until he knew the entire truth, he was at the

mercy of one very wary Witch who seemed intent on ignoring him. *Not bloody likely.*

"Thank you, Vasco, the cast was a difficult one, but I have done all I can for now. I am well, truly," she smiled up at her *friend* and Seff tensed. Her eyes had turned an intense violet color that usually meant she was pleased.

Seff frowned and narrowed his eyes at the pair of Witches. *Was the stranger her lover?* For a moment he could hardly breathe as his blood threatened to boil over.

It had been years since he could claim any rights to Sherry, but that didn't mean he wasn't jealous as hell at the thought that she might belong to that skinny punk! *Like hell. She is mine.*

Before he could shake off his disturbing train of thought, the dude in question whirled on Sherry, anger making his voice rise. *Fuck that.*

Seff tensed. It was true, his emotions were a little out of control, hell, they were running wild. Still, that didn't give the Witch leave to raise his voice at Sherry.

"Yes, and what will the Covens say about it? You shouldn't have done this, Sherry! Your loyalty to the *dogs* is sorely misplaced!" The Witch snarled and Seff growled and took a menacing step closer.

The Witch took no notice of him. He had an

obvious death-wish. He gestured in front of Sherry with an angry swipe of his hand as he continued to barrage her.

Maybe he was crazy? Seff could only conclude that the man wasn't all there. Especially since he continued to yell at Sherry.

As if that wasn't bad enough, as his tirade wound down, the skinny fuck had the nerve to stroke a long finger down the smooth, pale skin of her face. Sherry turned to look at him as if some inner sense made her realize he would not approve of the Witch's familiarity with her.

"Vasco, step away from me, please," she began, her eyes riveted to Seff.

But he wasn't looking at her. He was staring at the fucker with the hand problem. Seff's nostrils flared. He clamped down hard on his teeth before speaking, aware that he was vibrating with anger.

"First off, you need to back the hell up," his voice was a deep rumble, that caused both Witches to jump.

"Remove your hands from her or they will be removed for you. *Permanently.* Second, Ms. Morgan is on retainer with the Macconwood Pack, who are you to reprimand her for honoring our arrangement?" snarled Seff.

"Seriously, back up, crow-man," growled Liam, always one to follow his brother's lead.

"Foolish pup, you don't know what she's done for your brother there! She's given of herself. She will have no recourse now but to bow down to the demands of the *Elders Trust*. They will not give up in this-" he raged.

"What do you mean?" Seff spoke as he rubbed the hollow point in the middle of his chest that seemed to tug and pull at him in the general direction of where Sherry stood on her own two, if a tad wobbly, feet.

"Vasco, that is enough!" The power in her voice made the male Witch grit his teeth, but Seff was not affected in the least.

True, he was reeling, but it was from the idea that she had put herself in harm's way. *For him*. That did not sit well. *Not at fucking all.* His stomach threatened to revolt and, were it not utterly empty, he might have made a mess right where he stood.

And then he'd have to burn his fucking Wolf-card. Hurling on the feet of your lover, past, current, or future, it didn't matter, was definite cause for losing said card.

Not an option. Still, he couldn't just let this stand as it was. Sherry Morgan might be his ex, but she was still someone he cared about and, he would not have her put herself at risk. First, he needed to assess the danger and find out exactly what it was she did to save him. Then, he needed to make some plans.

"Sherry, what does he mean you *gave of yourself?*" Seff asked, clueing into the strange wording the male Witch had used.

She averted her gaze, but pride had her raising her now dark green eyes to meet his. Seff waited.

"You must understand, there was no other way. Your life force was being drained, I had to anchor you here."

"Alright–"

"How many days have we been out?" She turned her head and addressed the question to Vasco.

"Five days," he replied through clenched teeth.

"Five days," she shook her head, "Not since I was a young girl has a spell vexed me so."

"Sherry? You need to explain this to me," Seff insisted.

"Yes, Seff, you are right. Just give me a moment please," she swallowed some more tea.

"Well, honesty is best. *Okay then.* Seff, I've tried to battle the spell on you with potions and casting to no avail. The Dark magic used against you is most powerful and foul. To bring you out of your coma, I had to perform a *bondio enaid*, a *soul bonding* with you. Since he has attacked both aspects of your person, *Wolf and man*, I had to keep your human side from expiring, *soul bonding* was the only way," she bit her lower lip and frowned.

Her large eyes glowed green and she looked at him as if trying to gauge his response. She bit her lower lip and he sucked in a breath feeling her anxiety and wanting to soothe it.

He was so distracted by her mouth, he lost track of what she was saying. *Odd.* He'd been around her before, long after their breakup, and yet, this was the first time he wanted to cross that invisible barrier that separated them ever since the day he wrote her that stupid note.

Awareness tickled his senses. He inhaled again and this time he could only breathe in her scent, *cinnamon and spice.* The others in the room must have noticed his distraction because Conall cleared his throat and Liam nodded his head at him in anticipation. *Focus dammit.*

"Um, *soul bonding*? What does that mean?"

"It is nothing-"

"Nothing! Ha! Who will you mate with now that you have a bond with the *mongrel*!" Vasco spat the word at him like the insult it was.

"Did you seriously just call my brother a mongrel?" growled Liam.

"Did I? Sorry, I meant, *Wolf.* All better now?" said Vasco his sarcasm evident, even without the eye roll.

"What the hell are you talking about?" Seff's voice was loud even to his own ears in the suddenly quiet room.

"Don't you know what she's done? Don't you know of her promise? They will hold her to it, she has no choice now. They will force her-"

"Vasco!"

"No, Sherry, I won't let you go through this not without him understanding the cost to you!"

"Talk to me," Seff growled.

"Fine, *McAllister*, just so you understand the sacrifice she makes for you. It is a sacrifice of *free will*. You see, she will be seen as tainted, and none will want to forge an alliance with such a Witch, no matter how powerful. And since she's already agreed to their terms, she will have no bloody choice! They will seek to use her as a brood mare or worse, they will try and strip her of her magic!"

"What the fuck are you saying?"

"Don't you understand anything? *She* is the last Morrigan, the oldest and the strongest line of Witches, and the elders of all the Covens have her word that she will beget an heir by the next turn of the seasons. An heir, in her case a female Witch, to take up her mantle as it were. They will not take kindly to her diluting her essence by *soul bonding* with a *bloody dog*!"

In touch with his Wolf or not, Seff wasn't about to let that go unanswered. With one hand holding the sheet around his waist, he swung the other and with a resounding crack, the bird man went down. His body fell backwards, right onto the hardwood floor. He missed the plush, navy blue throw rug completely. Two points for the "bloody dog". *Grrr.*

"Now, look what you've done!" Sherry's accented voice met his ears, but all he could do was scowl.

"What the hell was that jerk talking about? *Brood mare? Soul bond?* Sherry speak to me!"

"Oh yes, because that worked out so well for Vasco," she crouched down on the floor next to Vasco's prone figure.

"You can't think I'd ever hurt you?"

"Vasco? Can you hear me?" She ignored Seff as she tried to revive the unconscious Witch on his floor.

He felt only slightly awkward at his unusual display of temper, but that embarrassment wore off when he looked at Sherry. Seff's gaze was riveted to her body in the almost see-through gown she wore.

The fabric pulled tight across her lush derriere as she checked the male Witch for injury. Seff had to bite his tongue to keep from reaching for her.

He wasn't the only one who noticed her enticing form. *Eyes off. Mine.* Liam and Conall didn't seem to notice his displeasure, until he growled at them and tossed a pillow at his brother's big head.

It connected with a satisfying thud, but that was short lived as he caught the second cushion Seff hurled at him. At least he had the good sense to avert his eyes and tug on Conall's arm to follow suit. Good thing too. Seff didn't want to punch his brother out for ogling her. *Sherry Morgan in his bedroom.*

"Here, we got him," the two Wolves lifted Vasco and dragged him to the couch while Seff shoved his legs into a pair of sweats. Sherry turned her head and bent to retrieve her robe which, when she put it on, managed to conceal her sweet little figure. *Boo.*

"Alright, let's get a few things clear," Seff's voice was raspy, and he appreciated Sherry offering him some of her tea. He hesitated, taking in her sad smile and, the small shrug of her shoulders.

"It is simply a restorative, nothing to harm you, Seff," she said apologetically.

He didn't think about it then. The last thing he wanted from her was an apology. She'd risked her neck for him!

He accepted the mug and drank the warm liquid without breaking eye contact. Her eyes widened at the gesture and he could see it pleased her. Trust was hard to come by in the supernatural world and he'd never been one to put any faith in magic. *But this was*

Sherry. Sherry who'd risked more than she should have for the likes of him.

"Thank you," he said, his voice already stronger with just a single sip of the tea.

"You're welcome."

"This *bond*, is it permanent?"

"That depends. Permanence is relative, I think. But you should know it was all I could do to wake you," Sherry bit her lip.

"And what he said about your elders, they will be angry?"

"Yes. He is correct. No respectable Witch family will forge an alliance with one who has willingly entered such a tie with another. It is a serious taboo. One that might cost me a chance at finding a mate. They will say I have purposely muddied my name in the hopes of getting out of my promise."

"What will they do?"

"It is not your concern."

"Yes, it is," he growled, his impatience growing.

"I will not discuss this with you. It is my business alone."

"Sherry, I owe you my life. I need to know how far the debt goes."

"You owe me nothing. I have a contract-"

"Fuck the contract. Let me help you."

"What are you saying?"

"I just want the truth," he murmured. The spicy cinnamon scent of her drifted into his nostrils making him sway on his feet.

He itched to touch her smooth ivory skin. She was like silk, perfection in the flesh. Seff longed to sink into her softness. Her nearness was driving him mad with desire. *Sherry.*

"You should sit, you are still weak-"

"That's not why I'm trembling like a newborn pup, Sherry. I can feel you, inside, calling to me, *Sherry*. You can't deny this *thing* between us anymore," his voice dropped to a low, deep grumble. She stopped in her tracks and Seff moved closer, purposely invading her space. He stared intently into her yellow eyes until she looked away.

"Seff, I appreciate the concern, but my deal with the Elders Trust is Witch business-"

"If it concerns you, it is my business."

"Seff, how much do you understand about the duality of your nature as a Werewolf?"

"What? That's quite the subject change," he began, "At any rate, there are things I can't share with you until I receive permission from my Alpha. You know that already, don't you?"

"Indeed, I do. Witches may not share their souls with another as Wolves do; however, those of us who are more in touch with the old ways do owe allegiance to our craft. This deal I have made was entered into with the intent of protecting my line, my craft, my magic."

"Okay, but what does that have to do with what he just said?"

"It is simple, you don't need to know–"

"Dammit Sherry, that isn't going to fly anymore. *You know me.*"

"Yes, I do, Seff, and I know how much you hate magic. Enough for you to leave me, to leave anything we might once have had. As for anything you might be feeling towards me now, I am sure it is a temporary side effect of the *soul bonding* cast, it will pass," she turned her head away and he had to stop himself for reaching for her.

"It was never hatred, Sherry. Confusion, uncertainty, but never, ever hatred," he whispered, hurting to see the sadness in her dove gray eyes. Seff cleared his throat and continued.

"At least tell me this, is what Vasco said true? Did you agree to be what, is it called *mated* for Witches like with Wolves, before the end of the year?"

"Yes, he spoke the truth. Those of us who follow the ancient ways use the term *mate*, though most modern Witches refuse such terminology, but really, Seff, this has nothing to do with you," she replied, her voice laced with sadness at what could have been.

"Have you found him then? Your mate, that is," fear gripped him as he asked. He didn't like the idea of her belonging to anyone else. Not one bit. *Because she is mine.*

"Yes and no, that is, no I have not claimed my mate. However, it is true that I agreed to produce an heir for my powers within the year as long as I could do so without any interference from the Covens. However, if I should fail to find my own mate, I agreed to let them choose someone to sire the child or I risk being stripped of my powers," she spoke without emotion, resigned to her fate as it were.

"Fuck that! Can they do that?" Seff wanted to rage at the bastards who dared threaten her.

"One Coven or two alone? Probably not. But this is the *Elders Trust*, they are many and powerful. Together they could theoretically do it. Not that I would allow it to come to that. I am a peaceful Witch for all intents and purposes," she smiled as if she had a secret and he wanted to beg her to let him in on it. *Not yet. You'll soon know all her secrets though, that's a promise.*

"You would really allow them to select a mate for you?"

"I may not have a choice anymore, Seff."

"So, what you are really saying is that in creating

this soul bond with me you've damaged your chances to find a mate on your own?"

"Seff, please, none of this is your concern-"

"Like hell it isn't, just answer me," he interrupted.

"Fine, it is true. Most Witch families will not take kindly to me sharing a *soul bond* with another. That is a ritual that usually only happens within a family or among mates. It seems incredible, doesn't it? That we are in the twenty-first century and some of my kind still harbor such medieval thoughts. It is true, I've seen it happen. Once word gets out that my soul is bound to another, I will be considered *damaged goods*."

"Fuck, Sherry, I am so sorry."

"You have no cause to apologize. I did so of my own free will. It was the only way to save you."

"And you risked all of this for me?"

"Of course."

"Why?"

"I think I have had enough questions for now, Seff," she tried to retreat, but he wasn't going to let her get away so easy.

Seff's blood heated at the way she looked at him. As if she actually cared about what happened to him. *Did she?* Her eyes were large in her pale face as she worried her lower lip with her teeth. Seff recalled what it felt like to have those lips, those teeth, on his bare skin. *Grrr.*

When did he lose control over his own thoughts? He'd spent time around her before, but now, he could barely stop the carnal images from flashing through his mind. His pulse sped up at just the thought of her. Sweet, warm, loving Sherry.

But how did she feel about him? His Wolf might be cut off from him, but he could see the way her breathing increased when he stood near. She desired him, even if she didn't want to.

The real question was, did she want to? He closed his eyes and fought the urge to wrap her in his arms. *Too soon.* He didn't want to spook her. He didn't deserve her trust. *God knows he didn't.* Not after he abandoned her after one night of heaven.

How many times had he replayed that night over and over in his mind? How many times had he wished that he tore up that note? He wished that he would have told both his foster father and his former Alpha to go to hell. Most of all, he wished he'd have just stayed with her.

He'd been half a man ever since he'd left her. Witch or not, Sherry was the best damn thing that ever happened to him. He'd met her by surprise, a chance encounter on the street.

She'd been carrying a box with seedlings and clay pots into her apartment and he'd bumped into her.

To repay her for breaking two of the clay pots, he'd offered to take her out for dinner.

"How about I cook for us instead?"

"Can you cook?"

"Yes. How do a couple of grilled steaks, baked potatoes, steamed asparagus, and a sliced tomato salad with sea salt and olive oil drizzled over the top sound?"

"Like heaven. I'll buy the groceries."

And he had. The meal was wonderful, the best he'd ever had. *She was wonderful.* Still is. He'd made excuse after excuse to keep running into her, until finally he grabbed his balls and asked her out.

They'd started dating. His Wolf senses had told him there was something different about her, something special, but he'd ignored them. Ignored all the signs that she was a Witch.

He was losing his heart for the first time in his life and damn he'd enjoyed every minute! She was the most unusual woman he'd ever met. Exotic with her lilting accent that faded in and out depending on her mood. She smelled of spices and her laughter reminded him of silver bells chiming in the clean air.

The females he'd known in the Pack tended to be a little bit hard. Perhaps it was because of their uber-chauvinistic leader at the time, but still, they hadn't appealed to him. Not then and not now.

Thank God, Rafe was the polar-opposite of his

father in that aspect. He believed Pack females, Wolves or not, were to be treated with respect and given an equal amount of freedom and the right to choose their own lives.

Something Zev Maccon abhorrently rejected. He was downright archaic in his treatment of girls and women. Women were to be kept barefoot, pregnant, and in the kitchen. Downright brutal. It was safe to say that no one missed the old alpha's ways.

As happy as he was for the she-Wolves in his Pack, Seff had eyes for one woman only. *Sherry Morgan.* And at the time, he'd thought she was just a woman. She'd been unlike anything in his experience. Sweet, kind and caring to a fault. Did he mention hot as fuck? With that gorgeous hair and her hazel eyes, not to mention her mouth-watering figure.

She could stop traffic when she walked around in those gauzy little dresses with sheer fabric in the sexiest of places. A strip of skin at her waist, low dip revealing the smooth skin of her back, a keyhole cutout just above the cleavage of her ample breasts, long slits up the sides of her skirts that revealed her luscious legs. *Grrr.*

She always wore the most vibrant colors. No grays or blacks for his little Witch. Nope. A rainbow of colors wherever she went. His own little piece of sunshine. *And he fucked it all up.*

He'd give anything to take back the hurt he'd caused her. He tried to apologize once she started working for the Pack, but she shut down every single attempt he made. For years, he thought she hated him.

Hell, he deserved her hatred. But if she truly did feel that way, why did she risk so much to save him? Could it be she still cared for him? *But how and why should she? When he fucked up so badly?*

He'd made the biggest mistake of his life the day he'd left her. It was the morning after they'd made love. Even the hours of talking and the sweet, steamy sex, didn't stop him from leaving in the morning. He simply wasn't strong enough to leave when she'd so willingly offered herself to him. *Fuck, Seff.* He'd been a greedy fool, and in the end, he'd hurt them both.

The moment he knew about her magic, he should have walked out, but no. He'd been too weak willed to leave her without having one taste. *And what a fucking taste.* She had single handedly ruined him for other women.

The few times he'd indulged in the opposite sex since then had left him feeling hollow and used. Not to mention guilty as fuck. His cheeks heated as he looked at her now.

He wondered if she'd been with other men since him. Of course, she probably had, but he trembled with rage just thinking about it. He might have had no claim on her before, but she linked them with this soul bonding thing, and he damn well wasn't letting her go without a fight. A plan began to take shape in his mind.

He had no right to ask this woman for anything. Especially not after the way he'd treated her. Still, he couldn't stop his next words from pouring out of his mouth.

"Look, Sherry, I have a request."

"You do? What is it you want then?"

"Since you obviously need someone to, *you know*, uh, *mate with*, I ask that you choose me."

"What are you talking about, Seff?"

"I should be the one, Sherry," he said it firmly, ignoring the shocked expression on her face.

"I'm sorry, am I understanding you? Are you saying I should allow you to mate and impregnate me as payment for bringing you out of a coma?"

"Yes. No. Not payment, but yes, I am saying you should take me as your mate."

HOLY. FUCKING. SHIT. Who said that? Me. I did. WTF?!

8

S herry could only stand there with her mouth hanging open. Her eyes narrowed, and closing said mouth, she turned her head away from the male in front of her. She could have screamed.

Who did he think he was making such an outrageous offer? As if she was that desperate. *Well, not for nothing, but the Wolf is correct, you are desperate.* Like bloody hell!

Energy flowed through her as her temper became riled. The restorative tea she'd drunk had done a lot in replenishing her spirit and healing her body after the long days of casting. Her reddish-gold hair danced around her shoulders and her eyes flashed.

The scent of magic, *her magic*, filled the air. She closed her eyes and tried to rein in her power. She could not afford to lose her temper with so many people nearby.

And yet the irony was just too much for her. With a wave of her hand she sent half of his belongings flying from the shelves. The jerk! How could he? *Choose me as your mate. Indeed!*

He had no idea how those words hurt. Like being shot in the gut. *Dammit, Seff, how could you?* She'd loved him once. Wanted him more than anything. Would have killed to have him offer for her. And now he asked her to mate him because of her stupid bargain with the Elders! *No freaking way! Just breathe.*

"Uh, Sherry?"

An unnatural wind whipped through Seff's bedroom causing his bedclothes and pillows to fly about. She smirked at the picture he made, hands gripping the sheet as it threatened to fly off him. She tempered down her powers. Her smirk turning into a full-on giggle as one of the pillows accidentally hit him in the head. *Oops. Not.*

"I suppose I should thank you, Seff, for your *offer*. However, if I find I am in need of the services of a *stud*, you can be certain that I will find one on my own."

She didn't need to look at him to know the grumbling sound came from his throat. Whether or not he was in contact with his Wolf, the man growled like the bloody beast he was at the mention of her finding her own stud.

Sherry had no intention of allowing either Seff or that group of old Witches to dictate her life to her. He offered himself as some sort of way to repay her. Like some sort of obligation. *Bit of a mood killer really.* And *they* feared and coveted her Magic, they wouldn't want to irritate her. At least not right away. She had time yet.

Time that she'd apparently be spending trying to break the spell on Seff. Despite his being heartier than when he first woke, she knew he wouldn't last without his Wolf. No Shifter could survive a forced disconnect for so long.

Werewolves might be stronger than most. They were used to some estrangement from their beasts, as per the effects of the Curse of St. Natalis which the entire Werewolf community had suffered from for a thousand years. That horrid curse kept the human side of a Werewolf from the Wolf side on all nights except that of the full moon. For a creature with a dual nature this was akin to torture.

That was why Sherry had offered aid to the young Wolf from Northern, New Jersey who'd been fated to end the curse. The poor child had gone through many trials in her journey to destroy it. It had taken years, but the curse that had plagued

Wolfkind for a millennium had finally been defeated just days ago.

Werewolves across the world were waking up to a new, stronger bond with their beasts. Some would need help. She'd already briefed Rafe on the situation as per a call from Grazi Kelly, the Werewolf who'd saved them. So, yes, Werewolves the world over were better off today than they were yesterday. But Seff was still in deep trouble.

The odds that he could survive a prolonged period without his Wolf were not in Seff's favor. Sherry needed to focus on the Darkness that still worked its power on him and forget about his outrageous offer to be her mate. Surely, all hope wasn't lost yet.

Perhaps there was a Witch somewhere who could overlook her *soul bond* with Seff? *Ugh.* Even if there was, would she want him? Sherry cursed her luck. How could she even look at another man when Seff was there and willing? He could be hers...

No. I won't fall into his trap again. I will find another way out of this. She sighed and rubbed her temples. This was not good.

Several hours and a few large containers of *general Tso chicken, beef lo mein, pork fried rice, broccoli in garlic sauce*, and many other assorted dishes later, the entire Macconwood Pack Wolf Guard, some of them with their mates, along with the Alpha, his mate Charley, and their three infants who slept in an enormous portable crib, crowded around the manor's enormous dining room table to eat and discuss matters. There were a few assorted others about, mostly Wolves, and of course, one red-headed Witch.

Though she wished for better circumstances, Sherry loved being amongst the animated group. Shifters were often a physical, loyal, and outspoken bunch. The Macconwood Pack took that and multiplied it to a much higher power.

The jests were all good natured as was the intentional ribbing between Packmates. Food was happily passed around and accepted with enthusiasm unlike anywhere else that Sherry had seen. And that was saying something.

A curvy girl herself, Sherry enjoyed food and drink as much as the next person. She fit right in with the group, eating her fair share of spicy eggplant and broccoli in garlic sauce over brown rice. Of course, she preferred to drink hot tea with her meal, a special blend of herbs and spices she crafted herself.

She laughed aloud when Conall, one of the Alpha's own Wolf Guard who looked like a cross between a linebacker and a punk rock singer with his spiked blonde hair and enormous frame, reached across the table and lifted her cup to his lips. After indulging in a huge gulp without asking permission he quite deserved the look of horror that crossed his otherwise affable face. *Priceless.* He spat the tea out behind his seat and jumped up screaming at which Sherry couldn't even try to hold in her laughter.

"That tastes like hot dirt! Oh man, Sherry, what the heck?"

"Well, Conall, serves you right grabbing without asking! Anyway, it is my own mixture of green and black tea leaves with a few added herbs that help to open my receptors and keeps me grounded at the same time. It is also good for digestion and purifies the blood."

"Well, it tastes like shit! I mean, uh, it isn't sweet or anything, err, damn, my bad," he murmured trying not to look aghast at the fact that he'd just insulted a powerful Witch.

"It's okay," she said when Seff frowned at him, "I admit, it is an acquired taste. And one not made for you, Conall. Now, if you start having strange cravings, such as a desire to eat spider stew, or to dance naked in the woods, anything unusual like that, you might let me know," she smiled wickedly at the blonde Wolf who looked as if he was about to puke.

"Cravings? Dance naked? Spider Stew?"

"Yes, you know, you may even want to eat the odd

rat or skunk, raw of course, you can probably find them anywhere on the property."

"Oh my God! Are you serious?"

"No, Conall, I'm not serious," she laughed.

"What if I- Wait, you're joking? That was harsh, man. I thought you liked me, Sherry," he managed to look hurt as he continued to wipe his tongue on a clean napkin. Sherry laughed again.

"Here, try this," Liam offered his cup and Conall chugged from the glass before spewing the liquid back into the cup.

"What the hell was that?!" roared Conall, but it was too late. Liam dashed across the room and headed towards the huge, restaurant equipped kitchen. Werewolves were serious about their food.

Poor Liam had obviously been caught as sounds of thumping and something crashing could be heard from the closed door. Seff stood up and covered the mess with a rag, but not before chuckling.

"Poor Conall, Liam gave him a glass full of white vinegar. He should have sniffed before he drank. Serves him right," his eyes met Sherry's and she got the oddest feeling he felt vindicated that Conall should suffer for having dared sip from her cup.

She shook her head. Surely, she was mistaken. Seff had no reason to act territorial or jealous of her. Not that it wasn't a huge turn on, but she was certainly beyond all that. *Wasn't she?*

"Seff, please drag those two back in here," Rafe's command was a pleasant distraction from her thoughts and the heated looks Seff was giving her.

The Pack Beta nodded and went towards the sounds of the scuffle. *He is as loyal as ever,* she thought, but for the first time her thoughts were kind and without injury. Given the generosity and honesty of their Alpha and his mate, Rafe and Charley Maccon, the Macconwood Pack was unusually close knit.

More of a family really. A pang of loneliness went through her, but she quickly dispelled the feeling. She missed having her own family. The closest thing she had left were the relations of her gigolo great-grand-father, but the Romani family headed by Madame Magdelena Kristos wanted nothing but a passing acknowledgement between them.

Oh well. She had tried to reach out to them many, many years ago. It hadn't ended well. Sherry always wanted a family of her own. It was simply something she would have to live without, she supposed. Magic could not help her with that.

Sherry watched as Charley turned to her mate with a look of such pure love that Sherry turned her head. The couple shared an intense and very special bond. It was not a surprise that Seff, as well as the entire Wolf Guard, was undoubtedly steadfast and loyal to them both.

Sherry could only imagine that the entire mini-squabble between Liam and Conall had been a ruse to lighten the mood. The gravity of why they were all gathered hit her. The Pack was on high alert. Seff had been attacked.

The fact that one of their own, the Macconwood Pack Beta and all-around good guy, had been attacked by Dark magic, *and on their property,* did not sit well with anyone. Sherry wholeheartedly approved of Conall and Liam throwing punches if only to see everyone relax a bit. They needed to go after the Dark Witch responsible for the attack with clear heads. There could be no foul ups.

The two red-headed giants, who sat on the opposite side of the table from Sherry with a petite brunette between them, seemed to breathe easier once the tussle was over and the three men came back to their seats.

The woman with them was an employee of sorts, Sherry guessed from her attire and the tablet that never left her side. She smiled at her and noted the way she ducked her head as if embarrassed. *Poor dear.*

Sherry couldn't help but notice as the tiny woman stole glances from beneath her lowered lashes at the quieter of the brothers. Dib did some computer work when he was younger, but he was better known as the Pack lawyer, if Sherry recalled correctly. Dressed in formal attire, his scowl never left his face throughout the entire meal.

He was the total opposite of his brother whose grin never left his boyishly charming face. He wore track pants and a t-shirt that read "Doin' It Doggy Style" with a picture of a Pomeranian sporting a 1950s pompadour.

Sherry shook her head and sighed, the Lowell brothers might be opposites in appearance, but they were as close as any two brothers could be. She could see their bonds clearly as she could see the pulsing aura of the woman who sat between them.

Sherry sensed there would be rough times ahead for that one. She'd pray to the goddess to be kind when that particular dam burst. *Poor thing.*

Kurt Lowell was renowned for his garish sense of humor, as his t-shirt so boldly stated, but Dib on the other hand, was a bit of a stick in the mud. Serious and goal oriented, the red-headed Wolf was an excellent attorney from everything Sherry had heard. If only he wasn't so solemn all the time. But then again, perhaps there was a reason for his stony-faced countenance.

After all, most people assumed Seff, with his good manners and easy-going personality, was the biggest tight-ass in the Wolf Guard. Sherry knew better. In fact, he was the exact opposite.

He had all the makings of an Alpha, with the good sense to know he was better as a Beta. A born negotiator, he had grit and style. Both traits she admired. Seff was a grounded individual, he was steadfast to his Pack, loyal and trustworthy.

But not to me. It dampened her spirits, but it was better she admitted the truth to herself than to build hopes on dreams and what-could-have-beens. *I won't go down that road. Not again.* She moved the food around her dish with her chopsticks but stopped once she realized she was no longer hungry.

Most everyone had finished eating by then. Though the Wolves at the table still picked at the little remaining food. Someone had brought in a tray of coffee and an assortment of cookies, but she declined.

Sherry sipped from her never empty teacup and listened to the chatter around the table. The regard and affection they held for each other was practically tangible. She exhaled a deep breath and tried to quell the longing she felt.

She noted, not for the first time, that Werewolves and Shifters had one up on the Witches in the world. Their sense of loyalty and comradery made them formidable. *There was power in that kind of bond.* Sure,

Witches had Covens, but they did not fulfill the same purpose as a Pack.

Pack was family. Sherry had none. Choosing not to belong to any one Coven, she was a nomad. Going from place to place, offering her services. No ties. No home.

How nice it must be to never have to question where you belong, she thought. She held herself still as Seff shifted in his seat. The tension between them was thick and uncomfortable. He looked at her with molten brown eyes and she felt a tingling sensation race up and down her spine.

Heat pooled in her abdomen and she clenched her legs tightly together. She wondered how they came to sit there, beside one another. He claimed the chair next to hers as if the years and circumstances between them had somehow melted away.

When they were called down to dinner, not only had he sat down beside her, but he also scowled fiercely at every male Wolf who tried to sit on her other side. The empty seat was finally filled by one of the Wolf Guard's mates, a lovely woman named Tulla Graves.

Of course, Seff's fierce scowl hadn't stopped Liam and Conall from sitting across from Sherry, much to her own amusement. The impertinent pups had developed a sort of soft spot for her after she'd proved she was trustworthy by bringing Seff back from his magic induced coma. She found their attention endearing, though she didn't read anything into it.

A fact, she noted, that Seff did not approve of. The two younger Wolves had spent the last few hours hovering at her side and volunteering to fetch her things when she asked. They were very sweet. Not that Seff thought so. She could tell by the way he narrowed his eyes and growled whenever they came too close. She laughed to herself.

"Now, if you know something funny, by all means tell me, honey, I sure could use a laugh," smiled the whiskey haired woman who sat on her left. Tulla was a forthright, honest woman and Sherry liked her a lot.

"Oh, I was just reading Kurt's t-shirt," Sherry smiled at the woman who then read the bold black print and laughed aloud. She had recently married to Randall Graves, the renowned software developer.

He was the creator of *Wolf Moon*. What started as a little role-playing game had quickly become an entire online universe that was used by both normals and supernatural folk alike. Sherry herself indulged in the fantasy world as none other than her famous ancestor, *Morgan Le Fey*.

It was a great place to engage with people. She found it gratifying to send those who looked for

Magical cures to worldly woes in other directions. Magic was not the easy answer for everything that most people assumed. Magic, on the contrary, always had a price. *Balance in all things*, she recalled her grandmother' words.

"Excuse me, ladies. Sherry, would you like something else?" Seff's voice roused her from her thoughts.

"Uh, no thanks," she said, but inside her mind was reeling.

Yes, you...

9

S itting next to Sherry Morgan proved to be more of a distraction than Seff could have ever imagined. At least, it was for him. She looked completely undisturbed by his nearness. Calm and collected as ever. *Well, damn. So much for her wanting me.*

He'd showered and dressed in a pair of old, worn jeans and a button-down shirt in an attempt to feel more like his old self, but who was he kidding? Seff might look refreshed and well on his way to healing, but inside he was in knots. And not just from missing his Wolf. It was *her*.

Being near the woman who'd haunted him since he'd walked out of her warm apartment on that cold morning so many years ago was wreaking havoc with

361

his emotions. Her spicy scent teased his senses in a way that made breathing difficult.

He couldn't be that close and not touch her, so he casually managed to brush up against her throughout the entire meal. His thigh pressed against hers, his hand accidentally skimmed hers as he reached for his water or napkin. Any excuse he could think of, he used. His pulse sped up every time they touched, and that wasn't the only part of him that noticed.

He wanted to toss his head back and howl at the way she seemed completely unaffected by his "accidental" touches, and yet, he noticed her look his way time and again. Occasionally, he saw a slightly lustful look in her gorgeous, ever-changing eyes.

There one second and gone the next. He tried to scent her arousal, but he couldn't. An annoying fact he attributed to his loss of his Wolf. *And yet she came after me. Almost as if she still cared.*

"How is Daniel?" Sherry's lightly accented voice sent shivers of awareness down his spine as she spoke with his fellow Wolf Guard's mate.

Tulla's son was gifted. He knew from Sherry that Daniel had "the sight" and all the makings of a Witch, *with the correct training of course*. It had been Seff who introduced the idea to the Graves' of hiring Sherry.

After they met with her, they readily agreed that

she was perfect for the job. They allowed her to see the boy several times. From Randall, Seff knew that Sherry had assessed the boy's talents and his magic.

Daniel was still very young, but Sherry had determined that his talents would only grow with the right environment. She'd given them the name of a local Witch who was happy to work with Daniel after school once a week.

From what Randall had told him, Sherry checked on Daniel's progress regularly and was pleased thus far. She frequently visited Macconwood Manor to see Daniel's parents in order to explain his progress and to answer any questions or issues the couple had with his lessons. A fact Seff exploited to "run into" her at least once a month at the manor.

He knew better than most what Randall had faced in trying to save the boy from a crazed Warlock who wanted to use him for his own purposes. Seff understood the dangers of magic. He spent most of his early life at the hands of a man who hated magic.

His old Alpha, Zev Maccon, hated all Witches. Of course, most of his fanatic views came from a dark and twisted place inside of himself. A cruel and hard Wolf, Zev had a zero-tolerance policy for Witches. Rafe had changed all that.

Of course, it took Seff only a little while after making the biggest mistake of his life, walking out on

Sherry, to discover that like with Wolves, Witches came in both good and evil. But by then it was too late. She'd gone away, and by the time he found her, she wouldn't listen. *I am a fucking idiot.*

He turned his attention back to Sherry's animated laughter as she spoke with Tulla. Seff looked past her to where Daniel sat with his new stepfather. Randall looked at home as he chatted with the small towheaded boy. Who knew the once gruff, solitary Werewolf would make an excellent father?

A pang of longing shot through Seff. Would he be a father one day? He'd never thought about it before, but suddenly, he could picture it. A tiny girl with long red curls laughing and jumping into his arms.

Seff's eyes shot to Sherry's abdomen. She'd make a wonderful mother. His heart sped up at the thought of her belly swollen with a child. *His child.* He couldn't help the rumble that came from his chest. Sherry's eyes flew up to meet his, a question in them. But he couldn't voice his thoughts. *Not yet.*

She turned back to her conversation and he noted how Sherry's eyes shone blue as she smiled at the boy. The child had recovered surprisingly well from his ordeal, but that was what having family and a good home did, Seff supposed.

Daniel sat next to his new father and together they played some game or other on his tablet. Randall enthused over the application as much as his son. The two of them shared a love of all things technology based and proved to be a good common ground for building a relationship.

Now the two were inseparable. With the recent news that Tulla was expecting an edition to the family, Seff was glad to see the boy would have no problems adjusting. Secure as he was with both his parents.

Seff wondered if he'd take to fatherhood as naturally as Randall had. Would he ever get the chance to find out? First his Alpha, with his three new babes, and with Tulla pregnant, the manor was going to be full to bursting with an entire new generation in a few years. *Would he get to be a part of that?*

Sherry was in a bind with this whole agreement with the Elders Trust. He didn't pretend to understand a lot about Witches, but he understood being bound by your word. At the time he left her, he'd given his word to his foster father that he would act in accordance with Pack law and hunt down and destroy all Witches. Finding out the sexy young woman he'd fallen for was in fact a Witch damn near broke him.

For the first time in his life, Seff had denied his duty. He'd broken a vow. One he'd made to his Pack and foster father to obey. When Zev Maccon confronted him about the woman he'd been dating and told him what she was, Seff felt as if the world had gone upside down. He'd been ordered to kill the Witch.

"Cut that bitch's heart out and burn it," Zev sneered at him.

He'd trembled and nodded his head. He'd feared that if he didn't agree, his then mad Alpha would have gone after her himself. He shuddered as he thought back to that night.

Seff went to her that night prepared to do his duty. But once in her presence, he could not. One thing led to another. In the heat of the moment he'd seen her eyes change color. She looked so fucking hot when in her passion they'd started to glow. He asked her then what she was, to trust him with her secret. She did. Sherry readily confirmed that she was, in fact, a Witch and Seff had wanted to howl his pain. *He could never claim her*, or so he'd thought.

Walking away was harder than he'd thought. *Especially after making love to her.* Loving Sherry Morgan was the sweetest bliss Seff had ever known. Sure, he'd lied to his Alpha. He'd told the crazed man that he'd killed the Witch in hopes of keeping him off her trail. And in writing her that damned note, he'd sent Sherry on her way and started to nurse his broken heart.

For the first time ever, Seff had lied and broken a vow to his Pack. All to keep her safe. Not that she'd believe him. *I'd do it again in a heartbeat.*

Despite all he'd done to hurt her, it was she who'd come for him when Darkness threatened. She who'd risked life and limb to bring him back from the brink of death. The knowledge both humbled him and gave him hope.

She insisted she'd helped him because of her contract with the Pack, but he knew better. His spirit had called to hers from where he'd been trapped inside of himself and she'd answered. *Without hesitation.*

Now, she needed his help. He wouldn't allow anyone to force her into becoming some kind of brood mare for their fucking selfish purposes. And they sure as shit weren't getting her magic! He'd help her, as she helped him. For one reason and one reason alone. *Sherry was his*. Now, he just had to prove it to her.

He looked over at her animated face and felt himself swell at the image that crept into his brain of her swollen with his young. *Holy. Fucking. Shit.*

Her reddish-gold hair hung about her shoulders and back in a glorious waterfall of colors and curls. He remembered the silky feel of it draped over his chest and wanted it again so fucking bad, he could taste it.

Her laughter rang out like silver bells and he closed his eyes to savor the sensation. She was still so beautiful. He'd been a fool to let her go.

"Thanks so much for asking, Sherry! Daniel is great! A handful, of course, but wonderful just the same. Excited about being a big brother, you know! And that woman you sent us to has been wonderful for him!"

"That's so wonderful for you all, Tulla! Congratulation! So, no more dreams then?" Sherry asked. Seff sat silently next to her and listened unashamedly to their conversation.

"Nope! Not so much as a peep in the last few weeks," Tulla answered. Her face beamed as her husband turned his head and kissed her lightly on the mouth.

Short as it was, the passion that flared between them was almost embarrassing for Seff to watch. He felt like a voyeur and almost fucking blushed until Sherry turned her head and her eyes met his. It was like being hit by a truck. The power of her gaze made him hungry for more.

The couple next to them were so obviously in love. Their shared kiss announced it to all, they were mates, a married couple, fated to always be together.

Like Rafe and Charley. Tate and Cat. Mason and Abigail. Fred and Callius. Mike and Claire. Cael and Rayne. And so many more recently mated Pack members. *Lucky bastards.*

Would Seff ever join their ranks? He'd never admit it because it made him sound like a sappy fuck, but he wanted a mate. Hell, he'd found her, he just needed her to accept him. To forgive him for the past and help him build a future.

Maybe he could use her whole situation to help move things along?

First, he needed his Wolf back. Though he felt better, he knew he was weaker than before. A fact he hated. It meant he wasn't in top form and couldn't offer her the best protection. *Grrr.*

Werewolves were pretty much Neanderthals when it came to the protection of their mates. Just because Seff was more levelheaded than most of the Wolves he knew, didn't mean he lacked that basic protective instinct. *Must protect.* That was kind of up there with, *must claim her now.*

"Randall are you ready for the next addition to your family?" Sherry teased.

"Oh, I'm getting there," the big man mused.

"Really? Then how come you fainted at the OB/GYN the other day, sugar?" Tulla laughed and more teasing ensued.

Randall was the unofficial Pack historian since he was responsible for uploading the ancient journals and records of the Macconwood onto a secure server for future generations. Seff spent a lot of time reading through them over the years as he'd often been called on by Rafe to research Pack law and precedence.

Rafe had done some outstanding work in getting the Pack to move with the times, and he relied on Seff's keen mind to help smooth out any foreseeable problems with research.

One of the things Seff had found interesting was records of a so-called *mating instinct* that once ruled Wolves without any thought for propriety or societal standards. Modern Werewolves, having been so consumed with the ancient and recently defeated Curse of St. Natalis, hadn't been as affected as Wolves of the past.

However, ever since that fiery teen, Grazi Kelly, broke the curse, Wolves have awakened all across the world, and as Seff himself was discovering, the long-lost *mating instinct* was starting to awaken as well.

Slowly. We must proceed slowly. Once he found the bastard that cursed him, Seff would get his Wolf back. Then he could formally ask Sherry to be his.

Easy-peasy.

10

S herry almost melted under the table over the
poignant look Randall and Tulla shared. So
much love between them. Like two halves of
one whole.

First Charley and Rafe and now these two. Aweee. But
within that sweet awe was just a tinge of the green-
eyed monster. Sherry frowned.

Jealousy was not a good look on her. Sure, she
would give just about anything she had for such a
look from a man. *Well, one man in particular.* But she
was nothing if not honest with herself. She would
never be on the receiving end of such blatant adora-
tion. *Not going to happen.*

Sherry had long ago resigned herself to a life
without Seff. He still held her heart, regardless of
how carelessly he threw it away. She wasn't a

masochist, but the heart wants what the heart wants. And her Witch's heart was nothing if not stubborn. It wanted Seff McAllister. *No. Bad heart.*

"Attention, everyone," Rafe cleared his throat and silence ensued. Everyone knew better than to interrupt the Pack Alpha when he spoke. Sherry included.

"I called you all here today because of recent events. First, let's give credit where it is due. Please, raise your glasses in honor of our friend, Sherry Morgan," a few wolf whistles and cheers rang out and Sherry's heart warmed as Rafe continued with his speech.

"Ms. Morgan, I want to thank you on behalf of the entire Macconwood Pack, from the bottoms of our hearts, for bringing our Packmate, Seff, back to the land of the living! Brother, it is so good to see you standing on your own two feet again!" More cheers and applause sounded as Rafe raised his glass and tipped his head to her and Seff.

Sherry nodded her thanks to the Alpha, humbled by his public acknowledgement. The Pack had only recently begun to work with Witches for the greater good. Suspicious by nature, each group of supernatural creatures tended to stay away from each other. Rafe was smart enough to realize they'd get further by working together than alone.

She didn't know why he'd had such a change of

heart, but whatever the reason, he had approached her some years ago and she'd developed a working relationship with the Macconwood Pack. Still, this was the first time she'd been to dinner at the manor.

She smiled as they continued to cheer and was shocked when Seff took her hand and firmly nestled it in his much larger one. He pushed his chair back and stood up, gently pulling her to her feet. He stood next to her with a large grin on his handsome face. He looked at her with eyes that shone with pride and something else.

Her breath caught in her throat as he squeezed her fingers gently in his big, warm hand and ran his thumb across her palm and Sherry was ready to swoon.

Stop it, you ninny. You aren't a schoolgirl any longer. Not like she could help it. Her mind might know better, but her body wasn't listening. She might as well admit it. Seff's touch still did things to her.

He looked down at her and his eyes glowed like amber fire for a second. Sherry had to drop her head back to keep eye contact. She always felt so small next to him, with his incredible height and wide shoulders. Though he was average for the Wolves at the table, to Sherry, he was enormous.

Distracted by the turn of her thoughts, she gasped when he brought her hand to his lips and placed a kiss on her palm in front of everyone there. Her skin sizzled at the brief contact between them. She trembled and prayed to the goddess he couldn't feel it. The sudden darkening of his eyes told her he did notice. *Uh oh.*

As the cheers died down, Seff seated her first and only after making sure she was comfortable did he take his own seat. If he moved his chair a little closer to her, she pretended not to notice. And yes, she also ignored the thrill that shot through her body when he took her hand in his again after sitting down.

Her own sense of pride had Sherry tugging her hand back. It was too much for her. The pull of attraction threatened to strangle her in the crowded room. Sitting next to him, holding his hand, allowing him to kiss her skin. *Are you losing your mind, silly Witch?*

He let her pull her hand free. *Drat.* She immediately missed his warmth. Okay, so she still desired him. But that didn't mean she should act on it. *No way.* She turned her head to listen to Rafe as he continued his speech.

"Second, I am pleased to report that, yes, it is true, our enemy, Skoll, is dead," more cheers erupted, and the Alpha waved a large hand to shush the crowd before he continued.

Sherry bit her lip and tried to ignore the warmth

pulsating from the man next to her. Each movement seemed to bring him into contact with her. His thigh innocently caressed hers under the table, his arm brushed against hers as he laughed at something his Alpha said. Sherry turned her head and took in the warm glow of his aura.

He radiated goodness. Except for the smoky tendrils of Dark magic that wound around that part of him that connected him to his Wolf. Anger raced through her body. She would end that spell or the Witch who dared cast it!

What fool thought he could harm that which I've claimed? She struggled against her possessive attitude and forced herself to calm down. Best focus on what Rafe was saying.

"Yes, Conall, *but*, there are more asses that need kicking! We are still in pursuit of the one he hired to cast a spell on one of our own. Ms. Morgan has investigated the spell and it is the work of Dark Magic. The Witch in question needs to be captured and brought in. We have men and women out trying to locate him, but so far we've come up blank."

This news was greeted with groans and exclamations that Sherry half-listened too. Seff had once again gotten hold of her hand and, weak-willed Witch that she was wherever he was concerned, she couldn't help but revel in his closeness. Such an abrupt about face was not something she should trust, but the woman in her wanted to believe that perhaps he felt something for her? The same something that left her dreaming about him a decade later.

Sherry lifted her teacup with her other hand and turned her head and chatted with Tulla and Randall some more. She could feel Seff's eyes on her, but she ignored him.

She didn't know what game Seff was playing, but she could not afford to let her heart run away with her. She must remain focused on her task. After a few more niceties, she excused herself from the table.

Seff had gotten up to speak to Rafe when she walked out of the dining room. He was safe. For now. As it was, she needed to retrieve her personal belongings from his room before moving into some guest quarters which she assumed were available. She waved an impatient hand that sent a pulse of magic into her belongings and had them packing themselves before she heard him enter the room.

"Holy shit, it's like *The Sword and the Stone* in here!" he exclaimed with a boyish grin on his face that made her knees turn to jelly.

Sherry yelped and lost her concentration causing her belongings to crash down to the hardwood floor.

"For the goddess's sake, Seff, you can't just sneak up on me like that!"

"Um, pardon me, but it is my room."

"Indeed, and I am doing my best to leave it the way I found it."

"I didn't ask you to go. Hey, I meant it though. That was really cool. Sorry I frightened you, baby."

"Cool? Are you sure you are the same Werewolf who shunned me for my magic?" *And did you just call me baby? She wanted to add.*

"Sherry," his voice dropped an octave as he stalked across the room and she found herself wishing for the buffer of the other Wolves. She'd even take Vasco at the moment, but her Witch friend had left her as soon as he found out she was staying at the manor until she finished decimating the magic that was separating Seff from his Wolf.

"I think I better get this out of the way before we continue on this mission," he growled as he advanced on her.

His steps were slow and determined. She hardly recognized him from the mild-mannered man she once knew. This Seff was different. Perhaps being separated from his Wolf left him feeling raw and *unfinished*, almost as if the human side of him took on a feral aspect that his Wolf normally harbored. *Interesting. Maybe a tad dangerous?*

"I was an idiot when we were together," his strong hands reached out and crushed her to his massive chest. Sherry was too stunned to utter much of a protest, "But I've since learned from the folly of my youth to never, ever take anyone for granted. Especially, not the only person I've ever known who can make this happen without even looking at me," he pressed his hard body, *and boy did she mean hard*, against hers and Sherry trembled helplessly in response.

"Seff, really, this isn't you, the *soul bonding*, may result in some unusual feelings-" She rushed to explain his behavior, but he cut her off with his mouth.

His lips slanted over hers and she gasped, giving him the perfect opening as his tongue slid inside. He tasted like chocolate and coffee, warm and sweet. She sighed as she kissed him back. Refusing to hide her true feelings.

"Oh no, don't you dare try and tell me that this is because of your magic, Sherry. *This* is because we belong together. It has nothing to do with my Wolf or your magic, *your beautiful fucking magic*, that shines from you like a rainbow in a city of blackness. You are a miracle, Sherry Morgan, and I've been thinking about this, about *you*, for years. I want you. I always have."

Any resolve she had to stay away from Seff McAllister crumbled in that moment.

"Oh, Seff," she sighed into his mouth and wrapped herself around him. He felt so good in her arms. Strong and solid. It was like coming home. Sherry trembled. Should she trust him again?

Did she even have a choice? Not likely, as her body took charge and she gave herself over to the pleasure that was kissing and touching Seff.

11

Seff growled deep in his throat as he locked his mouth onto the woman he held flush against his hard body. *Mine. My mate.*

He didn't question the possessive words that crowded his mind. He was drowning in the sensation of having her this close. It had been so long since he felt her, tasted her. *Too fucking long.*

He had no intention of stopping now. He'd already made too many mistakes with this woman. He needed her to know how he felt. And it wasn't because of her magic. He loved Sherry. Always had.

This wonderfully soft, sweet smelling, oh-so-fucking hot woman was finally his. The scent of apples and cinnamon wafted into his nostrils and he felt himself harden instantly. *Delicious.*

He wanted to lay her down and peel off the layers of clothing that separated them. He wanted to lick every delectable inch of her. He wanted to bury himself between her creamy white thighs. *Fuck.*

Seff wanted her so fucking bad he could hardly think straight. He ravaged her mouth with his. He needed to mark her, to scent her, to make sure no one made the fucking mistake of thinking she belonged to anyone other than him.

"No, Seff. It's just the *soul bonding* that's making you feel like this, it is not real," she whispered, but contrary to her words, her hands tugged on fabric.

Soon he was shirtless and the zipper to his jeans was down. He gasped as she cupped him, his breath coming in short, desperate pants. She tightened her grip and he almost lost control of himself. *Fuck me.*

"Does this feel fake to you," he pressed his arousal into her hand, and she purred against his mouth.

"Oh baby, I want you so fucking bad," he growled and tugged on her lower lip with his teeth.

Seff ran his hands up and down the length of her body as she stroked him firmly in her grip. He growled and inched away from her naughty little hand, divesting her of the layers of clothing she wore.

She giggled as his hands found the waistband of her skirt and skimmed the soft flesh of her stomach.

He'd almost forgotten how ticklish she was. He grinned and nibbled on her neck as he tugged the long material off her luscious frame. Her soft ivory skin was warm to the touch. *Finally, yes*, he thought as he touched every inch of it. He moved to follow his hands with his mouth.

"You're burning me alive with your hands," she gasped and strained towards his teasing fingers as they pinched and rubbed the pert buds of her nipples into hardened peaks.

"I need to taste you," he said and captured one round berry with his mouth. He suckled, and she went wild against him. Her beautiful breasts were just as sensitive as he remembered. Sweet as berries he licked and suckled her like a starving man.

She moaned and gasped, arousing little sounds that teased his senses. He wanted her to scream for him. To say his name as she came for him with her luscious legs wrapped around his waist. *Yes. Now. Mine.*

He pushed her back towards his couch and spread her thighs, taking in the sight of her pink cleft. It was so fucking beautiful it damn near stopped his heart. Moist and swollen he knelt before her. She was so lovely. All woman, mysterious and gorgeous. And all his.

He bent his head and brushed his bristly cheek

against her soft, sensitized thighs. Her sex was so close he inhaled her honey scent and licked his lips. He blew on her moist bud and reveled in the way she arched impatiently.

"Seff, please," she said her eyes glowing gold as she begged him for more.

He could hardly wait a second longer. He needed to taste her. *There.* He spread her knees wide apart and brought his mouth down over her hooded clit and sucked. Sherry gasped and writhed against him as his tongue laved at her sweet honey. *My honey.*

For years Seff had lived by a strong moral code. *Do not lose control. Pack first. Be the voice of reason.* But not now. For the first time in his life he was going to have what he wanted. *Her. Now.*

Sherry moaned his name aloud as he slid his tongue between the folds of her sex. He pushed two long fingers into her tight channel and found her sensitive nub with his teeth. He gently bit, sucked, and licked until she convulsed underneath the onslaught. Seff growled as he made love to her with his mouth.

"So beautiful," he groaned and felt her nether lips quiver in response, "I want to feel you when you cum on my tongue, Sherry. I want to taste you, to drink you in, Shereen mine. My own, yes, that's it, baby."

"Oh, Seff," she moaned as her body convulsed again.

"Now, baby, let yourself go for me, that's it, so fucking beautiful, you taste so good, *grrrr*," he growled and pushed another finger into her heat while laving at her clitoris with his long, raspy tongue.

He felt the second her sex tightened around his fingers in her climax. Sherry's entire body tensed, and she yelled while he pumped his fingers in and out all the while working her clit with his mouth.

"So, fucking perfect," he said and rose to wrap her legs around his waist.

He couldn't wait a second longer to join them. He took his cock in hand and rubbed the tip at the entrance of her sex. Sherry grasped his arms as he pushed his erection deep into her welcoming embrace.

Her whole body convulsed as the strength of her orgasm swept through her, tightening her channel around his hard shaft. Seff growled. *So fucking good*, he thought as he pumped himself deep, deeper into her heat.

He ground his hips against her, finding that sensitive spot where she craved his touch. He thrust harder, pumping his hips, filling her tight channel till he was fully seated inside of her.

Their slick bodies slapped against each other as

they moved in unison. He pumped as she undulated her hips, meeting him thrust for thrust. The sound they made was a symphony to his ears as Seff thrust wildly into Sherry's hot sex.

The past ten years had been so fucking empty. He'd been so stupid. *No more regrets. We begin now.* He had her here, now, and he wasn't letting go. Not ever. Her taste was tattooed on his tongue, branded on his very soul. He'd never touch another woman as long as he lived. *Mine.*

"I'll never let another man touch me," she said.

Seff growled and licked her skin where he'd pierced the sensitive flesh. He felt no shame even as he realized he must have spoken his thoughts aloud. No, he was proud. Dammit, he was downright cocky at the thought that she was all his.

He groaned loudly as he came, pumping his seed into her womb, marking her with his scent. He stiffened as he connected with his Wolf for the first time since he'd been cursed.

The connection was fleeting but in that second, he listened to his other half as his Wolf roared *MARK HER! SHE IS MINE!* Seff growled and did the only thing he could do. His fangs elongated. He nuzzled the skin where her shoulder met her neck and he bit down.

Lightning struck. He stiffened to the point of

pain as the taste of Sherry, *spicy cinnamon apple*, shot through his entire body. Electricity sizzled in the air as magic sparked between them. It wrapped around their fused bodies permeating the air with scents of ozone, Witch, and Wolf.

Seff growled deep in his chest at the intensity of it all. He could actually feel the *soul bond* between Sherry and himself. It pulsed with life as it too became stronger through the mating instinct of his Wolf.

His Wolf whom he missed with every second, but whose presence he felt in this moment even through their cursed disconnect. Seff grunted as Sherry cried out, scratching her long nails down his back as ecstasy claimed her.

Never like this before. He felt the intensity of her pleasure as her sex gripped him, milking his own satisfaction from him as he roared against her skin. *Mine!*

Loving her felt so right, Seff knew he was born for this woman. He needed her like no other. They lay clinging together, trying to catch their breaths. Sated smiles covered both their faces. Seff wrapped himself around her, *his Witch, his woman*, and kissed her until she was gasping once again.

"Mmm, Seff, I love this, but I need to breathe."

"Breathe me, baby, breathe me," he groaned and

kissed her again, shifting their positions so that she was on top of him.

Their lips fused together. He growled deep in his throat with satisfaction because this time it was all her. She was kissing him with everything inside her and he felt it down to his toes.

She was so sweet, so sexy, so fucking powerful, she sizzled in his arms. Seff groaned again as he felt his cock harden inside of her.

"Sherry, I need you."

"Yes," she sighed and straddled him. She arched her back as she settled her sex on top of him. Her heat encompassed his shaft, gripping him like a velvet vise. *Finally. Yes. Mine.*

Her passion glazed eyes met his as she rocked her hips, seating him more fully inside of her. She slowly swiveled around and around, sucking him deep into her core. Those long fingernails he loved raked down his chest, flicking his nipples as they went. He breathed in with an audible hiss, wanting to move, to take charge, but even more than that, he wanted to show her that he trusted her. *With all of him.*

"You look so perfect riding me, baby, with your hair hanging down around your shoulders like a curtain of fire, and your gorgeous breasts taut and high, you feel like fucking heaven, I want to taste you," he reached out and flicked his tongue over her puckered nipple.

"You feel so good inside me, Seff," she groaned and rocked her hips harder. Fueled by the volatile emotions he saw roiling in her eyes, Seff groaned her name.

When she looked at him her eyes glowed blue, as her channel tightened, Seff gripped her hips. Purple now her eyes bore into his as she licked her lips and leaned down, kissing him on the mouth. He could wait no longer, he thrust upwards and rocked her harder.

'Oh yes," she cried as he thrust his hips and slammed her down on his throbbing cock. Sherry cried out as her body convulsed in pleasure, her nails left marks on his arms. She felt boneless, but he wasn't done yet.

He wanted to wring every inch of pleasure from her that he could. He reached between them and thumbed her clit as he pumped his hips, slamming his hard shaft into her again and again until they both roared their pleasure as one.

The sensation like something between being hit by lightning and landing in heaven. His cock pulsed as he filled her once again with his seed. Relief coursed through his body.

A primal urge to bite her again, to rub his face all

over her to mark her with his teeth and his scent damn near overwhelmed him.

Sherry was his, but it was more than that, *he was hers*. Her mate, her lover, the one who would move heaven and earth for her, and he wanted the whole world to know it.

Mine.

12

"I can't believe we did that," Sherry lay on top of Seff in a tangle of arms and legs. Somehow, they made it to his bed, where they'd inevitably made love yet again. *Swoon.*

He was an even better lover than she'd remembered. Tender and attentive to her needs. He made her feel beautiful and wanted. But the feeling was fleeting. Sherry bit her lip as a heaviness settled inside of her heart. *Don't be fooled this time. This is not real.*

"Seff, we need to talk," she said and sat up. His protesting groan threatened to make her grin. Still, she pulled away from him, so she could look him in the eye when she spoke. It was necessary for the safety of her heart to lay down some rules.

"Okay," he nodded, his big, lust-glazed, brown

eyes bore into hers. Sherry lost her train of thought for a moment. *He was so beautiful.*

"Despite what we've done," she began.

"Several times," he interrupted with a grin.

"Yes, well, despite however many times, I am trying to explain that *this* is more than likely a side effect of the *soul bonding* cast I used to pull you back from the Dark magic that held you before, Seff. It's important we both acknowledge that so neither of us harbor any false expectations," she tried to further distance herself from his penetrating warmth, but arms like steel bands held her against the hard length of his body.

A body she'd licked from head to toe only moments ago. A body that had brought hers to ecstasy again and again. A body that she still wanted to kiss and taste and fill her from the inside. *Yes.*

"Sherry, I respect the hell out of you, but in this, you're wrong. *This* isn't a side effect," he turned on his side and pressed the splendid proof of his arousal against her soft belly, "I've never stopped wanting you."

"Yes, well, we both know that wanting is not the same as loving and I can't do this again, Seff," the note of sadness in her voice went deep.

Her heart threatened to break right then and there. She was not strong enough to survive him leaving her again. Best get it over with now. She turned her head away from him, ignoring the pleading look in his eyes.

Damn it, Sherry, why do you do this to yourself? You agreed to help him only. No strings. Definitely, no sex. Just break the spell. Foolish Witch!

"Look, baby, I know I never gave you a reason to trust me before, but we are meant to be. I love you," he placed his thumb and finger on her chin and turned her face towards him.

He looked at her with such tenderness she wanted to scream. *No, this isn't real. Please stop torturing me.*

"Sherry, you are my destined mate, I feel it, here," he placed her hand over his heart, and she exhaled.

She so desperately wanted to believe him, but she didn't dare. Not even when he looked at her like he could see through to her very soul. He had the most beautifully expressive eyes. *Eyes that had glowed amber when his fangs elongated and, he'd bitten her...*

"Um, Seff, can you feel your Wolf inside you now?" She changed the subject abruptly. Declarations of love aside, she needed to know how he'd called his Wolf forth in that moment of blind passion.

Besides, she couldn't concentrate on breaking the spell if she had to contend with him professing love for her now. Not when she couldn't be certain whether it was her cast that persuaded him to think he loved her or his true feelings.

"What do you mean?" he asked. She saw the exact moment when recognition dawned on him.

"I bit you! How? Wait, um, argh!" He sat up and slapped his hand against his head as he tried to concentrate and call his beast.

"No, I can't feel my Wolf now. Fuck it all to hell!" his frustrated roar stirred her heart. He was hurting, badly, and she wanted to stop it.

"Seff, if you can't feel your Wolf then how do you think, um, that is how could you-"

"How could I have marked you with my teeth?" he asked and rotated their positions so that she lay beneath him on the soft mattress.

Angry at his inability to connect with his Wolf or not, Seff's eyes glowed with possession as he pressed his body against hers. His nostrils flared as he pulled the sheet down, revealing her breast and the shoulder where he'd marked her.

"Mine," he growled and kissed the mark with his lips, then with his tongue, sucking the flesh into his warm mouth.

Sherry moaned at the sensations. She felt the connection between them. It pulsed from the bite mark on her shoulder to every nerve ending she possessed. He tore the sheet off her as he licked and kissed his way down her body. Sherry felt the cool air drift over her sweat slicked skin. She felt a charge of energy, her own magic feeding the bond that she'd cast to counter the spell on him.

She opened her eyes as his clever tongue found her sex and saw the air alight with shimmering tendrils of magic linking him to her. Seeing magic was a rare gift, but one that she'd had from birth.

The sparkling lengths that pulsed and moved and wound their way between the two of them, were beautiful and perfectly natural to her. Then again, she was a Witch, born and bred of magic. Her magic was as much a part of her as his Wolf was to him.

Sherry bucked her hips as he delved his tongue inside of her tight channel, his fingers bit into her flesh as he held her down. *Oh, Seff!* She moaned against his sensual onslaught, but still she held back. She was afraid, so afraid, to give him her heart a second time.

Werewolves were so stubborn, so set in their ways. Under Rafe, the Macconwood Pack were the most tolerant of Witches and magic in general, but still all change took time.

Would Seff ever realize that his bite marked her as her magic marked him? Would he understand that Wolves had their own brand of magic? Or like before, would he feel tricked and betrayed? *Would he reject her again?*

"Honestly, I don't know how my Wolf emerged long enough for me to mark you, baby, but I swear that nothing I have ever done in my entire life has ever felt so right. I told you, *Sherry Morgan*, Witch or not, *you are mine.*"

She tried to believe him. Wanted to with all her might but it was an impossible situation. She loved him. Always had. But he hated magic. Didn't he? It was so hard to think when he knelt at the apex of her thighs and pulled her legs up onto his shoulders. He pressed the tip of his cock against her entrance and teased her relentlessly until she practically begged him to take her.

"Seff, before you go further, understand that nothing will ever change the fact that I am a Witch. Not any Witch, I am the *Morrigan*. My clan descends from the goddess herself. I've a store of magic to rival entire Covens and they all want a piece of it. I have vowed to heal and serve others with my powers. I will never relinquish them," she narrowed her eyes to try and gauge his response to her statement.

She held her breath, fear stabbed at her heart. It would surely break in two if he pulled away from her now. *But wouldn't it be better now than before she lost her heart?*

Who the hell was she kidding? She was already so deep in love with him she could hardly see.

"I am going to say this to you now, and however many more times you need to hear it until you believe it, Sherry, I love every fucking inch of you from the top of your wild curly hair, to the tips of your toes, your heart, your soul, your magic, all of it, all of you. *Mine*," he growled the last word and thrust fully into her welcoming heat.

"Yes, *yours*," she moaned.

Hours later Sherry stood near the front door of the manor preparing to leave. She managed to withdraw from Seff's room while he slept. After showering and dressing in one of the guest rooms, she'd made a few calls and decided on a plan. She'd discussed it with Rafe and made to leave, but not before an angry male sauntered down the hallway bellowing her name.

"Sherry? Sherry!"

"Oh, uh Seff, I was just leaving–"

"The hell you are! What's going on?"

"Hey Seff," Conall greeted him with a smirk as he dangled a set of car keys from his meaty hands, "I'm taking Sherry here to see that Vamp dude, Balky or whatever."

"What the hell is he talking about?" Seff addressed Sherry alone.

"Look Seff, I have a lead. It occurred to me while your Pack was not having any luck finding the location of the Witch who bespelled you, a contact I know might have some information," she narrowed her eyes as she noted the glistening beads of sweat on Seff's forehead.

"Are you feeling, alright?"

"What do you mean? I feel fine," she could tell he lied, but it was just like him to try and deny his pain.

She looked deeper and when she blinked this time she saw that the black coils of dark magic were wrapped tightly around him, and they were growing thicker and stronger. *Oh no!*

"Seff!" She yelled his name as he blinked and staggered to the floor, his face contorted in pain.

13

For the first time in a long while, Seff woke up smiling. His smile grew even broader as he considered the reason for his current state of bliss.

He turned to find that reason and scowled as his hands met with empty sheets. He sprang up, the realization that the woman he'd spent hours loving with not only his body, but with every inch of his heart, mind, and soul, was gone.

Seff cursed soundly and jumped out of bed. He struggled to put on a pair of jeans and a semi-clean t-shirt before grabbing his sneakers and charging down the hallway. His chest squeezed painfully, and his stomach clenched.

The burning sensation in his chest grew worse with every passing minute. This was more than just him finding Sherry gone. Darkness hovered over him, but he didn't slow down.

He needed to find Sherry before she completely disappeared from his life. *Again.* Okay, last time was totally his fault, but he was young and stupid then.

Back then he thought he owed loyalty and obedience to his Pack alone. Now he knew better. In truth, he only ever owed anything to her. The sexy and oh-so-tempting Witch who held his heart and soul in her hands.

Pack would always be important. Pack was family. But Sherry was everything. The only woman he ever wanted. He'd do anything to keep her in his life.

Right then, Seff didn't give a fuck how it looked to his fellow Wolf Guard and Packmates who watched as he ran down the hall clutching at his chest and stomach like a madman, bellowing her name.

When he finally caught up to her, relief and anxiety coursed through his veins. Was she leaving him after all? He tried to sift through the words she was saying, but he needed to hold her to calm his inner panic.

Just as he reached for her, an invisible blade seemed to stab him straight through the heart. His knees buckled. *Fuck me!*

"Seff!" Sherry's cry reached his ears through the haze of pain.

"Conall, get me something for his head!"

Seff would have scoffed at the idea of having a pillow thrust under his head by the tall blonde goofball, but it was better than the marble-tiled hallway. Rafe and his aesthetic preferences be damned. Marble was cold and hard, and the way he was thrashing about from the pain, he'd probably give himself a concussion if it wasn't for his Sherry's quick thinking.

His Sherry. Damn straight she was his. When all this was over he'd show her just how fucking serious he was. This was one Witch who wasn't getting away again. Even if he had to chain her to the bed and make love to every sweet inch of her until she was too exhausted to move. *Good plan. Let's do that.*

Of course, they needed to fix the curse on him first. He needed his Wolf back. Then, when he was whole again, he could prove that it was all him and not some spell that made him confess his love for her. She was his mate. He knew it in his heart. He'd always known it.

He would come to her after he was healed. He would claim her and, he would vow in front of the whole damn world that she was his and he was hers, true mates, forever.

We'll see if she can dismiss what we have and walk away so easily then. No fucking way was he letting her get away from him again. That was a promise.

He didn't quite understand the words Sherry spoke in that sexy, lightly accented voice of hers, but it was clear from the spicy cinnamon scent that hit his nostrils what she was doing. The cool strength of her power seeped into his bones, soothing the fire of pain that had nearly rendered him unconscious.

He hated his weakness, but he was smart enough to understand he was no less a man for it. The Dark Witch who'd done this to him would suffer soon enough. Then he'd be joined with his Wolf once again and he'd have his woman, *his Witch*, at his side. It was a win-win, he just had to grin and bear with the annoying fucking pain until then.

"Seff, can you hear me?"

Her voice was like silver bells ringing through the air. Her sweet breath tickled his ear as she bent down and tucked a strand of hair behind his ear. Her cool hands felt his forehead for fever. Seff inhaled, *cinnamon and apples*. She smelled so damn good.

"I hear you, baby, you okay?"

"Am I okay? You were the one who hit the floor! Are you well enough to sit up?"

"Yes," he did and couldn't resist a peck on her pretty bow of a mouth before he went from sitting to standing, enjoying the shocked look on her face as she noted they were not alone in the hallway.

He watched her rise from the floor in a swirl of gauzy skirts and noted the flash of her cleavage in the cropped, skin-tight top that she wore with it. The shimmery gold fabric looked good against her pale skin and her fiery hair.

She oozed sexuality. She was woman, glorious and beautiful. A powerful Witch. Her power was a living part of her and for the first time he saw it. Shimmering about her like gold dust and silver stars.

He was in awe of her beauty. He growled as he realized they had quite the audience. He barely restrained himself from finding a blanket and throwing it over her delectable body. Seff did not like to share. *Mine.*

"You should go back to bed-"

"Not an option, now where are we headed?" he interrupted her with a gentle kiss on the mouth.

"Well, Conall was going to accompany me to the home of a friend of mine," she avoided his eyes when she said friend and Seff felt the hairs on the back of his neck stand up.

"A friend?"

"Well, actually, we used to date-"

Grrr. Seff stiffened as Sherry continued to speak,

but his mind was whirling. *An ex-boyfriend? WTF? And she wants me to stay here. No way.*

Still, he'd been raised a gentleman, so he allowed her to finish her little speech before he interrupted. Well, before he interrupted again anyway.

"So, you see, Seff, it is better you stay here."

"Not happening. Conall can come to, for back-up, but there is no way in hell you are walking into a den of Vampires without me."

"Fine, but you can't go dressed like that," Sherry smiled wickedly as she waved a hand and before he knew it, strait-laced Seff was dressed in a pair of black leather pants and a billowy white shirt with most of his chest exposed.

Conall laughed until with a wave of her hand he was similarly dressed. *Two points for Sherry's magic.* But where Seff could tell that his Packmate had been uncomfortable with the cast, Seff reveled in the cool comfort that was her magic wrapping itself around him. *Like a hug.*

"I look like a fucking pirate," he grumbled not for the first time as he followed Sherry through the woods at the back of the manor.

She ignored his griping, and he enjoyed the fact that she knew him so well. Her magic was just fine with him, tight leather pants not so much. Still, he was glad she didn't mind his complaints.

In fact, she seemed to be laughing at him. That made him smile between scowls. They'd need to be able to compromise as a couple if they were to have a future. *And they were going to have a future.*

Conall, however, didn't take the hint. Which was why he was rubbing his now sore arm after saying "ahoy matey" one too many times in a mock pirate voice. *Douche.*

Seff flexed his knuckles. Without his Wolf he was significantly weaker, but not enough that he couldn't cause some damage when he tried. That was one of the reasons he wasn't too worried about walking into a nest of Vamps.

"How do you know where to find this Vampire?"

"I told you, we used to date," was her noncommittal reply.

Seff wanted to growl and throw things. More than that, he wanted to rub himself all over her, to mark her with his scent. *There goes that primal mating instinct again.*

It was something modern Werewolves didn't normally indulge in, but he couldn't help it. His inner voice was screaming inside his head to pick her up and go home.

Sherry; however, was determined to go see this Vampire. There was no way he was letting her go without him. Only the thought that she bore his bite calmed him. *Mine.*

"Are we there yet?" Conall asked.

"Shut up," Seff said and punched him again.

"Ow! Dammit Seff, you don't have to hit me so hard!"

"Stop being a baby."

"Boys! Please, I need to concentrate," Sherry scolded them then turned to face a tall stand of pines with her arms raised and her eyes closed. They'd driven to the farthest part of the Macconwood property then proceeded on foot until she'd suddenly stopped.

He watched intently as the air around his shapely Witch began to shimmer and glow. *Beautiful.* As was she.

So perfectly lovely with her glorious hair blowing around her as if by some invisible wind. He guessed it was caused by her magic. The scent of ozone and cinnamon permeated the air as she concentrated.

He practically drooled on the forest floor. She was magnificent in her power. Everything he ever wanted. She looked and smelled so tempting.

Her skirts plastered to her long legs by that same invisible breeze. Outlining her luscious curves. *So perfect.*

Her *anima magicae* pulsed within her, the

fragrance growing stronger and stronger. *Like apple pie and ice cream in front of a warm fire. Like the thousands of flickering stars that dotted the night sky. Like home. My home. Mine.*

He was no longer surprised by the possessive thoughts he had whenever he was near this woman. In fact, for the first time, he accepted them, relished them even.

Being a Werewolf meant a lot of things, and though his Wolf was bespelled at the moment, Seff felt him rise whenever he savored thoughts of his Witch.

His eyes were glued to her. Hell, he never wanted to look away.

Mine.

14

Sherry tried to focus her mind on conjuring a portal to the Vampire's home, but it wasn't easy with two hundred pounds of sexy man standing behind her. She could feel Seff's perusal and tensed as doubts crept into her mind.

Did he regard her with disgust as she wove her spell? That idea was quickly dismissed as she opened her senses and searched out his aura. Multi-tasking was a specialty of hers.

His pleasure and, *yes*, arousal was more than evident in the brightly pulsating colors that flowed around his body despite the taint of the curse that was slowly suffocating his Wolf. The sight of those dark tendrils had her re-focusing her attention to the matter at hand. *His poor Wolf. She needed to end this curse, now. She needed to save Seff.*

That made her focus more intently on her task. Sherry continued to filter out the noise and concentrate on the magic necessary to open a portal to Bal's residence. The Vampire was notoriously secretive. She'd met him a year ago and had an ongoing flirtation with the tall blonde. She even dated him occasionally, but he'd never been able to really turn her head.

Because you already gave your heart to another. She opened herself to Seff's feelings and was thrilled to find he not only approved of her magic, but he seemed to hold her in awe.

Like you need his approval. She was a feminist at heart, but what woman didn't like knowing her man was proud of her? And he was her man, wasn't he? *Not now.*

It was a unique feeling. Knowing he watched with pride. He'd once shunned her for her magic, but now, he seemed to appreciate it, *and her*, on a deeper level. That boded well for their relationship. *Hmm. A future together? Shut it! Concentrate for the goddess' sake!*

The air hummed as she raised her hands up higher to the night sky. Invoking the magic that she controlled, asking it to do her bidding. She felt her power fluctuate and build within her.

She opened her eyes and felt the energy inside of her. Sherry knew from experience that they'd be glowing, a bright violet color as she spoke the words that called forth a portal that would take them to the Vampire.

"Ewch â ni lle byddaf i." Take us where I will to be.

The air in front of her began to swirl and shimmer, faster and faster until it appeared to suddenly stop. The very air in front of her was so still it was almost solid. She waved her hand again as it began to take shape.

She smiled, pleased with her accomplishments as she beckoned the two Wolves that accompanied her forward. Seff went immediately, proving once again that he was with her. *Mine.*

She was shocked at the possessive thought that pulsed through her. As if he read her mind, Seff looked right into her eyes. His own were heavy-lidded as he gazed at her. She knew that look. *Mm. Later.*

"What the hell is that?" Conall asked, his blonde eyebrows high on his forehead as he stared at the black door she'd conjured.

"It is the way in, of course," she replied.

"Into what?" he asked.

"Why Conall, you do trust me don't you?" she asked widening her sly grin.

"Um, yes?" it came out more question than answer, but Sherry just laughed.

She grew serious when she looked into Seff's

warm brown eyes. *What about him? Does he trust me? No time like the present to find out.*

"And you, do you trust me?" she asked, hating the desperation she heard in her own voice.

His answering smile warmed her heart. He was nothing if not honest, and she found herself unable to return the grin. Not until he said the words.

"With my life, baby. I trust you with my life," he said and walked through the portal without her.

Sherry stood for a moment, her eyes wide with shock. Conall shrugged and jumped in after Seff. She could hardly believe it, but here was the proof. They'd put their lives in her hands!

What the heck was she waiting for? She followed them through the portal and prayed she wasn't too late.

When she entered the room, she noted that Bal was indeed having another one of his famous parties. She rolled her eyes. The show-off knew she was coming.

She'd contacted him first of course. It was not wise to enter a Vampire's lair without his knowledge or permission. Though Sherry preferred not to think of it as that.

Her eyes quickly scanned the darkly lit surroundings. Bodies filled the opulent space, most writhing to the deep bass of the music that blared through invisible speakers.

She recognized immediately that the majority of the crowd were Vampires. That didn't bode well for her two companions. Where were they anyway?

She first spied Conall in the arms of a tall female Vamp who seemed to take a shine to the virile young Wolf. The black-haired Vamp had him pinned against a wall. They appeared to be talking and he was holding his own just fine. He caught her eye and nodded.

She scanned the crowd again. Where was Seff? Her heart pounded as she realized he'd leapt into the lion's den just to prove he trusted her. What if some Vampire decided he'd make a tasty treat? Without his Wolf he'd be hard-pressed to defend himself. Sherry's pulse tripled. Guest or not, she'd blast anyone who dared hurt him! She exhaled when she finally caught sight of his tousled brown hair.

He was facing away from her. He hid it well, but she could tell by the set of his shoulders that he was tense. That was when Sherry caught sight of the Vampire in short red-vinyl dress who'd taken a shine to her man. *That bitch!*

The whorishly dressed Vamp gyrated her hips against Seff's a little too aggressively. Sherry's lips thinned as she began to see red. Jealousy, a new feeling, welled up inside of her.

The female Vampire seemed to ignore the fact that Seff stood stock still. His disinterest evident, even insulting. That was when Sherry saw the trap. *Oh, damn you, Bal! Vampires and their foolish games!*

Sherry crossed the highly polished Italian marble floors, ignoring the elegant furniture, and the eclectic art collection. She waved towards Conall and soon he joined her in her pursuit of Seff who was now being sandwiched between two scantily clad Vamps. Sherry was in no mood for games.

"What do you want, bitch?" said the one in the painted on red dress.

"I supposed we should thank you for the snack, I always get the midnight munchies during one of Bal's parties!" the two of them smirked as they ran their long fingernails down Seff's chest.

"Take your hands off of him," Sherry said in a low voice.

The two Vampires hissed and stood in front of Seff as if he was theirs! Clearly, they both needed lessons in basic manners. *Mess with what is mine and you will regret it.*

"Let's see what you got then!" they said and showed their needle like fangs, eyes glazed with bloodlust.

Sherry smiled and not nicely. She drew her power to her and with barely a flick of a finger she sent the one in the red dress flying across the room. Her eyes turned to the other, but she clearly got the picture and relinquished her hold on Seff.

He went to Sherry's side immediately. For a second, she wondered if he would be angry that she'd saved him, but he grabbed her hand and squeezed. A smile on his kissable lips as he said, "You were freaking awesome, baby."

"Well, now! Is that anyway to behave in my home, *cara mia*?"

Sherry turned slowly around and stared at the six-foot-two-inch Vampire who stood regally in the center of the room. His long blonde hair shone in the dark lighting. It reached his impressive shoulders in gilded waves, his one true vanity, she knew.

"Baldassare di Capua, you arrogant bastard!" Sherry said.

15

Seff wished like hell his Wolf was on hand the second he entered the Vampire's lair. Okay, so it was his house, but *lair* fit better.

The dozens of cold bodies in the room seemed to zero in on him and Conall the second they entered through the portal Sherry had conjured.

Almost immediately, they were accosted by female Vamps who were as strong as they were demanding with their many attempts to glamour him and his Pack mate. *Hint, Werewolves weren't easy to cow, even with magic.*

Being cut off from his Wolf didn't diminish that ability, however, he was still at a disadvantage. Female or not, Vampires were notoriously strong. And he was a guest here.

As Pack Beta, he knew enough about the rules of

etiquette to determine he'd be insulting his host if he were to upset said host's guests. A risk he was willing to take as he had no intention of being a supple snack for either female.

Good thing Seff didn't have to ponder the problem for long. His beautiful Witch came right for him, guns, *or magic as it were,* blazing. Yup, Sherry came in and rescued his hairy ass. *Again.* Emasculating? Maybe to someone else, but to Seff it was ridiculously hot. In fact, the more he watched her the more he basked in her amazing talents.

She was freaking awesome and what's more, the fact that she fought for him meant she cared about him. A lot. *Heck yeah! Just a little while longer and she'll know she is mine!*

"Are you hurt?" her sultry voice interrupted his thoughts, but he didn't mind. He grinned broadly and stepped towards her, hands on is hips when another voice spoke, and Sherry turned her attention away from him. *Grrr.*

"Baldassare di Capua, you bastard!" Sherry said.

"Indeed! And yet here you are, my darling, Shereen Morgan, and I see you've brought a couple of your pets with you," the Vampire seemed to glide across the floor until he stood in front of them.

Conall barely contained his growl, but Seff did not act. He was used to dealing with other supernaturals. The fact that the Vampire was taller than him, and for the moment, stronger, made Seff edgy, but he kept that hidden by barely acknowledging the man's arrival.

"You dare insult me by having your harem attack these men when entering your home under my protection?" Sherry's voice rang clear throughout the suddenly quiet room.

Seff took in the moue of distaste on the Vampire's face. It lasted but a second before he broke out in a charming smile. *Sherry was right, he is a bastard.*

"Come, darling, let us not fight. Sit please," he captured her hand and brought it to his lips as he spoke. He didn't relinquish her hand, a fact Seff noted angrily, as he strode towards a pale sofa. The music started up again and the party resumed as Bal, Sherry, Seff, and Conall sat down.

"I hear you've got a problem, Shereen darling. The Covens are speeding up the deadline and demanding you honor your promise. Tell me, are you having trouble finding a mate? I could always volunteer-"

"That is not your concern," Seff growled between tight lips. He was vibrating with anger.

"Ah, I see, this is the one you are seeking to help? He is besotted then, the poor pup," this seemed to delight the Vampire who thought to reach out and touch a strand of Sherry's hair.

Seff didn't think first, he simply reacted. He shoved the offending hand off Sherry and grabbed the Vampire by the neck. The idiot smiled broadly at the gesture, clearly allowing the hold.

"You do realize, you are not yourself, don't you? No Wolf, silly pup, I could snap you like a twig," he said, but he made no move to do so. In fact, he wasn't even angry. Seff realized he'd been goaded.

He cursed to himself and reluctantly let go of the Vampire. He looked down, hated his weakness, missing his Wolf. A sound came from Sherry and his gaze swept to her. Immediately he felt a sort of calmness settle over him.

Was she using her magic? Or was it merely her nearness that soothed his ravaged soul? Either way his heart thudded in his chest as he gazed into her eyes. He liked the way her lips opened in response to that look.

Her eyes grew wide, the color changing to a dark grayish-blue that churned wildly like a sea storm. He could get lost in the depths of her eyes. Someone cleared their throat. *Conall*, he thought. But Seff didn't know of he was angry or grateful for the interruption.

"Bal," Sherry's soft voice infiltrated his mind, "My

companion here is not himself. You are correct in that. *Pax*, my friend, we come here in peace seeking your aid."

"She is right. I am sorry if my behavior has offended you," Seff hated the words, but he said them. For her sake.

Seff felt like an idiot. He was acting like some lovesick teenager for Pete's sake! He had no right to play the jealous fool and endanger their mission. Not when Sherry had so selflessly put herself on the line for him.

"*Hmm. Interesting.* Yes, well, I made the inquiries you asked me about, *belissima*, but why do you go looking for trouble when it so readily finds you?" Bal smiled wickedly and turned his head to the far side of the room. The three of them followed his gaze, all eyes falling on a tall, thin man dressed in black from head to toe.

Vasco. From the look of him, he'd just strolled into the Vampire's little party. He seemed agitated and reckless. Unusual, Seff was sure, even though he barely knew the male Witch.

One thing he knew, Vasco had not noticed them. He tilted his head back and drank heavily from a large black glass bottle that he held in his right hand. Then he dragged the first woman to walk past him against his body with his long, thin arms.

It was the female Vampire from before with the red vinyl dress. She writhed against him as he squeezed her, molding her long frame to his whipcord lean body. Seff growled. He didn't need his Wolf to tell him what was going on. *Traitor.*

From the second he'd spotted the Witch, Seff had known something was off. The man was clearly courting danger. That black glass bottle was surely *Black Market Brew*, a magical liquor created to allow any supernatural to feel the effects of drunkenness whereas they wouldn't otherwise due to their supernaturally enhanced metabolism. No one knew who made it, but most shifters knew to stay away from the concoction.

Seff's eyes narrowed. He should have known that bastard had something up his sleeve from the second he'd laid eyes on him. Hell, he would have known were it not for his disconnect from his Wolf.

Dammit. Not that any of that mattered now. Not when Sherry's lovely face wore the hard look of betrayal. Seeing that look on her face alone left Seff nearly rabid with fury.

"I should have known," she whispered.

"Sherry, I'm sorry about this," he began.

"Why should you be sorry?"

"I feel like I should have sensed something. *Goddammit!*" He growled.

"No, Seff, this is not on you. Vasco is a Witch and he has betrayed me by his own accord. He will answer for it," fury turned her eyes red and Seff sat in awe as her innate power began to change the atmosphere in the room.

"*Brava!* I always enjoyed watching you work, darling, perhaps you can use my office?" Bal inserted himself into the conversation.

A fact that made Seff want to howl in rage, but not any more than her smiling response did. *What the hell? She liked this guy?*

"Thank you, Bal. That would be lovely. Shall we?"

She stood up from her seat on the pristine couch and the entire room seemed to stop. Sherry had frozen everyone in place. *Holy shit.* She held Seff's eye for a moment as if to gauge his reaction.

When he smiled encouragingly, she slapped her hands over her head and she, Seff, Conall, Bal, and a stumbling Vasco were suddenly transported to an office that was decorated with more impeccable, high end furniture that could only belong to the Vampire.

The male Witch tripped as he went to grope the female Vamp who was no longer there. When he realized what had occurred, his long face grew even paler, if possible. Seff's lip curled in disgust as he watched the man drop to his knees in front of Sherry.

"Sherry, please, Sherry, you don't understand-"

"You are correct, Vasco, I don't understand."

"I had no choice-"

"Do not think you can lie to me! How could you?"

Her voice was ice cold, but no more than her eyes. They flashed white as she seethed with anger and betrayal before him. Seff had never seen this side of her. It was beyond his experience, but he felt no fear. In fact, quite the opposite. Her power was astonishing as was her anger. It was almost palpable in the small and suddenly ice-cold room.

"Please, mercy, mistress!"

"You knew about my contract with the Macconwood Pack, you knew about my, er, personal interest with them, and yet you deliberately set out to double-cross me! Me? *Shereen Morgan, the last Morrigan*! Surely not, Vasco," Sherry's eyes blazed green as she looked scathingly upon her former ally.

"No, never! I did not seek to betray you, Sherry! You had to let go of the Wolf, so you could fulfill your destiny! You needed to be free to choose a mate! *To choose me to mate!* Don't you see? You could never honor your promise to the elders if you still harbored feelings for that, *that cur*!" he wailed and fisted his hair.

It was not a good look for the Witch. Seff grabbed him by the color and flung him away from Sherry's feet. The idea that the sniveling scum stood anywhere near her made him want to rip the guy's head off. *Back away. Mine.*

Sherry's gaze remained on Vasco, but she stayed Seff with a touch of her hand on his arm. Heat seeped through the billowy fabric of his shirt to his skin. He felt her desire for him to remain still. He even understood through their connection what it was she meant to do.

Seff nodded his assent, but he remained at her side. He respected her enough to allow her to deal with the Witch her way. She was more than capable.

Seff snarled his displeasure at Vasco's prone form. He heard Conall's echoing growl. His Packmate was there for him should he need it. Seff signaled him to wait and had no doubt his order would be carried out. Bal sat quietly through all of it. Seff dismissed the Vampire as he watched Vasco grovel on his hands and knees.

How he wished his Wolf would come to him now! He wanted to tear out Vasco's throat! The bastard thought to keep him from his mate. His Sherry. *Mine.* He turned and addressed Sherry.

"You don't need to do this, I can take care of him for you," Seff wanted to spare her the pain of having to deal with a friend turned enemy.

The ugliness of the act contrasted vividly with the beauty of his Witch. This was, after all, his mess.

He didn't want her to sully her hands with the clean-up.

"It is alright, Seff," Sherry's hair swirled around her shoulders in wild disarray as she called on her powers.

"Wait, I will tell you all, I will tell you where to find the Dark Witch who cast the spell on your mongrel lover!" He spat the word and Seff took a step forward.

"Yes, Vasco, you will tell me his name, but not before this," she raised her hands and it was as if all the light in the room flowed directly into her. She looked down at the cowering man, still on his knees before she opened her mouth. When she did her voice rang out strong and clear, leaving the hairs on Seff's arms to stand on end and goosebumps to form along his exposed skin.

"Vasco Demerus of the Corvum Clan you have betrayed the sacred vow of all Witches. You have betrayed your own kind. You will face the Tribunal and be brought to justice. Until the day of your trial you will be stripped of your powers. They will be hereby bound and sealed, to be released only by me, as I will, so mote it be," her voice echoed in the confines of the office space.

Vasco wailed as if he were in pain. The man seemed to shrivel before Seff's eyes as his powers, whatever they may be, were pulled from him and bound into a glowing black sphere by Sherry's awesome magic. She waved her hand and the sphere disappeared. Vasco writhed on the floor and wailed as if he were in agony.

Still, Seff was not satisfied. It wasn't enough. He wanted the man to do more than beg for mercy. He wanted his blood.

"Well, it appears *mia bella signorina* has acted with mercy. Do not make the mistake of thinking that I will follow her lead. You will have one minute to vacate the premises *after* you tell us the name of the one you work for. Now, tell us," Bal, who was not as impartial as Seff had thought, leaned forward from his position in the white leather chair he'd occupied since they arrived in his office.

Seff could feel the power emanating from the Vampire and wondered at the way Vasco seemed to become even smaller as the glamour took hold. He'd heard of the magic ability of Vampires to possess and control weaker minded beings, but he'd never seen it actually work.

"Without his powers, Vasco is not immune to the Vampire's magic," Sherry explained.

"I, I, I don't know his name. only the place, master," Vasco sniveled before Bal.

"That is good, *my pet*, tell me then, where is he hiding?"

"In the dark, master, he hides from the Covens because they do not accept him as one of their own. He has used science and magic to break through the barrier of the supernatural world. He will remake us all."

"Will he now? Tell me, my pet, where can I find him?" Bal said. He spoke with a sort of innate patience, his stillness almost unnerving to the others in the room.

Seff focused on the male Witch instead. Vasco held vital information. Information that once garnered would lead him to the one who would end the curse that separated him from his beast. *And then I shall claim her for good.*

It was stunning to realize that Sherry consumed all his thoughts. Yes, he was still loyal to his Pack. He would continue as Rafe's Beta as long as the Wolf would have him, but *Sherry* was his mate.

Though Rafe may have a softer view on Witches than his father had, Seff had never really asked him how he felt about Werewolves mating with Witches. Not that it would matter. His mind was made up.

If he had to choose between the Pack or Sherry, he'd choose her. *Every. Single. Time.*

Seff was in love with Sherry. Desperately so. She

was his one true mate. He simply could not live without her. Hell, he wasn't sure he wanted to.

"I said name a location," Bal insisted. The glamour he cast proved strong as the male Witch began to whimper and jerk on the hard marble floor.

"He, he's holed up at the Ramapo Valley Reservation. You won't find him on any trail. He's hidden himself well with casts," Vasco's eyes were glazed as he spoke, but Seff had heard enough.

Vasco was handed over to a pair of Guardians, who assured both Sherry and Seff that they would escort him to the *Cells*. That place was feared by most supernaturals as it was nearly impenetrable and rendered most supes weak as newborns the second they entered the eternal fortress. That was where Vasco would await his Tribunal. The finality of it weighed on the rest of the group as they sat in silence after his departure.

Seff placed a hand on Sherry's shoulder, wondering how he could possibly comfort her after such a treachery. She linked her fingers with his and squeezed, almost as if she were seeking comfort or support. Either way he'd give it to her. *He'd give her anything she wanted if she would only let him.*

She turned her luminous hazel eyes on him and smiled as if she'd read his thoughts. That smile was like a sucker punch right to his gut. She was so fucking beautiful.

Blast these leather pants, he thought as he strained against the fabric. *When we're alone again.* The silence lasted only a moment before Conall opened his mouth.

"Hey, it just occurred to me, Sherry, you dated all these guys except me, huh? So, when's my turn?" Conall grinned for a moment. Just before he doubled over as the punch Seff sent into his stomach stole the air from his body.

"Idiot," Seff muttered, worried that he might have to hit his Packmate again for insulting his woman. Then Sherry laughed, and he knew all was forgiven.

"Oh Conall, try not to upset Seff, he doesn't appreciate your humor the way I do," she leaned over and kissed Seff on the cheek.

A kiss he wished was just a few centimeters to the right. She bit her lip and smiled again, her eyes promising more.

Later. Grrr.

❧ 16 ❧

The trip to Ramapo Valley Reservation took only moments as Sherry whipped up another portal. After a little begging, she also swapped Seff's and Conall's leather pants and pirate shirts for more practical outfits consisting of jeans and t-shirts.

Spoilsports, she thought with a grin. Maybe she'd keep that outfit handy for Seff for later. *If they had a later.* She hated to think how this little trip to the woods could end, but the fact was they were entering unknown territory to hunt down a powerful dark Witch with the power to almost sever the connection between shifter and beast.

She shivered in anticipation. *At least Bal stayed back*, she thought. She'd been relieved when with a low bow, Bal excused himself back to his guests. It was one thing for a Vampire to help you gather information, quite another for him to get wrapped up in the business of other supernaturals.

Besides, she could see Seff's tension when faced with the other male. They were better off without him. At least, she hoped they would be.

Seff knew of her previous relationship with Bal that was the obvious cause for his dislike of the Vamp, but she wondered if it would make a difference if Seff knew that she'd only dated Bal casually.

Oh well. This was not the time to explain all that and, if she were being honest, she kind of liked it when he got all jealous. She rolled her eyes at herself. *I am acting like a lovesick idiot and not the wielder of legendary power that I am. Focus.*

The moon hung low in the dark sky as they walked over the graveled parking lot to where a sign proclaimed the Ramapo Reservation wooded area as protected territory. The night air was brisk even for a New Jersey spring, but Sherry didn't mind it.

She inhaled the fresh air and smiled as she tilted her head back and allowed her senses to open. She sent magic forward into the beyond to scout the area that surrounded them.

"What is she doing?" Conall stage-whispered.

"Shh!" said Seff.

"I am looking for signs of traps or casts hidden in the forest. Do not wander off on your own, you must stay near me. The Dark Witch, or whatever he is since the readings I am getting are not at all clear as they should be, is dangerous, and these woods have been stained by his presence."

"He is here, I feel it, and the spell is getting stronger, Sherry," Seff clenched his jaw as he spoke.

She felt his pain and frustration through their bond. Worse than that, she felt his strength waning. Sherry opened her eyes and took in the figure of her lover. The normally robust man was slightly stooped. Beads of sweat dotted his forehead, his skin color was turning grayish.

Sherry frowned. It was almost as if his nearness to the one who cast the spell was making him even sicker. They started walking through the forest, careful not to make a sound, but with every step they took, Seff's condition worsened.

He tried to hide it from her, but after an hour of hiking through the forest at night, he was unable to keep the truth from her.

"Can you go on?" She asked, trying to keep her voice steady and smooth. It would not do him any good to know she worried.

"Of course, I'm a Werewolf you know, well most of the time I am," he smiled weakly.

Sherry forced herself to ignore his pain. It wasn't easy. The *soul bond* they shared allowed her to feel the stabbing pain and desolation that threatened to break him in two. He was in anguish, and yet he marched on. *Her brave and beautiful Wolf.*

She tried to feel for his beast through their connection, but it was already so faded she could barely make him out. His Wolf was silent and still, lying on the floor in that plane of reality where he waited for his human side to call him forth. He was still alive. For now.

Sherry grimaced. Every cell in her body wanted to turn around and help him, but she knew already that there was nothing she could do except find the bastard who was responsible for cursing him.

She concentrated on her magic, sending out signals, and waited. Each minute felt like an eon. Conall whined as Seff stumbled over some gnarled looking tree roots. He reached for his friend, lifting him gently before he could hit the ground. He placed him on a pile of fallen leaves and checked his pulse. *Pack looked out for each other*.

As a Witch without a Coven, Sherry had never had someone look out for her. She was glad she could trust Seff's care to his Packmate while she searched out the fiend behind this. Seff groaned aloud and Sherry tensed. Conall's eyes met hers. This wasn't good.

"Seff! You okay, buddy?" panic laced his voice.

Sherry couldn't help herself. She stopped her search and turned and ran to Seff's side. Her heart hammered inside of her chest as panic settled in the pit of her stomach. She couldn't lose him. *Not now*.

"Seff, can you hear me?" She spoke softly as her hands traced his brow and felt for fever.

She didn't know whether to be glad or terribly frightened as he continued to sweat and shake. Seff wasn't hot. He was cold and clammy. His body trembled and jerked uncontrollably on the forest floor. *Oh goddess, please, no, do not take him from me.*

"Sherry?" His voice sounded strained to her ears.

"I am here, Seff," she felt so useless as she said those words to him.

"Sherry, I am so sorry. Sorry I left you when I did-"

"No, we're not going to talk about this now, you are here with me and that is all that matters, do you hear me, Seff McAllister!"

"I feel it inside me. Fuck, it's like a knife slicing right through the center of me. *Agh, Goddammit*," Seff struggled to breathe as he grasped her hand.

"The end is close. I can feel it closing in like a vice around my neck! I am sorry, I need to tell you-"

"Don't you dare give up on me now, Seff McAllister! I swear I will never forgive you! Stay with me! Open your eyes," but it was too late, even as Sherry begged. Seff closed his eyes. Conall whined behind her.

"No, Seff, Seff! *Nooooooo!!*"

He exhaled once more, and Sherry cried out as his body shook violently before going utterly still.

"Oh fuck, man! Not Seff!" Conall moaned and knelt beside his friend, head in hands.

Sherry backed up. Her eyes went wide. She tossed her head back to the night sky, invoking all her powers. Lightning struck the ground mere inches from where she sat. The wind howled, and the creatures of the forest took flight as she roared her agony aloud.

"*Dewch â'm gelyn i mi,*" she spoke as if in tongues, her voice on a different decibel than was normal.

Sherry trembled with unbridled fury as she called her enemy to her. She stood in the suddenly quiet forest with her eyes ablaze with fury, as she sought the one responsible for her pain. Emptiness threatened to consume her. And with that void came the violence.

That of the *Morganna Witches* that had passed. Their ways were of blood and bone and vengeance. A path that she had renounced once she became both healer and teacher to those imbued with magic like herself. But that was when she had hope, now she had only a broken heart and her power. *Yes, she had her power. In spades.*

Her long skirts swirled around her. They began to change shape, growing thicker and shorter, molding themselves to her body until she was clad in something resembling a golden suit of armor. This war was not over.

Her eyes mimicked the bright gold as her hair wrapped itself in braids that hung down her back. *Warrior style.* She threw her head back and called out once more, "*Dewch â'm gelyn i mi! Bring my enemy to me!*"

As if the hounds of hell were at his feet, a man, cloaked in black came floating through the line of trees and into the clearing where Sherry stood. She looked once at Seff's prone body to where Conall crouched beside him, ready to defend his fallen mate. Satisfied that he would be protected, Sherry turned to the figure in front of her.

"You're the whore who chooses this dog over her own kind? How do you have the power to summon me?"

"Do you deny you have cursed the Wolf, Seff

McAllister, severing him from his beast and ending his life?" her voice multiplied as if several beings spoke as her braided hair swirled about her head.

She raised a finger to the now cowering male sending waves of pain into him with her magic. She ignored his pleas.

"But, but you should not be able to do this!"

"What is your name?"

"I am sponsored by Valac!"

"The child-Demon? And is he here now?" she asked.

"I, I, you cannot do this. I have made tapes of shifters! I am going to out them to the world! But not before I perfect this serum!"

"The one that you used on Seff? What is the spell you used?"

"It is too late for your boyfriend! Valac assured me I was safe!"

He raged on from his position on the floor, but Sherry only smiled at him. It was not a nice smile.

"Did they not tell you who I am?" She asked as she summoned power and sent it to him in a wave of lightning.

The male Witch shook as the spell hit him. Sherry vibrated with energy as she cast her rage at him. She waved her hands over her head and sent lightning bolts to strike him from all sides.

To her surprise the Witch seemed to enjoy the attack. He cackled and threw his head back. Magic charged the air. She watched as his hands reached under his cloak and he revealed his chest, covered in tattoos of ancient runes. She recognized the Dark magic cast and she clenched her jaw.

"It matters not! I am ready for you! Now you will suffer, Witch. Valac show me your splendor!" The Witch wailed.

Sherry went flying backwards as a crackling energy shot through the ground to where she'd been standing. The air was knocked out of her as she slammed into the trunk of a large pine tree. She slid to the floor limp and dazed.

What the hell? The strong smells of ozone, sulfur, and other noxious gasses permeated the air. *Bloody hell! He'd channeled the Demon!*

The Witch, or Warlock, as she'd better categorized him now stood, shaking off her hold as if it were nothing more than dust. Warlocks were renowned for breaking faith with the basic rules of magic. That meant he was not to be afforded the same niceties as Witches who'd slipped up.

No. There would be no mercy here. Madness shone in his eyes and she knew he'd not grant her any either. The whites of his eyes had turned completely black. He was not even human any longer. He cackled as he ambled forward.

"I know who you are, Sherry Morgan, but do you know me? I'm a descendant of *Mordred*, follower of *Valac*! A most devoted servant of his indeed!"

Sherry's eyes hardened to resemble diamonds as she stood gathering her powers. This was not good. Mordred had been a traitor and a downright evil bastard. The son of Morgan Le Fay, he'd killed his uncle, King Arthur, not his father by the way, and he murdered his mother in hopes of securing the crown for himself.

"That's right," the Warlock sneered, "We are family, dear Witch! I've been looking for ways to get back at *your kind* for decades! You see, I was not born with power. No, your descendants cursed all of my line to be born as *normals* to pay for the sins of Mordred! I was a nobody! A low-level scientist for a pharmaceutical company. I didn't know anything about Mordred until I was an adult already. Then he came to me in dreams through his ties to the great Valac!"

"The dead dreamwalked to communicate with you? This is not good," she whispered the last to herself.

"Tricking that dog, Skoll, into acting for me was easy. The Macconwood is the largest Pack in this hemisphere, it made sense I target them first. Getting to you and your boyfriend was just a bonus, *Sherry Morgan*."

"You are being tricked. You would forfeit your soul for a Demon?"

"Not just a Demon. He promised me greatness and vengeance! I will not go back to my boring little life anymore! I have discovered a way to end Shifters! But first, *Witch*," he sneered at her, "You must die! Or maybe I shall keep you for my own. See if that famous Morgan power will pass to our progeny?" His eyes grew glazed with greed and lust. Sherry felt sick.

"You will never have me," she replied as she gathered her strength.

"Yes, that is a great plan I think. You will bear my child and I will out shifters and give people an easy way to kill them! I will be famous!" He made to lunge for her, but he did not finish the move as he was lifted off his feet.

"No," a voice snarled from behind the Warlock and Sherry gasped as the man continued, "You will be dead!"

Sherry watched, her heart near to bursting as Seff appeared behind the deranged Warlock. One minute he was on two feet, the next he was on four.

His Wolf snarled as he clamped his jaws over the Warlock's neck and shook him violently until his head flew off his shoulders. His Wolf did not relent, even as blood and gore spouted all over the place.

The body continued to twitch, but Seff finally dropped it to the ground. A vicious snarl escaped his jaws as he did so. He turned and licked his muzzle to clean it from the taint of the Warlock's blood.

Sherry could not believe her eyes. Was it truly him? She blinked hard, but yes, Seff still walked forward to where she knelt. She sobbed as she reached out a trembling hand and touched him. Joy welled up inside her and she cried out as she ran her hands over his soft, thick fur.

"*Rydych chi wedi dychwelyd ataf.* You have returned to me, my love," she whispered and hugged him close to her chest.

The Wolf licked her face, cleaning the tears that flowed freely. Then brown fur rippled and soon she was embracing skin. Seff's skin. *Her Seff*. He was alive.

"I will never leave you," he whispered as he kissed her hair and her face.

"Oh Seff, I thought you died," she cried, returning his kisses.

"I thought I had to, but something held me back."

"What do you mean?" She asked, not really wanting to question the gift that was him, but still needing to understand it.

"You did, my sweet Sherry, our *soul bond* did. I could feel it, pulling me back to my body, to my Wolf, I couldn't go. Not without you. I love you, Sherry Morgan," he murmured into her mouth as they kissed.

EPILOGUE

"Wait, so the guy was a Witch, right?" Conall scratched his head as the entire Wolf Guard and their mates assembled over pizza and salads at the manor.

"No. He was a *Warlock*. Conall, how many freaking times have we gone over this?" Liam tossed his crust at the older Wolf's head and Conall snatched it out of the air before it could connect.

"I don't mind explaining again," Sherry said from her position on Seff's lap. He'd scooped her up and sat her there the second they'd entered the dining room after washing up and other things.

Her pulsed raced just thinking about the way they were in the shower only minutes earlier. Of course, the Pack Alpha demanded they come to the dining room to share what had happened and Sherry had agreed they should probably go. After all, they had time for all that later.

He nuzzled her neck as he lifted a slice of pizza smothered in sausage and onions to her lips. She took a bite and smiled as he answered for her. She enjoyed the way they seemed to be totally in sync. *No more secrets*, she thought.

"Conall, a male Witch who has broken the rules of magic, mainly to not cause harm, and who practices the Dark ways and consorts with Demons is then called a *Warlock*. The fact that this guy only received magic as a result of Demonic possession may mean the word is not exactly right, but whatever he was, he is gone now," Seff growled the last word.

"By the way, Sherry, thanks for saving my brother, *again*," Liam said with real sincerity despite his ribbing.

Sherry squeezed Seff's hand at the playful jibe and he readily returned the pressure. He smiled and tossed a piece of crust at his brother's head. She kissed his cheek and laughed, loving his strength as it pulsed into her through their bond. Sherry warmed at the feeling. He was fierce and proud. And man enough to not feel threatened by her powers.

"Okay, I think I get it," Conall continued, "But how do we know the Warlock wasn't working for anyone? We don't know anything about him, and we didn't find the potion he injected you with, Seff," Conall said.

"True, our information is limited. But we recovered this key from the body," Seff held up a small nondescript key that he, Sherry, and Conall had found amongst the Warlock's, er, body parts.

"Looks like a key to a bank deposit box," said Kurt thoughtfully. His serious expression was at odds with his t-shirt. Today's fashion marvel had a picture of a Dachshund with *"do you like my wiener"* written across the top in bold font.

"Could be. Why don't you see what you can find out," Seff tossed the key at Kurt and turned to his mate.

The fact that he had not yet officially gotten her to agree to be his was grating on his nerves. Sherry was not some little girl he could tell what to do. She was all woman first, a powerful Witch second, and she held his future in her hands.

Fuck. He needed to get her alone. He needed to make her his. But first he had to get through dinner. She squirmed on his lap and he felt himself swell immediately in response.

His body certainly had no problem stating the obvious. She was the one for him. Now he had to find the words. And he had to pray she would forgive him for the past.

"Are you finished eating?"

His fingers traced the sides of her torso in small tantalizing circles. He was still hungry. But not for pizza. His Wolf growled in his mind's eye. He couldn't wait any longer.

"Yes, I'm finished," she said.

Seff wasted no time. He stood up, dragging her with him to the amused glances of his Packmates and the few wives who ate with them. They both said their goodbyes before retiring to Seff's quarters.

The manor was made in such a way that his rooms were separate from the rest of the house, ensuring maximum privacy. He'd need it if his plan was going to work. *Make her cum until she saw stars, then hit her with the big question.*

She moved out of his arms as they entered the living room. Seff watched the sway of her hips as she walked away. What was that saying, *hate to see you go, but love to watch you leave?*

He'd never really understood it until now. His Witch sure had a fine way of moving. *Grrr.*

"What now?" she asked, her wide luminous eyes fixed on him. They were hazel just then and as open and honest as everything else about her.

"What do you mean?" Seff asked, completely hypnotized by the way she looked in the pale sea foam green confection that swirled around her more like mist than actual clothing.

He couldn't wait to peel her out of the thing. *Why was he waiting anyway?* He moved towards her, his arms reaching for her lush curves, but Sherry scurried away. Just out of reach. *Fuck.*

"Baby, why are you trying to drive me insane? Come here."

"Seff, I am serious. You are well now. The curse is broken. Your Wolf and human side are back in connection with each other."

"So?" he wasn't following her train of thought. How could he when she looked so damn tasty?

"*So*, we can ignore the *soul bond,* or I can even try to find a way to remove it. Your feelings for me, well, I understand if you they are *different* now," the set of her shoulders told him she was holding back.

He frowned. He wanted honesty from her at all times. And what was with this drivel she was spouting? *Hell to the no.*

"Okay. I guess I better say it then, Sherry. I do feel differently."

"It is okay, Seff, I do not blame you," her shoulders slumped even more.

She turned away from him and nodded her head sending her rust colored curls dancing down her back. He wanted to reach out and wrap the silky strands around his hand. *Ooh later, first I make her cum on my tongue.*

"I will try and break the bond, Seff. You have nothing to fear."

"Don't. You. Dare." He growled the words.

"What? But you said," she began.

His arms around her startled her into looking up at him. Unshed tears shone in her now blue eyes. Seff's stomach clenched at the sight. *Fuck.* He hadn't meant to make her cry. He'd better get on with it before he royally fucked things up.

"Sherry, my feelings *are* different. *I love you!* Now more than ever. Fuck, it's more than that, *I need you.* And God knows, *I want you.* So fucking much it hurts," this time when he bowed his head for a kiss, she didn't resist.

"But you said your feelings changed? I thought–"

"They did. They grew. I love you so much, Sherry Morgan, I want to spend the rest of our lives together."

"Oh, Seff," she moaned into his mouth, as his thick arms crushed her body to his. He broke off their kiss too soon.

"Say it, baby," he whispered as he teased the edges of her mouth with his lips. Her arousal made it hard for him to concentrate, but he needed an answer.

"Say what?" She asked in a breathless whisper.

"Say you'll be mine. My mate. My wife. Forever. Please, baby, I need to hear you say it," he begged. Not ashamed at all by how much he needed her.

"Yes! Seff, I will marry you. I will be your mate. I love you," she declared as he picked her up and swirled her around the room. Her laughter rang out and he locked his lips onto hers, sealing their promise to one another with a soul-searing kiss.

They didn't make it to the bedroom. Seff peeled her out of the gauzy dress and claimed every inch of his Witch. He kissed, licked, fondled, and loved every bit of her. From her beautiful body, to her powerful magic, and her gorgeous heart.

His Sherry. Mine. Forever.

Hours later they lay atop his bed in a tangle of limbs and sheets. An empty pizza box and a six pack of soda littered the floor after their second bout of lovemaking had caused some serious munchies leading Sherry to conjure some food from the kitchen to their bedroom.

She could say theirs now as the decision had been made that she would move in with him. She would be part of his Pack.

Her life had taken so many turns, but this was everything she had every wanted. She could open another salon in Maccon City, like the one she had in Northern, New Jersey. She could still work as a healer and teacher for Witches in the surrounding covens. But mostly she could be with her one true mate.

Seff loved her, and he accepted her. Magic and all. He was everything she ever wanted. She smiled as she listened to the sound of his heart while he slept.

The incessant knock of something on the window had her looking up. The first thing she'd done when they'd returned was she removed all of Vasco's charms and crystals. In her haste, she had not set up any magical blockers and now regretted the oversight.

She stood up and sighed as she clothed herself in a robe with a wave of her hand. Then she wandered over to the window. She opened it and was greeted to a portal where she could see the entire Elders Trust gathered.

The assembly of Witches looked her over, some amused, others not, as their leader, one Reginald Ardum, spoke to her.

"Shereen Morgan, we have been patiently waiting for you to update us on your progress in finding a mate, but you have been lax in your duties," he began, but was cut off by a growl coming from behind her.

She did not need to turn to know Seff was standing there ready to come to her aid should she need it. The fact that he didn't barge in made her heart swell with love. He trusted her, knew her capable, and waited until she asked for help before step-ping in. *That was so hot.*

"Yes, well, it has been a busy few weeks. At any rate, I am already mated-"

"To a dog?" Someone interrupted.

Sherry's eyes blazed red as anger seeped into her veins. She focused on the fool who uttered the foul question and with a wave of her hand the oversized Witch shrunk down to a tiny lap dog.

"That, ladies and gentlemen, is a dog. My mate is a Wolf," with that she closed the window and after a long incantation sealed the manor from all uninvited magical invasion.

"Are you alright, baby," Seff's voice brought her back down from the high of using so much magic at once.

She turned and fell into his embrace, out of breath and heady with the knowledge that he'd stood by her side. She nuzzled his lips and he opened his, ready for her.

Their tongues dueled with each other and Sherry felt her insides burn to be closer. Without releasing her hold on his wide shoulders, she soon had them both naked and panting.

She needed him. Now. His erection bobbed against the softness of her belly, and she knew he needed her just as much.

"I need you," she whispered urgently as she pushed him down into the mattress.

"And I you, Sherry, sweet, sweet Sherry," he growled her name as she sat astride him.

He kissed his way from her lips, down her throat to her heavy breasts. She loved the way he paid homage to them both. Licking and laving attention on each hard peak.

She grabbed hold of his cock and lifted her hips, impaling herself on him with one hard thrust. He bit down on the underside of her breast in his passion and her channel squeezed him tight.

Pleasure made her swoon, but Seff took charge. He grabbed her hips and moved her up and down until she cried out, "Harder, Seff."

He switched their positions, his muscles tight as he loomed over her.

"Anything you want," he growled as he pumped wildly into her heat.

He reached between them and found her clit with his thumb. He twisted and rubbed until she flew over the edge, only then did he take his pleasure.

"Seff, I love you," she cried out.

"You are mine. I love you, Sherry," he groaned.

Afterwards, Sherry snuggled in his arms as the sun rose from beyond the stand of trees outside his window. She smiled at the play of light as it streamed through the shades to the hardwood floor.

"What are you thinking about?" he whispered and pulled her closer.

"I was thinking that this is all like some kind of fairy tale," she smiled against his chest.

"What? Us?"

"Yeah, us, the Witch and the Werewolf, you know?"

"Well, I hope you like happy endings, cause I plan to keep you happy for a long, long time, baby."

"Oh, really? And how long is that then, Seff McAllister?" she teased.

"Forever, of course."

"Really now?" she sighed as his hands roamed over her body.

"Of course, *the Witch and the Werewolf live happily ever after*."

"I wouldn't have it any other way," she said.

The End.

WOLF BRIDE

THE MACCONWOOD PACK TALES 1

A MACCONWOOD PACK TALE

WOLF
bride

INTERNATIONAL BESTSELLING AUTHOR
C.D. GORRI

BLURB

One bride, two Wolves, and a love neither of them knew was possible.

He is the first son of the Alpha, a warrior, and a Hound of God. Duty bound to secure the future of his Pack.

He must sacrifice his freedom and marry the lass of his father's choosing, but a chance meeting changes his mind.

She is the property of her father. A woman with a secret and a yearning for the truth. Lies, threats, and betrayal are just some of the forces driving their future.

Will Eoghan and Ailis find true love in spite of it all?

Find out how it all began in this prequel to the Macconwood Pack Series.

PRONUNCIATION & TRANSLATIONS

Eoghan: *Owen*

Ailis: *Alice*

Leine: *Laynya* (a shirt or tunic on men, a dress on women)

Cota: *Coe Tah* (coat)

Inar: *Ee Nar* (Jacket)

Plaide: *Played* (blanket)

Failte: *Fal Cha* (Welcome)

Oidhre: *Ay Va* (Heir)

Baile na nGascioch Conriochtai: (Village of the Warrior Wolves)

Uisce Beatha: *Ishca Baha* (whiskey)

Benedicat omnis hic ambulare in nebula, nos ab hoste, protégé occulos: (Latin) *Curse all here to walk in the fog, protect us from their eyes!*

PROLOGUE

War, famine, blood feud, and more plague the Wolves of Northern Ireland. With the English tightening the noose, Dark Witches running amok, and the Hounds of God losing their foothold in Britannia, tensions are running high. A marriage to join Packs is the only way forward to foster peace amongst the Werewolves of the Emerald Isle, but for those closely involved, peace may come at too high a price.

Thunder sounded overhead and icy rain poured down from the darkening skies. Eoghan MacContire's blonde hair stuck to his forehead and neck from the vicious onslaught of weather. He tilted his head back and opened his mouth to the frigid yet refreshing water.

He sloshed it around and spit it out on the red-stained, muddy ground. The acrid stench of blood and dark magic was still strong in the air.

His mail was thick with the gory remnants of battle. With any luck, the rain would wash most of it away. Cleansing the Earth, but unfortunately, not his mind.

Eoghan wiped his sword on the bottom of his tunic and placed it back inside it's leather scabbard. He exhaled and pulled off the mail shirt that sat atop his plain, wool leine. The garment was heavy and wet with the blood of his enemies. It would need a good scrubbing.

Eoghan looked around in disgust at the hovel where they'd found the Dark Coven casting their forbidden magic. They chose a secluded part of the forest to practice their rituals. Dead animals hung from the trees that surrounded the enclosure.

He walked from corpse to hanging corpse and noted the shape his path made. The Witches' offerings formed an inverted pentacle. A sure sign of evil.

Most of the beasts were freshly killed, but some were rotten and decayed with their bones clearly visible. Runes were carved into the trunks of those trees from which they hung.

Eoghan did not recognize the markings as Irish or Celtic. *Must be Demonspeak*, he thought, *the tongue of the damned*. He crossed himself and continued his walk.

He spat on the ground next to the rotting corpse of the so-called Head Witch of this particular coven. She looked too young to be the mistress and yet she readily claimed the title when they attacked.

His gaze sharpened as he took in the self-mutilation evident on her corpse. She looked as if she'd been dead a fortnight instead of just a few hours. Still, her face was not as heavily lined as the last Head Witch he'd killed. Something was off, but he couldn't put a finger on it.

He kicked the ground and stalked away, mail shirt in hand. The battle was over, and they were victorious, he'd do well to focus on that. His men fought bravely, with speed and accuracy.

The world was a little bit safer this night because of it. He shouldn't worry over the small niggling feeling in the back of his mind that all was not settled.

There were other things that needed his attention. He tossed his heavy mail shirt and sword to one of his men.

"Oi there, Tom Kelly, see to it these are properly cleaned and looked after."

"Aye, I shall, sir."

"My thanks, son," Tom Kelly was a new Wolf, a

C.D. GORRI

lad of just sixteen years. He had his first Change only a few months ago, but his calling to the Hounds of God came immediately upon that Change. He was a loyal lad.

It was an honor to assign him such a detail as taking care of Eoghan's chain mail. 'Twas a valuable possession. He received it as tribute from a Scotsman. He was a mercenary Werewolf who hired himself out to the Gallowglass.

They'd fought a battle together and Eoghan saved the man's life. He in turn made him a gift of the mail shirt. It served him well every battle since then. This day was no exception.

He'd had a close call with a particularly nasty Witch who came at him with a sharpened spear and a crazed look in his black eyes. He was a shadow of a man, possessed by whatever Demon he'd sold his soul to. The Witch flung the weapon with the strength of Beelzebub himself.

His aim was true. It would have killed Eoghan had the tip not stuck in one of the small mail links right over his heart. Eoghan snapped the Witch's neck with his bare hands and only realized after the fact that he'd almost lost his life.

His stomach clenched at the thought. There was still so much he wanted to see and do. A dreadful unease settled over him. It was a nagging bitch of a feeling and he tried to shake it, but nothing worked.

Once all seven Witches' corpses were decapitated and burned, their Demons sent back to hell, Eoghan ordered his men to see to the cleansing of the wood surrounding the area. He normally took part in the healing ritual, but he was too restless. He couldn't focus enough to recite the Latin prayers needed for the ritual.

His head was reeling, he'd almost died. On top of that, the Witches magic had used up the strength of two full fields that were almost ready to harvest, one barley and one wheat. The failing crops alerted the Hounds to the presence of Witches in that area. A thing like that could mean starvation for the people in that area.

Eoghan volunteered for the mission and was glad he was the one who found the parasites before they sucked the land dry. Technically, it was not Greyback Pack territory, but this mission was overseen by the Hounds of God; therefore, he was granted access to the place.

Witches were a scourge on society. He'd see them all burn if he could. *Agh, enough*! He needed to calm his blood. He stilled himself and took a deep breath. The full moon was days away, but his Wolf already looked out of his eyes. He thanked God for it.

One of the worst things about being a Werewolf was missing that other intricate part of yerself in the long stretch of days between moons. He had to wait only a while longer and he'd be able to run as his Wolf. Only then would he be free as he never could be as a man.

As the first son of the Alpha, Eoghan was bound by his duties to his Pack because of his position. He didn't want to think about any of that now. He shook his wet head and stripped off the thick wool inar that sheltered him from the elements.

He tossed it to the same Kelly lad who held his mail and sword. He could stay in that place no longer and so he made his way deeper into the woods.

His men would take care of everything. The priests who travelled with them would put to rights the remnants of their battle. He'd have a few hours to himself. Well deserved, as they were, he still thought about going back to help.

'Twas his place as Lieutenant General in the Hounds' war party to stay with his men, but right then he needed to put some distance between himself and all that death. A moment alone, where he could breathe in something clean and untainted. The foul black-magicked air they'd been inhaling still clogged his lungs.

He walked nigh on five miles from the battle site

before slowing down. Perhaps it was far enough. The sound of running made him stop in his tracks. Eoghan stifled a growl and crouched behind a large, moss-covered boulder that sat on the bank of the small stream he'd found amongst the trees.

He strained to listen over the sounds of the running water and the icy rain. The pounding footsteps were nearer now. He peeked out from behind the large rock and found himself gazing at the most beautiful sight he'd ever seen.

His supernaturally enhanced eyesight allowed him to see the maiden clearly. *Aye, but she is a glorious sight,* he thought as he gazed upon her. The rain was coming down in earnest, but it didn't seem to bother the wood nymph.

She tossed her head back and lifted the hem of her long, plain dress to high enough to reveal long shapely legs. He barely got a look at them before she moved to stand knee deep in the rushing waters of the stream. He turned his body so he would be in a good position to act fast should she fall, but the lass was steady on her feet.

The wind howled around them and the rain dropped down even harder. Despite his Wolf-sharpened vision, Eoghan could barely make out her face. Especially with her head tilted back as it was. But by his oath, her *body*! That he had no trouble discerning for she wore neither cota nor plaide.

She had a trim waist that flared out to well-rounded hips. Her breasts were high and supple, her nipples visible through the thin layers of material as the fabric became soaked with rainwater. She laughed aloud, a bright, pleasant sound that created a yearning inside of his gut.

He was mesmerized. He watched her like a starving man gazed longingly at a loaf of bread. She danced in the stream, turning, round and round, in circles with her arms held out wide. Like some wild and untamed thing. By God's eyes, he wanted her then and there for his own.

He wanted more than just to possess her, he wanted to join her in her freedom. To taste the wildness on her lips. She had an unbroken beauty to her. Not bound by the constraints of society's definition of decorum.

It would be a shame to see her caged. He wondered what hell she'd escaped from to see her so joyous amidst a thunderstorm deep in the wood. But she was grand, he'd give her that.

Eoghan never felt such a longing. It was a deeply rooted sensation that made him want to do things he ne'er thought himself capable of. He had to still himself so as not to reach out and pull her to his chest.

Who is she? What mystery brought her now to this place? He licked his lips and studied the maiden as she reveled in the harsh Irish weather. As if she were part of it and the land around her.

Aye, go on then lass, drink it all in. Eoghan had never seen anything to match her in all his life. Not even his stallion, Bryn. At nineteen hands the beast was the largest in the land. Necessary for carrying a man who, as a Werewolf, stood a head taller than most and weighed almost half again the average man, for all the thick ropes of muscle that covered his body.

Right then, Eoghan's only concern was for the feminine body that danced but a short distance away. He focused on the small rivulets of rainwater that ran down her long neck and disappeared between the mounds of flesh visible from the top of her dress.

He felt a stirring in his loins as he watched her womanly curves perfectly outlined in her rain-soaked gown. She was just as a woman should be. That stirring turned to full on lust in a matter of moments as he imagined running his hands over the soft flesh hidden beneath the wet fabric.

Desire was something Eoghan was familiar with, but this time 'twas different. He never felt such a tightening in the pit of his stomach. His heart raced inside of his chest. What's more, he could see his

Wolf in his mind's eye. The great beast was standing at attention as he watched her.

Was it some kind of warning? This sudden intense awareness? He didn't know if he should trust it or not. Maybe she was a fairy and not to be trifled with by the likes of him. *A fantastical notion indeed, Eoghan MacContire.*

He cursed under his breath. He wasn't used to thinking like a fool. He almost missed it as she leaned down as if to grab something with her long delicate fingers. Her left foot slipped a fraction of a space and Eoghan started towards her before she completely lost her footing on the moss-covered rocks. He leapt forward like a stag and held her safe by her arm till she regained her composure.

"Are you in need of aid, my lady?"

Bright eyes, blue as a morning sky, flashed at him. He didn't know if she was more startled by her near miss or by his sudden presence. She looked like some sort of otherworldly being standing amidst the trees and the stream. The rain and the elements didn't seem to bother her one bit.

She was even better looking the closer he got to her. Soaked to the bone as she was, he couldn't imagine another who could even compare to the lass. Her pale skin was clear with a hint of rose in her cheeks, her big blue eyes were wide and surrounded by thick, dark lashes, and her hair wound down her back in a long braid. He wished he could tell what color it was, but 'twas far too wet for him to discern.

"Nay, sir, I am in no need of yer aid and I'll thank ye to release my arm," she said. Her voice was clear and strong, indicative of the woman who spoke. Eoghan's gaze roamed over the strangely enticing female from head to toe.

"I'd love to oblige ye, miss, but if I do that, ye'd fall clean over into the stream and I'd have to jump in after ye."

"Can't ye swim, sir?"

"Aye, but I'd much rather take hold of ye from solid ground than in that frigid water."

"I'll not ask ye again, sir, release my arm."

"Yer not very grateful. I say, would yer family be for yer safe return?"

"Wouldst thou be grateful if a great beast of a man first spied on ye then refused to let go of yer person though he was asked twice?"

"Let's out of the water then and I shall release yer arm, lady. Prithee, I cannot have it on my conscience were ye to be upended downstream when I could have prevented such."

"I am not entirely certain yer grasping the fact that I've no wish for a savior!"

"I don't think I'm the only one with very little

understanding on things, after all, tis not I who stands ankle deep in a running stream with lightning brewing in the heavens!"

"Prithee, tell me more about good sense when ye wear naught in all this wetness, but a leine! A thin one at that!"

"Doth thou judge me for the size of my purse then?"

"Nay, I've no right to judge ye for yer purse size. My apologies, sir, now my arm, please?"

His mystery maiden averted her eyes, away from his exposed torso, but Eoghan could see her interest. He grinned down at her. He supposed he should have done up his laces, but he liked the heat that he witnessed flashing in her blue eyes when she gazed upon his bare skin.

Indeed, he liked it just as much as her quick retorts. That was unique amongst the women he'd met. A man in his position was required to be seen at certain social functions with society's best and most eligible ladies. He'd had little use for those parties and often did not attend.

The few misses that he did meet were silly waspish things that he had no use for. *Aye, give me an honest lass as this*, he thought to himself. She stole another look at his exposed skin and Eoghan found his appetite for her increased. He held her elbow when she would have pulled away and was rewarded with the narrowing of her blue eyes.

His heart thudded heavily inside of his chest at that look. The lady was brave as well as beautiful. A mystery for certain. Curiosity burned inside of him like a wildfire. *What was she doing out here alone?*

"By yer leave, I shall escort ye to yer father's house, tis not safe for a lady-"

"Nay, sir, I shall take my leave alone, after all I got here without ye."

"Alone? Tis getting dark, I would see to yer safety."

"Stay, sir, I shall see to mine own safety."

"What is it you hide from me, lady?" Eoghan inhaled as he tried to get a read on the wild lass in his grip.

Alas, the smell of battle still lingered in his nostrils. He bent his head down to the nape of her neck, but his nose picked up nothing of *her*. Only a stream of fragrances that masked her real identity. Cloves, rosemary, heather, lavender, and some other exotic oils. *A kitchen or laundry maid perhaps?*

The combination of scents, blood, metal, spice, rain and wet earth, left him without the use of his Wolf's nose to tell him who or what she was. Still, he knew she was no Witch. Her bright eyes and healthy teeth told him that.

C.D. GORRI

"My lady, I would be glad to be of service to you. If it pleases you to know, my name-"

"Nay, sir, pray do not tell me yer name."

"Why? Don't ye wish to know me?" Eoghan bantered easily with the lass, but inside he was in turmoil.

His every instinct was to take her and possess her as his own. *Could this be matebonding*, he wondered? The ancient notion of a Wolf finding his mate upon first sight was sung about by minstrels and bards, but he'd never seen it in person.

Lust and longing raced through Eoghan's blood, and something more. A sort of heightened awareness of the lady in front of him, a tightening in his gut. It was a heady and strong feeling though he could not give it a name. The lightness in the atmosphere soon gave way to a dangerous sort of tension.

He leaned in closer, anticipation building up inside of him like steam in a kettle. He was just about ready to burst when she raised a slender hand and placed it gently on his chest. The light brush of her fingers on that part of his body revealed from the open ties of his soaked leine sent lightning shooting all through his body.

His breath came heavier now as his chest tightened in response to her light touch. In his mind's eye, he pictured her supple form moving wildly beneath him as he penetrated her soft velvet core over and over again. He could almost hear her groans and taste her honey on his tongue.

"I'll have an answer, lady."

"I know not how to answer thee, sir, soon I must leave and tis likely I'll not see ye again."

"Aye, but sweet lass, right now, we both are here in the wood, alone, in the rain, and Heaven's love is shining down on us right in this moment."

"It makes me sad, sir, for we have no time, all would be over before it even started."

Her softly spoken words touched him like a warm caress. Eoghan's heart thumped wildly in his chest for it meant she felt the attraction between them as did he. Perhaps there was hope then.

"Nay, my lady, tis not over yet. I shall continue to hold you here till I have had my fill of ye."

"I am not free. Ye must leave me as I am."

Eoghan felt his beast growl at the thought of who stood to gain this maid for a wife. He wanted to hunt down his rival and tear his throat out with his teeth, but who was he to argue. Eoghan himself was betrothed.

"This is all the time we have, lady, will ye not succumb?"

He took the maid by her chin and forced her eyes up to his. What he saw there reflected in her eyes were feelings as intense as his own. He stood a hair's breadth away from her, the pounding inside her chest audible to his supernatural ears.

"I am promised-"

"Damn the man who claims ye as his. He may have rights to yer future, lady, but yer present, *here and now*, is mine!"

Eoghan wrapped the lass close to his chest. The feel of her pressed against him sizzled through his body like a burning flame. There was no denying the intensity of his desire for her.

He bent his head and kissed her lips with all the pent-up passion he had inside of him. It was like being caught in the eye of the storm. Everything else faded away.

Deafening silence filled his ears as he tasted the sweet saltiness of her mouth. He growled deep inside his chest when she pressed herself more fully against him.

She sighed into the kiss, allowing him better access to her mouth. *Enchanting*. She wound her hands through his wet locks and held on as he delved inside of her heated mouth without fear or guile. No pretense or illusions. *Nay, no lying or falseness here*, his Wolf felt the honesty that made up her very being.

Wanton thoughts of lust and desire filled his

brain, but there was more to it as well. Something familiar about her, though he could not place it.

There was a freshness and tenderness there, but also something powerful and raw. He pressed his hardened arousal against her hips, expecting her to swoon, but she didn't move away. She was fierce in her stance, meeting him stroke for stroke with tongue, lips, and teeth. *I must have her.*

Her breath was fresh and sweet, her body sumptuous, and her response intoxicating as he dove headfirst into her embrace. The rain that fell on them trickled down to a stop. A thick fog began to rise from the ground, losing their feet and legs in the misty whiteness.

Huge droplets of rain clung to his clothes, hair, and eyelashes, but he cared not. He was lost in their kiss. Longing threatened to consume him. He wanted to throw her down on the muddied ground and bury himself inside of her.

"I am mad for you, lady, wilt thou have me?"

"Sir? I, I-"

The temptation to take her right then and there was almost too much for him. He dipped his head to take her lips once more, determined to claim this maid, but the call of his man, Kelly, brought him back to reality. *Far too soon.*

C.D. GORRI

"Tis finished, my lord! We are set to break camp! My lord, the fog grows thick, where art thou?!"

His Wolf growled in his mind's eye, *take her, claim her as mate.* He wanted too, sure as he needed to breathe air. The stomping footsteps of his men through the wood were getting closer and he'd not have her in front of an audience.

"Halt! I shall come to you!" Eoghan ended the kiss and called out to his men.

Glazed blue eyes met his dark ones. *Funny,* he thought, *her eyes are blue as are mine when I am Wolf. Mine,* the growled word reverberated through his head.

Perhaps he could bring her home with him, take her as his mistress? Even as the thought entered his mind, he dismissed it. She was not made to be a man's mistress and he could not live a lie.

While he was pondering the situation, the maiden raised a hand to her mouth. For some reason, the astonishment on her face was nearly his undoing.

Before he could speak, before he could put words to the tumultuous feelings inside of him, the lass reached out a trembling hand and brushed it across his face. Then she grabbed her sodden skirts and ran through the mist.

"There you are, my lord," Tom Kelly walked up to

him and tried to look to see what it was Eoghan was so intent on.

There was, fortunately, nothing there. Not even a trace of her in the fog. She was gone.

The Wolf in him demanded he make chase; the man ran his hands through his hair and stood there powerless.

"I let her go."

"Who, my lord?"

"*Her*, Kelly."

I

Three weeks later...

"I am *Chief of the Name*, Alpha of the Greyback, and I am also yer father! Ye will marry the Lady Dungannon!"

"Nay, I will marry none but the maid from the wood, father! Especially not some long-toothed pup for the sake of alliance!"

"The girl has but nineteen summers and that maid was naught but yer imagination! None of yer men saw the lass!"

"That many years and Dungannon's daughter has not wed nor received proposal? She must be some scabbed cur or slow of wit, either way she will not do for me. My sight is on the other."

"*Ye* will marry because *I* command it. Yer sight? *Yer sight*, indeed! Yer men take ye for a fool or perhaps bespelled! I had to assure them ye had been examined by Fr. Martin! The lass is of high birth and is a normal to boot! Now, obey, *pup of mine*, or doth ye challenge yer father and Alpha?" The first Eoghan MacContire stood his full height and flashed his eyes at his son.

"By my oath, I will do as you command if I cannot find the lady, but father, I don't want to give up my search yet. If she be the one, my *matebond*, then I shall not lose my freedom to another! Please–"

"God's blood, boy, I'll not say it again."

Power laced the words of Eoghan's father and forced the younger Wolf to avert his eyes. Anger and defiance refused to allow him to stoop his shoulders or bow his head, but he knew better than to stare down the man who was both his Alpha and sire.

He wanted more from life than to be a pawn for the Pack. He wanted adventure. He wanted to explore new worlds. And yes, he wanted to find the lass from the woods, to see if she was his heart's true desire. *Mine own true mate.*

Anyway, the Dungannon lass was more Brit than Irish! What care he is she be *normal* or Wolf or cat even? How could his father think she'd do for him?

The entire North of Ireland hated all things English. He had a special loathing for all who were favored by Bess including the bastard Raleigh for the lands he took and the Irish blood he spilled for his Virgin Queen.

Of course, he admitted to himself, he did admire the Queen's favorite for his ability to sail across the world and step on land untouched by corruption and greed. Eoghan would love to see the New World. To bring his father's Wolves there, to expand their territory, but his *da* would not hear of it. As he would not hear tales of Eoghan's maiden.

His father insisted their future was there, on Irish soil. Eoghan's shoulder's slumped. *A wife. What would he do with a wife, especially one he did not love?*

He'd have to give up the life he'd dreamt for himself. It was almost more than he could bear. The low growl emanating from his father's chest weighed down on him. The power of the Alpha demanded he get down on his knees in submission, but Eoghan fought back the urge. He was too angry to play the penitent child.

He kept his spine straight. His face a mask. Werewolves were too attuned to body language for him to let his guard down. He didn't want his father to guess what he was thinking. Nay, that would not do.

He inhaled steady breaths and wished he hadn't pulled his pale blonde hair back from his face that morning. If it was loose, least he could run his hands through it, and not stand there clenching his fists. His father hated that he kept his hair long.

'Twas not the popular hairstyle for young men of rank in society, but within the Pack, many a male allowed his hair to grow beyond the current fashion. Either way, it was his singular way of defying his father who preferred his sons to wear the trim hair of a monk.

His brother Lyall cut his hair in compliance with their da's wishes, but not he. He recalled many a maid who preferred his silky platinum locks to his brother's short, dark hair.

He hadn't even looked at a wench in weeks. These days, he found he could not without comparing her to his wood nymph. The image of her standing in her wet dress, arms wide twirling about in the stream on the day of that battle against the Dark Ones was ingrained in his memory.

Indeed, she haunted his dreams. Her pale skin and long hair, especially the taste of her. By God's eyes, he wanted her more for the time they had spent apart. He could still see her startling blue eyes gazing up at him from where her perfect form clung tightly to him. His body grew hard just thinking of her. *God's truth, she must be my mate.*

Did she think of him? Did she think him attractive

or enticing? His mother had called him fair many a time when she was alive. He had chiseled features, fair skin, pink lips, and a tall lean body roped with muscle and designed for speed and agility. Even his beard was flaxen.

Oddly enough, his Wolf was pure black except for one white forepaw, and where his eyes were dark as a man, they glowed ice blue as Wolf. *Still pretty*, however, that much was true. He inherited his silvery pale locks from his blessed mother.

He felt foolish for thinking of a wench he'd never see again in the face of his *da's* misery. His heart still ached at the thought of his ma's poor soul. She departed this world not a month passed.

She was a *normal* and as such was susceptible to human illness. She suffered from a disease of the lungs. Seeing her in pain was almost too much for him to bear, but he was a good son and he stayed by her side. *As did his father*.

His father who stood before him now angry as a, well, *as a Wolf*. Eoghan regretted that he was the cause of his ire. He respected his *da*. Loved him even. But how could he heed his command? Especially having seen the torment and pain his *da* went through at the loss of his mother.

Eoghan wondered if he would be able to stand the pain of losing a wife to such torture as his father had done. *Marriage? No.* How could he marry one when his dreams were consumed by another?

"The wedding will proceed."

"Nay, *da*!"

"It is done!"

Ever since his mother's death, his father was over-worried with seeing his eldest son married. Eoghan looked at his father, he was not the smiling *da* of his youth. *Nay*, gray and silver streaks shone in his hair where they never were before. Lines crinkled at the corners of his eyes and heavy, dark circles ringed them, telling of his pain and sleepless nights.

"Father, perhaps if you rested some you would come to see my side of it–"

"Enough! You will marry the Dungannon lass as was promised. What kind of man would break an oath such as this, son? Are you asking me to be liar and coward?"

"No, sir, of course Not, I just–"

A servant entered the room with parchment in hand. He was out of breath. The smell of human sweat, and dirt filled Eoghan's nostrils. He was a messenger, one of those trusted to present to his da, Chief of the name to all normals in the village. He bowed and handed the rolled paper to Eoghan's father.

The interruption gave Eoghan time to think. *Tis*

true, a bond was made, he admitted silently. He was betrothed to the Dungannon's daughter before he went to fight that battle in the woods. The one that had changed his life.

The facts were against him, but he left his heart in the woods that day. He would be a liar if he wed another. But how did he tell his *da*? 'Twas hopeless to argue for love. Loyalty and duty were paramount.

He had to make him see they had no need to adhere to some backward tradition that forced marriage between strangers. *And for what? Land? Silver? Weapons? Meat? Tis not the price of his freedom worth far more than that?* He wanted to choose his mate, to explore the brave New World, and to claim a piece of it for the Pack.

His Pack, *the Greyback*, was plenty wealthy. They had land, cattle, pigs, and bountiful fields of grain. They'd recently started cultivating a crop of potatoes that hailed from the New World.

They could feed their people through the next ten winters without aid. He had no need for that trifle of a dowry the Dungannon had sent with his man. It was a damned pittance!

"Da, you know the Dungannon insults us with that lowly dowry. The lands and money were not what was promised, tis a breach of contract, sir-"

"The dowry is of no import."

"But da-"

"Son, land and money are not the entirety of it. The Dungannon clan holds sway with Britain and the lords of the Virgin Queen. Tis necessary to protect the Hounds!"

It was true then, just as Eoghan had feared. This match was not personal. Dungannon's influence in England was what they, the Greyback, with their roots in the Catholic Church and their vows to the Hounds of God, did greatly need. It was a dangerous time for Catholics in Britannia. All the more dangerous for Werewolves who worked for the Church.

No matter how great the deed, no matter how many times the Hounds saved mankind, they were the rivals of many in Britain simply because of their faith. Their strong ties to Rome made them the enemy of the Queen.

The Dungannon, though raised a Catholic, had since converted to Protestant when he took his English wife. Eoghan had no love for the English, but as far as faith was concerned his attitude was, more or less, to each his own.

He was proud to be Catholic. Proud to be associated with the Hounds of God. His duty was to ensure the flourishment of not only Werewolves, but normals too. And what of his wife-to-be? She was half-English, probably Protestant too. Would she look down on him and his Catholic faith?

He would not care either way what religion his wife kept, as long as he loved the lady. But he did not love this maid. He did not even know her. That was the whole of it.

If he needs choose a wife then why not the lady of the wood? Were she the lass he was to wed, then by God, he'd dance all the way down the aisle! He'd take her to wife without hesitation!

A beautiful normal like her would bear many a fine son, no doubt! She was luscious and lively. Definitely fit for the kinds of adventures he had in mind.

He'd never thought about it much before, but many Werewolves preferred normals to wife. Some Packs were strict about that kind of thing. Female Wolves were mostly kept quiet and out of sight. Never was there a highborn lass who was she-Wolf to his knowledge.

Though how they managed that, he did not know. Mayhaps it came from wedding and breeding with so many normals. Either way, he wanted no part of the Dungannon's daughter.

His mind was set on the mystery maiden who managed to capture his heart with one kiss. He didn't mind the idea that his lady was not familiar with the supernatural world. Though he imagined it would be a difficult conversation between them.

He was a skilled and trained warrior of his Pack. That would not cease upon taking his vows. Eoghan's life was fraught with danger.

He was responsible for sending many a Demon back to Hell. And all for a world that would never know his sacrifice. Still, he could protect his own. That much, he was sure of.

"The contract is signed by the Dungannon. There is naught to be done by yer whining here. Now leave me or, by yer sainted mother, I will deliver my wrath upon yer head the likes of which you have never seen."

"The Dungannon has neglected the terms of the contract! He's sent not half of what was promised!"

"I know that, son, do ye think me daft? Tis matters not one bit! Ye will meet the Lady Ailis and ye will enter into the handfasting with an honest and loyal heart."

"But father-"

"That is all. Yer bride comes soon. Ready yerself."

The hallway that opened to the kitchen stores was doubly wide. It had to be for the cooks and their carts and trays that made their way up and down the path throughout the course of a day. At this hour, however, it was empty, dark, and quiet.

The servants had all gone to bed and the fires had been banked down for the night. Still, it would be just another hour or two before the first wave of kitchen help came to start the morning baking.

They would in turn be followed by another group of servants responsible for the preparation of the vast selection of fowl and game that would be roasted throughout the day. This was the way of such places where hundreds needed to be fed each morning and evening.

Castle MacContire, as the house was affectionately known by members of Greyback Pack and normals in the surrounding villages on their land, was a well-kept stronghold. Indeed, those who knew their truth, called their village *Baile na nGascioch Conriochtai*, or Village of the Warrior Wolves.

'Twas a modern village and a thriving one. All the old timber and sod huts had been replaced in the last hundred years or so with strong and durable stone dwellings. There were two large towers, a stone wall, and several smaller outer buildings. Presently, there were smithies working on the construction of an enormous stone and iron gate.

The design was supposed to praise the Wolves of the Pack and their connection to the Church and God. It was foolish to wave a red flag in the face of that bull of a Tudor monarch, but, though it be a sin, pride was abundant among those who dwelt in Northern Ireland. *Wolf or not.*

Inside, the castle was opulently decorated with enormous tapestries woven with golden thread. They graced the walls of the great banquet hall and throughout the bedrooms and sitting rooms of the family and honored guests.

The furnishings were just as fine, draped with gold and heavy brocade fabrics. Fine linens made up every bed and they were topped with fur lined blankets. Heavily lacquered tables and benches, as well as sturdy upholstered chairs, were placed throughout to accommodate the number and size of the Pack's Wolves.

The Castle was especially known for its excellent privies or garderobes. Unlike other castles, where human waste was left for months at a time, the sensitive noses of the Werewolves required them to be emptied and cleaned daily. The Chief of the Name forbade the disposal of human waste in the local streams as well. Overall, the village was fresh smelling and common illness hardly affected any who lived there.

It was a grand place, it's visage much like the old Irish royal castles across the countryside. Lyall MacContire approved of the buildings. He relished the thought that one day, Castle MacContire and everything inside of it would be his.

He crept across the freshly swept stone floor on leather soled boots. The smells of grain and fresh killed fowl and deer were faint in the air. His Wolf was smallish, but cunning in his senses. It disturbed him that he found no trace of the one he sought. Neither by scent nor sound.

The lingering odor of the human servants from the village, who came and went daily was still in the air. Some of them lived inside the castle itself. Lyall sneered at the thought, those vermin did not deserve to sleep in the same place where he did.

The present Greyback Alpha, his revered *da*, took too much care of the local *normals*. Lyall sneered at the thought of their treatment. Such respect should be reserved for the Werewolves alone.

'Twas an absurdity he'd pondered his entire life. He recognized his superiority amongst the beasts that roamed the Earth and aimed to best those who would look down on him as second son. Every single one of them would bow to him. Including that dolt of a brother that he was forced to endure.

That pale-haired oaf was little more than a weapon with a heartbeat. He was all brawn and no brains. Lyall studied and read their histories, even those scrolls taken down in the ancient language of the Celts that many of the Pack had long since forgotten. He studied long and hard. When he brought his findings to his father, he was told that the Pack had no room for old stories about deals with Witches and ancient prophecies.

"Why can't ye take an interest in wrestling and handling a sword like yer brother, eh? Put down those dusty tomes, Lyall, and prove yer worth as a man should! Yer my second son, ye must earn yer place here."

Lyall retreated into himself after that. He knew he could never best Eoghan in strength, so he began studying even harder to his father's consternation. As they grew older, Eoghan received all the attention and accolades. That pretty face of his was just another nail in his coffin as far as Lyall was concerned.

Eoghan had been born blessed and lucky, but he had not the brains to attempt the ideals to which Lyall himself aimed. He didn't deserve his position. The fool would never get the chance to run this Pack. He'd make sure of it. Even if it meant getting in bed with the Devil himself.

He smiled at the thought of his brother's bloodied corpse hanging from a rope. Even better, his father's right next to him. The old man had overlooked him far too often for Lyall to feel anything but hostility and rage, but his time would soon come.

He stilled and waited. The person whose audience he sought would know he was there, but there was often the show of making him, *second son of the Alpha*, wait for her. He rolled his dark eyes. He'd keep up the pretenses for now. The ends were well worth the means after all.

He stood straight; he'd not sully his fine shirt with whatever grime clung to these walls. Lyall frowned at the thought of soot from the kitchen fires blackening the leather soles of his fine made boots. *When he was Alpha the floor would be scrubbed thrice daily! Maybe he'd have servants carry around carpets just for him to stand on! Ha! That would be grand!*

"Has all been made ready?" A raspy voice sounded in the dark causing him to gasp.

"You are late, lady, I have waited for you some time now." Lyall straightened his tunic. He did not like being caught unawares.

"Aye, my lord, but what I can give you is worth the wait is it not, he who should be *Alpha*," the woman said.

She stepped out of the shadows and Lyall kept his face still. Her dark hair was limp and dull. The bosoms that heaved with each breath over the neckline of her dress were covered in dirt and grime. She stunk of decay, blood, and offal. But all of those were nothing compared to the horror of her face.

The Witch smiled at him, but he managed to keep his disdain inside for he knew it would not please her. She was missing several teeth and what remained were blackened and produced a foul and sickening stench.

One eye was sewn shut, he'd made the mistake of asking about it once, and after she tore out the stitches and showed him the rotting hole, she told him that she gave it to her master as offering. *So, I may better see the truths of my master, Wolf pup.*

"Ye know what I need from ye."

"Yay verily, I am aware of yer needs." He swallowed and closed his eyes a second.

"Are ye prepared to give it then?" The grin on her face was as nasty as the rest of her. Lyall tried not to breathe deeply. He nodded his head.

"Aye, I shall give it ye."

She smiled wide and Lyall backed up a step. This was not going to be an easy feat. The Witch lifted herself onto the side table and pulled up her stained and frayed skirts. She hiked them up over her bruised and scabbed legs to reveal herself to him in a most base manner. Lyall felt his dinner surge in his stomach, but he forced it down.

"Why doth ye tarry, sir? It needs be now. The seed. Now!"

"Don't talk and for God's sake don't smile." He clenched is teeth as he spoke and reached for the bottom of his tunic.

'Twas no use, he was limp and soft as freshly kneaded dough. *Damn it all,* he cursed himself.

"Well? Find yer manhood, then! The door is closing!"

"Aye, hush now!" Lyall took himself in hand. He closed his eyes and thought of his prize. *Riches, land, fame, power, control, his rightful place.* Suddenly, his manhood became engorged. He pumped himself a few times to be sure.

"Yes, I will be Alpha. I will be Alpha," he continued with his mantra until he felt himself harden to the point 'twas needed. He kept both eyes shut and found the entrance to the Witch's slit.

"Grrr. I am the rightful son," he said and impaled the Witch on his staff. Manic with the idea of his own success, Lyall thrust himself into her foul and shriveled body. She was dry and rough and though it pained him, he kept on, ignoring all else.

She cackled deep in her throat and Lyall's eyes flew open. He muffled his scream on the long sleeves of his leine and tried to pull away, but the Witch's claws were on his back and he could not move a muscle.

"Nay, wench! Yer eye, tis black as a bottomless hole!"

"As yer soul, now keep at it, pup. Tis yer youthful seed I require, here," she touched his forehead with her finger and muttered a spell. Where his dick fell limp a moment ago, it once again became hard.

The picture in his head was of a lovely maid with blonde hair and a wet, soft cunny. He pushed himself in and out believing in the bespelled vision, choosing to see the fine lass instead of the foul Dark One. Lyall moaned as pleasure began tingling up his spine. It sickened him, for he knew the truth of it, but he quieted his conscience. He needed to finish his fuck to get what he wanted.

"I will be Alpha!" His final thrust was deep, and he poured himself inside of her foulness.

"Tis done," her gravelly voice echoed in his ears. When he opened his eyes, he was alone in the hallway. His manhood was once again in his hand. Coming from the tip was a thick, putrid, black sludge. He wanted to scream, maybe even to cry, but he bit his tongue.

Lyall's breath hissed in and out of him. He never felt more physically alive. Elated and disgusted at once. He covered himself with his clothes and quickly left the place.

'Twas only a matter of time now.

The road to *Tyrone* was far more perilous than Ailis Dungannon prepared for. They hit many a hole and rock along the well-worn path through that part of the woods where the heather seemed to bloom year-round and the trees grew tall as mountains.

'Twas not a terribly far journey, but an arduous one indeed. They arrived at the gates of the Village of the Warrior Wolves and Castle MacContire at just past midnight.

Ailis felt as though the excursion had lasted a fortnight instead of just a few days. Her stomach turned over itself, nerves ate away whatever measure of composure she had feigned the trip over. She looked to her maid and bit her lower lip. At least she had the comfort of going straight to her rooms.

She was to remain hidden from sight until the ceremony. A surprise for her betrothed as it were. She had no audience with the head of the household upon her arrival. *Thank the Lord.*

She was shown the way to a handsomely decorated chamber by an older house servant. The slight woman had a mean air about her. She never glanced back or spoke a word, just gave them nasty looks as she walked ahead of Ailis and her own lady's maid.

When she left them at the door to her chamber, the maid simply held her rather large nose in the air and walked away. Ailis shot a look to Gwinnie who just shrugged.

She opened the door herself and took a walk around the room. It was decorated richly with intricate tapestries depicting the moon in all her phases and a pack of Wolves in a variety of colors from coal black to a brilliant yellow.

Her lady's maid fetched her a wooden tub and readied pots of hot water for her bath. Ailis enjoyed a nightly bath though many thought she would catch her death. Bathing was a ritual of hers, 'twas the only time she could take off the harsh scent her father bade her wear.

She used the time in the warm water to ready her mind for what was to come. Afterwards, she lay down in the enormous four-post bed with its thick hanging curtains and its intricate carvings of high Celtic crosses and, of course, Wolves.

'Twas beautiful workmanship. The room was a statement, as these things were, of the riches of the household. Clearly, she was highly thought of by the head of the house. *If not by the servants.*

A thick, feather stuffed mattress sat atop a stronger one filled with straw. 'Twas covered with soft linen sheets and a fur lined blanket that was done in a rich, heavy fabric dyed a deep blue and embroidered with golden thread. The bed itself was large enough for more than two people and much finer than anything she had back home.

She felt so small just sitting there in her long night shift with her hair loose down her back. Her mind was still reeling from the idea that soon she'd be someone's wife. If only she knew all that would entail.

Ailis made the sign of the cross and said a quick prayer before diving under the thick blankets. It was cold in the room. Drafty as castles tended to be.

"May the Lord keep you well through the night, my lady," Gwinnie said as she snuffed out the candle.

"Aye, you too Gwinnie. Tomorrow, we shall see just what it is my father has sold me to."

"Don't fret, my lady, all will be well." She curtsied and retreated to her chamber for the night.

Ailis wished she could put faith in her maid's words, but after what she'd been through the past few weeks, it was difficult. Her life and everything she knew was about to change yet again. And not necessarily for the better. She closed her eyes and practiced the breathing exercises Gwinnie had taught her.

They were most useful on nights when she missed that internal contact with her Wolf. She said another quick prayer for forgiveness, for she felt none of the shame her father told her she should feel after her first Change. Her heart was sick with the memory of her father's harsh words to her.

"Nay, it cannot be. How couldst thou betray me like this?! False creature! Thou art cursed!"

She'd somehow shamed him, for all she could not control her very nature. He was Werewolf as men should be, but female Wolves were frowned upon. She felt her stomach tightened and closed her yes. The breathing techniques greatly helped her let go of the stress of it all.

She never understood what her father's Wolves meant when they talked about *the waiting*. Now she knew. The *waiting* was what her *da's* people called the time in-between moons. When Werewolves were cut off from that other part of themselves, the curse of St. Natalis, as it were.

She was new to being Wolf. Her father's Pack did

not value females for one simple reason. They had a difficult time bearing young. *Barren women did not make good matches.* Hence his fury when she had her first Change just a few weeks ago.

The MacContire had sent his second son, a shifty smallish man with dark hair and a nasty look about him to their house. He came to visit her father to negotiate the terms of the contract.

She was told to stay hidden, but there were secret places where she could observe and that is what she did. She prayed her husband to be did not resemble his brother, for the man sent shivers of dread up her spine.

On the second day of his visit Ailis had been hiding in the secret hallway watching when she heard him accuse her father of trying to trick them. Her dad had sent less than the promised dowry. *Cheap bastard.*

The Dungannon was furious to be caught at such a thing. That night he came to her chambers to be sure she hid herself from sight and scent. When she asked him about the dowry, he struck her hard across her face.

She did not cry out. She'd not give the brutal man the satisfaction. The next day, for some unknown reason, the second son of the MacContire was swayed to forgive the discrepancy. *A bribe no doubt.*

Ailis had no feelings on the matter besides relief. She could not stay at her father's house any longer. When she left, he told her one final thing that would secure her hatred for the man who was her father.

"Ye must conceal yer true self, Ailis, for if the marriage fails to go through, I'll take it out on yer mother's hide one day at a time."

Ailis agreed to obey her da, not out of any great love for the woman who bore her, but because she could not bear to be responsible for her mother's pain.

The delicate woman fled to England when Ailis was quite young. Mary Elizabeth Dungannon was a normal, a human woman. *Nothing at all like Ailis.*

Her mother was a great beauty. She was soft and curvy, medium height, with lovely dark hair, and bright blue eyes. Ailis inherited the eyes, but that was all she got from the woman.

She did not blame her mother for leaving. The reality of living with a Pack of wild Irish Werewolves was too much for her. There were rules, hierarchies, she simply couldn't understand.

Ailis was fine without her mother, at least that was what she told herself often when things got too tough for her. She had Gwinnie, who was both teacher and protector. Servants who were female and

Wolf were afforded almost the same respect as male Wolves.

It was those in the upper class who were to *rise above the Change*, her father's exact words. As if it were a choice she had! Gwinnie was the one who helped Ailis when it was evident her Change was to take place and soon.

She'd heard the call of the moon and went through the agonizing transformation from maid to beast during a night when it was at its fullest. The song in her head was so beautiful she cried thinking about it.

She assumed her Change would mean freedom. Her father would surely toss her out, *but no*. After his initial rage, he informed Ailis that she was still being shipped off for marriage.

"Cursed ye are, Ailis, but he will still take thee to wed. You will speak of nothing, be hidden from sight, until the ceremony, and ye shall continue to apply this every night after yer bath."

"But why?"

"Because I command it! Take the bottle, lass."

"What is in it, father? Makes my eyes sting, it does!"

"Tis a special tincture, a covering scent. It'll mask yer she-Wolf from the MacContire. Be sure and wear it well, girl, or that mother who whelped me such a wrong bitch as ye are, shall feel pain like ye never imagined possible."

Her father did not smile when he sent her from his house just days ago. He simply went back to his rooms. Going over the contracts that allowed him to fall under the protection of the mighty Greyback Pack.

That was why he sold his only child. For solid ties to a Wolf Pack whose warriors were renowned for their skill at killing the evil forces who walked the Earth. *Fierce warriors indeed.*

Her father's lands were being destroyed by Witches. They cursed the land they sucked dry to fuel their magic. They'd lost countless fields and crops due to their ways. Dungannon needed the Greyback to clear them out.

Ailis shivered in her bed. She was no more than a cow sold by her *da*! Even when he knew 'twas most likely that, when her husband found out what she was, she'd be killed or imprisoned.

Nightmares of her husband-to-be kept her awake most of the night in the strange house. *What was he like? Would he be cruel?*

She'd heard tales of women, Werewolves such as she, who were ordered by their husbands to be confined to dark iron cells lined with silver panels, during nights of the full moon. Others were less fortunate, tossed out to become prostitutes or beggars, and some were even killed by beheading or hanged as traitors.

'Twas thought unladylike and unlucky for high-born females to Change, undignified for them to run free with the Pack. They were scorned and mocked. *Only those who were cuckolded lived to raise she-Wolves.* 'Twas one of the more popular sayings.

Only female servants and some families in trade who Changed were left alone to be what they were. But she, *a lady of status*, well, she was expected to follow the rules of society. The rules today said Were-wolves were to be male only. She-Wolves were uncouth and undesirable.

As if she had a choice in the matter? *Nay, but even if I did*, Ailis narrowed her eyebrows in defiance, *I'd choose Wolf!* Damn any man who made her sorry for what she was!

Would her new husband practice such barbarism with her? Would she be chained and locked away when she was just learning what it was to be free? Would he slit her throat one night as her father's cousin, the Scotsman, Laird McKellen did to his Wolf bride? The stories of her murder were gruesome indeed and McKellen was still on the run.

Ailis cringed as she recalled the sting of her father's backhand after her first Change. He'd cursed her for what she thought was her greatest gift. The betrayal still stung.

For weeks, she hardly ate or left her room. The night before that next full moon, Ailis watched from her window as rain poured from the sky that whole day. Such a sight it was, why she ran out from the house into the woods just to feel soak into her skin.

Of course, she found more than rain in the woods. She found a man. A poor one by the state of his dress, aye, but he was incredible, nonetheless.

He wore only the simplest leine, but his hair was the color of the finest silk ribbon she owned. A pale yellow it shone like moonlight. *Was he real?* Sometimes she thought she dreamed him.

Most nights, she curled up and shed tears for the memory of their shared kiss. *Oh Fie!* Fate was a cruel mistress to tease her with such an experience! To have the passion of love shown to you so you were sure it existed, but for far too short a time!

Why did she ever run from him? *Foolish lass.* She may have missed the only opportunity she'd ever have to feel love. What now for her? What would her future hold? Another man who may see her in irons yet!

She'd surely die if she was locked up in a cage! Bless Gwinnie's heart for telling her the truth of such things. She'd heard similar tales from the wives and daughters of visiting clans and Packs. Her husband-to-be was a warrior and brutal man to be sure.

Why, he was told to have carved the eyes out of six Witches before he hung them and burnt them to cinders and ash! A horror of a man for certain. What will he do when he finds out what she is? She shook her head and bade her brain be quiet. Worrying would do for naught.

Ailis' dreams that night were loosely woven images of thick iron chains, a ruin of a tower hidden deep in the woods, a black Wolf with a white paw, and silver moonlight shining through a narrow slit of a window. A snarl then, and blood, and at last an ear-piercing howl.

She gasped and jumped up in bed. *Just a dream, Ailis, tis only a nightmare of sorts.* She looked around at the unfamiliar room. She was in *Castle MacContire*, she was safe, for now.

The smell of freshly cooked meat invaded her nostrils. Her stomach growled. She saw the tray laden with food on the small table. A jug of thick milk was in the center, her personal favorite.

Some boiled grain and a small round bread near to bursting with dried currants sat next to a plate piled high with steaming slices of meat. Ailis was used to much simpler fare and sighed at her good fortune. She ate the food with an appetite as hearty as any young lad a hundred miles out.

"My lady, ye must not eat so!"

"Tis normal for Werewolves, Gwinnie! I've had my Change and find I am most ravenous in the mornings!"

"Nay, lady, do not speak of such!"

"Oh, he will know soon enough. And this may be my last meal as it were, besides, ye must have known I was hungry otherwise you'd have brought naught, but the thick milk and a crust of brown bread on my tray."

"Aye, my lady, but the handfasting ceremony is tonight! Ye must look yer best!"

"I can assure you, Gwin, I will not go hungry till then," Ailis tried not to smile in the face of her maid's horror.

'Twas true, ladies were expected to eat less than a bird, but Ailis was no bird. She was a Wolf and she was hungry.

"Ye will be safe, lady, I promise thee. Prithee, allow old Gwin to brush yer hair and braid it. Ye will look so beautiful yer new master wilt have no other thought than to keep ye fer his own."

"Thank ye, Gwinnie, but I think not."

"But we shall scent you over and hide yer Wolf's musk from yer lord husband and he'll not know the difference. Ye must seduce him in bed with yer lady's wiles then he'll not be able to live without ye. Now let me to yer hair, miss!"

Gwinnie spoke with a slight bit of demand in her voice. 'Twas unlike her, but Ailis smiled. She was more than maid; she was a trusted friend and devoutly loyal to her mistress.

Ailis felt tears fill her eyes and felt her throat grow thick. She disguised her sudden emotion with a laugh and her quick tongue as she continued to eat though her stomach suddenly felt full.

"Gwinnie, I shall look well enough. I soaked myself in that tub for an hour last night and scrubbed my hair and skin to a high polish, I did. I even brushed it, but I don't have a fondness for knots or ribbons today. I'll thank ye to leave it alone. Nay, no braids! I beg ye, I much prefer it down."

"But ye must let me! Yer hair, tis so long and unruly when ye leave it down! What kind of seduction wilt thou make looking like a demon?! Yer father sent no laced caul or jeweled hood to cover it either, the scoundrel, oh, what shall they think?"

"Mayhaps I shall cut it off then and worry it no more!" Ailis hid her grin behind her cup and drank the refreshing, tangy milk. She sighed after swallowing it down. *'Twas brilliant!*

"No, please, my lady, tis fine I swear, I shall just

braid the sides and ye will still be wanting yer plain veil?"

"If it will stop yer griping then yes, Gwinnie, you may that, indeed."

Ailis smiled at her lady's maid and finished her meal. She sat still while the buxom, yet nimble-fingered Gwinnie brushed out her naturally unruly hair and braided each side into long complicated twists before securing them to the back of her head with a bit of ribbon.

The rest of her locks hung down her straight back all the way to her hips in long large curls that were not any one color, but rather a combination of browns, reds, and golds. Some strands so pale they were as silver in the light, *like the man from the woods who haunted her dreams*, but others dark as slate.

"I will try and make ye respectable, my lady, but ye must know tis a heathen who sits and wears her hair down such as yers!"

"Oh, Gwinnie!" she laughed at her lady's maid and drank the last from her mug of thick milk. The cool, sour liquid tasted fine going down her throat. *A heathen indeed! She was as good a Catholic as any!*

To the horror of her English mother, her Irish father refused to have his daughter raised a heretic. Her upbringing was Catholic. The priest of her village saw to her christening and education.

Ailis spent most of her life in seclusion at her father's house. She longed for those days when she lived beneath her father's notice. She'd run and play outside all the day long.

A *wild thing*, that was what Gwinnie called her. Nothing like the lady a proper lord, *countrified or not*, would allow for a wife. Even should he not discover her secret, he may still prove a wretch. Ailis had worried over her predicament till the wee hours of the morning.

Would he permit her to run barefoot through the wood or swim in the moonlight with naught on but her skin? Would she be allowed to read the plays and poems she brought with her hidden in her trunk under layers of linen and wool? Especially if they were written by an Englishman?

Ailis frowned. Women were property. 'Twas simply the way of things. Oh, but how she longed for the freedom that was inherent for man. She wanted to do and say the things on her mind without fear of repercussion. The one and only time she spoke out against her father's will she was punished severely. But that did not stop her from rebelling in her own ways.

Before her Change, Ailis dreamt of leaving her father's house, but only for a man who was certain to understand her. She would not be owned. She would have her life. She closed her eyes as the pain that squeezed her chest grew sharp only to abide once more.

She no longer dreamt of happily ever afters with a knightly prince to take her away from the oppressive house of her father. Nay, now she wondered how her husband would let her live? Would he choose to cage her, or would she be killed?

Curse it all! She missed her Wolf, the red-gold furred she-beast who lived inside of her but was hidden as if in a fog from her during those days that led up to the moon.

"My lady, let's put yer scent on, then I shall help ye dress."

"Yea, thank thee, Gwinnie."

Her father insisted she wear the twenty pounds of stiff perfumed fabric that had been packaged and sent along with her for the ceremony. He had spies everywhere and she dared not disobey him.

She suddenly wanted to leave, to disappear into the woods that surrounded her new prison. She wondered if she could just carelessly fling her responsibilities to the wind.

Was it possible for her to simply vanish on her own? To use her new improved senses to explore the world around her. Much like those who dared to sail across the vast sea to that exotic shore called the New World.

What would her new husband say if she told him she longed to see and hear and taste and touch the world around her on two feet as well as four. Would he think her a heathen? A demon, perhaps?

She bit her lip until she tasted blood. All her wild yearnings would come to naught. There would be no revealing her secret, no exploring the world around her, no poor lad in the woods with whom she could steal another kiss. Ailis exhaled.

She knew all her daydreaming would yield nothing except heartache. Ailis wondered if that fist-sized organ in her chest would ever know happiness. Would she ever know love? She should stop all her foolish wonderings! *Poor fool,* she sighed again. It would seem Ailis simply could not help herself.

"Oh my, lovely you are! Beauty is a kindness, my lady!"

"Oh, Gwin, I hope tis not the only kindness in Castle MacContire."

⚜ 4 ⚜

"**H**ow long have ye been in yer cups, brother?"

"What is it you want, Lyall?"

"Ah, well for one, father is furious. Tell old Lyall now, what ails ye so this evening? Can it be the beggarly maid you're betrothed to or is it yer Wolf that plagues yer mind?"

Eoghan raised his head from the scarred wooden table and looked into the dark gray eyes of his younger brother, Lyall. *Hmm*, he seemed happy, an odd thing for his younger brother.

Eoghan saw no trace of the Wolf within the man. Lyall always was hard to read, but even more so when it was between moons as it was now. He wished he too had mastered the art of hiding his troubles in public.

Mayhaps he should ask him for lessons in the matter for future reference. 'Twas too late for now, Eoghan wore his heart and his woes on his sleeve. What a sad and sorry wretch he felt!

"My lord, shall I help ye to yer quarters?"

"Nay, Tom, I shall remain with my brother. Ye may go."

"Aye, sir." Tom Kelly had proved a loyal lad and brave too. Eoghan wondered why he stared at them for a moment before heading out the doors to the courtyard.

"You know brother, wallowing in self-pity is not a pretty thing. Even for a Werewolf who looks like Adonis."

"Oh, shut up, Lyall, I am not in the mood for yer sarcastic comments. Can't you see my heart is torn asunder?"

"Ah. So, tis the other than? The mystery wench? Perhaps she was of the Coven you destroyed and haunts yer dreams as a form of revenge?"

Eoghan glared at his brother from over the top of his mug. He'd been drinking for three straight hours, but as was the way with Werewolves the ale had little effect. And none that was lasting.

Eoghan took in is brother and wondered at their differences. How was it he had hair as pale and fair as silver while his own brother's sheared locks were dark as midnight. Like night and day, they were opposite in looks as with dress.

Eoghan favored the plain wool leines and trews of the common folk. He hardly ever wore the mantle his father had bestowed on him. It was a fine cloak of the softest wool dyed and stitched with great care, but Eoghan was a warrior and preferred to dress lightly to assure swift and unobstructed movement.

Lyall dressed to show his wealth and opulence. As if to announce his status to all. There was no doubt in his finely sewn inar and the exaggerated sleeves of his leine that he was the son of the Chief and Alpha.

"Nay, she was no Witch and I'll have words with any who says otherwise," Eoghan said.

His growl was fierce. Lyall moved quickly to expose his throat. Indeed, dress was not the only way in which he differed from his older brother. The Wolf in Eoghan knew prey when he saw it. Lyall sneered at the ground and Eoghan turned his head to regain his composure.

"We two have so little in common. That reminds me, I wanted to ask where you got the information on the location of the Coven? 'Twas quite useful knowledge."

"A peasant girl told one of my spies that a Witch

had passed in the wood where they were discovered. I never meant for ye to go yerself, Eoghan, those were Dungannon lands after all, wasn't it dangerous?"

Eoghan scowled. His brother was always coming across tidbits of information that proved useful in their search against the Dark Ones. Though Lyall was not a Hound himself, he aided their fight against evil.

"When will ye heed father and join the priesthood, Lyall?"

"Thanks, brother, but thus far, I have resisted the call to serve the Lord. After all, who could be above mine own father in my eyes?"

Eoghan missed the flash of anger in his brother. He agreed with him though. Lyall did not have the temperament for priesthood. He was quick to anger, though his rage displayed itself not in physical challenges, but in more subtle ways.

Eoghan recalled the Wolf who made the mistake of calling his brother a dandy. The man was assigned to clean the garderobes for six straight months.

The typical time for that particular duty was no more than a fortnight per assignment for all members of the Pack. But Lyall kept the ledgers and told the foremen who was to work which detail. 'Twas only when Eoghan became aware of it, did he order the lad to another post. *An error*, Lyall had said.

"The danger came not from the Witches, but from the wondrous maiden who stepped softly through the woods like an angel on Earth. She stole my heart, I swear it, brother, and I am to wed another. Curse me for a fool!"

"Ease your mind, now, perhaps father would be willing to change his mind."

"Nay, he cares not for my ordeal."

"Let me think on it then, man, perhaps I can help."

Eoghan grasped his brother's shoulder and squeezed though he feared there was naught he could do to sway their *da's* mind. *We are so different*, he thought. Lyall believed he could influence their father where Eoghan knew there was little chance of that.

Lyall's dark hair gleamed in the dim firelight. He was smallish for a male Werewolf. Thin and slight despite is long sleeved leine and puffed inar. He lacked the physical prowess to fight his way to the top of the Pack, and so Lyall leaned heavily on his status to exert influence among others. He was cunning in the ways of man and court.

Eoghan had no use for such things. His father used to joke that he was born more Wolf than man. His only desire to run free. When they were pups, Eoghan often reveled in exerting dominance and strength over his younger brother. He competed against any who would rise to the challenge and won many a fight on their training grounds.

"If my position in the Pack was as secure as yours, mayhaps I would not listen to father."

"Oh, Lyall, ye don't understand. I am father's *oidhre*, his heir, by blood and by dominance. Tis I who must obey the most, for all watch me and act as I do."

"Mayhaps a challenge then?"

"Nay! How could ye think it? I'd never harm father, if I even could. He is much loved by all. His sons included!"

"Yea, tis true."

"Father has a grace and dignity reserved for very few in his position and yet he is much respected by his men and the Pack. Nay, I would die for father, I'd never dream of challenging him. I admit I am surprised ye would suggest it."

"Aye, forget it. I just hate to see you so pained."

Eoghan's reputation for being good and brave was almost as well-known as his fair face. His brother was not as easily trusted among the men. These days he shut down rumors about Lyall with little more than a look.

His mother bade him on her deathbed to watch her second son. He readily agreed as he saw how anxious it made her. Werewolves were naturally attuned to body language. Eoghan was no exception, but his brother was not so easily understood.

Eoghan chalked it up to differences in their nature. He was a leader of Wolves, both Pack and Hound. Lyall was a scholar.

He marched into battle with them against their true enemies. The Dark Witches and Demons who sought to rule the world. Lyall studied law and kept the Pack finances in order.

The destructive ways of the Dark Witches caused chaos, disease, and famine. The last fifty years had been filled with political and religious unrest across all of Britain. It was just the type of atmosphere those devils flourished in. Sometimes hiding in plain sight, even taking the role of village priest or counsel.

Eoghan was their judge, jury, and executioner. He'd been tasked by his *da* to hunt the Demons and burn the Witches who dared practice on their lands. He did so with pleasure in the name of the Almighty and for the security of his Pack.

His little brother was more bookish and less warrior. He studied ancient texts and worked as chief negotiator for his father. Though lately, he'd not been seen at many of the trade meetings and business dealings that took place on MacContire land.

Eoghan proved long ago he was the better warrior

of the two of them. He was a valued fighter, the heir to his father's seat as Alpha and Chief of the Name, and the single most sought-after man in the entire county. Everything was his, and yet sometimes he envied Lyall.

He was fond of him. His sly and sarcastic younger brother was free to choose his life be it as priest, husband, lawyer, what have ye. Sure, he spent his days with scroll or book in hand, but 'twas his choice to do so.

Eoghan cared little for the written word. He was more a man of action. Though, truth be told, he enjoyed the odd group of players who passed their village every now and again. Especially the wenches who travelled with them.

He looked at his brother's unsmiling face and frowned. Lyall was handsome in his way. When had Eoghan last seen him with a lass or two? Why, was his saintly brother too good for the company of the village wenches?

"Tell me Lyall, why is it that yer always alone with a ledger in hand and never with a young miss on yer arm?"

"I have things of more import to whittle away my time, and besides, you are the one who is fair of face. You've had many of the village wenches and yet you long for one who for all ye know could have been a figment of yer imagination. Ha!"

Eoghan missed the fire in Lyall's eyes as he tossed back the rest of the thick brew in his mug. Still he sympathized with him. It could not be easy for the lad being the second son. Eoghan would inherit all and Lyall, well, he was left to work for him.

"I drink to yer freedom, Lyall, may ye never waste it."

Too many chains came with Eoghan's position in the Pack. Lyall, bless his heart, would have naught to worry his dark head over. One thing he vowed upon his life, Eoghan would always take care of his brother. Blood was blood.

"Is it freedom ye long for? I fear ye shall be free when ye are dead, brother, so do not worry now," Lyall reached forward and poured more dark ale into Eoghan's mug.

"Aye. To death! Ha!" Eoghan's laughter echoed through the hall and Lyall narrowed his eyes.

"Tis really worth the trouble of drowning yerself in ale??"

"You know damn well it is! I must marry the Dungannon lass."

"Is that all?"

"Is that all?! Are ye daft? Tis agony! It pains my heart thus!"

"Eoghan, mayhaps you should find some means to soothe yer troubled heart?" Lyall reached for the arm of the hearty maid who'd been strutting past him for the past hour. He gave her buxom figure a generous squeeze and whispered in her ear whilst she giggled.

"Do not trouble yerself so, Eoghan, marrying the lass is easy. She'll not interfere much. Ye can search for the other when the vows are said, after all, there is naught she can do to stop you, is there?"

Eoghan watched his brother with lifted eyebrow. Lyall continued to hold the wench in one strong arm while he licked the side of her neck and, wait, did he just bite her? She squealed and pushed at him, but he was immovable.

He reached up her skirts in view of all in the place. 'Twas most unlike him. Eoghan frowned. Whatever Lyall was about, the maid looked scared and cried aloud.

Eoghan was about to intervene, but suddenly, Lyall released her. She hurried off, wiping her eyes as she fled. Mayhap Eoghan needed to discuss the occurrence with Lyall, but he was distracted by his brother's words.

"Don't forget Eoghan that 'twas I who met with the Dungannon on yer and father's behalf. On father's orders, of course. The cut in dowry was necessary I am afraid, but the maiden is pure and

fresh, a *normal* and a virgin! Our own priest had it
from her maid and surgeon."

"That is fine for her. At this point I'd not care
whether she be Wolf, Dog or Bear!"

"What say you? Are ye daft? A normal who knows
about Wolves and understands the way of things? Tis
a blessing!"

"Aye, Lyall, but what of the rest of her? Is she
intelligent? Is she kind? Thoughtful? Does she have
good humor?"

"Ye mean how does she fair in looks?"

"Tis of no import. There is but one maid I can see
in my mind."

"Well, come to think of it, she was veiled when I
saw her, but her form was very comely. She was
neither too plump nor too thin."

"Oh, that's reassuring!"

"Worry not, fair brother, worry not. I have it on
the best authority that you will have all that is yer
due."

Lyall grunted when Eoghan clapped him on the
shoulder and stood to leave. Whatever was wrong
with Lyall, Eoghan had little time for it now. He
wished he could bury his sorrows somehow, but it was
time for him to act a man.

He was promised and, though he had not made
the vow himself, it was just as sacred. He would

forget the lady of the woods and prepare himself for his marriage.

He hastened to the chapel and sought prayer and solitude. Perhaps he'd find the answer there. If not, there was always the training grounds. *Hmm.* Perhaps he'd go there first.

5

Eoghan stared at his father with a look of disbelief on his face. 'Twas bad enough he was betrothed where his heart had no currency. Was he to play the fool now as well and marry a faceless bride?

"What do you mean she wishes to be veiled throughout the ceremony and the feast afterwards?"

"As I understand it, the lady wishes to wear a veil, so you are persuaded by no other outside force, only the strength of yer word and yer commitment to make good yer oath and proceed with this match."

"I will keep my word or yers as it were, father! Does the Dungannon question my honor?"

"'Tis done, Eoghan, calm yerself. She will wear the veil."

"Nay, I'll not-"

The altercation between father and son continued with silent growls and even a bit of posturing. Were-wolves tended to be quite keen on displays of power and the younger Eoghan MacContire was no exception.

What he did not know, was that Lyall sat in the corner with his head down as his brother and father growled across his father's sitting room. A wicked grin spread across his pale face with both none the wiser.

His plans were going exceedingly well. His pact with the Dark Witch working as she said it would. What was it she told him after he spilled his seed inside of her foul body that cursed night? *Ah yes*, he recalled her raspy voice in his ear before she vanished from the empty corridor.

"Now to feed the spell with yer seed, I cast this night and ye shall watch it unfold as I tell it now. Strife will sow between first son and father, the veiled bride shall be wed, she must not be unmasked, and ye will rise from yer station to that which is yer heart's desire. Heed me, the Wolf Bride must ne'er take off her veil in his sights or all will be lost."

It seemed as if Lyall would not have to lift a finger. His father already agreed the lady would be veiled and his brother, well, he'd have no say in the matter. Everything was going according to plan. He turned his dark head to see his father order both his sons out of the room. *Soon, old man, it will be me in command and all will obey my word! Soon.*

"Tis done, be gone with ye both!"

At their father's dismissal both brothers stalked off from the room. Eoghan's hands were clenched into fists. He was anxious after all that had taken place.

"I'd like to dip my head in a vat of *uisce beatha* for all that man does not listen!" Eoghan pushed his golden locks out of his face and exhaled.

Lyall noted that his eyes were glowing an icy blue that was almost white in color. The same color they were when he was Wolf. He must have been angrier than he knew. He was careful not to look directly at Eoghan.

He didn't need to scuffle with his older sibling. Physical prowess was not the means by which he'd win his right to Alpha. Nay, he had more brains than that. Eoghan in a state would beat the tar out of him and he knew it. *Best to lighten his mood altogether.*

"Come, brother, let us find yer whiskey! Ye shall need yer courage to wed a masked lady, perhaps a little something else to take the edge off as well."

"Nay, I'll take whiskey only. I've had my fill of wenches as of late. First, a mystery woman in the woods and, now, a masked bride."

"Yes, I wonder why father allowed it," Lyall agreed.

"Can you imagine? A veil? For what purpose? Does she hide a scar? Is she disfigured in some way? Is she just another English patsy in our midst to try and cure me of my Roman affiliations and plan to bid me as dog to her queen?"

"Perhaps it is just she has more than nineteen summers and wishes to hide her age from you, brother!"

"Yer the one who had dealings with Dungannon! Did ye not get one good look at the lass?" Eoghan shoved Lyall playfully as the pair went down the hall in search of their sustenance.

"Nay, she was kept from mine eyes, but he assured me she is all the things a wife should be!" Lyall wiped that part of his tunic that Eoghan wrinkled with his push.

He could barely contain his snarl, but again was too intelligent to challenge his brother outright. *Nay, be still.* He tried to focus on Eoghan's words.

What did he ask again? Ah! 'Twas true he visited the Dungannon a fortnight ago to finish the terms of the betrothal contract. Lyall volunteered for the mission as it were, much to the surprise of his father.

The old fool thought he was taking an interest in

becoming Eoghan's bloody secretary! The insinuation enraged him to no end.

Soon he'd be the one in charge and not some lackey! Before his journey to Dungannon lands, Lyall met with the Dark Witch. She led him to believe that the lady betrothed to his brother was not the English miss her father spoke of. Nay, she was just a common *bitch*.

A fine match for his pig of a brother! *Ha!* She told him to sweeten the deal with the Dungannon and Lyall heeded her words. Her powers, whatever they were, best be worth it. Lyall could hardly piss worth a damn since his cock entered her wretched slit.

'Twas the price he paid for his kingdom and he'd likely do it again, he reminded himself. Lost in his own thoughts, Eoghan missed the malice hidden behind his brother's dark coal eyes.

"Come let us drown yer sorrows in a jug of golden whiskey," Lyall's tongue was honeyed and sweet as he poured jar after jar for his fair-haired brother.

"One more for strength, yes?"

"Nay! I am done! And you, when shall ye trade yer milk for this then?"

Lyall smiled his serpentine grin and shook his head. Eoghan failed to notice the powdery substance his brother added to his beverage time and again. A half an hour later and the effects were evident.

"Lyall, I feel ill, Ly-" His blonde head hit the wooden table with a thump.

Lyall sneered and slapped his brother across the face. He moved to repeat his action, but a servant, *his servant*, interrupted. He was a sniveling wretch, but he kept Lyall's secrets and was paid well for the trouble.

"Take this note to my father," he took a rolled letter from out of his sleeve and lifted Eoghan's hand, it was imperative that his scent be on the paper.

"It seems my brother is well and happy to marry the Dungannon lass on the morrow. May he be damned for all the remainder of his days and may those days be brief!" He spat on his brother's sleeping form and thrust the missive at the servant.

"Aye, sir."

Lyall's head snapped round and he bared his teeth at the wretch before him.

"Pardon, I mean, *my lord*, of course."

"Tis best you remember that, boy. Now wait upon my word. As for you, brother mine, for once in yer perfect life I've the upper hand. Come now, tis time for you to wake!" Lyall lifted the jug of whiskey and splashed it across Eoghan's face.

Werewolves metabolized potions and poisons far quicker than normals. He had roughly a minute or two before his brother would awaken.

"Oy, what is this? My head throbs murderously."

"Nay, tis only yer nerves. Come, go and bathe. Yer betrothal shall be announced and ye shall make yer promise to the lass among all soon enough. Now, I'll get a servant to fetch some water."

Sometime later...

Eoghan stood up too quickly. He sipped from the jug of water Lyall's man had fetched for him, but the water was too tepid for his tastes. The slow thud that plaguing his brain suddenly peaked and he howled his pain.

"How dost thou fare?"

"What brew was in this cup? Lyall! What time is it?"

"It is almost time for the ceremony! Come you must bathe and dress the part," Lyall was immaculate in his finely stitched wool. His dark hair gleamed, and his shoes were polished.

Eoghan looked like a commoner in comparison. Even his mouth felt mealy and sick. He took a long swallow from a mug of fresh water and spit it into a waiting bowl.

"Ugh, I feel I've been bespelled by some Witch or Devil!"

"Come Now, in our house? Who would dare such a thing? Tis husbandly nerves is all."

Eoghan wiped his face with a square of cloth and

followed his brother to his chambers. He needed to at least dress the part, or his father would have his hide for a rug. He would wear the traditional *leine* of his clan.

His affluence would be recognizable in both the fine dying of the wool with saffron till it shone as yellow as his hair. Golden thread embroidered the hem and sleeves, it sparkled in the sunlight. His *inar* was a red-brown color and fit tightly over his broad chest. Hundreds of small pleats were neatly stitched and ironed into the soft wool.

It was further decorated with the crest of his family, the *MacContire*, it depicted a Wolf, head thrust back mid-howl and claw raised. His clan were warriors. The crest was ancient with few modern touches. The newest addition was a high Celtic cross behind the Wolf.

It signified their clan's loyalty to the Hounds of God, and the Werewolf blood that kept them strong. Though normals had no idea the MacContire were actually more beast than man.

Eoghan was proud of his crest. Proud of his land. Of his people. He was both Wolf and Hound. Warrior and heir to the Pack. Eoghan may not want to marry the English miss, but he would at that. Honor was everything.

The handfasting would soon begin, and he would

go to his betrothed in the dress of his people. 'Twas the custom of both his Irish and Werewolf descendants. The Catholic priest overseeing the match agreed that their ancient custom would be honored. The real marriage ceremony, the legally binding one, would not be held for weeks.

Many things could happen in that time. Eoghan wondered if the lass fancied taking herself to London after the ceremony, as her English mother before her did.

His dark eyes narrowed. He'd not allow it. She could just as well forget her fancy notions of English life. No sir, not here. She was in the wilds of Ireland. His home. And he was the only master he'd tolerate in his house.

Betrothals aside. Eoghan was a man. He intended to get a few things straight with his bride before the ceremony.

6

"**G**winnie, is that you? Just come in then and help me with my laces!"

Ailis was bent over the side of the bed. She attempted to retrieve her sleeve from the floor, but the cumbersome skirts of her English dress were simply too big for her. Especially unlaced as they were now.

Whatever her mother had assured her about fashion, she felt large as three people in the multi-layered skirts that would go under the gown itself. The dark green color was fetching and all, but she didn't even have it on yet and already the dress weighed a ton. She was not even certain of all the pieces.

There were several underskirts on top of the thin chemise she wore. An outer gown with hard pieces of bone sewn inside, a stiff collar, separate sleeves, wool stockings, and the veil her father insisted she wear, made up the rest. The gown itself was heavily embroidered with silvery thread and brocade adornments.

Ailis wondered if she'd look as ridiculous as she felt. If only she could wear the much simpler gowns she was used to wearing at home. But this ceremony was about more than her comfort. It was about power and standing.

She was the currency her father used to buy his good standing in County Tyrone. *And now I go from one man's rule to another's. Will I never be free?*

What was taking her lady's maid so long? She could not even put on the outer gown without her help. She turned around at the sound of footsteps.

"Gwi- Ooh, you, you leave this room at once!" Ailis shrieked at the tall man standing in her doorway.

She was very aware of the fact that an indecent amount of her breasts and shoulders were on display. She wanted to cover them and hide, but something told her she'd never outrun the brute. He was big as an ox and took up most of the space of the large doorway.

His dark eyes seemed to eat every inch of her exposed skin and she fought not to shield herself from his sight with her hands. Instead, she stood tall and straight, after all she was well over five foot five inches at her full height.

She looked down her straight nose at him with clear blue eyes. A difficult feat since he was at least ten inches taller than she. Still, she managed it.

"I said leave here, sir. Can ye not see that I am not dressed yet?"

"Indeed, I see that and more, lady, tis the reason I cannot look away."

Ailis' blue eyes widened. She'd never been addressed in such a way before. And by a man! Her heart sped up in her chest as he continued his thorough perusal.

"Wondrous and lovely, thou art, lady, forgive the intrusion," his eyes that had been dark a moment ago suddenly shone a light blue and Ailis stepped back.

He stared at her face for one moment before recognition spread across each of them. *Tis cannot be? And what she, a servant then? For she is undone in my eyes and puts her mistresses gown out on the bed.*

"Tis you! The lady of the wood! I am pleased to see you are well," Eoghan's words were calm, but inside he felt anything but.

"Oh my! Tis you as well! But how? Is MacContire yer master?"

"Yea, lady, he is." 'Twas not a lie. His father was the MacContire still and Eoghan was his servant above all else. What mad God resided in Heaven that He would send temptation on the day of his hand-fasting?

"I have thought about you all the days since our last meeting. Yer face has haunted my dreams, lady. Do I ever cross yer mind, I wonder?"

"I should not speak of such things, sir."

"Why not? Ye are here now, woman, but I've dreamt of you here so often that I question if yer real or not."

"I am real, sir. I confess, you have been in my dreams as well."

"Have I, now?" He asked and stepped further into her room. He closed the door behind him.

Ailis stood her ground and watched the man with hair as gold and light as the sunshine itself walk towards her. Her heart thudded in her chest.

Her stomach tightened as he approached. It was as if all her nerves were standing at attention. She looked down, feeling her Wolf surge forward. She must needs keep that secret! She was almost grateful for the heavy scent Gwinnie had insisted she put on before she left to fetch some food for Ailis.

"I have wondered about ye. Prithee, lass, may I have yer name?"

"For what purpose, sir, tis nothing can come of this. Ye must go now."

"Do not send me away, not before I've had a taste of ye. By my eyes, I feel as if my soul has been sieged upon just by the sight of you."

Ailis raised a hand to her throat. Was it possible to fall in love in a blink of an eye? She inhaled and a sea of fragrance assailed her nostrils.

Salt of the earth, a pure musky scent, accompanied by fields of heather, golden sunshine, the wind and more. He was all those things. Earth and heaven combined. *And Wolf.* She smelled that too. Mayhaps he was of her new Pack?

Wolf and servant, maybe, but one thing she knew for certain, she'd never seen a man as fair. And yet he reeked of masculinity. His simple Irish dress only made him more appealing. She bit her lip and was shocked when his eyes zeroed in on the action. He moved forward.

"If that needs doing, I beg you, leave me the honor?" He stepped forward. His big body wrapped around hers. Heat seeped through the fabric of her dress into her skin and Ailis sighed. She felt incredibly small and protected.

She leaned into his strength and tipped her head back for him. She knew all the reasons she shouldn't allow this, but for once in her life she knew what she wanted. If she was to be given to a man, she didn't even know like she was naught but cattle, then Ailis would not spurn an opportunity to taste true love.

Her body tingled in anticipation as he leaned down and covered her mouth with his own. She tasted the faint remnants of whiskey and something else that was very sweet and fleeting on his breath.

After that it was all *him*. That earthy Wolf scent that was sweeter on her lips than honey. This kiss was even better than the first.

"Sweet, I need you," he crushed her breasts to his chest and Ailis was lost. Heat pooled in her belly and her heart raced as he continued his exploration of her mouth.

Instinctively, she wrapped her arms about him and tipped her head back further as his lips left hers to trail kisses down her neck and throat, all the way to the deliciously exposed flesh of breasts.

He was her other half. She knew it instinctively. Every touch, every caress, as if he knew exactly where she needed to feel him.

He reached for her skirts and she allowed it. The feel of his hard body making her burn with curiosity and desire. He stroked her thighs and she sucked in a breath.

It was as if a huge void she never realized she had, opened deep inside of her. The empty hollows of her being were howling to be filled. *By him. Only him. Mine.*

Their kiss was not just a joining of lips, it was a communion of like souls. Recognition stirred on the edges of her consciousness. Their lips met, tender and sweet, with long curious strokes of their tongues. Quickly, it became something more. Something urgent and hurried.

"I must have you, I am mad for you, lass. What say ye?"

"Sir, I've never felt such a rush of excitement. Tis deep in my blood. A raging fire that hungers for you, will you satiate me?"

"As if my life depended on it, lady," he freed her breast from its scanty confines and took the plump nipple in his mouth.

Ailis bucked against him as he suckled the pebbled nipple. His hand moved under her skirt towards the juncture of her thighs. He parted her tender skin and did things she'd never dreamed possible.

He stroked and dipped with subtle masterful movements. Ailis shuddered and her stomach clenched as he gently parted her curls and with one thick finger pushed inside of her.

Ailis moved a little out of reach and held his wrist. Fear and excitement battled within her. Should she push his hand away?

A tremble shook her body. As she debated with herself, he lowered himself to the ground in front of her. She gazed into his beautiful face before speaking.

"What are ye doing?"

He knelt on the floor and gently pushed her backwards onto the bed. He smiled up at her. Like a Wolf.

A predator, indeed, as he inched her skirts up around her knees, then her thighs. He lifted her ankles and placed them on his broad shoulders. She made to sit up, but he gently held her in place with one large hand flat against her stomach.

"Trust me, lass, I'm only going to taste ye."

"Taste me?"

"Aye, yer sweet as honey, I'd swear it. I'm ravenous for you, my lady."

He lifted her skirts until she was quite bare in front of him. Ailis felt as if her body was aflame. Shame warred with curiosity. *What would Gwinnie say?*

Then his hands stroked her thighs and that place where she was most feminine. She exhaled and leaned back against the cushions. Trusting him to do her no harm. Then, her fair-haired lover dipped his head and *kissed her.*

Ailis felt as if her whole body had ignited. And that was only the beginning. His long tongue snaked out of his mouth and brushed across her sensitive nether lips. Inciting passions to heights she never dreamed existed. Ailis bucked against him. Unsure of the sensations that were taking control of her body.

"Oh, I feel things I fear I should not. Tis a sin, surely!"

"I promise there is nothing sinful about you. Let me worship yer body, lady, as I do in my heart."

He dipped his head again and suckled on that tiny nub that seemed to control her every feeling. Ailis stuck a hand in her mouth to keep from crying out as sensation after sensation overwhelmed her to the point where she thought she'd explode.

And then she did. By the time she opened her eyes the man of the wood was kissing her breast and then her mouth. She felt something big and hard against her slick folds and she knew what was about to happen. She welcomed it.

"Are you sure, lass, I cannot undo it once it is done."

"Yea, sir, for wherever I be tomorrow I am with ye now."

He growled in his throat and thrust past the barrier that held her intact. The Wolf in him surged forward. Icy blue eyes glowed from his head as he bit down on her shoulder.

He impaled her on his long, hard shaft and Ailis reveled in the tingling sensations that ran through her body. His accompanying groan was loud in her ear. A sound so deep and guttural it was akin to pain.

Ailis sucked in a breath. It hurt but for a brief, fleeting second. Once he moved inside of her again the pain lessened. He thrust his hips with detailed precision and she soon found herself riding another wave of pleasure unlike any her untried body ever felt.

"I feel everything new," she held his face in her hands and kissed him as he drove into her.

Her muscles tightened as she felt that same dizzying feeling come over her again only this time, she knew he was feeling it too. Sensation after sensation exploded inside of her body until it reached a pinnacle.

She moaned and scratched her nails down his back. She almost didn't hear his possessive words as he spilled his hot seed inside of her, filling her and causing no end of pleasure.

"*Mine*," he growled.

Ailis gasped for breath. She never felt so complete in her life. She stroked the silvery gold locks of his hair back and kissed his head.

"By God's eyes, what have I done?"

"Only what I wanted you to, sir."

"Still, sir, am I? Shall we not call each other by our names now?"

"I agree I am compelled but let us keep this secret." Ailis spoke through tears that misted her eyes and made her voice thick with sadness.

"I fear I shall never be the same again."

"Nor I."

Eoghan stared at the maid in the bed and kissed her sweet lips before helping his lady fix her disheveled clothing. He knew the instant he spied her who she was. *His lady of the wood.*

Though her hair was different, he recognized her instantly. She was beautiful as he remembered. Only now he knew her hair was a multitude of colors from ash brown and reddish-gold, to a silvery-blonde pale as his own. The color having been unrecognizable in the rain upon their first meeting.

He'd not been able to control himself. He needed her. *What have I done?* Guilt warred with pride as Eoghan took in what had just happened.

His head was no longer pounding, his stomach felt slightly queasy, and his heart thudded inside of his chest. This was no common conquest. He was sure of it.

What was she doing here? She must be a new servant or lady's maid. His bad luck, she was maid to his betrothed!

The idea left him sick to his stomach. He wanted

no one, except this lass. He'd have to tell his father immediately.

He felt his Wolf surge forward and knew that she was his. *Mine.* The need to protect her and claim her again were overwhelmingly strong.

"Thou art lovely."

"As are you."

"Ha! I am glad you find me so, lady mine."

"I will remember you better, sir, in my dreams now that I have seen you again. I am sorry this is goodbye."

"Nay, I shall find a way for us. Promise me you will wait."

"You do not understand. I am not my own to promise."

"Whatever price yer father sets, I shall pay it."

"Tis not dowry or payment that separate us."

"I mean to make you mine."

"I cannot." Her tears were nearly his undoing. He wanted to scream in rage.

"I promise to make this right."

Eoghan cursed as the Church bells chimed the hour. He had little time left. He needed to dress first then he would see his father.

"Prithee, believe my words. I shall be back for ye."

Eoghan left the room like a man ready to throw down and face Hell. Surely, that was what his father would send him to once he told him his plans to wed a common girl!

"Brother! Come, tis time you dressed for the ceremony, where have ye been?" Lyall waylaid him on the way to his chambers, but Eoghan planned to see his father first.

"Nay, I need an audience with father."

"He is with the priest now, dress first, please brother, or he'll be in no mood to hear ye!"

"Ah! You are right! Fine, but quickly then."

Eoghan hurried to his chamber with Lyall on his heels. Breaking a contract would not be easy, but he was determined to risk all for his heart's desire. The lady of the wood was here, and he knew in his heart she was the only one for him.

His mate for life. *Mine.*

7

"Calm yerself," Lyall could barely contain his brother as they waited in the hall to speak with their father.

"I cannot wait, Lyall."

"There is little choice but to wait. What has brought ye to this state?"

Eoghan ignored the question and paced back and forth. He stopped suddenly. As if he felt a certain something, *a presence*, behind him. When he turned his face was unreadable.

A lady in a fine green gown with rich brocade adornments stood at the end of the long hallway. She was familiar somehow though her face and hair were covered from his eyes with a heavy veil. Her head was bowed so he was sure she did not see him.

Her lady's maid stepped forward. A buxom wench

with sharp eyes and a haughty air. *What is this? If she be the maid, then who is the lady?*

"Tis yer betrothed," Lyall sneered in his brother's ear. If Eoghan didn't know better, he'd think his brother was laughing at him.

As it were, he was too preoccupied with pondering the identity of the veiled lady to pay any heed to his younger sibling. The lady stepped forward.

She raised her head hesitantly under the opaque fabric. Once she did, her head shot up and down. She gasped and Eoghan understood entirely. He shrugged off his brother's arm just as the priest and his father strode down the hall.

"Ah, my boy, my lady, we are all gathered! Wonderful! Let us commence."

Before Eoghan could reach her, his father had him by the arm and brought him inside the doors to down the aisle, to a podium where, now, stood the priest.

"Why dost thou smile so, forget ye are to be hand fasted to a masked thing? This only enforces the conclusion that ye and she shall wed, Eoghan!"

"Nay, I do not forget, Lyall, mayhaps I even look forward to it!"

"What–"

"May I present the Lady Dungannon," the

MacContire, *Eoghan's da*, raised his hand and the Lady progressed slowly to the front of the room.

Her lady's maid led the way, she was stern looking and raised an eyebrow at Eoghan. He imagined she knew of his, er, earlier indiscretions and he bowed slightly to her out of respect for so well guarding his lady. *And she was his. Finally! Mine.*

A few more people settled inside, Pack members and such, but Eoghan only had eyes for his veiled bride. Her scent was still masked by the perfume she wore and yet he could find no fault with it. It was nice enough, though it hid her from him much like the mask she wore.

The priest had them join their hands. The MacContire took out a gold threaded length of silk with which he bound them. Next, he presented a ring to the priest who mumbled some Latin over it to bless and sanctify the handfasting, Eoghan assumed.

The metal was pale like silver. It was engraved with ageless runes sacred to the Pack. In the center was an enormous blue sapphire. *The MacContire Stone.*

Ailis heard tell of the precious ring. It was hundreds of years old and passed down to each female Alpha of the line. Tears welled up in her eyes as the man she was betrothed to, the one she had given her body and soul to, slid it onto her finger. She hardly heard anything the priest said.

"We are bound to each other then?" It sounded like a question to her, but when she looked from priest to betrothed, she realized something had happened when she was daydreaming.

"I must see you," despite the gasps he removed her veil to see her face and his smile was like the sun coming out!

"But this is just the handfasting?"

"Nay, I have sanctified this union in the presence of the Lord, ye two are wed!" exclaimed the priest.

Both bride and groom looked from one to the other. Their feelings masked behind surprise. Tension was thick in the air.

Lyall stood, a nasty smile on his face, just to the side of them. But when he saw Eoghan's own expression lighten, he grew angry.

"Did ye not hear? You two are married!"

"Yea, I heard though I don't know how or why tis so all I know is I am truly blessed, brother, for this is *my lady*," he leaned down and kissed her on the mouth to everyone's astonishment.

"Tis true, my lord?" Ailis looked into the face of her husband and tears of joy slipped past her eyes and rolled down her pale cheeks. She was lovely as ever.

"Aye, *wife*," Eoghan brushed the wetness from her face and kissed her cheeks then her lips again. His father slapped him on the back and laughed.

"What? But she was veiled? You did not know her?"

"Brother, don't you see, I have known her for eternity! She is mine own true mate!"

"Tis true, sir, I have met my husband before, in the wood."

"You mean, you, a high-born lady, was traipsing about the wood like a common wench?"

"Careful Lyall," Eoghan moved to block Ailis and bared his teeth at his brother. When he faced him though, he found he no longer recognized his sibling.

Lyall's face was contorted with rage. He looked at Ailis and then at Eoghan and snarled before taking a long sharp knife out of his waistband.

"Out everyone! We've family things to attend here," The MacContire's command was obeyed by all except an old woman who stood at the back.

Priests and villagers all left, but she walked to the back door and raised her left hand. She muttered something Eoghan could not here. He watched in horror as she thick, black ropes of magic poured from her fingers and locked the door.

"Witch! Be gone from here!" His father yelled.

The Witch cackled and turned around to reveal a hideous mockery of a smile. She was missing several teeth and what was left were rotted black and stunk up the room.

Her skin was pock-marked and sallow. She raised a hand to Eoghan's father and with a swipe the Alpha was overcome! He sank to the floor.

"What is this? I never said I wanted to harm father!"

"Of course, ye wanted to harm *father*! How else might ye be Alpha? Now grab the bitch!"

"Do not touch her, Lyall! As for ye, Witch, I'll end you the now!"

"I think not, pup! Yer brother is mine and in my debt! He will do what he can to secure his position. A greedy bastard he may be, but then again yer mother would know all about that, wouldn't she?"

"What say ye about our mother?" Eoghan growled and his da groaned from his position on the floor.

"'Tis no MacContire there, I assure ye. Lyall is the bastard son of the mercenary soldier who raped yer mother when the village was invaded by the English nigh on thirty years ago. 'Tis the truth, ask the MacContire!"

"What? Art, thou saying I am a bastard, Witch?" Lyall stuttered but held firm to the knife in his hand. Eoghan moved to help his father who had just fallen to the floor when Lyall screamed his fury.

He turned to shield Ailis, but Lyall had her. His knife pointed to her pale throat. She looked at him with fear brimming in her wide blue eyes and he felt all the rage inside of him desperate to take shape. *If only 'twas the night of the full moon!*

"You deceived me, Witch!"

"Nay, I saved you. Now you've the bitch come to me, we must away."

"Is it true, am I what she says I am?"

"Son, she is a lying foul mou‑ Ahhhh!" the MacContire groaned as the Witch hit him with another spell. Eoghan leapt to his feet. He could not believe the betrayal before his very eyes. *His own brother. But why?*

"Back away, Eoghan!" Lyall held the blade at Ailis' throat. She gulped and looked to him for aid, but he was helpless. Eoghan could barely contain his growl.

"She has you bespelled, Lyall. We do not side with the Dark Ones! Let her go, now."

"Can't you see she changes my life? From servant to Alpha, and from bastard to more, but ye were s'pposed to suffer! Not marry a lass ye favored! Now, I'll take her as mine and you will watch my victory from afar!"

"Why Lyall? Just tell me."

"You could never understand, *first son*, *the heir*! And now I am shamed! That cuckold of a father should have never let our mother live! He knew! Don't you see that? Damn ye, Eoghan! Now I'll take what ye treasure the most!"

8

Eoghan looked at his bride. Her fear was tangible. A living thing between them. Almost as strong as his rage at his own impotence.

"Ailis, I'll come for thee."

"The next time you see this woman she will be swollen with my heir and ye shall be hanging from a noose!"

"We must away the now! *Benedicat omnis hic ambulare in nebula, nos ab hoste, protégé occulos!*"

"Eoghan!"

"Ailis!"

Eoghan collapsed as the Witch hissed in his direction. His head felt as if it were being crushed between two stones. He howled in pain and then everything went black.

When he woke some thirty minutes later it was with sweat running down his face. His fever had broken, but he was not altogether well.

Eoghan drank some water and paced the hall to clear his head. The priest and Pack healer were with his father. He was suffering from a dark curse placed on him by the Witch. *As they all were*.

After she screeched her last spell a thick, white fog encircled Castle MacContire. It was impenetrable and made it exceedingly dangerous to try and navigate across the rough terrain in such a state. Eoghan's rage threatened to consume him.

"My lord, yer father asks for thee," the lad, Tom Kelly, bade him enter his father's rooms.

"Son, my son. The Witch speaks the truth. Yer father was molested by an English bastard, a rogue Wolf, who raped her one night whilst I fought to protect us. But she, she was my life, I promised to love her and to raise the child as mine own. Lyall is not my blood, but I believed him my son. I am sorry-"

"Nay, da, do not speak thus. Ye are good and brave and will be fine. I will see to Lyall and his Witch."

"Do not harm him, I promised yer mother."

"I shall do my best, but my loyalty is now to wife. I must find Ailis!"

Eoghan left the room abruptly. He went to the

front door of the castle. Misty ropes of cursed fog blocked every available path from view. Yet he knew in his heart he had not a moment to lose.

"Sir? How shall ye travel in all this and where?"

"They have what is mine, Tom, and I mean to get her back."

Eoghan raised his blonde head to the skies. The sun was setting, but 'twas weeks still to the full moon. He needed his Wolf more than ever, but the curse of St. Natalis forbade the connection between man and beast during the between times.

Eoghan growled and snarled. He had to focus. He went deep inside himself to that place in his mind's eye where his black Wolf rested and waited for him to call.

The silvery bonds of his Packmates were glowing as always, but they seemed almost dim compared to one. *That line leads to her. My mate. Mine.*

He knew instinctively tis the matebond he'd heard tales about from the Pack elders. His heart thudded in his chest as he settled back into the present. Then suddenly, as if through the mist, Eoghan saw a path. He raised his head. When he did his eyes were the familiar icy white blue of his Wolf.

"Sir!" Tom gasped.

"Ready yerself and my men. Bid them follow me. We go to fetch yer mistress and to save my father and yer Alpha." He threw his head back and howled for all the Pack to hear.

"Grab the bitch by her hair and drag her if ye have to. We must lock the doors now!"

Ailis struggled against Lyall's hold. He had six men loyal to him acting as guards, the Witch, and himself. They raced through the woods on horseback until they came to a decayed and crumbling tower.

"I saw this in my dreams," she whispered. The Witch, having heard her, grabbed her by the chin and hissed.

"Ye have sight, I'll grant ye, but shut that whore mouth or I'll snap yer neck!"

"Nay! She is mine now, Witch. Have a care!" Lyall snaked his tongue out and licked the side of her face. Ailis cringed and moved away.

"Tis a fine perfume to cover that particular canid scent ye carry, but I know what ye are, *she-Wolf*! Dost thou think Eoghan would care to be married to such a *bitch*?"

"Let me go, foolish pup!" She spat at Lyall's feet only to be slapped across the face hard enough to split her lip. The taste of blood in her mouth was familiar though unwelcome.

"Come, we must to the tower room. The ritual needs completing."

"I'll not give ye any more of my seed, Witch. It is

for the lass now. No doubt, my brother will miss the honor of taking that pie for himself!"

Ailis gasped in pain as he tied a rope around her wrists and pulled her up the stairs. The rotting stone steps combined with mold, damp moss, and dead things invaded her nostrils. She wanted to gag.

For the first time ever, she wished she had applied more of that confounding scent. It was a nasty place and an even nastier future lay in wait for her. If only Eoghan would hurry!

Could he make it past the fog? The Witch was strong and cast a powerful spell. Nay, she'd not give in to those thoughts.

Her mate would come for her. She believed that with all her soul. She repeated it to herself over and again like the chanting monks she'd read about. *Eoghan, love, come to me. Find me. I'm waiting for ye.*

Her husband's half-brother, *half a man was more like*, pushed her onto a seat in the center of the tower room. He fastened a chain to the rope that bound her wrists together and linked it to the hard seat. She could barely move her arms.

"Lyall, tis not too late to stop this."

"Stop this? Why on earth would I stop this. Now that I look on ye, Lady Ailis, I must say my brother has taste at least. Yer fine English gown and yer sparkling blue eyes are fetching indeed. Mayhaps I shall enjoy deflowering you!" He said with a guttural snarl in his voice that made her skin crawl.

He ran a hand down her hair as if testing its weight, then lifted her face by her chin. His eyes seemed to undress her and Ailis suddenly wished for something with which to cover herself. He made her feel foul and used and that was just with his eyes.

"Aye, lass, you'll do for me. I'll have my brother's wife first, ha! How's that for a bastard second son, eh?"

"Yer Witch is scowling at ye, go tend her and leave me to find my peace afore yer brother comes to tear your throat out."

What started out as bravado, ended with the strength of her belief. Ailis did not doubt that her beloved would be coming for her. It was there in the vehemence with which she spoke. Her kidnapper must have agreed for she noticed a twitch in his lip before he went to his Witch.

A foul and evil thing she was. Ailis knew of her kind, those who practiced the Dark Arts had been cavorting on Dungannon lands for months now. 'Twas Eoghan who burned their last habitat. No doubt she'd been stolen as some sort of revenge.

Her only hope now was to wait for her husband of but a few hours. Would their tie be strong enough to lead him to her? She wondered. She'd heard of such things amongst Werewolves, a *matebond* strong enough to link the two people as if they were one.

But she'd kept secrets from her man. She'd lied. Well, she had no choice at the time, but still. Would their bond be strong with deceit between them? Would he reject her?

Doubts and fear plagued her mind. Tears rolled down her cheeks. She was always a useless thing, wasn't she? No good to anyone. Not worth what her father paid for her in dowry. *Nay, Ailis, tis not yer own thoughts that besiege yer mind.*

The voice of her Wolf sounded clear in her mind. Ailis closed her eyes and saw her clearly. Wrapped lovingly around her forepaw was a silvery glowing cord that travelled into the mist. She knew instinctively where it would lead.

Mine own mate. Tis true we are joined. He shall come for ye. Focus, Ailis. Stay at the ready.

Ailis opened her eyes and saw the Witch bent over a dark flame candle. Her one good eye peered at her and Ailis knew she was trying to invade her thoughts again. *Nay, she will not get inside of my mind again!*

Lyall paced around the small room and peeked through a small slit of a window that looked down on the ground below. He'd placed two of his men outside and four inside. *Closest to him. The coward.*

"Tis not right. He'll come! I know it!" Lyall rubbed his head, his agitation increasing.

"I cursed him with a fever, he'll not rouse in time. Take her, mark her now and make her yours!"

"Ye cannot just bite a wench! I must be in the act of consummation to mark her."

"Well then, get to fornicating with the bitch, but do it now! The signs are not unchangeable, ye must make the wench yers and then stake yer claim to Alpha! If he finds us tis lost."

"But ye cursed the path?"

"Yay, but the bitch here is pretty bait! He'll come!"

"Grrr," Lyall growled a pitiful sound and stalked to Ailis. He grabbed for her hands when suddenly a noise, more roar than howl sounded from outside.

"Tis not possible!"

9

Eoghan did not know exactly how it happened, but he found himself staring out of Castle MacContire at a path that seemed lined with a silvery rope. He did not wait for anything else; he took off at full speed.

He felt his Wolf keenly inside of him. His two legs trod through dirt path and thick tall grass until he was running faster than any deer he'd ever tracked. One thought was on his mind and one thought only. *Ailis. Mine.*

The need to have her in his sights, to see her safe and feel her heartbeat under his own was a powerful motivation. 'Twas like he was half a person without her near him. The idea that his own blood, half or not, could harm a hair on his bride's head was not easily swallowed.

He heard his men following behind. They were a mile or so out, but he did not slow down. He could not afford to waste a moment. There was no telling what would happen.

His feet took him down a path he'd never seen in his own forest. Every step he took further into the darkness was like fighting his own nature. Everything about the place was warning him away. Telling him to leave, but he kept on.

Finally, he found himself running up a stone walkway. A tower was hidden under tall trees, 'Twas old and crumbling. A ruin of a thing. Any other day he'd have passed it by, but not this day.

When two armed men, friends of his brother, came forward, Eoghan knew he'd found them. His heart thudded in his chest. He'd right the wrongs done to him. And how.

"Sir! He is here! Yer brother is here!" One of them bellowed to the tower behind them.

Eoghan expected to see something happen in the topmost room, but to his surprise a voice sounded from below. There was a thin slit in the stone wall where he saw familiar dark eyes peer at him.

'Ah! Come to wish *me* well with yer bride on yer wedding night? Forgive me if we get too loud, brother, but I'll have her filled and fucked in no time!"

"Lyall! Ye will not touch her!"

"Come now! I will plunder her slit with my cock until she weeps with joy of it! I do you a favor, Eoghan, she's not the lady ye think her!"

"I am warning you, Lyall. Surrender now or there is no hope for ye."

"Men! Hold the bitch down and lift her skirts high. I want to see what I've stolen from this fool out here!"

"Taunt him not and fuck the bitch! Yer window is almost passed!" Lyall grabbed the Witch round her neck and slammed her against the wall.

"Ye will remember who I am! I am Alpha, I am in charge! Yer naught, but a vile demon whore!"

"Curse ye, fool! The Maccon comes and there is naught to do but run!" She threw her revolting head backward until her neck almost snapped then she ran straight up the wall and out the rooftop to Ailis' horror and fascination. She watched as the Witch was swallowed by the shadows.

"That vile bitch!" Lyall wrenched Ailis from the chair and held her face to the tiny opening.

"Lyall! Release her!" Eoghan bellowed from where he stood. He felt like a wounded animal though the fight had not even started yet.

"Eoghan!" Her scream sent shivers down his spine. This would not end well for his brother.

Lyall shoved Ailis back at his men. They held her by her hair and the chains that bound her. She struggled but it was difficult.

"We shall see this to the end! Guards! Maim my brother so he may hear me take this whore, then kill him!"

Lyall's men charged Eoghan. He recognized one, but not the other. The lout was a Wolf who was thrown out of the Pack for heinous crimes against his family. His wife and children were kept and protected from his abuse. Eoghan was the one who tossed him outside the village gates upon is father's orders.

"Remember me, lad?"

"Gerald the wife-beater and child abuser, how could I forget?"

"How's my wife been? When Lyall is Alpha I'll have the bitch and my pups back and I'll wipe the bloody floor with them all! As is my right as father and husband!"

"Gerald, this is not yer fight. Leave this place and ye will live a while longer."

"Nay, I'm going to rip you apart!"

Up to that point, Eoghan had been trying to find a way in the fortress. The thing was well-built. Iron bars, stone walls, no large windows or openings of any kind. Would be nigh on impossible.

At the sound of Gerald's charge, Eoghan readied

himself. The guards had swords in one hand and short knives in the other. Eoghan had not stopped to put on weapons once he found the path.

He braced himself. Speed, strength, and accuracy were on his side. Gerald attacked first. He lunged with all his brutish strength and the man was at least three stones heavier than Eoghan. He sidestepped and kicked him in the backside, using the man's own momentum to force him to the ground.

"Stay down, Gerald. Live another day at least."

The man growled his fury and got to his feet. Eoghan kept him in his sight though he didn't turn his back on the other. Sounds of a struggle coming from inside the tower momentarily distracted him.

"Ailis?!" he yelled just as the other guard stabbed at him with his knife.

Eoghan hissed as the blade sliced the skin of his forearm. He grabbed the guard and quieted his screams with one quick twist of his neck. That was his Ailis yelling now, the fear in her voice evident. He couldn't wait a moment longer.

He crouched down and waited for Gerald to make his move. The man spit on the floor and growled. He swung his sword first. Eoghan ducked it easily. 'Twas not the sword that worried him, 'twas the knife.

Gerald came at him like a man possessed. He lunged and stabbed at Eoghan until he almost succeeded in plunging his blade straight through his chest. Eoghan grabbed him by the forearm, allowing the blade to slice into the skin just to the right of his heart. He twisted and heard the pop of the bone breaking.

"Ye bastard! Yer brother is taking yer bride the now! Ha! I have my revenge!"

"I gave you a choice, Gerald. You chose wrong."

He took his head in both hands and twisted. The snapping of his neck made a sickening sound, but Eoghan was not stranger to battle. He did not even flinch.

He turned frantic. His Ailis was there, trapped by magic and worse, his mad half-brother! He needed in now. He ran to the door and pushed with all his might, but it would not budge.

Frustration warred with rage! If only the moon was full! He'd break down the bloody walls if he had to!

"Ailis!" he yelled.

"Shut up, bitch! Wait, ye cannot leave!" Lyall screamed at Ailis and stared at the place where the Witch had been swallowed by darkness.

She'd left him. Abandoned him. Well, how was he supposed to take control of the Pack now.

"You two, guard the door! You hold this one down. I'll have my brother's wife the now! Do ya hear me Eoghan, I'll plow her fields within yer hearing! I'll use the bitch and leave her with nothing left!"

The sound of Eoghan banging against the outside walls and pounding against the door was constant. *He's here!* Ailis was almost relieved, but she was still trapped in the tower. She needed to get out. She needed Eoghan.

Two huge, stinking guards grabbed her by her restraints. They made to pull her up, but something was happening. She looked at them, blue eyes glowing silver and snapped her teeth.

"What is this?"

"Sir, she be possessed!"

"Nay, fools! She is Wolf like we, and the moon is weeks away. Come now this is how you take a bitch to heel!"

Lyall stalked towards her, but Ailis' Wolf was in charge for the moment. She'd not be used by the likes of him. She whipped her head side to side and snapped her teeth again, catching his finger. She spit out the appendage and ignored the metallic taste of his blood in her mouth.

His screams were like fuel to her fire. The sound of her mate drawing close was greater now. Ailis knew what she needed to do to help him get to her.

He heart roared inside her chest. Love for the man, her husband, overwhelmed her. She tossed back her still human head, though her Wolf was clearly in charge, and she howled.

She recognized a sort of ethereal glow emanating from her entire body as she howled and howled. A cry so loud and fierce that the men in the room all fell to their knees.

Those guards who would have held her while she was raped began to sob and scream, blood poured from their ears, but still she howled. Lyall yelled for them to seize her, but they were helpless.

Then the miracle happened. The huge wooden door, that was minutes ago held shut with black ropes of magic, fell open to the cold stone floor. *Eoghan!*

"What? How?" Lyall sputtered and backed up till he hit the wall behind him.

Eoghan snarled and growled his lupine jaws inches from the four guards. Only one remained conscious and he bowed to the floor in submission, wailing and crying, as Ailis' howl came to an end.

He looked down his ice blue Wolf eyes at Lyall. The lecherous bastard already had his clothes undone. He cradled his hand where Ailis had bitten his finger off in his lap and he was sobbing incoherently.

The Wolf that was Eoghan was huge and black, his fangs a good three inches long. Saliva dripped from them as he growled and barked at his brother.

He was furious as he moved to stand in front of Ailis.

He turned his back on his brother and bit through the cords and chains that bound her. She stood, her eyes still glowing, her Wolf near. She wanted to rejoice in him, in them, but then movement to their left startled her.

Eoghan turned just in time to see Lyall lunge towards them with a dagger in his hand. Eoghan had no choice. He reacted as any mated Wolf would. He charged his brother.

His great jaws closed around Lyall's neck. He took no time to think about the fragility of his brother in human form. No, he had taken what was his, and now he would pay.

As his long, sharp teeth came into contact with the soft flesh, he bit down. With a mighty tug, he tore out Lyall's throat, ending him quickly and succinctly. The blood that spewed forth was black, tainted as he was with Dark Magic.

Eoghan continued to snarl and snap his teeth at Lyall's gaping mouth and shocked expression. His eyes were glazed over, the life drained from them. And still he growled.

Until he felt a hand on his back. Without turning he know it was his mate. *Mine.* The connection between them was bright and strong. He wanted to

Change back to man, but his Wolf insisted he remain. To see her to their home.

Together, they left the fortress and met with Eoghan's men along the path back to Castle MacContire. They gasped and started when they saw the familiar black Wolf with one white paw.

"How can this be?"

"Are you Tom?" Ailis spoke with her hand still on the back of the Wolf who was her husband.

"Aye, lady, I am Tom Kelly, at yer service."

"There are bodies that need gathering ahead. A search party of Hounds to go after the Witch as well. Oh, and Eoghan says you are to lead them."

"Y-yes, my lady," he bowed deep and turned to his duties.

No one dared get close to the them. Some crossed themselves and muttered prayers, others smiled through tears. Seeing their leader as Wolf on a night other than the full moon was amazing indeed.

They continued side by side the way back, as fog and mist cast by the Witch lifted from the ground. The stars and half-moon shone above them. Lighting their way.

10

Eoghan and Ailis settled into the large
wooden tub filled to the brim with hot
water, thanks to Gwinnie. They soaped
each other and bathed until both were free of the
grime and blood of their ordeal.

"On the morrow, I shall stand before my father,
Ailis. I shall have to answer for my crimes."

"Nay, we shall stand together."

"Are ye certain?"

"Oh, aye. Blood was spilt by us both, but not
without provocation."

"Tis true, but I acted without the Alpha's orders.
And I killed my brother."

"I am sorry, Eoghan."

"Nay. I am sorry for I did not see what he truly
was sooner. I am only glad you are okay."

"Thanks to you."

"Thanks to *us*."

Once clean and dry, they settled in front of the fire under blankets and furs aplenty. Eoghan stared at the face of his beloved bride with wonder in his eyes. She was free of the heavy scent she wore, and he was able to smell *her*. All of her. *Wolf and woman*.

"Why did ye hide yerself from me?"

"Tis not fashionable for a lady to be Wolf. My father was afraid the match would be called off."

"Damn fashion! The fool. Did he not think ye were special?"

"Nay, my father has never had a kind thought or care for me. I, I only wonder, now that ye know the truth, will ye still keep me?"

Eoghan ran his hand over her soft skin exposed from her thin chemise. She was beautiful. Her long hair in its multitude of colors swirled around her shoulders and hips. It was soft as down feathers from a goose.

He followed his hands with his lips. If he could not tell her how much he loved her, he'd show her. Kisses trailed along her sweet body soon turned into something more.

"Eoghan," she groaned and grabbed his face and brought his lips to hers.

"I love ye, Ailis, and I'd die for ye, don't ye know that?"

"Yea, my love, as I would for you."

He leaned his head and met her lips with his. Their kiss was long and deep. She wound her hands through his long flaxen hair and over the soft whiskers that covered his face.

His hands were skilled and gentle as he removed her thin layer of clothing. The heat of his body seeped into her skin as he licked his way from her neck to her breasts.

He feasted on her creamy flesh. Kissing and teasing, then nibbling the peaks with his teeth. His Wolf growled deep inside of him. He recognized her beast and demanded he claim her again as mate with a bite on her shoulder.

Eoghan recognized the command now for what it was. *Mine.* He reveled in the knowledge that their bond brought him to her and allowed him to carry her away to safety. Now he'd show her his love.

"Aye, my Ailis, I love ye," he breathed the words as he suckled her. His hands found their way down her thighs and parted them.

She was smooth and warm and so ready for him by the time he reached the nest of soft brown curls that graced her body with his long fingers. She was a fine form of a woman. And she was his.

In every sense of the word. His own, his mate, his Wolf bride. His mind went cloudy with lust as he smelled her sweet musk when he smoothed her slit open. He dipped a finger in and smiled at her moan.

Pleasure at the sounds and feel of her swept through his body. He wanted to make her howl again, this time with satisfaction. He nudged her legs open a bit wider so he could more fully attend to her.

She was slick and hot, ready for him. Eoghan could wait no longer. His cock was full to bursting. He entered her with a swift flex of his hips. Her inner muscles squeezed him as he pumped in and out of her body.

An eruption of feelings flowed inside of him as he buried himself inside of her. She was fire and light, strength and goodness, everything he ever wanted. He rolled her onto her back and sank even further, lifting her legs and wrapping them tightly around him. He lowered his head and kissed her mouth. Her tongue met his and together they explored each other.

She was naked beneath him as she'd never been before. Her Wolf scent invading his nostrils and making him hungry for more. She smelled like lavender fields and fresh Irish rain, like home and something more. He couldn't put a name to it.

He'd never experienced pleasure so intense and so

right as this before. Nay, she was the only one to make him feel so. She writhed underneath him, meeting him stroke for stroke.

She was earthy and sensual. Unafraid of the intense connection between them. His Ailis ran her hands around his chest then down his back to his buttocks. She stroked and cupped and squeezed.

He pumped and pounded until she moaned out his name in her completion. Aye, she was beautiful like that. Sweat glistened on her body and he licked the saltiness from her skin as he pumped once then twice more.

He growled his pleasure and spilled himself inside of her. She was his everything. Tomorrow they would face his father and their future, together.

"Eoghan! Aye, ye feel so good when ye fill me like this."

"We are matebonded, Ailis, can ye feel the connection?"

"Yea, feel it and see it, in my mind's eye."

"As can I, love. You feel like heaven. I never want to stop loving ye like this."

"Then don't, husband."

"I never shall, my Wolf bride."

The following day…

"Though it pains me to give ye both this sentence, it is by our laws that I, Chief of the Name, banish ye from our

lands, Eoghan MacContire and yer bride, the Lady Ailis Dungannon..."

The speech ordering their banishment for the crime of fratricide was made to the entire village, then again to the Pack and the Hounds. It differed a trifle from audience to audience, but nothing said was a lie.

He killed his half-brother. And, to protect Ailis, he would do it again. It was what was whispered in Eoghan's ear by his father that would stay with him for a lifetime.

"Son now is yer chance to go explore yer new worlds with yer Wolf Bride. Take her to a new place where she and ye will both thrive and be safe. Know in yer heart that I am with ye. I am only sorry I have failed yer mother in caring for her sons."

"Nay, father, ye were a fine father. I shall not forget all yer teachings."

"Aye. Go now, lad, or I might not let ye."

"Fare thee well, father, God keep thee."

"And thee."

EPILOGUE

any years later.

Eoghan looked at his wife with a wide smile on his face. Her belly was swollen with their second child and she was radiant with it. They were lucky that in their long lifetimes they had known so much happiness.

Her Wolf was strong and beautiful as she and he had no course for complaint. They'd lost one babe months before the infant was ready for birth, as She-Wolves were wont to do. It pained him to think of it, but this one was strong inside of her.

He stood to lift the crate she was looking through so she wouldn't strain herself. He kissed her head as she nodded her thanks. Ailis was still unpacking their belongings after their recent move from Jamestown to the new Dutch settlement just north of where they lived the past twenty years.

They were known as Eoghan and Ailis Maccon in the New World. A shortened name, one Ailis recalled the Witch had called him with fear when he found her in the tower. *Maccon.* In Irish it meant the *son of a Wolf* and that he was.

Letters from Ireland reached them from the lad who had once cleaned his mail, Tom Kelly. He informed them that his da had passed on some years after their banishment, the Witch had never been found, but the Greyback Pack was strong, and a new Alpha placed. There was no mention of the Dungannon, other than that he too has passed. Ailis wept not for her stern father.

They closed the door on their past with that letter. Content with each other and strong in their bond. They settled into a wonderful life together of adventure and love.

Young Nathaniel's giggles could be heard from outside. He was running amok with Gwinnie as she hung the wash. Ailis' lady's maid had insisted on accompanying them in their exile.

The small village they'd built was thriving. He built his house with good timber and thatching for the roof. He'd encountered few Werewolves since uprooting his family. Those he had joined them on their journey.

The Wolves were restless without a leader. They were uncertain in their new home, but they all agreed they recognized his natural dominance. Before he knew it, they named him Alpha and swore loyalty to him and his.

He swallowed to stop the tears that naturally sprung to his eyes when he thought of his da and all he taught him about being an Alpha. He'd make his father proud and he'd only lead his Wolves to prosperity.

Ailis called them the Macconwood Pack in honor of their new name and the place where they two first met. It could not be more perfect. *Another adventure indeed.*

"Well, love, is this new land agreeing with my son that you carry?"

Eoghan wrapped his arms around his wife's increased girth and nuzzled her neck. Pride and contentment filled his chest as he inhaled her sweet musk. *Mine.*

"What makes you think tis not a daughter then, sir?"

Ailis said and leaned into him. His manhood stood at attention as it did whenever she was near, but suddenly his mind went black. *Did she say daughter?*

"Aye, well, wait- a daughter?"

"There is a chance, you do recognize that?"

"Uh-"

"Oh, Eoghan!" She laughed and swatted at him. He ignored her and picked her up.

"I swear, Ailis, I love ye more each and every day. You've given me a fine son, and if this here be a daughter, then I'll strive to be an even better man for ye both."

"As if you could be any better, my love."

Their lips met and Eoghan lost himself in her kiss. This woman, his wife, who had braved Witches, Wolves, banishment, oceans, settlers, natives, strange lands, childbirth, and more. And all just to be with him.

She was still his wild thing, his lady of the wood. Beautiful and fierce.

And his.

His Wolf Bride.

Dear Readers,

I wanted to thank you for taking this journey back in time with me to the start of the Macconwood Pack. This remains my only historical paranormal romance to date, but if you are interested in continuing the tales featuring more of our contemporary Wolves check out the whole series The Macconwood Pack Tales on my website www.cdgorri.com.

Looking for more about the Macconwood Wolves try my Maccon City Shifters books.

Or catch up on how the Alpha and his Wolf Guard found their mates in the Macconwood Pack Novel Series from book1, Charley's Christmas Wolf, to book 8, Werewolf Fever.

Thank you so much for reading!
Del mare alla stella,
C.D. Gorri

BEWARE... HERE BE DRAGONS!

The Falk Clan Tales are my stories surrounding four Dragon Shifter brothers and how they find their one true mates!

Each brother's chest is marked with his rose, the magical link to his heart and his magic. They each have a matching gemstone to go with it.

In *The Dragon's Valentine* we meet the eldest Falk brother, Callius. He is on a mission to find a Castle and his one true mate, one he can trust with his diamond rose....

She's given up on love, but he's just begun...

In *The Dragon's Christmas Gift* our attention shifts to Alexsander, the youngest brother of the four. He has resigned himself to a life alone, until he meets *her*...

His heart is frozen. Can she change his mind about love?

The Dragon's Heart is the story of Edric Falk who has vowed never to love again, but that changes when he meets his feisty mate, Joselyn Curacao.

Some wounds run deep. Can a Dragon's heart be unbroken?

Meet Nikolai Falk in the last Falk Clan Tale, *The Dragon's Secret*.

She just wants a little fun, he's looking for a lifetime.

*These first four books are now available in one convenient set. Look for Dragon Mates today.

Meet another long lost Falk brother in *The Dragon's Treasure*. Castor Falk breaks free from his prison in search of his kin, he finds his mate instead.

She doesn't believe in fairytales, until a Dragon comes knocking on her door.

The Dragon's Surprise features a new Dragon, Devine Graystone, and a female Werewolf who makes him think twice about his lonely state of being...

Nothing can surprise this six hundred-year-old Dragon, except maybe her.

Lastly, in *The Dragon's Dream* we meet a spunky she-Wolf who gives Nicholas Graystone a run for his money when it comes to romance. Can a Dragon really have it all?

He's a hardcore realist until she dares him to dream.

HAVE YOU MET THE BARVALE CLAN BEARS?

Looking for a Paranormal Romance series that is loads of growly fun?

Meet the Barvale Clan first in the Bear Claw Tales! A complete shifter romance series about 4 brothers who discover and need to win their fated mates!
Titles are:
Bearly Breathing
Bearly There
Bearly Tamed
Bearly Mated

Followed by two more spin off series, the Barvale Clan Tales, featuring:
Polar Opposites
Polar Outbreak

Polar Compound
Polar Curve

and, of course, the Barvale Holiday Tales, beginning
with A Bear For Christmas
Hers to Bear
Thank You Beary Much
&
Bearing Gifts!
Look for more of these sexy, heartwarming holiday
inspired tales soon!

No cliffhangers. Steamy PNR fun.
Go and read your next happily ever after today!

OTHER TITLES BY C.D. GORRI

Pack Tale 1

Summer Bite: A Macconwood Pack Tale 2

His Winter Mate: A Macconwood Pack Tale 3

Snow Angel: A Macconwood Pack Tale 4

Charley's Baby Surprise: A Macconwood Pack Tale 5

Home for the Howlidays: A Macconwood Pack Tale 6

A Silver Wedding: A Macconwood Pack Tale 7

Mine Furever: A Macconwood Pack Tale 8

A Furry Little Christmas: A Macconwood Pack Tale 9

Also available in two boxed sets:

The Macconwood Pack Tales Volume 1

Shifters Furever: The Macconwood Pack Tales Volume 2

The Falk Clan Tales:

The Dragon's Valentine: A Falk Clan Novel 1

The Dragon's Christmas Gift: A Falk Clan Novel 2

The Dragon's Heart: A Falk Clan Novel 3

The Dragon's Secret: A Falk Clan Novel 4

The Dragon's Treasure: A Falk Clan Novel 5

The Dragon's Surprise: A Falk Clan Novel 6

The Dragon's Dream: A Falk Clan Novel 7

Dragon Mates: The Falk Clan Series Boxed Set Books 1-4

The Bear Claw Tales:

Bearly Breathing: A Bear Claw Tale 1

Bearly There: A Bear Claw Tale 2

Bearly Tamed: A Bear Claw Tale 3

Bearly Mated: A Bear Claw Tale 4

Also available in a boxed set:

The Complete Bear Claw Tales (Books 1-4)

The Barvale Clan Tales:

Polar Opposites: The Barvale Clan Tales 1

Polar Outbreak: The Barvale Clan Tales 2

Polar Compound: A Barvale Clan Tale 3

Polar Curve: A Barvale Clan Tale 4

Also available in a boxed set:

The Barvale Clan Tales (Books 1-4)

Barvale Holiday Tales:

A Bear For Christmas

Hers To Bear

Thank You Beary Much

Bearing Gifts

Also available in a boxed set:

The Barvale Holiday Tales (Books 1-3)

Purely Paranormal Romance Books:

Marked by the Devil: Purely Paranormal Romance Books

Mated to the Dragon King: Purely Paranormal Romance Books

Claimed by the Demon: Purely Paranormal Romance Books

Christmas with a Devil, a Dragon King, & a Demon: Purely Paranormal Romance Books

Vampire Lover: Purely Paranormal Romance Books

Grizzly Lover: Purely Paranormal Romance Books

Christmas With Her Chupacabra: Purely Paranormal Romance Books

Purely Paranormal Romance Books Anthology

The Wardens of Terra:

Bound by Air: The Wardens of Terra Book 1

Star Kissed: A Wardens of Terra Short

Waterlocked: The Wardens of Terra Book 2

Moon Kissed: A Wardens of Terra Short

*Now in a boxed set and in audio!

The Maverick Pride Tales:

Purrfectly Mated

Purrfectly Kissed

Purrfectly Trapped

Purrfectly Caught

Purrfectly Naughty

Purrfectly Bound

Hungry Fur Love

Hungry Like Her Wolf: Magic and Mayhem Universe

Hungry For Her Bear: Magic and Mayhem Universe

Shifters Unleashed Boxed Sets

Check out these amazing anthologies where you can find some of my books and the works of other awesome authors!

Midnight Magic Anthology (Water Witch)

Rituals & Runes Anthology (Air Witch)

Island Stripe Pride

Tiger Claimed

Tiger Denied

NYC Shifter Tales

Cuff Linked

Sealed Fate

A Howlin' Good Fairytale Retelling

Sweet As Candy (as seen in Once Upon An Ever After)

Coming Soon:

Asterion

Vampire Shield: Guardians of Chaos 6

Tiger Rejected

For Fangs Sake

Hungry As Her Python: Magic and Mayhem Universe

If The Shoe Fits: A Howlin' Good Fairytale Retelling

Chickee and the Paparazzi: FUCN'A

The Wolf's Winter Wish: A Macconwood Pack Tale

The Hybrid Assassin

Tempted By Her Protector: WPU 2

Alien Protector: WPU 3

Elvish Protector: WPU 4

Thrilled By Her Protector: WPU 5

Young Adult Urban Fantasy Books:

Wolf Moon: A Grazi Kelly Novel Book 1

Hunter Moon: A Grazi Kelly Novel Book 2

Rebel Moon: A Grazi Kelly Novel Book 3

Winter Moon: A Grazi Kelly Novel Book 4

Chasing The Moon: A Grazi Kelly Short 5

Blood Moon: A Grazi Kelly Novel 6

*Get all 6 books NOW AVAILABLE IN A BOXED SET:

The Complete Grazi Kelly Novel Series

Casting Magic: The Angela Tanner Files 1

Keeping Magic: The Angela Tanner Files 2

G'Witches Magical Mysteries Series

Co-written with P. Mattern

G'Witches

EXCERPT FROM PURRFECTLY
MATED

How the fuck did I wind up here?

It was all Elissa could do not to slam her face down on the table as she pondered that question for the umpteenth time since leaving her cozy Hoboken apartment to go on this so called date.

"So, babe," the over-stuffed, heavily-cologned, and downright fugly man said.

Her date of the evening looked like something out of a bad sitcom as he tried to lean over the stained tablecloth of the rundown hotel buffet room, he'd driven two hours to get to. Waggling his caterpillar-like eyebrows, he gave her the once over and Elissa's skin crawled.

Oh, hell no.

"I got a room upstairs, you know, for *after*," he

told her, nodding his head, and biting his lower lip in a manner she assumed he thought was provocative.

At best, it was nauseating.

FML.

How was this guy Elissa's date for the evening? What had she done to deserve this?

Little Gianni. Yup, that was how he'd introduced himself. And here she was. On a blind date with a guy who had the word 'little' in front of his name.

Well, what did she expect? Roses and champagne? In this economy? She didn't know where Cinder-fuck-ing-ella got her prince, but it sure as fuck wasn't in Jersey.

Elissa could only blame herself for agreeing to go on this blind date. Initially, the whole Little Gianni fiasco had been intended for her roommate.

Wait a second. Scratch that thought.

It *was* all Gretchen's fault. That ungrateful cow!

She tried to play it off like she was some sweet little homegrown maiden. Oh, just wait till Elissa got home. Gretchen was never going to hear the end of it.

She owed Elissa. Big time. Like a whole month of washing the dishes big time. The rat trap they shared in her hometown of Hoboken was all the two women could afford, and for the most part, they got along just fine.

In fact, they'd grown to be close friends over the three years they'd lived together. It was the only reason she'd ever agreed to this date from Hell.

Elissa sighed and looked over at Little Gianni. Maybe he wasn't all that bad?

"*BEEEELLLLLLLLCHHH!* 'Scuse me, doll. Better out, am I right?"

Gianni winked and Elissa wished for a black hole to open up and swallow her up right through the floor.

OMFG.

The man just burped out loud like he was in a frat boy belting contest, only those days passed him up about thirty years ago.

For fuck's sake. Gretchen, you so owe me.

Elissa cursed her roommate and tried not to groan. But Little Gianni wasn't quite done. The grown ass man lifted his leg and let one rip.

Right. Fucking. There.

Elissa was going to die before the end of the night.

Literally.

This is what you get when you do a friend a favor without asking for details! Idiota!

The voice of her Italian grandmother sounded in her brain. She tried to ignore it, willing herself not to wince at the man while he sucked air, and who knows what else, noisily through his coffee-stained teeth.

Ew. So gross.

That was the perfect word to describe it. The only word, in fact. The entire date was just so fucking gross. She still couldn't believe her sweet little roommate from Iowa, *Gretchen Kaepernick*, she of the wispy hair and baby blues, had set her up with this guy!

What the actual fuck was up with that?

Little Gianni was a slob. Actually, he looked just like her Uncle Nico, and that was not a good thing. Seriously, not good at all.

He wore his hair slicked back in a too tight ponytail that emphasized his rapidly receding hairline. As if that wasn't enough to put her off, he was sporting an enormous paunch. Now, being a curvy girl, Elissa appreciated food and was in no way against men showing the same appreciation.

She liked bigger men. Always had. But bigger did not mean you had to be sloppy. Little Gianni's stomach was literally hanging out from under a tight tan golf shirt that had definitely seen better days.

The man didn't even look like he had ever played a sport of any kind. With it, he wore brown polyester pants that were three inches above his ankles and unbuttoned at the waist.

He didn't look like he tried at all for this date.

What kind of guy did that? His shirt collar was bent and wrinkled, and all three buttons were open to his chest, revealing a mat of oily, dark hair and pimples.

Somehow, he'd managed to tuck the back of the shirt in, but the front simply would not hold in that stomach. What worried her more were the tight brown pants.

As he sat back and stretched, she wondered if she should take cover. They looked like they were one bite from exploding off his body. Elissa shuddered at the image.

Please God, if You have an ounce of mercy, don't let that happen, she prayed.

"Hang on, doll, I gotta take this," he said, and turned to answer his cell phone.

It was ringing to the tune of '70s disco music she hadn't heard since the last family reunion. Her eyes kept going to the huge stain on the front of his shirt. It was a little game she liked to call *what the hell is that*.

Coffee, she guessed.

"Up your ass, Bruno. I gotta have it by Monday," he cursed into the receiver.

Elissa winced at the spectacle he was making of them both. There were only a handful of people there, but still.

Deep breaths.

Ew. Maybe not.

She coughed as the strong body spray, that he'd obviously used a ton of in lieu of a shower, bad move in her opinion, invaded her lungs.

Oh, this was so bad.

Elissa was, by no means, a snob. But this guy looked like he'd stepped out of a bad 1980s mafia spoof film. What's worse, he kept smacking his lips together as he hung up the phone and looked her over from head to chest.

Thank fuck for the table, she thought, wishing she could hide her bosoms from his view.

"Sssssss," he hissed, like it was sexy or something.

She just grimaced. Elissa might be able to forgive a lot of quirks, but she hated mouth noises. Really hated them. It was a super pet peeve of hers. Never mind his totally inappropriate and unwelcomed leer.

She started counting the minutes, willing the date to be over already. Plenty of people would tell her she shouldn't be so choosy, but really? She was not this desperate.

Not yet anyway.

So, she was curvy and a little mouthy too. But was it wrong to want a man with good table manners? Even if men were thin on the ground for someone like her.

As a chef, she'd worked in a lot of restaurants

and even as a personal cook for professional couples. She'd seen her fair share of unhappy couples and downright uncomfortable marriages. But as far as she was concerned, all relationships went downhill when good table manners were dismissed.

Good manners were merely a sign that a person was thoughtful and respectful. At least, that was what Nonna had told her. Gianni here had clearly missed that lesson as a child. Elissa had to work not to groan in disgust as he slurped a raw clam down his gullet.

Shudder.

Was there no end to his feeding? That's what it reminded her of. Feeding time at the zoo.

OMG. That was rude, she scolded herself. But it wasn't like she said it out loud.

All she wanted to do was go home. At least she was comfortable. *She'd* worn her softest pair of black leggings for this disaster date, paired with one of her favorite tunics on top.

It was dark green with tiny black buttons down the front and showed just the right amount of cleavage. She'd gone for neat and tidy as opposed to downright sexy.

Good call, in her opinion. Elissa looked perfectly fine for a nice *getting to know you* dinner, which is what she thought she was getting when her roommate asked her to step in for her on a blind date that one of her best client's had set up for her.

Elissa shuddered now, thinking how good old Gianni here would've reacted to the red dress and heels she'd contemplated before checking the weather report.

Gulp.

The lewd man was already salivating, and she was so not having it. Fending off his unwanted advances was not how she wanted to finish the night.

Ew again.

Elissa shivered, slightly chilled despite the fact they were indoors. It was a cold, gloomy evening, and the forecast called for even more rain later that night. Not at all unusual for this time of year in the Garden State.

November was always chilly in the evenings, rainy too. Elissa tended to run warm, but she was glad she'd brought a jacket with her. Especially since her date refused to turn the heat on in the car.

When she'd asked, he'd looked offended and told her it wasted gas.

Um. Okay.

She checked her phone. It was only seven o'clock, but the two hour drive was still ahead of them. Maybe they could make it home before ten if they left soon.

Ugh. Did he just blow his nose?

"Allergies, doll. Say, you gonna eat that?" he asked before scooping a fry from her dish and swallowing it down.

Elissa was gonna kill her roomie. Gretchen was a hair and nail stylist. A lot of her clients were elderly, and they just loved her. They were always offering to set her up on blind dates with their nephews and grandsons.

Mostly, the sweet old ladies were kind. They swore they could find her curvy roommate the right man, assuming she was single because she was new to town. Well, when Elissa got home tonight, she was going to tell Gretchen she needed to fire the old lady who set this date up from being her client.

Like *ASAP*.

No one who liked Gretchen would've sent her out with this guy. Gianni reached over and touched her hand and Elissa pulled back, reaching for the napkin.

Gross.

"I sure hope you ain't a cold one, doll," he said, shaking his head.

"What?"

"Ain't gonna matter. I know just what you need, doll."

She was still wiping the greasy residue he'd transferred to her skin from the food he ate sans utensils.

This was too much. Elissa was beyond uncomfortable with all the leering and bad attempts at innuendo.

Plus, she was starving. One look at the dump he'd taken her to, and she knew she could never eat there. The chef in her wouldn't allow it.

To think they drove two hours for this! She'd practically frozen to death in his maroon Cadillac, listening to a CD of the Rat Pack, while Gianni crooned loudly, and off key, to the music.

Normally, she was a fan of the famous group of legendary singers. Having grown up in Hoboken, she couldn't not be a Sinatra fan. Though, to be honest, Dean Martin had always been her favorite.

Still, Elissa was a firm believer that there were just some people you did not try to imitate. Especially not if you were Little Gianni. While he was belting his heart out, he'd been trying to get his right hand on her thigh. She'd asked him politely to stop.

Twice.

Then she'd been forced to try something a little more drastic. Like spilling her hot tea on the offending hand the third time he'd tried it. Finally, he'd removed his hand from her leg. Not making a fourth attempt, which she was grateful for.

Elissa should've taken that behavior as a sign and gotten out of the car. But no. She'd wanted to do

Gretchen a solid. So, against her better judgement, she gave the creep another chance.

Idiota, her grandmother's voice echoed in her brain again.

The old woman had loved her. Elissa knew that without a doubt. She'd raised her after her own parents had passed on in a tragic automobile accident when Elissa was just twelve.

Her grandmother was a no-nonsense kind of lady who dished out priceless wisdom with brutally honest insights. It was the same way she dished out huge bowls of pasta with her amazing meatballs and home-made sauce. Not to mention a side order of back-breaking hugs that Elissa still missed.

Nonna cooked like that all the time. She made a huge pot of sauce every weekend, and she was happy to serve it to Elissa and her teammates and friends, especially after games and tournaments.

Soccer had been her sport of choice, and cooking had soon become her favorite hobby. Her grand-mother had encouraged her in both pursuits. Guiding her in one and cheering her on in the other. Elissa still missed her terribly.

"Hey babe, ain't you gonna eat nothin'? You know they charge twenty dollars just to sit down," Little Gianni interrupted her train of thought.

Elissa was forced to turn her mind back to the

present, which unfortunately included watching, *and hearing*, him as he sucked on his teeth and stuffed another breaded shrimp down his throat.

"I'm fine," she answered with a polite smile plastered on her face.

Just get home, Lissa. Just get him to take you home.

Elissa closed her eyes when he looked back down at his dish. Thank God for small favors, she mused. At least he was more interested in eating at the moment.

He'd taken her to the rattiest looking hotel and casino she'd ever seen in her life. And the buffet room?

Ew.

Seriously, the place had to be violating at least a dozen health codes. When Gianni had said Atlantic City, she'd thought at least the atmosphere would be exciting. But they were so far from the real glitz and entertainment, they might as well be anywhere else.

She sighed, looking at the plate she'd made for herself. Elissa couldn't even fake an interest in the food. As a chef, it was hard enough to dine out.

She was always judging the food, the service, the ingredients. How could she not? It was her business. And that was when the food was good!

This was not good. Not at all.

She'd been to hospitals that served better food.

Old yellow lights buzzed and blinked around the buffet, giving it an abandoned kind of feel. The menu was made up of mostly frozen then fried or baked cuisine.

Reheated actually. It was like a giant TV dinner buffet where every item was previously frozen when already cooked and warmed up in an oven.

It was the kind of food sold cheap at restaurant supply stores in bulk. Yeah, this was much worse than hospital food, in her opinion.

There was a worn carpet on the floor, a handful of scattered tables in the dining room, elevator music on in the background, and the entire place smelled like canned soup.

Not to mention not one of the five people there besides them was under sixty years old.

"Gianni," she said, leaning forward so as not to hurt his feelings.

"I thought you mentioned something about seeing a show tonight. Is it here?"

Please don't be here.

If he was taking her somewhere else, she could beg off and hire a cab to take her home. There was no way she was sitting through anything else with this man. Not now. Not ever.

"Ah, I see, babe, you want some entertainment first, I get it," he snickered loudly, and she blanched.

Whatever he thought was going to happen wasn't. She needed to disabuse him of the notion, and fast.

"Alright, alright. Lemme finish this, babe. Then we'll go up to the room I got for us," he said.

Before she could make sense of the ludicrous statement, he slurped another fried shrimp, don't ask how. Then he grabbed her arm and yanked her from the seat before she could even react.

Elissa tugged on his hold, but the man was immovable. Tossing a five-dollar bill on the table, Little Gianni snatched a toothpick from the hostess stand before dragging her outside.

Great, he was a cheap tipper, too.

All she wanted was to go home. Figuring the best way to do that would probably be to get him to the car, she let him lead the way.

Once inside, she would ask him to drive back to Hoboken so she could wring Gretchen's neck. Fuming, she pulled her arm out of his hand and walked behind him.

The rain was really pouring, and the cheap bastard had refused valet. Elissa ducked her head so she wouldn't get so wet. Of course, the jacket she'd brought was light and had no hood.

Gianni had an umbrella, but he didn't offer to hold it for her, and honestly, she did not relish the idea of getting any closer to him than necessary.

Seriously, not happening.

Now all she had to do was break the news. She had no intention of watching a show or returning to the hotel with him.

What could go wrong?

GRAB PURRFECTLY MATED TODAY.

EXCERPT FROM GRIZZLY LOVER

"Resa," Oliver fisted the note he'd found tucked under the secondhand keyboard he'd just finished paying off.

The instrument sat against one wall of the cramped room, right beside the only window in the small Brooklyn Heights apartment he'd been renting the past six months since he came to the city.

For a Grizzly Bear Shifter used to the wilds of the woods as his backyard, it was quite the change, but he just had to try to see if he could make a go of his music. Oliver had always been gifted with a good ear, but even as a cub, his mother had encouraged him to go and seek his destiny.

Brooklyn Heights was as close to Manhattan as he could afford with his meager savings, but what did money matter anyway? Especially when there was music to be written. The window faced the south brick wall of another small apartment complex identical to his.

It didn't matter what it looked like outside, as long as he was able to breathe some fresh air. At least on the fifth floor, it was somewhat fresher than the heavily congested streets below.

She was gone. His mind registered that fact as he took in the empty room. She'd left.

"No," he growled, and aimed his fist at the tiled counter top, cracking a few of the old ceramic squares in the process. Mrs. Goldstein, the landlady, would be pissed when she saw that.

Oliver's Bear roared inside of him and his heart contracted painfully in his chest. It was worse than being sucker punched by Thor his idiot cousin, who was as big and strong as his namesake. Why would Teresa say such cruel things? He couldn't believe it, couldn't fathom his sweet Resa saying such foul callous words about their relationship. He read the hated missive one more time.

Oliver,

It was fun while it lasted, but even you can't be so naïve as to think I could find true love with a nobody. I just wanted to get back at my father. Don't bother looking for me or calling, I will have already changed my number.

Teresa

Yes, it was her handwriting. He closed his eyes on the wave of anguish that washed over him. Gasping, he sunk to his knees while the beast inside of him roared and sTimped his massive claws in fury.

Mate, his Bear cried out, but Oliver refused to answer his other half.

How could she just leave him like this? He'd been so sure of her, of them. He was positive that she loved him too. Being with her was everything to him. She was his fated mate. It was the first time he had ever tasted happiness. A taste that was bitter now that he knew it was all one-sided.

The first time he'd seen the golden-haired beauty, Oliver's Grizzly Bear had stood up and taken notice. The second he'd breathed in her peaches and cream scent, his animal had roared one single word in his mind's eye that would change Oliver's life forever.

Mate.

Following his heart, he'd approached the soft spoken, elegantly dressed Teresa Witherspoon after spying her at the park day after day. She'd sit on one of the cleaner benches and read from a book of seventeenth century cavalier poets.

"You like Lovelace? Looking at you I pictured a Donne fan," Oliver said when he'd finally found the nerve to approach her.

"Spiritualist poetry doesn't appeal as much to me I guess. I like Lovelace and Suckling. They're fun and witty."

"But they're just trying to get in a girl's pants with their poetry. You approve?" he grinned.

"It's not so much the seduction that appeals to me, it's the living in the moment. Carpe diem and all that," she shrugged.

There was something so tragically sad about her that his heart had squeezed in his chest with longing. He'd wanted to make her smile. Heck, he even pretended to stumble in the grass, laid himself flat just to get her to walk over and touch him. And she had, put her soft, long hands right on him to see if he was alright. He'd stolen a kiss and had never looked back. Until now. The dream was over. She'd left him.

Oliver's Bear roared in his grief. That last night they were together, he'd told her the truth about what he was. The fact that there were more things in the world than she had ever imagined.

Oliver Pax had committed a most grievous sin against his Clan. He'd confessed to a normal, a human woman, that he was a Grizzly Bear Shifter.

It was allowed under certain circumstances, like when the woman in question was your fated mate. He'd thought she'd taken it well, after all, they'd made wild, passionate love immediately after. Hell, he'd been so caught up in the moment, he'd marked her with his bite, tying himself to her irrevocably, but now she was gone.

What would become of him? Would he go mad like so many other Shifters who'd lost their mates? He had heard the stories. The tales of broken matings and rogue Shifters who needed to be put down.

Oliver tipped the bottle of whiskey back emptying its fiery contents down his throat. Then he threw the hated thing across the room. Something about the muted violence of the act satisfied his animal's need for savagery. The Bear inside of him wanted to tear the whole world down, but maybe work would be a better outlet, he thought.

Oliver sat down at his banged-up keyboard and began to play. He poured out his bruised heart. Wrote lyrics and tied them together with a fairy tale as old as they come. The Beast of Brooklyn Heights was born that day. And the rest, as they say, was history.

GRAB GRIZZLY LOVER NOW.

EXCERPT FROM BEARING
GIFTS

"Thanks for coming tonight, Charity," Abigail Jensen, a nurse who worked at the Barvale Senior Center spoke softly as Charity hung her coat and hat on the rack near the desk.

It was already snowing, and she only had a few minutes, but Abigail never called her if it wasn't an emergency. Charity just had a way with people, and she enjoyed spending her time helping put others at ease if she could. True, she had about fifteen minutes before she needed to leave on time, otherwise she would be late for her shift, and tonight was important.

"No worries. You know I enjoy spending time with the residents, Abigail."

"I know, but normally you come on the weekends.

Mr. K is a special case, and we have tried everything to make him feel at ease. His wife had to have emergency hip replacement surgery, and he is only here while she recovers, but he's been despondent without her."

"Wow, he must really love her," Charity whispered. She shuffled the box that held a single bear claw inside and followed Abby down the hall. Seated in a wheelchair in the middle of his room was an elderly man with white hair and a beard. He had a hand-knitted red scarf draped around his neck, and his hands were clasped together.

"Good evening, Mr. K. I brought you a visitor," Abigail announced, and Charity walked in.

"Hello, I'm Charity—"

"I don't need any charity, I need my Elaine," he muttered grumpily.

"I understand. If I had a wife or husband, I would miss her too, but the center isn't all bad, you know. I usually come by on weekends and bring treats like this and crafts or movies. Sometimes, we play card games and once we had a talent show."

"A talent show? And what can you do, my dear?" he asked, engaging already, and Charity smiled at the win.

"Well, Mr. K, not to brag, but I am a terrible dancer, and I can't carry a tune," she confided.

"I will leave you two to it," Abigail said and turned to leave.

For the next fifteen minutes, Charity chatted with the exceedingly kind Mr. K, answering questions, and getting the older gentleman to open up about his wife. Her recovery was slow going, but he talked to her every single day. That kind of devotion was really touching, and Charity's heart swelled hoping someday, she would have that kind of love for herself.

"So, do you still believe in Santa?" he asked.

"Oh, I don't know. When I was little, I used to stay up and wait to hear him, but I never did. I think that would be amazing—"

"Even now that you are a grownup? I am surprised."

"Why? Adults need magic too," she told him.

"That is true, my dear. This was so lovely, Charity. Thank you for visiting me," Mr. K said, taking her hand as she stood to leave.

"It was my pleasure."

"You know, Christmas is in just a few days. I hope you sent your letter to Santa already," he whispered conspiratorially, and she laughed.

"I sure did," she replied, and kissed his weathered cheek.

"Oh, how nice! I am going to tell my Elaine she

must get well faster, a younger woman has her sights on me," he teased.

"You do that, and I bet she will be better in no time. You are quite the catch, Mr. K!" Charity chuckled.

"Seriously, my child, I want to thank you, very much so. I do not know many young women who would stop by to chat with a grumpy old stranger."

"You're not grumpy, Mr. K, just sad, and it is understandable. I bet you're worried something awful about your wife, and I want you to know I will be praying for her speedy recovery. I am sorry to cut our talk short, though, but I have to go."

"I see. Hot date?" he asked.

"Ha! No, I have to go to work."

"And after, is that when you will meet your boyfriend?"

"Actually, I am single—"

"I can see from the look in your eyes that is not exactly a choice, is it, Charity?"

"Well, I have a crush on someone, and tonight I am going to tell him. I'm kinda nervous," she confessed.

"My dear, if he has even one brain cell still functioning in his head, he will scoop you up and run away with you. I know quality when I see it, and you have it, child. Yes, indeed," he said and patted her hand. "You be a good girl now."

"Yes, sir. Thank you, Mr. K. I hope I will get to see you before your stay is over. Merry Christmas," she said, and waved goodbye as she raced to her car.

She did not hear the elderly man whisper his reply softly as he watched her go with sparkling blue eyes, "I'll be watching you, Charity Smith."

He knows if you've been bad or good...

GRAB YOUR COPY OF BEARING GIFTS TODAY.

ABOUT THE AUTHOR

C.D. Gorri is a USA Today Bestselling author of steamy paranormal romance and urban fantasy. She is the creator of the Grazi Kelly Universe.

Join her mailing list here: https://www.cdgorri.com/newsletter

An avid reader with a profound love for books and literature, when she is not writing or taking care of her family, she can usually be found with a book or tablet in hand. C.D. lives in her home state of New Jersey where many of her characters or stories are based. Her tales are fast paced yet detailed with satisfying conclusions.

If you enjoy powerful heroines and loyal heroes who face relatable problems in supernatural settings, journey into the Grazi Kelly Universe today. You will find sassy, curvy heroines and sexy, love-driven heroes who find their HEAs between the pages. Were-wolves, Bears, Dragons, Tigers, Witches, Romani, Lynxes, Foxes, Thunderbirds, Vampires, and many more Shifters and supernatural creatures dwell within her worlds. The most important thing is every mate in this universe is fated, loyal, and true lovers always get their happily ever afters.

Want to know how it all began? Enter the Grazi Kelly Universe with Wolf Moon: A Grazi Kelly Novel or pick up Charley's Christmas Wolf and dive into the Macconwood Pack Novel Series today.

For a complete list of C.D. Gorri's books visit her website here:

https://www.cdgorri.com/complete-book-list/

Thank you and happy reading!

del mare alla stella,
    C.D. Gorri

Follow C.D. Gorri here:
    http://www.cdgorri.com
    https://www.facebook.com/Cdgorribooks
    https://www.bookbub.com/authors/c-d-gorri

https://twitter.com/cgor22
https://instagram.com/cdgorri/
https://www.goodreads.com/cdgorri
https://www.tiktok.com/@cdgorriauthor

CPSIA information can be obtained
at www.ICGtesting.com
Printed in the USA
LVHW082256180123
737433LV00006B/574

9 781960 294043